PENGUIN CLASSICS

THUS SPOKE ZARATHUSTRA

FRIEDRICH NIETZSCHE was born near Leipzig in 1844, the son of a Lutheran clergyman. He attended the famous Pforta School, then went to university at Bonn and at Leipzig, where he studied philology and read Schopenhauer. When he was only twenty-four he was appointed to the chair of classical philology at Basle University; he stayed there until his health forced him into retirement in 1879. While at Basle he made and broke his friendship with Wagner, participated as an ambulance orderly in the Franco-Prussian War, and published *The Birth of Tragedy* (1872), *Untimely Meditations* (1873–6) and the first part of *Human, All Too Human* (1878; two supplements entitled *Assorted Opinions and Maxims* and *The Wanderer and his Shadow* followed in 1879 and 1880 respectively). From 1880 until his final collapse in 1889, except for brief interludes, he divorced himself from everyday life and, supported by his university pension, he lived mainly in France, Italy and Switzerland. *The Dawn* appeared in 1881 followed by *The Gay Science* in the autumn of 1882. *Thus Spoke Zarathustra* was written between 1883 and 1885, and his last completed books were *Ecce Homo*, an autobiography, and *Nietzsche contra Wagner*. He became insane in 1889 and remained in a condition of mental and physical paralysis until his death in 1900.

R. J. HOLLINGDALE translated eleven of Nietzsche's books and published two books about him; he also translated works by, among others, Schopenhauer, Goethe, E. T. A. Hoffman, Lichtenberg and Theodor Fontane, many of these for Penguin Classics. He was the honorary president of the British Nietzsche Society. R. J. Hollingdale died on 28 September 2001. In its obituary *The Times* described him as 'Britain's foremost postwar Nietzsche specialist' and the *Guardian* paid tribute to his 'inspired gift for German translation'. Richard Gott wrote that he 'brought fresh generations – through fluent and intelligent translation – to read and relish Nietzsche's inestimable thought'.

NIETZSCHE

Thus Spoke Zarathustra

A BOOK FOR EVERYONE
AND NO ONE

TRANSLATED
WITH AN INTRODUCTION BY
R. J. Hollingdale

PENGUIN BOOKS

PENGUIN BOOKS

Published by the Penguin Group
Penguin Books Ltd, 80 Strand, London WC2R 0RL, England
Penguin Putnam Inc., 375 Hudson Street, New York, New York 10014, USA
Penguin Books Australia Ltd, 250 Camberwell Road, Camberwell, Victoria 3124, Australia
Penguin Books Canada Ltd, 10 Alcorn Avenue, Toronto, Ontario, Canada M4V 3B2
Penguin Books India (P) Ltd, 11 Community Centre, Panchsheel Park, New Delhi – 110 017, India
Penguin Books (NZ) Ltd, Cnr Rosedale and Airborne Roads, Albany, Auckland, New Zealand
Penguin Books (South Africa) (Pty) Ltd, 24 Sturdee Avenue, Rosebank 2196, South Africa

Penguin Books Ltd, Registered Offices: 80 Strand, London WC2R 0RL, England

www.penguin.com

This translation first published 1961
Reprinted with new Introduction 1969
Reprinted with new Chronology and Further Reading 2003

087

Copyright © R. J. Hollingdale, 1961, 1969
All rights reserved

Printed and bound in Great Britain by Clays Ltd, Elcograf S.p.A.
Set in Monotype Garamond

ISBN-13: 978-0-140-44118-5
ISBN-10: 0-140-44118-2

www.greenpenguin.co.uk

MIX
Paper from
responsible sources
FSC® C018179

Penguin Books is committed to a sustainable
future for our business, our readers and our planet.
This book is made from Forest Stewardship
Council™ certified paper.

CONTENTS

Part Two

Part Three

Part Four

CHRONOLOGY

1844   15 October. Friedrich Wilhelm Nietzsche born in the parsonage at Röcken, near Lützen, Germany, the first of three children of Karl Ludwig, the village pastor, and Fraziska Nietzsche, daughter of the pastor of a nearby village.

1849   27 July. Nietzsche's father dies.

1850   The Nietzsche family moves to Naumberg, in Thuringia, in April. Arthur Schopenhauer publishes *Essays, Aphorisms and Maxims*.

1856   Birth of Freud.

1858   The family moves to No. 18 Weingarten. Nietzsche wins a place at the prestigious Pforta grammar school.

1860   Forms a literary society, 'Germania', with two Naumberg friends. Jacob Burckhardt publishes *The Civilization of the Renaissance in Italy*.

1864   Enters Bonn University as a student of theology and philology.

1865   At Easter, Nietzsche abandons the study of theology having lost his Christian belief. Leaves Bonn for Leipzig, following his former tutor of philology, Friedrich Ritschl. Begins to read Schopenhauer.

1867   First publication, 'Zur Geschichte der Theognideischen Spruchsammlung' (The History of the Theognidia Collection) in the *Rheinische Museum für Philiogie*. Begins military service.

1868   Discharged from the army. Meets Richard Wagner.

1869   Appointed to the chair of classical philology at Basle University having been recommended by Ritschl. Awarded a doctorate by Leipzig. Regular visitor at Wagners' home in Tribschen.

1870   Delivers public lectures on 'The Greek Music Drama' and 'Socrates and Tragedy'. Serves as a medical orderly with the Prussian army where he is taken ill with diphtheria.

1871   Applies unsuccessfully for the chair of philology at Basle. His health deteriorates. Takes leave to recover and works on *The Birth of Tragedy*.

1872   *The Birth of Tragedy* published (January). Public lectures 'On the Future of our Educational Institutions'.

1873   *Untimely Meditations I: David Strauss* published.

1874   *Untimely Meditations II: On the Use and Disadvantage of History for*

Life and *III: Schopenhauer as Educator* published.

1875 Meets Peter Gast, who is to become his earliest 'disciple'. Suffers from ill-health leading to a general collapse at Christmas.

1876 Granted a long absence from Basle due to continuing ill-health. Proposes marriage to Mathilde Trampedach but is rejected. *Untimely Meditations IV: Richard Wagner in Bayreuth* published. Travels to Italy.

1878 *Human, All Too Human* published. His friendship with the Wagners comes to an end.

1879 *Assorted Opinions and Maxims* published. Retires on a pension from Basle due to sickness.

1880 *The Wanderer and his Shadow* and *Human, All Too Human* II published.

1881 *Dawn* published.

1882 *The Gay Science* published. Proposes to Lou Andreas Salomé and is rejected.

1883 13 February. Wagner dies in Venice. *Thus Spoke Zarathustra* I and II published.

1884 *Thus Spoke Zarathustra* III published.

1885 *Zarathustra* IV privately printed.

1886 *Beyond Good and Evil* published.

1887 *On the Genealogy of Morals* published.

1888 *The Wagner Case* published. First review of his work as a whole published in the Bern *Bund.* Experiences some improvement in health but this is short-lived.

1889 Suffers mental collapse in Turin and is admitted to a psychiatric clinic at the University of Jena. *Twilight of the Idols* published and *Nietzsche contra Wagner* privately printed.

1890 Nietzsche returns to his mother's home.

1891 *Dithyrambs of Dionysus* published.

1894 *The Anti-Christ* published. The 'Nietzsche Archive' founded by his sister, Elisabeth.

1895 *Nietzsche contra Wagner* published.

1897 20 April. Nietzsche's mother dies; and Elisabeth moves Nietzsche to Weimar.

1900 25 August. Nietzsche dies. Freud publishes *Interpretation of Dreams.*

1901 Publication of *The Will to Power*, papers selected by Elisabeth and Peter Gast.

1908 *Ecce Homo* published.

I

THE first thing a reader of *Thus Spoke Zarathustra* will notice, even before he/she notices what is being said, is the manner of saying it: or rather, the *excess* of manner. The book's worst fault is excess. That this is the most forgivable of faults doesn't change the fact that it *is* a fault. As it happens, excess is the one fault no one could impute to Nietzsche's subsequent works: there concision, brevity, directness of statement are present to a degree not even approximated by any other German philosopher (and hardly equalled by any writer of any kind). It is clear that the rhetorical-oratorical is something Nietzsche was impelled to, gave way to and thus *got rid of* in *Zarathustra*: the eruption of words, metaphors, figures and word-play suggests an eruption of feeling. It will be our job here to try to discover why this eruption became necessary, and why just at this time (i.e. January 1883), and thus to understand better what this great odd book is really about.

2

Thus Spoke Zarathustra is (to anticipate our conclusion somewhat) the resolution of a long-sustained intellectual crisis. Let the word 'intellectual' not mislead: unlike most people, even most philosophers, Nietzsche lived with his intellectual problems as with realities, he experienced a similar emotional commitment to them as other men experience to their wife and children. It is this, indeed, which is the badge of his uniqueness and the key to understanding him. He makes clear what he means by intellectual problems in these few posthumously-published notes:

As soon as you feel yourself *against me* you have ceased to understand my position and consequently my arguments! You have to be the victim of the *same passion*!

I want to awaken the greatest mistrust of myself: I speak only of things I have *experienced* and do not offer only events in the head.

One must want to experience the great problems with one's body and one's soul.

I have at all times written my writings with my whole heart and soul: I do not know what purely intellectual problems are.

You know these things as thoughts, but your thoughts are not your experiences, they are an echo and after-effect of your experiences: as when your room trembles when a carriage goes past. I however am sitting in the carriage, and often I am the carriage itself.

In a man who thinks like this, the dichotomy between thinking and feeling, intellect and passion, has really disappeared. He feels his thoughts. He can fall in love with an idea. An idea can make him ill.

His forbears were Lutherans. Many were in the Lutheran church: his father and both grandfathers were Lutheran ministers, and his paternal grandfather was a Superintendent, the Lutheran equivalent of a bishop. As a boy he was, as befitted a pastor's son, intensely pious, but he lost his faith during his late teens and abandoned the study of theology. He replaced religious belief with freelance philosophizing, upon which he brought to bear the intensity of involvement he had withdrawn from religion. The path away from the family parsonage was the path of scepticism. Schopenhaueran metaphysics and Wagnerian music were detours, *ersatz* religion. In the summer of 1876, in his thirty-second year, he returned to the sceptical path and started on the series of aphoristic books which constitute probably the most thorough course in scepticism produced in the nineteenth century. *Human, All Too Human* appeared in 1878, *Assorted Opinions and Maxims* in 1879, *The Wanderer and his Shadow* in 1880; in June 1881 he published *Dawn*. These books embody reflexions on a very wide range of subjects, but the controlling tendency of his thought during all these five years is nonetheless unmistakable: it is to break down all the concepts and qualities in which mankind takes pride and pleasure into a few simple qualities in which no one takes pride or pleasure and to see in the latter the origin of the former; likewise to undermine morality by exposing its non-moral basis and rationality by exposing its irrational basis; likewise to abolish the 'higher' world, the metaphysical, by accounting for all its supposed manifestations in terms of the human, phenomenal, and even animal world; in brief, the controlling tendency of his thought is *nihilist*. The cheerful tone, the stylistic beauty, the coolness of the performance cannot conceal that what is taking place is destruction. The fact was, in any event, obvious to Nietzsche himself; and of all his problems this became the greatest, the most pressing, the one with which his 'passion' was most engaged. He had come close to a total devaluation of humanity and because he could as yet see no way of halting this movement he took the only course open to him: he pushed it on to its limit.

The earlier parts of his next book, *The Gay Science*, were intended for *Dawn*; they were excluded partly because he thought that book had grown sufficiently bulky, but also, I would say, because of the enhanced vehemence of what he was now thinking and writing. The nihilism of his position is now stated frankly:

The four errors. Man has been reared by his errors: first he never saw himself other than imperfectly, second he attributed to himself imaginary qualities, third he felt himself in a false order of rank with animal and nature, fourth he continually invented new tables of values and for a time took each of them to be eternal and unconditional, so that now this, now that human drive and state took first place and was, as a consequence of this evaluation, ennobled. If one deducts the effect of these four errors, one has also deducted away humanity, humaneness and 'human dignity'. (115).

He looks more squarely in the face and discusses more urgently the question whether 'truth' is in any way discoverable or whether mankind is not *necessitated* to error:

Life no argument. We have arranged for ourselves a world in which we are able to live – with the postulation of bodies, lines, surfaces, causes and effects, motion and rest, form and content: without these articles of faith nobody could now endure to live! But that does not yet mean they are something proved and demonstrated. Life is no argument; among the conditions of life could be error. (121).

He reaches what seems to be the final term in this line of argument:

Ultimate scepticism. What then in the last resort are the truths of mankind? – They are the *irrefutable* errors of mankind. (265).

His conception of the world as meaningless and chaotic is rounded off. That God is dead is announced in a famous passage:

The madman. Have you not heard of that madman who lit a lantern in the bright morning hours, ran to the market place and cried incessantly: 'I am looking for God! I am looking for God!' – As many of those who did not believe in God were standing together there he excited considerable laughter. Have you lost him then? said one. Did he lose his way like a child? said another. Or is he hiding? Is he afraid of us? Has he gone on a voyage? or emigrated? – thus they shouted and laughed. The madman sprang into their midst and pierced them with his glances. 'Where has God gone?' he cried. 'I shall tell you. *We have killed him* – you and I. We are all his murderers. But how have we done this? How were we able to drink up the sea? Who gave us the sponge to wipe away the entire horizon? What did we do when we unchained this earth from its sun? Whither is it moving now? Whither are we moving now? Away from all suns? Are we not perpetually falling? Backward, sideward, forward, in all directions? Is there any up or down left? Are we not straying as through an infinite nothing? Do we not feel the breath of empty space? Has it not become colder? Is more and more night not coming on all the time? Must not lanterns be lit in the morning? Do we not hear anything yet of the noise of the gravediggers who are burying God? Do we not smell anything yet of God's decomposition? – gods too decompose. God is dead. God remains dead. And we have killed him. How shall we, the murderers of all murderers, console ourselves? That which was holiest and mightiest of all that the world has yet possessed has bled to death under our knives – who will wipe this blood off us? With what water could we purify ourselves? What festivals of atonement, what sacred games shall we need to invent?

Is not the greatness of this deed too great for us? Must not we ourselves become gods simply to seem worthy of it? There has never been a greater deed – and whoever shall be born after us, for the sake of this deed he shall be part of a higher history than all history hitherto.'...(125).

Not only is there no God, there is no other ordering principle either:

Let us beware! Let us beware of thinking the world is a living being. Whither should it spread itself? What should it nourish itself with? How could it grow and multiply? We know indeed more or less what the organic is: and shall we reinterpret the unspeakably derivative, late, rare, chance phenomena which we perceive only on the surface of the earth into the essential, universal, eternal, as they do who call the universe an organism? I find that disgusting. Let us likewise beware of believing the universe is a machine; it is certainly not constructed so as to perform some operation, we do it far too great honour with the word 'machine'. Let us beware of presupposing that something so orderly as the cyclical motions of our planetary neighbours are the general and universal case; even a glance at the Milky Way gives rise to doubt whether there may not there exist far more crude and contradictory motions, likewise stars with eternally straight trajectories, and the like. The astral order in which we live is an exception; this order and the apparent permanence which is conditional upon it is in its turn made possible by the exception of exceptions: the formation of the organic. The total nature of the world is, on the other hand, to all eternity chaos, not in the sense that necessity is lacking but in that order, structure, form, beauty, wisdom, and whatever other human aesthetic notions we may have are lacking. Judged from the viewpoint of our reason, the unsuccessful cases are far and away the rule, the exceptions are not the secret objective, and the whole contraption repeats its theme, which can never be called a melody, over and over again to eternity – and ultimately even the term 'unsuccessful case' is already a humanization which contains a reproof. But how can we venture to reprove or praise the universe! Let us beware of attributing to it heartlessness and unreason or their opposites: it is neither perfect nor beautiful nor noble, and has no desire to become any of these; it is by no means striving to imitate mankind! It is quite impervious to all our aesthetic and moral judgements! It has likewise no impulse to self-preservation or impulses of any kind; neither does it know any laws. Let us beware of saying there are laws in nature. There are only necessities: there is no one to command, no one to obey, no one to transgress. .... Let us beware of saying that death is the opposite of life. The living being is only a species of the dead, and a very rare species.... (109).

These passages and very many more like them are included in the first three of the four books which constitute the original edition of *The Gay Science*: they seem to me to mark the end of the road on which Nietzsche set out when he left his forefathers' faith and went off alone. I do not see how he or anyone could go further in this direction. If he had not found some other direction he would at this time – the second half of 1881 – have reached his end station: and it is his knowledge that this is so that constitutes the intellectual crisis of which *Zarathustra* is the resolution.

3

We must now take a look at another aspect of Nietzsche's authorship. So far as modern Europe is concerned he was very much a pioneer in the demolition of ancient habits of mind and moral prejudices, and he was moreover very little read during his active life: so that to a great degree he had to be his own commentator and critic. There is an element in his work which derives directly from this fact. You will often hear not one voice but two: one asserts, the other objects and qualifies. Or one draws a sombre, the other a happy conclusion from the same premisses. Now one important duty of the second voice is to intimate, at strategic points in the books, that all the demolition going on *may* be only the essential preliminary and prerequisite for new construction; and none of these passages is more eloquent or revealing than that which stands at the end of *Dawn*:

We aeronauts of the spirit! All those brave birds which fly out into the distance, into the farthest distance – it is certain! somewhere or other they will be unable to go on and will perch down on a mast or a bare cliff-face – and they will even be thankful for this miserable accommodation! But who could venture to infer from that, that there was *not* an immense open space before them, that they had flown as far as one *could* fly! All our great teachers and predecessors have at last come to a stop . . .; it will be the same with you and me! But what does that matter to you and me! *Other birds will fly farther!* This insight and faith of ours vies with them in flying up and away; it rises above our heads and above our impotence into the heights and from there surveys the distance and sees before it the flocks of birds which, far stronger than we, still strive whither we have striven, and where everything is sea, sea, sea! – And whither then would we go? Would we *cross* the sea? Whither does this mighty longing draw us, this longing that is worth more to us than any pleasure? Why just in this direction, thither where all the suns of humanity have hitherto *gone down*? Will it perhaps be said of us one day that we too, *steering westward, hoped to reach an India* – but that it was our fate to be wrecked against infinity? Or, my brothers? Or? – (575).

This makes a brave sound, and the feeling that it expresses – that there are new worlds to be opened up – came to dominate more and more from the summer of 1881 onwards. 'Ideas have arisen on my horizon the like of which I have never seen before . . .', Nietzsche wrote to Peter Gast on 14 August 1881. 'I shall certainly have to live a *few* years more! . . . The intensity of my feelings makes me shudder and laugh – a couple of times I couldn't leave my room for the ludicrous reason that my eyes were inflamed. . . . Each time I had been weeping too much on my walks the day before, not sentimental tears but tears of rejoicing; and as I wept I sang and talked nonsense, filled with a new vision . . .'

This is not an altogether new note, but the intensity is new and the 'ideas' alluded to are also new and new in this sense that they are direct attempts to go beyond the nihilist conclusions of the past five years without being obliged to retract any of them.

The fourth book of *The Gay Science* is a signpost pointing the way Nietzsche is going. Always under the influence of significant dates, he opens it with a passage written on New Year's Day 1882:

For the New Year. I am still living, I am still thinking: I have to go on living because I have to go on thinking. *Sum, ergo cogito: cogito, ergo sum*. Today everyone is permitted to express his desire and dearest thoughts: so I too would like to say what I have desired of myself today and what thought was the first to cross my heart this year – what thought shall be the basis, guarantee and sweetness of all my future life! I want to learn more and more to see what is necessary in things as the beautiful in them – thus I shall become one of those who make things beautiful. *Amor fati:* may that be my love from now on! I want to wage no war against the ugly. I do not want to accuse, I do not want even to accuse the accusers. May *looking away* be my only form of negation! And, all in all: I want to be at all times hereafter only an affirmer (*ein Ja-sagender*)! (276).

This challenge to everything nihilist in his nature is followed a little later by a call to action, battle and positive commitment phrased in one of his most famous coinages – perhaps actually the most famous phrase in all his works:

I greet all the signs that a more manly, warlike age is coming, which will, above all, bring valour again into honour! For it has to prepare the way for a yet higher age, and assemble the force which that age will one day have need of – that age which will carry heroism into knowledge and *wage war* for the sake of ideas and their consequences. To that end many brave pioneers are needed now ...: men who know how to be silent, solitary, resolute, ... who have an innate disposition to seek in all things that which must be *overcome* in them: men to whom cheerfulness, patience, simplicity and contempt for the great vanities belong just as much as do generosity in victory and indulgence towards the little vanities of the defeated: ... men with their own festivals, their own work-days, their own days of mourning, accustomed to and assured in command and equally ready to obey when necessary, equally proud in the one case as in the other, equally serving their own cause: men more imperilled, men more fruitful, happier men! For believe me! – the secret of realizing the greatest fruitfulness and the greatest enjoyment of existence is: to *live dangerously*! Build your cities on the slopes of Vesuvius! Send your ships out into uncharted seas! Live in conflict with your equals and with your-selves! Be robbers and ravagers as long as you cannot be rulers and owners, you men of knowledge! ... (283).

A new image of man, of what mankind might be, begins to appear:

Excelsior! 'You will never again pray, never again worship, never again repose in limitless trust – you deny it to yourself to remain halted before an ultimate wisdom, ultimate good, ultimate power, and there unharness your thoughts – you have no perpetual guardian and friend for your seven solitudes ... there is no longer for you any rewarder and recompenser, no final corrector – there is no longer any reason in what happens, no longer any love in what happens to you – there is no longer any resting-place open to your heart where it has only to find and no longer to seek, you resist any kind of ultimate peace, you want the eternal recurrence of war and peace – man of renunciation, will you renounce in all this? Who will give you the strength for it? No one has yet possessed this strength!' – There is a lake which one day denied it to itself to flow away and threw up a dam at the place where it formerly flowed away: since then this lake has risen higher and higher. Perhaps it is precisely that renunciation which will also lend us the strength by which the renunciation itself can be endured; perhaps man will rise higher and higher from that time when he no longer *flows out* into a god. (285).

And the penultimate section of the book is a very curious suggestion for a formula of self- and life-affirmation:

The heaviest burden. What if a demon crept after you one day or night in your loneliest solitude and said to you: 'This life, as you live it now and have lived it, you will have to live again and again, times without number; and there will be nothing new in it, but every pain and every joy and every thought and sigh and all the unspeakably small and great in your life must return to you, and everything in the same series and sequence – and in the same way this spider and this moonlight among the trees, and in the same way this moment and I myself. The eternal hour-glass of existence will be turned again and again – and you with it, you dust of dust!' – Would you not throw yourself down and gnash your teeth and curse the demon who thus spoke? Or have you experienced a tremendous moment in which you would have answered him: 'You are a god and never did I hear anything more divine!' If this thought gained power over you it would, as you are now, transform and perhaps crush you; the question in all and everything: 'do you want this again and again, times without number?' would lie as the heaviest burden upon all your actions. Or how well disposed towards yourself and towards life would you have to become to have *no greater desire* than for this ultimate eternal sanction and seal? (341).

In April 1882 began the one wholly serious sexual involvement of Nietzsche's life: his brief and humiliating affair with Lou Salomé. This is not the place to go into the details of that affair; I discuss it here at all only because it has some bearing on the 'man in solitude' aspect of *Zarathustra* and because it is part of the general state of crisis in which Nietzsche existed during the eighteen months from the summer of 1881 to the beginning of 1883. Only two points need to be made. Firstly, Nietzsche thought that the solitude in which he had been living since his enforced retirement from Basel University at Easter 1879 and which had been weighing more and more heavily upon him was about to come to an end. In a letter to Lou Salomé (2 July 1882) he says that the previous day 'it seemed as if it must be my birthday: *you* sent me your assent [i.e. to come and stay with him for three weeks], the best present anyone could have given me ... Teubner [a printer] sent the first three proof-sheets of the *Gay Science*, and in addition to all this the last part of the manuscript of the *Gay Science* was completed, and therewith the work of six years (1876 to 1882), my entire "free-thought"!'

This means that when he wrote this letter he had just made a fair copy of the following passage, which closes *The Gay Science* in its original version:

Incipit tragoedia. When Zarathustra was thirty years old, he left his home and Lake Urmi and went into the mountains. Here he had the enjoyment of his spirit and his solitude and he did not weary of it for ten years. But at last his heart turned – and one morning he rose with the dawn, stepped before the sun, and spoke to it thus: 'Great star! What would your happiness be, if you had not those for whom you shine! You have come up here to my cave for ten years: you would have grown weary of your light and of this journey, without me, my eagle and my serpent; but we waited for you every morning, took from you your superfluity and blessed you for it. Behold! I am weary of my wisdom, like a bee that has gathered too much honey; I need hands outstretched to take it; I should like to give it away and distribute it, until the wise among men have again become happy in their folly and the poor happy in their wealth. To that end, I must descend into the depths: as you do at evening, when you go behind the sea and bring light to the underworld too, superabundant star! – like you, I must *go down* – as men, to whom I want to descend, call it. So bless me then, tranquil eye, that can behold without envy even an excessive happiness! Bless the cup that wants to overflow, that the waters may flow golden from him and bear the reflexion of your joy over all the world! Behold! This cup wants to be empty again, and Zarathustra wants to be man again.' – Thus began Zarathustra's down-going. (342).

The sense of this passage is repeated in other words at the end of the above-quoted letter: 'I don't want to be lonely any more; I want to learn to be human again. Alas, in *this* field I have almost everything still to learn!'

Undoubtedly Nietzsche at this point identified himself with another 'teacher' who came down out of solitude around his fortieth year.

The second point is that, after he was abandoned during the following October by Lou Salomé and had to realize that his hope of marrying her was definitely not going to be fulfilled, he fell into an abyss of despair. I am not underrating the emotional effect which such a disappointment might normally be expected to produce, but its effect on Nietzsche was certainly very violent indeed, especially considering that his disposition was usually a cheerful one. It should be recalled that he had been recurrently ill since 1871 – almost certainly a consequence of a syphilitic infection contracted when a student – and the inability of these attacks to depress him or do more than delay his work is a witness to the resilience of his temperament. His failure with Lou, however, threw him for a time completely off balance – how far off balance can be gauged, for example, from this letter to Franz Overbeck, posted on Christmas Day 1882:

I have suffered from the disgraceful and anguishing recollections of this past summer as from a kind of madness. ... They involve a conflict of contrary emotions which I am not equal to. ... If only I could sleep! But the strongest sleeping-draughts help as little as do the six to eight hour walks I take. If I cannot find the magic formula to turn all this – muck to *gold,* I am lost. . . . I now mistrust everybody: I sense in everything I hear contempt towards me. . . . Sometimes I think of renting a small room in Basel, visiting you now and then and attending lectures. Sometimes I think of doing the opposite: of driving my solitude and resignation to the ultimate limit and –

The ground of this violent reaction was, as other letters but especially *Zarathustra* show, the realization he was back in solitude and that he was going to stay there.

With the benefit of hindsight we can see that by the turn of the year 1882–83 there had been assembled in Nietzsche the material for an explosion of some sort – or rather, as we shall discover, an *eruption.* Intellectually, emotionally and physically he was all but exhausted; but the 'ideas' of the summer of 1881 as they had received tentative expression in the fourth book of *The Gay Science* are preliminary rumblings which indicate what is coming. In January – 'as a result of ten absolutely fresh and cheerful January days' – the tension broke, inhibition gave way, and the first part of *Zarathustra* came furiously out.

'Has anyone at the end of the nineteenth century a distinct conception of what poets of strong ages called inspiration?' he asked in *Ecce Homo, a propos* of *Zarathustra.*

If not, I will describe it. – If one had the slightest residue of super-stition left in one, one would hardly be able to set aside the idea that one is merely incarnation, merely mouthpiece, merely medium of overwhelming forces. The concept of revelation, in the sense that something suddenly, with unspeakable certainty and subtlety, becomes *visible,* audible, something that shakes and overturns one to the depths, simply describes the fact. One hears, one does not seek; one takes, one does not ask who gives; a thought flashes up like lightning, with necessity, unfalteringly formed – I have never had any choice. An ecstasy whose tremendous tension sometimes dis-charges itself in a flood of tears, while one's steps now involuntarily rush along, now involuntarily lag; . . . a depth of happiness in which the most painful and gloomy things appear, not as an antithesis, but as conditioned, demanded, as a *necessary* colour within such a superfluity of light; . . . Everything is in the highest degree in-voluntary but takes place as in a tempest of a feeling of freedom, of absoluteness, of power, of divinity. The involuntary nature of image, of metaphor is the most remarkable thing of all; one no longer has any idea what is image, what metaphor, everything presents itself as the readiest, the truest, the simplest means of expression. It really does seem, to allude to an expression of Zarathustra's, as if the things themselves approached and offered themselves as metaphors ... This is *my* experience of inspiration; I do not doubt that one has to go back thousands of years to find anyone who could say to me 'it is mine also'.

Zarathustra again emerges from his ten-year solitude, but now the mankind to whom he wants to address himself rejects him and he turns from it; subsequently he deserts even the chosen few who have remained with him and goes back into solitude. His message to mankind is:

I teach you the Superman. Man is something that should be overcome.

And:

The Superman is the meaning of the earth. Let your will say: The Superman *shall be* the meaning of the earth.

And:

All gods are dead: now we want the Superman to live – let this be our last will one day at the great noontide!

Then:

A table of values hangs over every people. Behold, it is the table of its overcomings; behold, it is the voice of its will to power.

And (in the second part, written in a similar state of excitement in the following June and July):

Of Self-Overcoming ... Where I found a living creature, there I found will to power ... And life itself told me this secret: 'Behold,' it said, 'I am that *which must overcome itself again and again*. ... Where there is perishing and the falling of leaves, behold, there life sacrifices itself – for the sake of power! ... And you too, enlightened man, are only a path and footstep of my will: truly, my will to power walks with the feet of your will to truth! ... The living creature values many things higher than life itself; yet out of this evaluation itself speaks – the will to power!' ...

And (in the third part, written in a state of even greater excitement in January 1884):

O my Will! ... Preserve me from all petty victories! ... That I may one day be ready and ripe in the great noontide ... a bow eager for its arrow, an arrow eager for its star – a star, ready and ripe in its noontide, glowing, transpierced ... Spare me for one great victory!

And:

Sing and bubble over, O Zarathustra, heal your soul with new songs, so that you may bear your great destiny ... behold, *you are the teacher of the eternal recurrence* ... And if you should die now, O Zarathustra: behold, we know too what you would then say to yourself ... 'Now I die and decay ... and in an instant I shall be nothingness ... But the complex of causes in which I am entangled will recur – it will create me again! ... I shall return ... *not* to a new life or a better life or a similar life: I shall return eternally to this identical and self-same life ... to teach once more the eternal recurrence of all things, to speak once more the teaching of the great noontide of earth and man, to tell man of the Superman once more ...

Finally:

> O Man! Attend!
> What does deep midnight's voice contend?
> 'I slept my sleep,
> And now awake at dreaming's end:
> The world is deep,
> Deeper than day can comprehend.
> Deep is its woe,
> Joy – deeper than heart's agony:
> Woe says: Fade! Go!
> But all joy wants eternity,
> – wants deep, deep, deep eternity!'

And, in an immense expansion of this poem, written a year later:

Did you ever say Yes to one joy? O my friends, then you said Yes to *all* woe as well. All things are chained and entwined together, all things are in love; if you ever wanted one moment twice, if

24

you ever said: 'You please me, happiness, instant, moment!'
then you wanted *everything* to return! you wanted everything anew,
everything eternal, everything chained, entwined together, everything in love, O that is how you *loved* the world, you everlasting
men, loved it eternally, and for all time: and you say even to woe:
'Go, but return!' *For all joy wants – eternity!*

The Superman, the will to the Superman, the will to power
and self-overcoming. Live dangerously! *Amor fati*, eternal
recurrence, total affirmation of life. The great noontide. These
are the slogans, the 'signs', by which Nietzsche surmounted
his nihilism and resolved his crisis.

4

Let's now try to get to the heart of this book and discover the
real meaning of its central concepts.

What is truth? said jesting Pilate; and would not stay for an
answer. If he had stayed, what answer would he have received?
There cannot be any doubt: Jesus would have said: *I* am the
truth. This too is Zarathustra's answer to the question 'what is
truth?' For what, at this level, *is* truth, 'the truth'? Isn't it the
discovery that no truth is discoverable except the truth which
you yourself are? that there is no truth (sense, meaning) in the
world except the truth (sense, meaning) *you yourself give it*?
that 'truth' is a concept belonging to the human mind and
will and that apart from the human mind and will there is no
such thing as 'truth'? finally, that the resolute determination
that your own truth shall be *the* truth is the sole origin of '*the*
truth' on earth? To give life a meaning: that has been the
grand endeavour of all who have preached 'truth'; for unless
life is *given* a meaning it has none. At this level, truth is not
something that can be proved or disproved: it is something
which you *determine upon*, which, in the language of the old
psychology, you *will*. It is not something waiting to be discovered, something to which you submit or at which you halt:
it is something you *create*, it is the expression of a particular
kind of life and being which has, in you, ventured to assert
itself. Thus Zarathustra declares: 'The Superman is the mean-

ing of the earth. Let your will say: The Superman *shall be* the meaning of the earth.' He is a prophet, not of the truth that *is*, but of the truth that *shall be*. What determines the nature of 'truth'? The nature of the I which asserts '*I* am the truth'. *Why* truth, and not rather untruth or indifference to truth? Because each particular life and being needs a fortress within which to preserve and protect itself and from which to reach out in search of aggrandizement and more power, and truth is this fortress. Or, as life says to thinking mankind: 'my will to power walks with the feet of your will to truth.' What then ultimately is the answer to Pilate's question? It is: truth is will to power. Thus – by my reading at any rate – spoke Zarathustra.

The great need, the 'one thing needful', was to overcome the nihilistic devaluation of life and man which had followed the destruction of the metaphysical world (the 'death of God'). This devaluation had been effected chiefly by a psychological theory, namely the theory that primitive drives can be *sublimated*, so that distinctively human qualities, 'humane' qualities, can be understood as sublimated forms of drives which mankind has in common with the animals. The motive for formulating such a theory was the need to account for what is distinctively human without recourse to the metaphysical or supernatural. From a very large number of experiments, two primitive drives emerged as dominant: the desire for power and the emotion of fear. And when Nietzsche came to understand fear as *the feeling of the absence of power*, he was left with a single motivating principle for all human actions: the will to power.

Sublimated will to power was now the Ariadne's thread tracing the way out of the labyrinth of nihilism. 'A table of values' – i.e. a *morality* – 'hangs over every people': it is the table of the self-imposed commands which have turned a herd and rabble into a nation: primitive aggression has been directed back upon itself, sublimated into *self*-control. When the same thing happens in an individual, when he imposes commands upon himself, and obeys them, so that he too as it were changes from a rabble into a nation, the result is 'the Superman', the man who is master of *himself*. But to master *oneself* is the hardest of all tasks, that which requires the greatest amount of power: he who can do it has experienced the greatest increase in power, and if (as Nietzsche later says explicitly but here implies) happiness (in *Zarathustra* 'joy') is the feeling that power increases, that a resistance is overcome, then the Superman will be the happiest man and, as such, the meaning and justification of existence. Through continual increase of power to transmute the chaos of life into a continual self-overcoming of life and thus to experience in an ever greater degree the joy which is synonymous with this self-overcoming: that would now be the meaning of life – for joy is to Nietzsche, as it is to commonsense, the one thing that requires no justification, that is its own justification. He who had attained that joy would affirm life and love it however much pain it contained, because he would know that 'all things are chained and entwined together' and that everything is therefore part of a whole which he must accept *as a whole*. To express this feeling of life-affirmation Nietzsche formulated a theorem of 'the eternal recurrence of the same events' to which he gave rhapsodic expression in *Zarathustra*. To be sure, only the Superman could be so well-disposed towards his life as to want it again and again for ever: but that precisely is the reason for willing his creation. The joy of the Superman in being as he is, now and ever, is the ultimate sublimation of the will to power and the final overcoming of an otherwise inexorable and inevitable nihilism.

5

These conceptions constitute the heart of *Thus Spoke Zarathustra*; these, and the extended hymn to solitude and individuality to which the book owes its peculiar tone and pathos. I have described the process of their formation as an eruption; what I mean is an eruption from the subconscious of ideas belonging to Nietzsche's earliest years, an eruption brought about by the very fact that at this time he had arrived at the *end* of the path which led away from them. He could go no further forward, so he had to go back. But since he likewise could not retract what he had been asserting for the previous five years, these earliest ideas which now came up again came up transformed and distorted almost beyond recognition. What is involved is the operation of something like the psychic censor of psychoanalysis: so that I doubt whether Nietzsche himself was altogether aware of the provenance of the grand and grandiose positive conceptions to the elaboration of which he began to apply his exceptional rhetorical gifts.

These 'earliest ideas' are of course Christian, and specifically Lutheran. The teaching of Lutheran Pietism is before all that the events of life are divinely willed and that it is thus impiety to desire that things should be different from what they are:* but the other tenets of Christian belief are naturally also firmly adhered to by Lutherans. Here, without more ado, are what I take to be the Christian parallels to the conceptions which dominated Nietzsche's mind during the period from the summer of 1881 to the year January 1883–January 1884, when they found full expression in *Zarathustra*.

Amor fati: Lutheran acceptance of the events of life as divinely willed, with the consequent affirmation of life as such as *divine*, as a product of the divine will, and the implication that to hate life is blasphemous.

Eternal recurrence: as a consequence of *amor fati* the extremest formula of life-affirmation, strongly influenced by the Christian concepts of eternal life and the unalterable nature of God: what is, 'is now and ever shall be, world without end.'

Will to power: divine grace. The clue to the connexion is the concept of 'self-overcoming', which is one of Nietzsche's terms for sublimation and the hinge upon which the theory of the will to power turns from being a nihilist to a positive

*I owe this insight to Mr Marvin Rintala, who in his review of my biography of Nietzsche in *The Review of Politics*, January 1969, said I had failed to understand in what the essence of Lutheran Pietism consisted, which was true, and then went on to expound it. 'The great petition of the Lord's Prayer,' says Mr Rintala, 'is for Pietists: "Thy will be done"'. This is so much in line with the Christian origin of the conceptions of *Zarathustra* that I ought to have *guessed* it even if I did not know it.

and joyful conception. The corresponding Christian conception is that of unregenerate nature redeemed by the force of
God's grace. In both conceptions the central idea is that a
certain inner quality (grace/sublimated will to power) elevates
man (or some men) above the rest of nature. The pathos with
which 'will to power' is invested derives to some extent from
'Thy will be done' and the juxtaposition of 'power' and
'glory', together with the Christian doctrine that to God's
will all things are possible.

Live dangerously!: 'Take up thy Cross, and follow me' –
Christian deprecation of the easy life.

Great noontide: the Second Coming, the Last Judgement,
the division of the sheep from the goats, the wheat from the
chaff.

Superman: God as creator and 'highest being', the 'Son of
Man' as God, man as the receptacle of divine grace who rejoices at the idea of eternity: the embodiment and actualization of everything regarded as desirable. What the Christian
says of God, Nietzsche says in very nearly the same words of
the Superman, namely: 'Thine is the kingdom, and the power,
and the glory, for ever and ever.'

6

Zarathustra's posture as inspired prophet and reader of riddles
would itself suggest an atavism in Nietzsche's mind even if
we were unable clearly to identify the earlier stage to which it
had reverted. But it was an atavism whose effect was curative,
like an electrical storm that breaks up the cloud and bad
weather which has caused it. The theme of joy in existence, of
the self-sufficiency-in-joy of the sovereign individual, of this
joyful self-sufficiency as the aim and meaning of life is what
finally reigns as the paramount theme of the book: and this
theme derives, not from the grand but ultimately overpowering and stifling conceptions of Christianity, but from
someone Nietzsche was later to celebrate as an actualization
of the Superman: Goethe.

When the sound and wholesome nature of man acts as an entirety, when he feels himself in the world as in a grand, beautiful, worthy and worthwhile whole, when this harmonious comfort affords him a pure, untrammeled delight: then the universe, if it could be sensible of itself, would shout for joy at having attained its goal and wonder at the pinnacle of its own essence and evolution. For what end is served by all the expenditure of suns and planets and moons, of stars and Milky Ways, of comets and nebula, of worlds evolving and passing away, if at last a happy man does not involuntarily rejoice in his existence?

This passage, from Goethe's essay on Winckelmann (1805), which Nietzsche certainly knew, could stand as the motto of *Thus Spoke Zarathustra*. It is the distillation of the great benevolent spirit of Goethe, a spirit Nietzsche called 'dionysian' and with which, for all its tremendous difference in emphasis, *Zarathustra* is in accordance.

7

I now offer a brief survey of *Zarathustra* chapter by chapter and comment on a few individual points about which the reader may like some enlightenment.

Zarathustra (*Greek* Zoroastres) is the founder of the ancient Persian religion, and the book with which he is credited, the Zend-Avesta, is its Bible. Scholars of the nineteenth century questioned whether Zarathustra existed, as they questioned whether Homer existed (probably a side-effect of 'evolutionism'): both are now rehabilitated. Nietzsche protested at the dissolution of Homer: 'We gain nothing with our theory of the poetising soul of the people, we are always referred back to the poetical individual' (*Homer and Classical Philology*, 1869). So with Zarathustra. He is conjectured to have lived in the seventh century B.C. The heart of his religion is a conflict between Ahura Mazda (Ormuzd), the god of light and good, and Angra Mainyu (Ahriman), the god of darkness and evil. Nietzsche's explanation of why he appropriated his name for his own hero:

I have not been asked, as I should have been asked, what the name
Zarathustra means in precisely my mouth, in the mouth of the first
immoralist: for what constitutes the tremendous uniqueness of that
Persian in history is precisely the opposite of this. Zarathustra
was the first to see in the struggle between good and evil the
actual wheel in the working of things: the translation of morality
into the realm of metaphysics, as force, cause, end-in-itself, is *his*
work. But this question is itself at bottom its own answer. Zarathustra *created* this most fateful of errors, morality: consequently
he must also be the first to *recognize* it. Not only has he had longer
and greater experience here than any other thinker ... what is
more important is that Zarathustra is more truthful than any other
thinker. His teaching, and his alone, upholds truthfulness as the
supreme virtue. ... To tell the truth and *to shoot well with arrows:*
that is Persian virtue. – Have I been understood? The self-
overcoming of morality through truthfulness, the self-overcoming
of the moralist into his opposite – *into me* – that is what the name
Zarathustra means in my mouth. (*Ecce Homo*).

The book is very loosely constructed, but it does possess
direction and a plot of sorts.

PART ONE. *Prologue.* (1) Zarathustra comes down out of
solitude, announces (2) that God is dead and (3) preaches
God's successor, the Superman. Mankind fails to understand
him, even when he (4) expounds his beatitudes (cf. Matthew
5, 3–11) and (5) appeals to their pride by describing the Superman's antithesis, the 'Ultimate Man', the man who sacrifices
the future to his own present. The (6) overtoppling of the
tightrope walker (mankind balanced over an abyss) by the
buffoon (Zarathustra himself perhaps, an unannounced attrac-
tion) brings home to Zarathustra (7) that human existence is
'uncanny' (cf. the second chorus of *Antigone*: 'Many things
are uncanny, but none more uncanny than man'), and after a
bad night (8) he resolves (9) to desert the market place and
speak his message only to the individual.

The twenty-two 'discourses' which follow are addressed
by Zarathustra to his band of disciples. Five of the discourses
are enclosed in a miniature dramatic scene, the remainder are
direct address. Each is an epitome of Nietzsche's views on the
subject in question:

1: the 'education of the spirit': self-discipline, independence, creativity (for another account, in quite different language, see *Human, All Too Human*, Preface to volume I (1886), sections 3–7); 2: 'negative virtue', virtue which consists in *not doing wrong* and which has as its reward 'peace of soul'; 3: 'the metaphysical world' (including a renunciation of his earlier view (*The Birth of Tragedy*, 1872) that aesthetic values are the only true values); 4: the relation between mind and body (a prologue to the theory of the will to power); 5: the nature of virtue; 6: its opposite, the 'criminal instinct'; 7: aphorisms on authorship, happiness and laughter (introduces 'the Spirit of Gravity'); 8: 'nobility of soul'; 9: pessimism; 10: 'Live dangerously!'; 11: the State; 12: nausea at mankind, '*l'enfer, c'est les autres*'; 13: sensuality and its disguises; 14: how to be a true friend; 15: the relativity of moral values (introduces the will to power); 16: critique of 'love thy neighbour as thyself'; 17: the need for solitude and the danger of solitude; 18: the nature of women; 19: the nature of justice; 20: bad marriages and good ones; 21: bad deaths and good ones.

Over all these discourses hovers Zarathustra's dictum 'Man is something that must be overcome.' The final chapter reverts to the Prologue, to the death of God and the need for the Superman to give significance to the earth; Zarathustra extols the magnanimous man, the man so full of strength and well-being he bestows gifts on others because he has to, and exhorts his disciples to independence. Then he leaves them.

PART TWO. Much more various than Part One. Zarathustra is more of a dramatic character and eight of the twenty-two chapters involve action.

1: corresponds to the Prologue of Part One: Zarathustra's return; 2: a much-expanded recapitulation of the 'God is dead' theme, and the reintroduction of the Superman as God's successor; 3: pity for mankind and the need to overcome it; 4: organized religion and the priesthood; 5: another essay on virtue, true and false; 6: another essay on nausea at

mankind and how to avoid it; 7: another essay on justice and
a polemic against revengefulness disguised as justice; 8: philosophy, true and false; 9–11: prose poems, autobiographical,
for the most part fretful, plaintive, disgruntled (cf. Part
Three 3–4 and 14–16); 12: the will to power in full; 13: re-
sumes and completes 8; 14: critique of contemporary culture;
15: critique of the contemplative life and the search for 'pure
knowledge'; 16: critique of the scholarly life; 17: critique of the
artistic nature; 18: dramatically, the book's turning-point. A
discourse on revolution and anarchism is allied to an uncommon amount of action and a fantastical story told by
sailors. Zarathustra's disciples 'hardly listened' to his discourse, we are told, because of their anxiety to repeat the
sailors' story, the point of which is that Zarathustra's alter ego
has been seen flying through the air crying 'It is time! It is
high time!' 'For what is it high time?' Zarathustra asks himself when he learns this: the answer (suppressed for the moment but henceforward never absent from his mind) is: 'Time
to declare the eternal recurrence.'; 19: continues the fantastical
atmosphere of 18 and intensifies it into nightmare; Zarathustra is now in a nervous and depressed condition very different from the state of ebullient optimism which has chiefly
characterized him hitherto; a 'dark night of the soul', which
persists into Part Three; 20: a discourse on 'great men' leads
to reflexions on the nature of will in the midst of which Zarathustra is struck dumb when he realizes the implications of
what he is saying for the theory of eternal recurrence; 21: on
the desirability of masks – a beautifully shaped chapter, in
this respect perhaps the finest; but it belongs in spirit earlier
in the book, it interrupts the steady descent from 18 to 22, in
which Zarathustra, as the consequence of a second nightmare
which robs him of all self-confidence and almost of self-
control, again deserts his disciples, this time, however, in a
mood of profound misery, and this time for good.

PART THREE. For the most part Zarathustra is alone and
addressing himself. Earlier themes are taken up and woven
into a texture which sometimes grows too tight. Imagery be-

comes clotted at times. But the intensity of expression aimed at is superbly achieved and maintained.

1: Zarathustra has just left his disciples and is making his way home, his depression still upon him; 2: on board ship, he expounds the eternal recurrence as a riddle and in language which recalls the nightmare of Part Two 18; although all is still shrouded in obscurity and mystery, that he has now brought himself to raise the veil even to this limited extent is sufficient to restore him to his normal cheerfulness; 3 and 4: prose poems, introspective, cheerful, calm; half way between the melancholy of Part Two 9–11 and the Dionysian ecstasy of Part Three 14–16; 5: back on firm land, Zarathustra experiences again his familiar nausea at mankind; 6: self-portrait of Zarathustra as a solitary; 7: extended exegesis of the text 'May *looking away* be my only form of negation!'; 8: polemic against piety; 9: Zarathustra arrives back at his cave: a hymn to solitude; 10: a model 'revaluation' of three vices; 11: exhortation to cheerfulness; 12–16: the climax of the book, a supreme exhibition of the sustained intellectual passion which gives Nietzsche his place among the world's great men. 12 is a re-exposition in brief of Zarathustra's teachings, up to but not including the theory of the eternal recurrence, which is reserved for 13, in which the theory is at last stated in full and without disguise, and joyfully accepted and embraced. With this act Zarathustra's self-education reaches its appointed end. The fulfilment is celebrated with a trilogy of prose poems, 14–16, of great exuberance and intensity. At this culmination of his course, Zarathustra is, as aforesaid, entirely alone, so that when he wishes to give vent to his feelings of unbounded joy and gratitude in dithyrambic poetry there is no one to whom he can address these dithyrambs except himself. Thus 14 is addressed to his own soul, 15 to the life he feels within him, 16 to himself in his future reincarnation. The eternity referred to in 16 is of course the eternal recurrence, and the child he wants to have by 'eternity' is – himself.

PART FOUR. When, in January 1884, he closed his book with Seven Seals, Nietzsche thought *Zarathustra* was finished.

But in the following winter he took up the theme again, and planned a further three parts. In the first of them, Zarathustra is visited by sundry 'higher men' who, as a consequence of Zarathustra's instruction, become conscious of their inadequacy. At the conclusion of this part Zarathustra receives the call to go out into the world again, and in the following part he accumulates a large following, to whom he preaches his now triumphant message. In the final part he dies, although Nietzsche could not decide in what manner. Of these three new parts only the first was written, slowly and with interruptions, in the winter of 1884–85. Nietzsche had it privately printed but withheld it from publication, and it first appeared, as 'the Fourth and Last Part' of *Zarathustra* in 1892, as part of the first collected edition of Nietzsche.

Stylistically, Part Four is quite different from the earlier parts and on a lower level of inspiration. The 'higher men' are at once types and individuals. The gloomy prophet is Schopenhauer. The two kings are any kings. The conscientious man of the spirit is probably Darwin, although any scientific specialist would do. The sorcerer is Wagner (the sorcerer's poems are parodies of Wagner's later poetic manner). The last pope is of course (as yet) imaginary. The ugliest man and the shadow are representations of the atheist and the freethinker respectively. The voluntary beggar is either the Buddha or Tolstoy.

The eternal recurrence remains in the background, but emerges at the conclusion, where it receives its most sonorous and ecstatic affirmation.

June 1969   R.J.H.

FURTHER READING

David B. Allison, *Reading the New Nietzsche* (2001)

MaudeMarie Clark, *Nietzsche on Truth and Morality* (1990)

R. J. Hollingdale, *Nietzsche: The Man and His Philosophy* (1965; 1999)

Brian Leiter, *Nietzsche on Morality* (2002)

Bernd Magnus and Kathleen Higgins (eds.), *The Cambridge Companion to Nietzsche* (1996)

Alexander Nehemas, *Nietzsche: Life as Literature* (1985)

F. Nietzsche, *Daybreak: Thoughts on the Prejudices of Morality*, trans. R. J. Hollingdale, introduction by M. Tanner (1982)

——, *Dithyrambs of Dionysus*, trans. with introduction and notes R. J. Hollingdale (1984; 2001)

——, *Untimely Meditations*, trans. R. J. Hollingdale, introduction by J. P. Stern (1983)

John Richardson and Brian Leiter (eds.), *Nietzsche* (2001)

Rudiger Safranski, *Nietzsche: A Philosophical Biography*, trans. Shelley Frisch (2002)

Henry Staten, *Nietzsche's Voice* (1990)

Tracy Strong, *Friedrich Nietzsche and the Politics of Transfiguration* (1988)

PART ONE

✤

ZARATHUSTRA'S PROLOGUE

I

WHEN Zarathustra was thirty years old, he left his home and the lake of his home and went into the mountains. Here he had the enjoyment of his spirit and his solitude and he did not weary of it for ten years. But at last his heart turned – and one morning he rose with the dawn, stepped before the sun, and spoke to it thus:

Great star! What would your happiness be, if you had not those for whom you shine!

You have come up here to my cave for ten years: you would have grown weary of your light and of this journey, without me, my eagle and my serpent.

But we waited for you every morning, took from you your superfluity and blessed you for it.

Behold! I am weary of my wisdom, like a bee that has gathered too much honey; I need hands outstretched to take it.

I should like to give it away and distribute it, until the wise among men have again become happy in their folly and the poor happy in their wealth.

To that end, I must descend into the depths: as you do at evening, when you go behind the sea and bring light to the underworld too, superabundant star!

Like you, I must *go down*[1] – as men, to whom I want to descend, call it.

So bless me then, tranquil eye, that can behold without envy even an excessive happiness!

Bless the cup that wants to overflow, that the waters may flow golden from him and bear the reflection of your joy over all the world!

Behold! This cup wants to be empty again, and Zarathustra wants to be man again.

Thus began Zarathustra's down-going.

2

Zarathustra went down the mountain alone, and no one met him. But when he entered the forest, an old man, who had left his holy hut to look for roots in the forest, suddenly stood before him. And the old man spoke thus to Zarathustra:

'This wanderer is no stranger to me: he passed by here many years ago. He was called Zarathustra; but he has changed.

'Then you carried your ashes to the mountains: will you today carry your fire into the valleys? Do you not fear an incendiary's punishment?

'Yes, I recognize Zarathustra. His eyes are clear, and no disgust lurks about his mouth. Does he not go along like a dancer?

'How changed Zarathustra is! Zarathustra has become – a child, an awakened-one: what do you want now with the sleepers?

'You lived in solitude as in the sea, and the sea bore you. Alas, do you want to go ashore? Alas, do you want again to drag your body yourself?'

Zarathustra answered: 'I love mankind.'

'Why', said the saint, 'did I go into the forest and the desert? Was it not because I loved mankind all too much?

'Now I love God: mankind I do not love. Man is too imperfect a thing for me. Love of mankind would destroy me.'

Zarathustra answered: 'What did I say of love? I am bringing mankind a gift.'

'Give them nothing,' said the saint. 'Rather take something off them and bear it with them – that will please them best; if only it be pleasing to you!

'And if you want to give to them, give no more than an alms, and let them beg for that!'

'No,' answered Zarathustra, 'I give no alms. I am not poor enough for that.'

The saint laughed at Zarathustra, and spoke thus: 'See to it that they accept your treasures! They are mistrustful of hermits, and do not believe that we come to give.

'Our steps ring too lonely through their streets. And when at night they hear in their beds a man going by long before the sun has risen, they probably ask themselves: Where is that thief going?

'Do not go to men, but stay in the forest! Go rather to the animals! Why will you not be as I am – a bear among bears, a bird among birds?'

'And what does the saint do in the forest?' asked Zarathustra.

The saint answered: 'I make songs and sing them, and when I make songs, I laugh, weep, and mutter: thus I praise God.

'With singing, weeping, laughing, and muttering I praise the God who is my God. But what do you bring us as a gift?'

When Zarathustra heard these words, he saluted the saint and said: 'What should I have to give you! But let me go quickly, that I may take nothing from you!' And thus they parted from one another, the old man and Zarathustra, laughing as two boys laugh.

But when Zarathustra was alone, he spoke thus to his heart: 'Could it be possible! This old saint has not yet heard in his forest that *God is dead*!'

3

When Zarathustra arrived at the nearest of the towns lying against the forest, he found in that very place many people assembled in the market square: for it had been announced that a tight-rope walker would be appearing. And Zarathustra spoke thus to the people:

I teach you the Superman. Man is something that should be overcome. What have you done to overcome him?

All creatures hitherto have created something beyond themselves: and do you want to be the ebb of this great tide, and return to the animals rather than overcome man?

What is the ape to men? A laughing-stock or a painful

embarrassment. And just so shall man be to the Superman: a laughing-stock or a painful embarrassment.

You have made your way from worm to man, and much in you is still worm. Once you were apes, and even now man is more of an ape than any ape.

But he who is the wisest among you, he also is only a discord and hybrid of plant and of ghost. But do I bid you become ghosts or plants?

Behold, I teach you the Superman.

The Superman is the meaning of the earth. Let your will say: The Superman *shall be* the meaning of the earth!

I entreat you, my brothers, *remain true to the earth,* and do not believe those who speak to you of superterrestrial hopes! They are poisoners, whether they know it or not.

They are despisers of life, atrophying and self-poisoned men, of whom the earth is weary: so let them be gone!

Once blasphemy against God was the greatest blasphemy, but God died, and thereupon these blasphemers died too. To blaspheme the earth is now the most dreadful offence, and to esteem the bowels of the Inscrutable more highly than the meaning of the earth.

Once the soul looked contemptuously upon the body: and then this contempt was the supreme good – the soul wanted the body lean, monstrous, famished. So the soul thought to escape from the body and from the earth.

Oh, this soul was itself lean, monstrous, and famished: and cruelty was the delight of this soul!

But tell me, my brothers: What does your body say about your soul? Is your soul not poverty and dirt and a miserable ease?

In truth, man is a polluted river. One must be a sea, to receive a polluted river and not be defiled.

Behold, I teach you the Superman: he is this sea, in him your great contempt can go under.

What is the greatest thing you can experience? It is the hour of the great contempt. The hour in which even your happiness grows loathsome to you, and your reason and your virtue also.

The hour when you say: 'What good is my happiness? It is poverty and dirt and a miserable ease. But my happiness should justify existence itself!'

The hour when you say: 'What good is my reason? Does it long for knowledge as the lion for its food? It is poverty and dirt and a miserable ease!'

The hour when you say: 'What good is my virtue? It has not yet driven me mad! How tired I am of my good and my evil! It is all poverty and dirt and a miserable ease!'

The hour when you say: 'What good is my justice? I do not see that I am fire and hot coals. But the just man is fire and hot coals!'

The hour when you say: 'What good is my pity? Is not pity the cross upon which he who loves man is nailed? But my pity is no crucifixion!'

Have you ever spoken thus? Have you ever cried thus? Ah, that I had heard you crying thus!

It is not your sin, but your moderation that cries to heaven, your very meanness in sinning cries to heaven!

Where is the lightning to lick you with its tongue? Where is the madness, with which you should be cleansed?

Behold, I teach you the Superman: he is this lightning, he is this madness!

When Zarathustra had spoken thus, one of the people cried: 'Now we have heard enough of the tight-rope walker; let us see him, too!' And all the people laughed at Zarathustra. But the tight-rope walker, who thought that the words applied to him, set to work.

4

But Zarathustra looked at the people and marvelled. Then he spoke thus:

Man is a rope, fastened between animal and Superman – a rope over an abyss.

A dangerous going-across, a dangerous wayfaring, a dangerous looking-back, a dangerous shuddering and staying-still.

What is great in man is that he is a bridge and not a goal; what can be loved in man is that he is a *going-across* and a *down-going*.[2]

I love those who do not know how to live except their lives be a down-going, for they are those who are going across.

I love the great despisers, for they are the great venerators and arrows of longing for the other bank.

I love those who do not first seek beyond the stars for reasons to go down and to be sacrifices: but who sacrifice themselves to the earth, that the earth may one day belong to the Superman.

I love him who lives for knowledge and who wants knowledge that one day the Superman may live. And thus he wills his own downfall.

I love him who works and invents that he may build a house for the Superman and prepare earth, animals, and plants for him: for thus he wills his own downfall.

I love him who loves his virtue: for virtue is will to downfall and an arrow of longing.

I love him who keeps back no drop of spirit for himself, but wants to be the spirit of his virtue entirely: thus he steps as spirit over the bridge.

I love him who makes a predilection and a fate of his virtue: thus for his virtue's sake he will live or not live.

I love him who does not want too many virtues. One virtue is more virtue than two, because it is more of a knot for fate to cling to.

I love him whose soul is lavish, who neither wants nor returns thanks: for he always gives and will not preserve himself.

I love him who is ashamed when the dice fall in his favour and who then asks: Am I then a cheat? – for he wants to perish.

I love him who throws golden words in advance of his deeds and always performs more than he promised: for he wills his own downfall.

I love him who justifies the men of the future and redeems

the men of the past: for he wants to perish by the men of the present.

I love him who chastises his God because he loves his God: for he must perish by the anger of his God.

I love him whose soul is deep even in its ability to be wounded, and whom even a little thing can destroy: thus he is glad to go over the bridge.

I love him whose soul is overfull, so that he forgets himself and all things are in him: thus all things become his downfall.

I love him who is of a free spirit and a free heart: thus his head is only the bowels of his heart, but his heart drives him to his downfall.

I love all those who are like heavy drops falling singly from the dark cloud that hangs over mankind: they prophesy the coming of the lightning and as prophets they perish.

Behold, I am a prophet of the lightning and a heavy drop from the cloud: but this lightning is called *Superman*.

5

When Zarathustra had spoken these words he looked again at the people and fell silent. There they stand (he said to his heart), there they laugh: they do not understand me, I am not the mouth for these ears.

Must one first shatter their ears to teach them to hear with their eyes? Must one rumble like drums and Lenten preachers? Or do they believe only those who stammer?

They have something of which they are proud. What is it called that makes them proud? They call it culture, it distinguishes them from the goatherds.

Therefore they dislike hearing the word 'contempt' spoken of them. So I shall speak to their pride.

So I shall speak to them of the most contemptible man: and that is the *Ultimate Man*.

And thus spoke Zarathustra to the people:

It is time for man to fix his goal. It is time for man to plant the seed of his highest hope.

His soil is still rich enough for it. But this soil will one day be poor and weak; no longer will a high tree be able to grow from it.

Alas! The time is coming when man will no more shoot the arrow of his longing out over mankind, and the string of his bow will have forgotten how to twang!

I tell you: one must have chaos in one, to give birth to a dancing star. I tell you: you still have chaos in you.

Alas! The time is coming when man will give birth to no more stars. Alas! The time of the most contemptible man is coming, the man who can no longer despise himself.

Behold! I shall show you the *Ultimate Man*.

'What is love? What is creation? What is longing? What is a star?' thus asks the Ultimate Man and blinks.

The earth has become small, and upon it hops the Ultimate Man, who makes everything small. His race is as inexterminable as the flea; the Ultimate Man lives longest.

'We have discovered happiness,' say the Ultimate Men and blink.

They have left the places where living was hard: for one needs warmth. One still loves one's neighbour and rubs oneself against him: for one needs warmth.

Sickness and mistrust count as sins with them: one should go about warily. He is a fool who still stumbles over stones or over men!

A little poison now and then: that produces pleasant dreams. And a lot of poison at last, for a pleasant death.

They still work, for work is entertainment. But they take care the entertainment does not exhaust them.

Nobody grows rich or poor any more: both are too much of a burden. Who still wants to rule? Who obey? Both are too much of a burden.

No herdsman and one herd. Everyone wants the same thing, everyone is the same: whoever thinks otherwise goes voluntarily into the madhouse.

'Formerly all the world was mad,' say the most acute of them and blink.

They are clever and know everything that has ever happened: so there is no end to their mockery. They still quarrel, but they soon make up – otherwise indigestion would result.

They have their little pleasure for the day and their little pleasure for the night: but they respect health.

'We have discovered happiness,' say the Ultimate Men and blink.

And here ended Zarathustra's first discourse, which is also called 'The Prologue':[3] for at this point the shouting and mirth of the crowd interrupted him. 'Give us this Ultimate Man, O Zarathustra' – so they cried – 'make us into this Ultimate Man! You can have the Superman!' And all the people laughed and shouted. But Zarathustra grew sad and said to his heart:

They do not understand me: I am not the mouth for these ears.

Perhaps I lived too long in the mountains, listened too much to the trees and the streams: now I speak to them as to goatherds.

Unmoved is my soul and bright as the mountains in the morning. But they think me cold and a mocker with fearful jokes.

And now they look at me and laugh: and laughing, they still hate me. There is ice in their laughter.

6

But then something happened that silenced every mouth and fixed every eye. In the meantime, of course, the tight-rope walker had begun his work: he had emerged from a little door and was proceeding across the rope, which was stretched between two towers and thus hung over the people and the market square. Just as he had reached the middle of his course the little door opened again and a brightly-dressed fellow like a buffoon sprang out and followed the former with rapid steps. 'Forward, lame-foot!' cried his fearsome voice, 'forward sluggard, intruder, pallid-face! Lest I tickle you with my heels! What are you doing here between towers? You belong in the tower, you should be locked up, you are blocking the way of a better man than you!' And with each word he came nearer and nearer to him: but when he was only a single pace behind him, there occurred the dreadful thing that silenced every mouth and fixed every eye: he emitted a cry like a devil and sprang over the man standing in his path. But the latter, when he saw his rival thus triumph, lost his head and the rope; he threw away his pole and fell, faster even than it, like a vortex of legs and arms. The market square and the people were like a sea in a storm: they flew apart in disorder, especially where the body would come crashing down.

But Zarathustra remained still and the body fell quite close to him, badly injured and broken but not yet dead. After a while, consciousness returned to the shattered man and he saw Zarathustra kneeling beside him. 'What are you doing?' he asked at length. 'I've known for a long time that the Devil would trip me up. Now he's dragging me to Hell: are you trying to prevent him?'

'On my honour, friend,' answered Zarathustra, 'all you have spoken of does not exist: there is no Devil and no Hell. Your soul will be dead even before your body: therefore fear nothing any more!'

The man looked up mistrustfully. 'If you are speaking the truth,' he said then, 'I leave nothing when I leave life. I am not much more than an animal which has been taught to dance by blows and starvation.'

'Not so,' said Zarathustra. 'You have made danger your calling, there is nothing in that to despise. Now you perish through your calling: so I will bury you with my own hands.'

When Zarathustra had said this the dying man replied no more; but he motioned with his hand, as if he sought Zarathustra's hand to thank him.

7

In the meanwhile, evening had come and the market square was hidden in darkness: then the people dispersed, for even curiosity and terror grow tired. But Zarathustra sat on the ground beside the dead man and was sunk in thought: thus he forgot the time. But at length it became night and a cold wind blew over the solitary figure. Then Zarathustra arose and said to his heart:

Truly, Zarathustra has had a handsome catch today! He caught no man, but he did catch a corpse.

Uncanny is human existence and still without meaning: a buffoon can be fatal to it.

I want to teach men the meaning of their existence: which is the Superman, the lightning from the dark cloud man.

But I am still distant from them, and my meaning does not speak to their minds. To men, I am still a cross between a fool and a corpse.

Dark is the night, dark are Zarathustra's ways. Come, cold and stiff companion! I am going to carry you to the place where I shall bury you with my own hands.

8

When Zarathustra had said this to his heart he loaded the corpse on to his back and set forth. He had not gone a hundred paces when a man crept up to him and whispered in his ear – and behold! it was the buffoon of the tower who spoke to him. 'Go away from this town, O Zarathustra,' he said. 'Too many here hate you. The good and the just hate you and call you their enemy and despiser; the faithful of the true faith hate you, and they call you a danger to the people. It was lucky for you that they laughed at you: and truly you spoke like a buffoon. It was lucky for you that you made company with the dead dog; by so abasing yourself you have saved yourself for today. But leave this town – or tomorrow I shall jump over you, a living man over a dead one.' And when he had said this, the man disappeared; Zarathustra, however, went on through the dark streets.

At the town gate the gravediggers accosted him: they shone their torch in his face, recognized Zarathustra and greatly derided him. 'Zarathustra is carrying the dead dog away: excellent that Zarathustra has become a gravedigger! For our hands are too clean for this roast. Does Zarathustra want to rob the Devil of his morsel? Good luck then! A hearty appetite! But if the Devil is a better thief than Zarathustra! – he will steal them both, he will eat them both!' And they laughed and put their heads together.

Zarathustra said nothing and went his way. When he had walked for two hours past woods and swamps he had heard too much hungry howling of wolves and he grew hungry himself. So he stopped at a lonely house in which a light was burning.

'Hunger has waylaid me', said Zarathustra, 'like a robber. My hunger has waylaid me in woods and swamps, and in the depth of night.

'My hunger has astonishing moods. Often it comes to me only after mealtimes, and today it did not come at all: where has it been?'

And with that, Zarathustra knocked on the door of the house. An old man appeared; he carried a light and asked: 'Who comes here to me and to my uneasy sleep?'

'A living man and a dead,' said Zarathustra. 'Give me food and drink, I forgot about them during the day. He who feeds the hungry refreshes his own soul: thus speaks wisdom.'

The old man went away, but returned at once and offered Zarathustra bread and wine. 'This is a bad country for hungry people,' he said. 'That is why I live here. Animals and men come here to me, the hermit. But bid your companion eat and drink, he is wearier than you.' Zarathustra answered: 'My companion is dead, I shall hardly be able to persuade him.' 'That is nothing to do with me,' said the old man morosely. 'Whoever knocks at my door must take what I offer him. Eat, and fare you well!'

After that, Zarathustra walked two hours more and trusted to the road and to the light of the stars: for he was used to walking abroad at night and liked to look into the face of all that slept. But when morning dawned, Zarathustra found himself in a thick forest and the road disappeared. Then he laid the dead man in a hollow tree at his head – for he wanted to protect him from the wolves – and laid himself down on the mossy ground. And straightway he fell asleep, weary in body but with a soul at rest.

9

Zarathustra slept long, and not only the dawn but the morning too passed over his head. But at length he opened his eyes: in surprise Zarathustra gazed into the forest and the stillness, in surprise he gazed into himself. Then he arose quickly, like a seafarer who suddenly sees land, and rejoiced: for he beheld a new truth. And then he spoke to his heart thus:

A light has dawned for me: I need companions, living ones, not dead companions and corpses which I carry with me wherever I wish.

But I need living companions who follow me because they want to follow themselves – and who want to go where I want to go.

A light has dawned for me: Zarathustra shall not speak to the people but to companions! Zarathustra shall not be herdsman and dog to the herd!

To lure many away from the herd – that is why I have come. The people and the herd shall be angry with me: the herdsmen shall call Zarathustra a robber.

I say herdsmen, but they call themselves the good and the just. I say herdsmen: but they call themselves the faithful of the true faith.

Behold the good and the just! Whom do they hate most? Him who smashes their tables of values, the breaker, the law-breaker[4] – but he is the creator.

Behold the faithful of all faiths! Whom do they hate the

most? Him who smashes their tables of values, the breaker, the law-breaker – but he is the creator.

The creator seeks companions, not corpses or herds or believers. The creator seeks fellow-creators, those who inscribe new values on new tables.

The creator seeks companions and fellow-harvesters: for with him everything is ripe for harvesting. But he lacks his hundred sickles: so he tears off the ears of corn and is vexed.

The creator seeks companions and such as know how to whet their sickles. They will be called destroyers and despisers of good and evil. But they are harvesters and rejoicers.

Zarathustra seeks fellow-creators, fellow-harvesters, and fellow-rejoicers: what has he to do with herds and herdsmen and corpses!

And you, my first companion, fare you well! I have buried you well in your hollow tree, I have hidden you well from the wolves.

But I am leaving you, the time has come. Between dawn and dawn a new truth has come to me.

I will not be herdsman or gravedigger. I will not speak again to the people: I have spoken to a dead man for the last time.

I will make company with creators, with harvesters, with rejoicers: I will show them the rainbow and the stairway to the Superman.

I shall sing my song to the lone hermit and to the hermits in pairs; and I will make the heart of him who still has ears for unheard-of things heavy with my happiness.

I make for my goal, I go my way; I shall leap over the hesitating and the indolent. Thus may my going-forward be their going-down!

10

Zarathustra said this to his heart as the sun stood at noon: then he looked inquiringly into the sky – for he heard above him the sharp cry of a bird. And behold! An eagle was sweeping through the air in wide circles, and from it was hanging a serpent, not like a prey but like a friend: for it was coiled around the eagle's neck.

'It is my animals!' said Zarathustra and rejoiced in his heart.

'The proudest animal under the sun and the wisest animal under the sun – they have come scouting.

'They wanted to learn if Zarathustra was still alive. Am I in fact alive?

'I found it more dangerous among men than among animals; Zarathustra is following dangerous paths. May my animals lead me!'

When Zarathustra had said this he recalled the words of the saint in the forest, sighed, and spoke thus to his heart:

'I wish I were wise! I wish I were wise from the heart of me, like my serpent!

'But I am asking the impossible: therefore I ask my pride always to go along with my wisdom!

'And if one day my wisdom should desert me – ah, it loves to fly away! – then may my pride too fly with my folly!'

Thus began Zarathustra's down-going.

Of the Three Metamorphoses

I NAME you three metamorphoses of the spirit: how the spirit shall become a camel, and the camel a lion, and the lion at last a child.

There are many heavy things for the spirit, for the strong, weight-bearing spirit in which dwell respect and awe: its strength longs for the heavy, for the heaviest.

What is heavy? thus asks the weight-bearing spirit, thus it kneels down like the camel and wants to be well laden.

What is the heaviest thing, you heroes? so asks the weight-bearing spirit, that I may take it upon me and rejoice in my strength.

Is it not this: to debase yourself in order to injure your pride? To let your folly shine out in order to mock your wisdom?

Or is it this: to desert our cause when it is celebrating its victory? To climb high mountains in order to tempt the tempter?

Or is it this: to feed upon the acorns and grass of knowledge and for the sake of truth to suffer hunger of the soul?

Or is it this: to be sick and to send away comforters and make friends with the deaf, who never hear what you ask?

Or is it this: to wade into dirty water when it is the water of truth, and not to disdain cold frogs and hot toads?

Or is it this: to love those who despise us and to offer our hand to the ghost when it wants to frighten us?

The weight-bearing spirit takes upon itself all these heaviest things: like a camel hurrying laden into the desert, thus it hurries into its desert.

But in the loneliest desert the second metamorphosis occurs: the spirit here becomes a lion; it wants to capture freedom and be lord in its own desert.

It seeks here its ultimate lord: it will be an enemy to him

and to its ultimate God, it will struggle for victory with the great dragon.

What is the great dragon which the spirit no longer wants to call lord and God? The great dragon is called 'Thou shalt'. But the spirit of the lion says 'I will!'

'Thou shalt' lies in its path, sparkling with gold, a scale-covered beast, and on every scale glitters golden 'Thou shalt'.

Values of a thousand years glitter on the scales, and thus speaks the mightiest of all dragons: 'All the values of things – glitter on me.

'All values have already been created, and all created values – are in me. Truly, there shall be no more "I will"!' Thus speaks the dragon.

My brothers, why is the lion needed in the spirit? Why does the beast of burden, that renounces and is reverent, not suffice?

To create new values – even the lion is incapable of that: but to create itself freedom for new creation – that the might of the lion can do.

To create freedom for itself and a sacred No even to duty: the lion is needed for that, my brothers.

To seize the right to new values – that is the most terrible proceeding for a weight-bearing and reverential spirit. Truly, to this spirit it is a theft and a work for an animal of prey.

Once it loved this 'Thou shalt' as its holiest thing: now it has to find illusion and caprice even in the holiest, that it may steal freedom from its love: the lion is needed for this theft.

But tell me, my brothers, what can the child do that even the lion cannot? Why must the preying lion still become a child?

The child is innocence and forgetfulness, a new beginning, a sport, a self-propelling wheel, a first motion, a sacred Yes.

Yes, a sacred Yes is needed, my brothers, for the sport of creation: the spirit now wills *its own* will, the spirit sundered from the world now wins *its own* world.

I have named you three metamorphoses of the spirit: how

the spirit became a camel, and the camel a lion, and the lion at last a child.

Thus spoke Zarathustra. And at that time he was living in the town called The Pied Cow.

Of the Chairs of Virtue

ZARATHUSTRA heard a wise man praised who was said to discourse well on sleep and virtue: he was greatly honoured and rewarded for it, and all the young men sat before his chair. Zarathustra went to him and sat before his chair with all the young men. And thus spoke the wise man:

Honour to sleep and modesty before it! That is the first thing! And avoid all those who sleep badly and are awake at night!

Even the thief is shamed when confronted with sleep: he always steals softly through the night. But shameless is the night-watchman, shamelessly he bears his horn.

Sleeping is no mean art: you need to stay awake all day to do it.

You must overcome yourself ten times a day: that causes a fine weariness and is opium to the soul.

Ten times must you be reconciled to yourself again: for overcoming is bitterness and the unreconciled man sleeps badly.

You must discover ten truths a day: otherwise you will seek truth in the night too, with your soul still hungry.

You must laugh and be cheerful ten times a day: or your stomach, that father of affliction, will disturb you in the night.

Few know it, but one must have all the virtues in order to sleep well. Shall I bear false witness? Shall I commit adultery?

Shall I covet my neighbour's maidservant? None of this would be consistent with good sleep.

And even when one has all the virtues, there is still one thing to remember: to send even these virtues to sleep at the proper time.

That they may not quarrel among themselves, the pretty little women! And over you, unhappy man!

Peace with God and with your neighbour: thus good sleep will have it. And peace too with your neighbour's devil. Otherwise he will haunt you at night.

Honour and obedience to the authorities, and even to the crooked authorities! Thus good sleep will have it. How can I help it that power likes to walk on crooked legs?

I shall always call him the best herdsman who leads his sheep to the greenest meadows: that accords with good sleep.

I do not desire much honour, nor great treasure: they excite spleen. But one sleeps badly without a good name and a small treasure.

The company of a few is more welcome to me than bad company: but they must come and go at the proper time. That accords with good sleep.

The poor in spirit, too, please me greatly: they further sleep. Blessed and happy they are indeed, especially if one always agrees with their views.

Thus for the virtuous man does the day pass. And when night comes I take good care not to summon sleep! He, the lord of virtues, does not like to be summoned!

But I remember what I have done and thought during the day. Ruminating I ask myself, patient as a cow: What were your ten overcomings?

And which were the ten reconciliations and the ten truths and the ten fits of laughter with which my heart enjoyed itself?

As I ponder such things rocked by my forty thoughts, sleep, the lord of virtue, suddenly overtakes me uncalled.

Sleep knocks on my eyes: they grow heavy. Sleep touches my mouth: it stays open.

Truly, he comes to me on soft soles, the dearest of thieves, and steals my thoughts from me: I stand as silent as this chair.

But I do not stand for long: already I am lying down.

When Zarathustra heard the wise man's words he laughed

in his heart: for through them a light had dawned upon him. And he spoke thus to his heart:

This wise man with his forty thoughts seems to me a fool: but I believe he knows well enough how to sleep.

Happy is he who lives in this wise man's neighbourhood. Such sleep is contagious, even through a thick wall.

A spell dwells even in his chair. And the young men have not sat in vain before the preacher of virtue.

His wisdom is: stay awake in order to sleep well. And truly, if life had no sense and I had to choose nonsense, this would be the most desirable nonsense for me, too.

Now it is clear to me what people were once seeking above all when they sought the teachers of virtue. They sought good sleep and opium virtues to bring it about!

To all of these lauded wise men of the academic chairs, wisdom meant sleep without dreams: they knew no better meaning of life.

And today too there are some like this preacher of virtue, and not always so honourable: but their time is up. And they shall not stand for much longer: already they are lying down.

Blessed are these drowsy men: for they shall soon drop off.

Thus spoke Zarathustra.

Of the Afterworldsmen

ONCE Zarathustra too cast his deluded fancy beyond mankind, like all afterworldsmen.[5] Then the world seemed to me the work of a suffering and tormented God.

Then the world seemed to me the dream and fiction of a God; coloured vapour before the eyes of a discontented God.

Good and evil and joy and sorrow and I and You – I thought them coloured vapour before the creator's eyes. The creator wanted to look away from himself, so he created the world.

It is intoxicating joy for the sufferer to look away from his suffering and to forget himself. Intoxicating joy and self-forgetting – that is what I once thought the world.

This world, the eternally imperfect, the eternal and imperfect image of a contradiction – an intoxicating joy to its imperfect creator – that is what I once thought the world.

Thus I too once cast my deluded fancy beyond mankind, like all afterworldsmen. Beyond mankind in reality?

Ah, brothers, this God which I created was human work and human madness, like all gods!

He was human, and only a poor piece of man and Ego: this phantom came to me from my own fire and ashes, that is the truth! It did not come to me from the 'beyond'!

What happened, my brothers? I, the sufferer, overcame myself, I carried my own ashes to the mountains, I made for myself a brighter flame. And behold! the phantom *fled* from me!

Now to me, the convalescent, it would be suffering and torment to believe in such phantoms: it would be suffering to me now and humiliation. Thus I speak to the afterworldsmen.

It was suffering and impotence – that created all afterworlds; and that brief madness of happiness that only the greatest sufferer experiences.

Weariness, which wants to reach the ultimate with a single leap, with a death-leap,[6] a poor ignorant weariness, which no longer wants even to want: that created all gods and afterworlds.

Believe me, my brothers! It was the body that despaired of the body – that touched the ultimate walls with the fingers of its deluded spirit.

Believe me, my brothers! It was the body that despaired of the earth – that heard the belly of being speak to it.

And then it wanted to get its head through the ultimate walls – and not its head only[7] – over into the 'other world'.

But that 'other world', that inhuman, dehumanized world which is a heavenly Nothing, is well hidden from men; and the belly of being does not speak to man, except as man.

Truly, all being is hard to demonstrate; it is hard to make

it speak. Yet, tell me, brothers, is not the most wonderful of all things most clearly demonstrated?

Yes, this Ego, with its contradiction and confusion, speaks most honestly of its being – this creating, willing, evaluating Ego, which is the measure and value of things.

And this most honest being, the Ego – it speaks of the body, and it insists upon the body, even when it fables and fabricates and flutters with broken wings.

Ever more honestly it learns to speak, the Ego: and the more it learns, the more it finds titles and honours for the body and the earth.

My Ego taught me a new pride, I teach it to men: No longer to bury the head in the sand of heavenly things, but to carry it freely, an earthly head which creates meaning for the earth!

I teach mankind a new will: to desire this path that men have followed blindly, and to call it good and no more to creep aside from it, like the sick and dying!

It was the sick and dying who despised the body and the earth and invented the things of heaven and the redeeming drops of blood: but even these sweet and dismal poisons they took from the body and the earth!

They wanted to escape from their misery and the stars were too far for them. Then they sighed: 'Oh if only there were heavenly paths by which to creep into another existence and into happiness!' – then they contrived for themselves their secret ways and their draughts of blood!

Now they thought themselves transported from their bodies and from this earth, these ingrates. Yet to what do they owe the convulsion and joy of their transport? To their bodies and to this earth.

Zarathustra is gentle with the sick. Truly, he is not angry at their manner of consolation and ingratitude. May they become convalescents and overcomers and make for themselves a higher body!

Neither is Zarathustra angry with the convalescent if he glances tenderly at his illusions and creeps at midnight around the grave of his God: but even his tears still speak to me of sickness and a sick body.

There have always been many sickly people among those who invent fables and long for God: they have a raging hate for the enlightened man and for that youngest of virtues which is called honesty.

They are always looking back to dark ages: then, indeed, illusion and faith were a different question; raving of the reason was likeness to God, and doubt was sin.

I know these Godlike people all too well: they want to be believed in, and doubt to be sin. I also know all too well what it is they themselves most firmly believe in.

Truly not in afterworlds and redeeming drops of blood: they believe most firmly in the body, and their own body is for them their thing-in-itself.

But it is a sickly thing to them: and they would dearly like to get out of their skins. That is why they hearken to preachers of death and themselves preach afterworlds.

Listen rather, my brothers, to the voice of the healthy body: this is a purer voice and a more honest one.

Purer and more honest of speech is the healthy body, perfect and square-built: and it speaks of the meaning of the earth.

Thus spoke Zarathustra.

Of the Despisers of the Body

I WISH to speak to the despisers of the body. Let them not learn differently nor teach differently, but only bid farewell to their own bodies – and so become dumb.

'I am body and soul' – so speaks the child. And why should one not speak like children?

But the awakened, the enlightened man says: I am body entirely, and nothing beside; and soul is only a word for something in the body.

The body is a great intelligence, a multiplicity with one sense, a war and a peace, a herd and a herdsman.

Your little intelligence, my brother, which you call 'spirit', is also an instrument of your body, a little instrument and toy of your great intelligence.

You say 'I' and you are proud of this word. But greater than this – although you will not believe in it – is your body and its great intelligence, which does not say 'I' but performs 'I'.

What the sense feels, what the spirit perceives, is never an end in itself. But sense and spirit would like to persuade you that they are the end of all things: they are as vain as that.

Sense and spirit are instruments and toys: behind them still lies the Self. The Self seeks with the eyes of the sense, it listens too with the ears of the spirit.

The Self is always listening and seeking: it compares, subdues, conquers, destroys. It rules and is also the Ego's ruler.

Behind your thoughts and feelings, my brother, stands a mighty commander, an unknown sage – he is called Self. He lives in your body, he is your body.

There is more reason in your body than in your best wisdom. And who knows for what purpose your body requires precisely your best wisdom?

Your Self laughs at your Ego and its proud leapings. 'What are these leapings and flights of thought to me?' it says to itself. 'A by-way to my goal. I am the Ego's leading-string and I prompt its conceptions.'

The Self says to the Ego: 'Feel pain!' Thereupon it suffers and gives thought how to end its suffering – and it is *meant* to think for just that purpose.

The Self says to the Ego: 'Feel joy!' Thereupon it rejoices and gives thought how it may often rejoice – and it is *meant* to think for just that purpose.

I want to say a word to the despisers of the body. It is their esteem that produces this disesteem. What is it that created esteem and disesteem and value and will?

The creative Self created for itself esteem and disesteem, it created for itself joy and sorrow. The creative body created spirit for itself, as a hand of its will.

Even in your folly and contempt, you despisers of the body,

you serve your Self. I tell you: your Self itself wants to die and turn away from life.

Your Self can no longer perform that act which it most desires to perform: to create beyond itself. That is what it most wishes to do, that is its whole ardour.

But now it has grown too late for that: so your Self wants to perish, you despisers of the body.

Your Self wants to perish, and that is why you have become despisers of the body! For no longer are you able to create beyond yourselves.

And therefore you are now angry with life and with the earth. An unconscious envy lies in the sidelong glance of your contempt.

I do not go your way, you despisers of the body! You are not bridges to the Superman!

Thus spoke Zarathustra.

Of Joys and Passions

MY brother, if you have a virtue and it is your own virtue, you have it in common with no one.

To be sure, you want to call it by a name and caress it; you want to pull its ears and amuse yourself with it.

And behold! Now you have its name in common with the people and have become of the people and the herd with your virtue!

You would do better to say: 'Unutterable and nameless is that which torments and delights my soul and is also the hunger of my belly.'

Let your virtue be too exalted for the familiarity of names: and if you have to speak of it, do not be ashamed to stammer.

Thus say and stammer: 'This is *my* good, this I love, just thus do I like it, only thus do *I* wish the good.

'I do not want it as a law of God, I do not want it as a human statute: let it be no sign-post to superearths and paradises.

'It is an earthly virtue that I love: there is little prudence in it, and least of all common wisdom.

'But this bird has built its nest beneath my roof: therefore I love and cherish it – now it sits there upon its golden eggs.'

Thus should you stammer and praise your virtue.

Once you had passions and called them evil. But now you have only your virtues: they grew from out your passions.

You laid your highest aim in the heart of these passions: then they became your virtues and joys.

And though you came from the race of the hot-tempered or of the lustful or of the fanatical or of the vindictive:

At last all your passions have become virtues and all your devils angels.

Once you had fierce dogs in your cellar: but they changed at last into birds and sweet singers.

From your poison you brewed your balsam; you milked your cow, affliction, now you drink the sweet milk of her udder.

And henceforward nothing evil shall come out of you, except it be the evil that comes from the conflict of your virtues.

My brother, if you are lucky you will have one virtue and no more: thus you will go more easily over the bridge.

To have many virtues is to be distinguished, but it is a hard fate; and many a man has gone into the desert and killed himself because he was tired of being a battle and battle-ground of virtues.

My brother, are war and battle evil? But this evil is necessary, envy and mistrust and calumny among your virtues is necessary.

Behold how each of your virtues desires the highest place: it wants your entire spirit, that your spirit may be *its* herald, it wants your entire strength in anger, hate, and love.

Every virtue is jealous of the others, and jealousy is a terrible thing. Even virtues can be destroyed through jealousy.

He whom the flames of jealousy surround at last turns his poisoned sting against himself, like the scorpion.

Ah my brother, have you never yet seen a virtue turn upon itself and stab itself?

Man is something that must be overcome: and for that reason you must love your virtues – for you will perish by them.

Thus spoke Zarathustra.

Of the Pale Criminal

You do not intend to kill, you judges and sacrificers, before the beast has bowed its neck? Behold, the pale criminal has bowed his neck: from his eye speaks the great contempt.

'My Ego is something that should be overcome: my Ego is to me the great contempt of man': that is what this eye says.

He judged himself – that was his supreme moment: do not let the exalted man relapse again into his lowly condition!

There is no redemption for him who thus suffers from himself, except it be a quick death.

Your killing, you judges, should be a mercy and not a revenge. And since you kill, see to it that you yourselves justify life!

It is not sufficient that you should be reconciled with him you kill. May your sorrow be love for the Superman: thus will you justify your continuing to live!

You should say 'enemy', but not 'miscreant'; you should say 'invalid', but not 'scoundrel'; you should say 'fool', but not 'sinner'.

And you, scarlet judge, if you would speak aloud all you have done in thought, everyone would cry: 'Away with this filth and poisonous snake!'

But the thought is one thing, the deed is another, and another yet is the image of the deed. The wheel of causality does not roll between them.

An image made this pale man pale. He was equal to his deed when he did it: but he could not endure its image after it was done.

Now for evermore he saw himself as the perpetrator of one deed. I call this madness: in him the exception has become the rule.

The chalk-line charmed the hen; the blow he struck charmed his simple mind – I call this madness *after* the deed.

Listen, you judges! There is another madness as well; and it comes *before* the deed. Ah, you have not crept deep enough into this soul!

Thus says the scarlet judge: 'Why did this criminal murder? He wanted to steal.' But I tell you: his soul wanted blood not booty: he thirsted for the joy of the knife!

But his simple mind did not understand this madness and it persuaded him otherwise. 'What is the good of blood?' it said. 'Will you not at least commit a theft too? Take a revenge?'

And he hearkened to his simple mind: its words lay like lead upon him – then he robbed as he murdered. He did not want to be ashamed of his madness.

And now again the lead of his guilt lies upon him, and again his simple mind is so numb, so paralysed, so heavy.

If only he could shake his head his burden would roll off: but who can shake this head?

What is this man? A heap of diseases that reach out into the world through the spirit: there they want to catch their prey.

What is this man? A knot of savage serpents that are seldom at peace among themselves – thus they go forth alone to seek prey in the world.

Behold this poor body! This poor soul interpreted to itself what this body suffered and desired – it interpreted it as lust for murder and greed for the joy of the knife.

The evil which is now evil overtakes him who now becomes sick: he wants to do harm with that which harms him. But there have been other ages and another evil and good.

Once doubt and the will to Self were evil. Then the invalid became heretic and witch: as heretic and witch he suffered and wanted to cause suffering.

But this will not enter your ears: you tell me it hurts your good people. But what are your good people to me?

Much about your good people moves me to disgust, and it is not their evil I mean. How I wish they possessed a madness through which they could perish, like this pale criminal.

Truly, I wish their madness were called truth or loyalty or justice: but they possess their virtue in order to live long and in a miserable ease.

I am a railing beside the stream: he who can grasp me, let him grasp me! I am not, however, your crutch.

Thus spoke Zarathustra.

Of Reading and Writing

OF all writings I love only that which is written with blood. Write with blood: and you will discover that blood is spirit.

It is not an easy thing to understand unfamiliar blood: I hate the reading idler.

He who knows the reader, does nothing further for the reader. Another century of readers – and spirit itself will stink.

That everyone can learn to read will ruin in the long run not only writing, but thinking too.

Once spirit was God, then it became man, and now it is even becoming mob.

He who writes in blood and aphorisms does not want to be read, he wants to be learned by heart.

In the mountains the shortest route is from peak to peak, but for that you must have long legs. Aphorisms should be peaks, and those to whom they are spoken should be big and tall of stature.

The air thin and pure, danger near, and the spirit full of a joyful wickedness: these things suit one another.

I want hobgoblins around me, for I am courageous. Courage that scares away phantoms makes hobgoblins for itself – courage wants to laugh.

I no longer feel as you do: this cloud which I see under me, this blackness and heaviness at which I laugh – precisely this is your thunder-cloud.

You look up when you desire to be exalted. And I look down, because I am exalted.

Who among you can at the same time laugh and be exalted?

He who climbs upon the highest mountains laughs at all tragedies, real or imaginary.

Untroubled, scornful, outrageous – that is how wisdom wants us to be: she is a woman and never loves anyone but a warrior.

You tell me: 'Life is hard to bear.' But if it were otherwise why should you have your pride in the morning and your resignation in the evening?

Life is hard to bear: but do not pretend to be so tender! We are all of us pretty fine asses and assesses of burden!

What have we in common with the rosebud, which trembles because a drop of dew is lying upon it?

It is true: we love life, not because we are used to living but because we are used to loving.

There is always a certain madness in love. But also there is always a certain method in madness.

And to me too, who love life, it seems that butterflies and soap-bubbles, and whatever is like them among men, know most about happiness.

To see these light, foolish, dainty, affecting little souls flutter about – that moves Zarathustra to tears and to song.

I should believe only in a God who understood how to dance.

And when I beheld my devil, I found him serious, thorough, profound, solemn: it was the Spirit of Gravity – through him all things are ruined.

One does not kill by anger but by laughter. Come, let us kill the Spirit of Gravity!

I have learned to walk: since then I have run. I have learned to fly: since then I do not have to be pushed in order to move.

Now I am nimble, now I fly, now I see myself under myself, now a god dances within me.

Thus spoke Zarathustra.

Of the Tree on the Mountainside

ZARATHUSTRA had noticed that a young man was avoiding him. And as he was walking alone one evening through the mountains surrounding the town called The Pied Cow, behold! he found this young man leaning against a tree and gazing wearily into the valley. Zarathustra grasped the tree beside which the young man was sitting and spoke thus:

'If I wanted to shake this tree with my hands I should be unable to do it.

'But the wind, which we cannot see, torments it and bends it where it wishes. It is invisible hands that torment and bend us the worst.'

At that the young man stood up in confusion and said: 'I hear Zarathustra and I was just thinking of him.'

Zarathustra replied: 'Why are you alarmed on that account? – Now it is with men as with this tree.

'The more it wants to rise into the heights and the light, the more determinedly do its roots strive earthwards, downwards, into the darkness, into the depths – into evil.'

'Yes, into evil!' cried the young man. 'How is it possible you can uncover my soul?'

Zarathustra smiled and said: 'There are many souls one will never uncover, unless one invents them first.'

'Yes, into evil!' cried the young man again.

'You have spoken the truth, Zarathustra. Since I wanted to rise into the heights I have no longer trusted myself, and no one trusts me any more. How did this happen?

'I change too quickly: my today refutes my yesterday. When I ascend I often jump over steps, and no step forgives me that.

'When I am aloft, I always find myself alone. No one

speaks to me, the frost of solitude makes me tremble. What do I want in the heights?

'My contempt and my desire increase together; the higher I climb, the more do I despise him who climbs. What do I want in the heights?

'How ashamed I am of my climbing and stumbling! How I scorn my violent panting! How I hate the man who can fly! How weary I am in the heights!'

Here the young man fell silent. And Zarathustra contemplated the tree beside which they were standing, and spoke thus:

'This tree stands here alone on the mountainside; it has grown up high above man and animal.

'And if it wished to speak, it would find no one who understood it: so high has it grown.

'Now it waits and waits – yet what is it waiting for? It lives too near the seat of the clouds: is it waiting, perhaps, for the first lightning?'

When Zarathustra said this, the young man cried with violent gestures: 'Yes, Zarathustra, you speak true. I desired my destruction when I wanted to ascend into the heights, and you are the lightning for which I have been waiting! Behold, what have I been since you appeared among us? It is *envy* of you which has destroyed me!' Thus spoke the young man and wept bitterly. But Zarathustra laid his arm about him and drew him along with him.

And when they had been walking together for a while, Zarathustra began to speak thus:

It breaks my heart. Better than your words, your eye tells me all your peril.

You are not yet free, you still *search* for freedom. Your search has fatigued you and made you too wakeful.

You long for the open heights, your soul thirsts for the stars. But your bad instincts too thirst for freedom.

Your fierce dogs long for freedom; they bark for joy in their cellar when your spirit aspires to break open all prisons.

To me you are still a prisoner who imagines freedom: ah,

such prisoners of the soul become clever, but also deceitful and base.

The free man of the spirit, too, must still purify himself. Much of the prison and rottenness still remain within him: his eye still has to become pure.

Yes, I know your peril. But, by my love and hope I entreat you: do not reject your love and hope!

You still feel yourself noble, and the others, too, who dislike you and cast evil glances at you, still feel you are noble. Learn that everyone finds the noble man an obstruction.

The good, too, find the noble man an obstruction: and even when they call him a good man they do so in order to make away with him.

The noble man wants to create new things and a new virtue. The good man wants the old things and that the old things shall be preserved.

But that is not the danger for the noble man – that he may become a good man – but that he may become an impudent one, a derider, a destroyer.

Alas, I have known noble men who lost their highest hope. And henceforth they slandered all high hopes.

Henceforth they lived impudently in brief pleasures, and they had hardly an aim beyond the day.

'Spirit is also sensual pleasure' – thus they spoke. Then the wings of their spirit broke: now it creeps around and it makes dirty what it feeds on.

Once they thought of becoming heroes: now they are sensualists. The hero is to them an affliction and a terror.

But, by my love and hope I entreat you: do not reject the hero in your soul! Keep holy your highest hope!

Thus spoke Zarathustra.

Of the Preachers of Death

THERE are preachers of death: and the earth is full of those to whom departure from life must be preached.

The earth is full of the superfluous, life has been corrupted by the many-too-many. Let them be lured by 'eternal life' out of this life!

Yellow men or black men: that is what the preachers of death are called. But I want to show them to you in other colours.

There are the dreadful creatures who carry a beast of prey around within them, and have no choice except lusts or self-mortification. And even their lusts are self-mortification.

They have not yet even become men, these dreadful creatures. Let them preach departure from life and depart themselves!

There are the consumptives of the soul: they are hardly born before they begin to die and to long for doctrines of weariness and renunciation.

They would like to be dead, and we should approve their wish! Let us guard against awakening these dead men and damaging these living coffins.

They encounter an invalid or an old man or a corpse; and straightway they say 'Life is refuted!'

But only they are refuted, they and their eye that sees only one aspect of existence.

Muffled in deep depression, and longing for the little accidents that bring about death: thus they wait and clench their teeth.

Or: they snatch at sweets and in doing so mock their childishness: they cling to their straw of life and mock that they are still clinging to a straw.

Their wisdom runs: 'He who goes on living is a fool, but we are such fools! And precisely that is the most foolish thing in life!'

'Life is only suffering' – thus others of them speak, and they do not lie: so see to it that *you* cease to live! So see to it that the life which is only suffering ceases!

And let the teaching of your virtue be: 'You shall kill yourself! You shall steal away from yourself!'

'Lust is sin' – thus say some who preach death – 'let us go aside and beget no children!'

'Giving birth is laborious' – say others – 'why go on giving birth? One gives birth only to unhappy children!' And they too are preachers of death.

'Men are to be pitied' – thus say others again. 'Take what I have! Take what I am! By so much less am I bound to life!'

If they were compassionate from the very heart they would seek to make their neighbours disgusted with life. To be evil – that would be their true good.

But they want to escape from life: what is it to them that, with their chains and gifts, they bind others still more firmly to it?

And you too, you to whom life is unrestrained labour and anxiety: are you not very weary of life? Are you not very ripe for the sermon of death?

All of you, to whom unrestrained labour, and the swift, the new, the strange, are dear, you endure yourselves ill, your industry is flight and will to forget yourselves.

If you believed more in life, you would devote yourselves less to the moment. But you have insufficient capacity for waiting – or even for laziness!

Everywhere resound the voices of those who preach death: and the earth is full of those to whom death must be preached.

Or 'eternal life': it is all the same to me – provided they pass away quickly!

Thus spoke Zarathustra.

Of War and Warriors

WE do not wish to be spared by our best enemies, nor by those whom we love from the very heart. So let me tell you the truth!

My brothers in war! I love you from the very heart, I am and have always been of your kind. And I am also your best enemy. So let me tell you the truth!

I know the hatred and envy of your hearts. You are not

great enough not to know hatred and envy. So be great enough not to be ashamed of them!

And if you cannot be saints of knowledge, at least be its warriors. They are the companions and forerunners of such sainthood.

I see many soldiers: if only I could see many warriors! What they wear is called uniform: may what they conceal with it not be uniform too!

You should be such men as are always looking for an enemy – for *your* enemy. And with some of you there is hate at first sight.

You should seek your enemy, you should wage your war – a war for your opinions. And if your opinion is defeated, your honesty should still cry triumph over that!

You should love peace as a means to new wars. And the short peace more than the long.

I do not exhort you to work but to battle. I do not exhort you to peace, but to victory. May your work be a battle, may your peace be a victory!

One can be silent and sit still only when one has arrow and bow: otherwise one babbles and quarrels. May your peace be a victory!

You say it is the good cause that hallows even war? I tell you: it is the good war that hallows every cause.

War and courage have done more great things than charity. Not your pity but your bravery has saved the unfortunate up to now.

'What is good?' you ask. To be brave is good. Let the little girls say: 'To be good is to be what is pretty and at the same time touching.'

They call you heartless: but your heart is true, and I love the modesty of your kind-heartedness. You feel ashamed of your flow, while others feel ashamed of their ebb.

Are you ugly? Very well, my brothers! Take the sublime about you, the mantle of the ugly!

And when your soul grows great, it grows arrogant, and there is wickedness in your sublimity. I know you.

In wickedness, the arrogant and the weak man meet. But they misunderstand one another. I know you.

You may have enemies whom you hate, but not enemies whom you despise. You must be proud of your enemy: then the success of your enemy shall be your success too.

To rebel – that shows nobility in a slave. Let your nobility show itself in obeying! Let even your commanding be an obeying!

To a good warrior, 'thou shalt' sounds more agreeable than 'I will'. And everything that is dear to you, you should first have commanded to you.

Let your love towards life be love towards your highest hope: and let your highest hope be the highest idea of life!

But you should let me commend to you your highest idea – and it is: Man is something that should be overcome.

Thus live your life of obedience and war! What good is long life? What warrior wants to be spared?

I do not spare you, I love you from the very heart, my brothers in war!

Thus spoke Zarathustra.

Of the New Idol

THERE are still peoples and herds somewhere, but not with us, my brothers: here there are states.

The state? What is that? Well then! Now open your ears, for now I shall speak to you of the death of peoples.

The state is the coldest of all cold monsters. Coldly it lies, too; and this lie creeps from its mouth: 'I, the state, am the people.'

It is a lie! It was creators who created peoples and hung a faith and a love over them: thus they served life.

It is destroyers who set snares for many and call it the state: they hang a sword and a hundred desires over them.

Where a people still exists, there the people do not understand the state and hate it as the evil eye and sin against custom and law.

I offer you this sign: every people speaks its own language of good and evil: its neighbour does not understand this language. It invented this language for itself in custom and law.

But the state lies in all languages of good and evil; and whatever it says, it lies – and whatever it has, it has stolen.

Everything about it is false; it bites with stolen teeth. Even its belly is false.

Confusion of the language of good and evil; I offer you this sign as the sign of the state. Truly, this sign indicates the will to death! Truly, it beckons to the preachers of death!

Many too many are born: the state was invented for the superfluous!

Just see how it lures them, the many-too-many! How it devours them, and chews them, and re-chews them!

'There is nothing greater on earth than I, the regulating finger of God' – thus the monster bellows. And not only the long-eared and short-sighted sink to their knees!

Ah, it whispers its dismal lies to you too, you great souls! Ah, it divines the abundant hearts that like to squander themselves!

Yes, it divines you too, you conquerors of the old God! You grew weary in battle and now your weariness serves the new idol!

It would like to range heroes and honourable men about it, this new idol! It likes to sun itself in the sunshine of good consciences – this cold monster!

It will give *you* everything if *you* worship it, this new idol: thus it buys for itself the lustre of your virtues and the glance of your proud eyes.

It wants to use you to lure the many-too-many. Yes, a cunning device of Hell has here been devised, a horse of death jingling with the trappings of divine honours!

Yes, a death for many has here been devised that glorifies itself as life: truly, a heart-felt service to all preachers of death!

I call it the state where everyone, good and bad, is a poison-drinker: the state where everyone, good and bad, loses himself: the state where universal slow suicide is called – life.

Just look at these superfluous people! They steal for themselves the works of inventors and the treasures of the wise: they call their theft culture – and they turn everything to sickness and calamity.

Just look at these superfluous people! They are always ill, they vomit their bile and call it a newspaper. They devour one another and cannot even digest themselves.

Just look at these superfluous people! They acquire wealth and make themselves poorer with it. They desire power and especially the lever of power, plenty of money – these impotent people!

See them clamber, these nimble apes! They clamber over one another and so scuffle into the mud and the abyss.

They all strive towards the throne: it is a madness they have – as if happiness sat upon the throne! Often filth sits upon the throne – and often the throne upon filth, too.

They all seem madmen to me and clambering apes and too vehement. Their idol, that cold monster, smells unpleasant to me: all of them, all these idolators, smell unpleasant to me.

My brothers, do you then want to suffocate in the fumes of their animal mouths and appetites? Better to break the window and leap into the open air.

Avoid this bad odour! Leave the idolatry of the superfluous!

Avoid this bad odour! Leave the smoke of these human sacrifices!

The earth still remains free for great souls. Many places – the odour of tranquil seas blowing about them – are still empty for solitaries and solitary couples.

A free life still remains for great souls. Truly, he who possesses little is so much the less possessed: praised be a moderate poverty!

Only there, where the state ceases, does the man who is not superfluous begin: does the song of the necessary man, the unique and irreplaceable melody, begin.

There, where the state *ceases* – look there, my brothers. Do you not see it: the rainbow and the bridges to the Superman?

Thus spoke Zarathustra.

Of the Flies of the Market-place

FLEE, my friend, into your solitude! I see you deafened by the uproar of the great men and pricked by the stings of the small ones.

Forest and rock know well how to be silent with you. Be like the tree again, the wide-branching tree that you love: calmly and attentively it leans out over the sea.

Where solitude ceases, there the market-place begins; and where the market-place begins, there begins the uproar of the great actors and the buzzing of the poisonous flies.

In the world even the best things are worthless apart from him who first presents them: people call these presenters 'great men'.

The people have little idea of greatness, that is to say: creativeness. But they have a taste for all presenters and actors of great things.

The world revolves about the inventor of new values: imperceptibly it revolves. But the people and the glory revolve around the actor: that is 'the way of the world'.

The actor possesses spirit but little conscience of the spirit.[8] He always believes in that with which he most powerfully produces belief – produces belief in *himself*!

Tomorrow he will have a new faith and the day after tomorrow a newer one. He has a quick perception, as the people have, and a capricious temperament.

To overthrow – to him that means: to prove. To drive frantic – to him that means: to convince. And blood is to him the best of all arguments.

A truth that penetrates only sensitive ears he calls a lie and a thing of nothing. Truly, he believes only in gods who make a great noise in the world!

The market-place is full of solemn buffoons – and the people boast of their great men! These are their heroes of the hour.

But the hour presses them: so they press you. And from you too they require a Yes or a No. And woe to you if you want to set your chair between For and Against.

Do not be jealous, lover of truth, because of these inflexible and oppressive men! Truth has never yet clung to the arm of an inflexible man.

Return to your security because of these abrupt men: only in the market-place is one assailed with Yes? or No?

The experience of all deep wells is slow: they must wait long until they know *what* has fallen into their depths.

All great things occur away from glory and the market-place: the inventors of new values have always lived away from glory and the market-place.

Flee, my friend, into your solitude: I see you stung by poisonous flies. Flee to where the raw, rough breeze blows!

Flee into your solitude! You have lived too near the small and the pitiable men. Flee from their hidden vengeance! Towards you they are nothing but vengeance.

No longer lift your arm against them! They are innumerable and it is not your fate to be a fly-swat.

Innumerable are these small and pitiable men; and rain-drops and weeds have already brought about the destruction of many a proud building.

You are no stone, but already these many drops have made you hollow. You will yet break and burst apart through these many drops.

I see you wearied by poisonous flies, I see you bloodily torn in a hundred places; and your pride refuses even to be angry.

They want blood from you in all innocence, their bloodless souls thirst for blood – and therefore they sting in all innocence.

But you, profound man, you suffer too profoundly even from small wounds; and before you have recovered, the same poison-worm is again crawling over your hand.

You are too proud to kill these sweet-toothed creatures.

But take care that it does not become your fate to bear all their poisonous injustice!

They buzz around you even with their praise: and their praise is importunity. They want to be near your skin and your blood.

They flatter you as if you were a god or a devil; they whine before you as before a god or a devil. What of it! They are flatterers and whiners, and nothing more.

And they are often kind to you. But that has always been the prudence of the cowardly. Yes, the cowardly are prudent!

They think about you a great deal with their narrow souls – you are always suspicious to them. Everything that is thought about a great deal is finally thought suspicious.[9]

They punish you for all your virtues. Fundamentally they forgive you only – your mistakes.

Because you are gentle and just-minded, you say: 'They are not to be blamed for their little existence.' But their little souls think: 'All great existence is blameworthy.'

Even when you are gentle towards them, they still feel you despise them; and they return your kindness with secret unkindness.

Your silent pride always offends their taste; they rejoice if you are ever modest enough to be vain.

When we recognize a peculiarity in a man we also inflame that peculiarity. So guard yourself against the small men!

Before you, they feel themselves small, and their baseness glimmers and glows against you in hidden vengeance.

Have you not noticed how often they became silent when you approached them, and how their strength left them like smoke from a dying fire?

Yes, my friend, you are a bad conscience to your neighbours: for they are unworthy of you. Thus they hate you and would dearly like to suck your blood.

Your neighbours will always be poisonous flies: that about you which is great, that itself must make them more poisonous and ever more fly-like.

Flee, my friend, into your solitude and to where the raw, rough breeze blows! It is not your fate to be a fly-swat.

Thus spoke Zarathustra.

Of Chastity

I LOVE the forest. It is bad to live in towns: too many of the lustful live there.

Is it not better to fall into the hands of a murderer than into the dreams of a lustful woman?

And just look at these men: their eye reveals it – they know of nothing better on earth than to lie with a woman.

There is filth at the bottom of their souls; and it is worse if this filth still has something of the spirit in it!

If only you had become perfect at least as animals! But to animals belongs innocence.

Do I exhort you to kill your senses? I exhort you to an innocence of the senses.

Do I exhort you to chastity? With some, chastity is a virtue, but with many it is almost a vice.

These people abstain, it is true: but the bitch Sensuality glares enviously out of all they do.

This restless beast follows them even into the heights of their virtue and the depths of their cold spirit.

And how nicely the bitch Sensuality knows how to beg for a piece of spirit, when a piece of flesh is denied her.

Do you love tragedies and all that is heartbreaking? But I mistrust your bitch Sensuality.

Your eyes are too cruel for me; you look upon sufferers lustfully. Has your lasciviousness not merely disguised itself and called itself pity?

And I offer you this parable: Not a few who sought to drive out their devil entered into the swine themselves.

Those to whom chastity is difficult should be dissuaded from it, lest it become the way to Hell – that is, to filth and lust of the soul.

Am I speaking of dirty things? That does not seem to me the worst I could do.

Not when truth is dirty, but when it is shallow, does the enlightened man dislike to wade into its waters.

Truly, there are those who are chaste from the very heart: they are more gentle of heart and they laugh more often and more heartily than you.

They laugh at chastity too, and ask: 'What is chastity?

'Is chastity not folly? But this folly came to us and not we to it.

'We offered this guest love and shelter: now it lives with us – let it stay as long as it wishes!'

Thus spoke Zarathustra.

Of the Friend

'ONE is always one too many around me' – thus speaks the hermit. 'Always once one – in the long run that makes two!'

I and Me are always too earnestly in conversation with one another: how could it be endured, if there were not a friend?

For the hermit the friend is always the third person: the third person is the cork that prevents the conversation of the other two from sinking to the depths.

Alas, for all hermits there are too many depths. That is why they long so much for a friend and for his heights.

Our faith in others betrays wherein we would dearly like to have faith in ourselves. Our longing for a friend is our betrayer.

And often with our love we only want to leap over envy. And often we attack and make an enemy in order to conceal that we are vulnerable to attack.

'At least be my enemy!' – thus speaks the true reverence, that does not venture to ask for friendship.

If you want a friend, you must also be willing to wage war for him: and to wage war, you must be *capable* of being an enemy.

You should honour even the enemy in your friend. Can you go near to your friend without going over to him?

In your friend you should possess your best enemy. Your heart should feel closest to him when you oppose him.

Do you wish to go naked before your friend? Is it in honour of your friend that you show yourself to him as you are? But he wishes you to the Devil for it!

He who makes no secret of himself excites anger in others: that is how much reason you have to fear nakedness! If you were gods you could then be ashamed of your clothes!

You cannot adorn yourself too well for your friend: for you should be to him an arrow and a longing for the Superman.

Have you ever watched your friend asleep – to discover what he looked like? Yet your friend's face is something else beside. It is your own face, in a rough and imperfect mirror.

Have you ever watched your friend asleep? Were you not startled to see what he looked like? O my friend, man is something that must be overcome.

The friend should be a master in conjecture and in keeping silence: you must not want to see everything. Your dream should tell you what your friend does when awake.

May your pity be a conjecture: that you may first know if your friend wants pity. Perhaps what he loves in you is the undimmed eye and the glance of eternity.

Let your pity for your friend conceal itself under a hard shell; you should break a tooth biting upon it. Thus it will have delicacy and sweetness.

Are you pure air and solitude and bread and medicine to your friend? Many a one cannot deliver himself from his own chains and yet he is his friend's deliverer.

Are you a slave? If so, you cannot be a friend. Are you a tyrant? If so, you cannot have friends.

In woman, a slave and a tyrant have all too long been concealed. For that reason, woman is not yet capable of friendship: she knows only love.

In a woman's love is injustice and blindness towards all that she does not love. And in the enlightened love of a woman, too, there is still the unexpected attack and lightning and night, along with the light.

Woman is not yet capable of friendship: women are still cats and birds. Or, at best, cows.

Woman is not yet capable of friendship. But tell me, you men, which of you is yet capable of friendship?

Oh your poverty, you men, and your avarice of soul! As much as you give to your friend I will give even to my enemy, and will not have grown poorer in doing so.

There is comradeship: may there be friendship!

Thus spoke Zarathustra.

Of the Thousand and One Goals

ZARATHUSTRA has seen many lands and many peoples: thus he has discovered the good and evil of many peoples. Zarathustra has found no greater power on earth than good and evil.

No people could live without evaluating; but if it wishes to maintain itself it must not evaluate as its neighbour evaluates.

Much that seemed good to one people seemed shame and disgrace to another: thus I found. I found much that was called evil in one place was in another decked with purple honours.

One neighbour never understood another: his soul was always amazed at his neighbour's madness and wickedness.

A table of values hangs over every people. Behold, it is the table of its overcomings; behold, it is the voice of its will to power.

What it accounts hard it calls praiseworthy; what it accounts indispensable and hard it calls good; and that which relieves the greatest need, the rare, the hardest of all – it glorifies as holy.

Whatever causes it to rule and conquer and glitter, to the dread and envy of its neighbour, that it accounts the sublimest, the paramount, the evaluation and the meaning of all things.

Truly, my brother, if you only knew a people's need and land and sky and neighbour, you could surely divine the law of its overcomings, and why it is upon this ladder that it mounts towards its hope.

'You should always be the first and outrival all others: your jealous soul should love no one, except your friend' – this precept made the soul of a Greek tremble: in following it he followed his path to greatness.

'To speak the truth and to know well how to handle bow and arrow' – this seemed both estimable and hard to that people from whom I got my name – a name which is both estimable and hard to me.[10]

'To honour father and mother and to do their will even from the roots of the soul': another people hung this table of overcoming over itself and became mighty and eternal with it.

'To practise loyalty and for the sake of loyalty to risk honour and blood even in evil and dangerous causes': another people mastered itself with such teaching, and thus mastering itself it became pregnant and heavy with great hopes.

Truly, men have given themselves all their good and evil. Truly, they did not take it, they did not find it, it did not descend to them as a voice from heaven.

Man first implanted values into things to maintain himself – he created the meaning of things, a human meaning! Therefore he calls himself: 'Man', that is: the evaluator.

Evaluation is creation: hear it, you creative men! Valuating is itself the value and jewel of all valued things.

Only through evaluation is there value: and without evaluation the nut of existence would be hollow. Hear it, you creative men!

A change in values – that means a change in the creators of values. He who has to be a creator always has to destroy.

Peoples were the creators at first; only later were individuals creators. Indeed, the individual himself is still the latest creation.

Once the peoples hung a table of values over themselves. The love that wants to rule and the love that wants to obey created together such tables as these.

Joy in the herd is older than joy in the Ego: and as long as the good conscience is called herd, only the bad conscience says: I.

Truly, the cunning, loveless Ego, that seeks its advantage in the advantage of many – that is not the origin of the herd, but the herd's destruction.

It has always been creators and loving men who created good and evil. Fire of love and fire of anger glow in the names of all virtues.

Zarathustra has seen many lands and many peoples: Zarathustra has found no greater power on earth than the works of these loving men: these works are named 'good' and 'evil'.

Truly, the power of this praising and blaming is a monster. Tell me, who will subdue it for me, brothers? Tell me, who will fasten fetters upon the thousand necks of this beast?

Hitherto there have been a thousand goals, for there have been a thousand peoples. Only fetters are still lacking for these thousand necks, the one goal is still lacking.

Yet tell me, my brothers: if a goal for humanity is still lacking, is there not still lacking – humanity itself?

Thus spoke Zarathustra.

Of Love of One's Neighbour

You crowd together with your neighbours and have beautiful words for it. But I tell you: Your love of your neighbour is your bad love of yourselves.

You flee to your neighbour away from yourselves and would like to make a virtue of it: but I see through your 'selflessness'.

The 'You' is older than the 'I'; the 'You' has been consecrated, but not yet the 'I': so man crowds towards his neighbour.

Do I exhort you to love of your neighbour? I exhort you rather to flight from your neighbour and to love of the most distant! [11]

Higher than love of one's neighbour stands love of the most distant man and of the man of the future; higher still than love of man I account love of causes and of phantoms.

This phantom that runs along behind you, my brother, is fairer than you; why do you not give it your flesh and bones? But you are afraid and you run to your neighbour.

You cannot endure to be alone with yourselves and do not love yourselves enough: now you want to mislead your neighbour into love and gild yourselves with his mistake.

I wish rather that you could not endure to be with any kind of neighbour or with your neighbour's neighbour; then you would have to create your friend and his overflowing heart out of yourselves.

You invite in a witness when you want to speak well of yourselves; and when you have misled him into thinking well of you, you then think well of yourselves.

It is not only he who speaks contrary to what he knows who lies, but even more he who speaks contrary to what he does not know. And thus you speak of yourselves in your dealings with others and deceive your neighbour with yourselves.

Thus speaks the fool: 'Mixing with people ruins the character, especially when one has none.'

One man runs to his neighbour because he is looking for himself, and another because he wants to lose himself. Your bad love of yourselves makes solitude a prison to you.

It is the distant man who pays for your love of your neighbour; and when there are five of you together, a sixth always has to die.

I do not like your festivals, either: I have found too many actors there, and the audience, too, behaved like actors.

I do not teach you the neighbour but the friend. May the friend be to you a festival of the earth and a foretaste of the Superman.

I teach you the friend and his overflowing heart. But you must understand how to be a sponge if you want to be loved by overflowing hearts.

I teach you the friend in whom the world stands complete, a vessel of the good – the creative friend, who always has a complete world to bestow.

And as the world once dispersed for him, so it comes back to him again, as the evolution of good through evil, as the evolution of design from chance.

May the future and the most distant be the principle of your today: in your friend you should love the Superman as your principle.

My brothers, I do not exhort you to love of your neighbour: I exhort you to love of the most distant.

Thus spoke Zarathustra.

Of the Way of the Creator

MY brother, do you want to go apart and be alone? Do you want to seek the way to yourself? Pause just a moment and listen to me.

'He who seeks may easily get lost himself. It is a crime to go apart and be alone' – thus speaks the herd.

The voice of the herd will still ring within you. And when you say: 'We have no longer the same conscience, you and I', it will be a lament and a grief.

For see, it is still this same conscience that causes your grief: and the last glimmer of this conscience still glows in your affliction.

But you want to go the way of your affliction, which is the way to yourself? If so, show me your strength for it and your right to it!

Are you a new strength and a new right? A first motion? A self-propelling wheel? Can you also compel stars to revolve about you?

Alas, there is so much lusting for eminence! There is so

much convulsion of the ambitious! Show me that you are not one of the lustful or ambitious!

Alas, there are so many great ideas that do no more than a bellows: they inflate and make emptier.

Do you call yourself free? I want to hear your ruling idea, and not that you have escaped from a yoke.

Are you such a man as *ought* to escape a yoke? There are many who threw off their final worth when they threw off their bondage.

Free from what? Zarathustra does not care about that! But your eye should clearly tell me: free *for* what?

Can you furnish yourself with your own good and evil and hang up your own will above yourself as a law? Can you be judge of yourself and avenger of your law?

It is terrible to be alone with the judge and avenger of one's own law. It is to be like a star thrown forth into empty space and into the icy breath of solitude.

Today you still suffer from the many, O man set apart: today you still have your courage whole and your hopes.

But one day solitude will make you weary, one day your pride will bend and your courage break. One day you will cry: 'I am alone!'

One day you will no longer see what is exalted in you; and what is base in you, you will see all too closely; your sublimity itself will make you afraid, as if it were a phantom. One day you will cry: 'Everything is false!'

There are emotions that seek to kill the solitary; if they do not succeed, well, they must die themselves! But are you capable of being a murderer?

My brother, have you ever known the word 'contempt'? And the anguish of your justice in being just to those who despise you?

You compel many to change their opinion about you; they hold that very much against you. You approached them and yet went on past them: that they will never forgive you.

You go above and beyond them: but the higher you climb, the smaller you appear to the eye of envy. And he who flies is hated most of all.

'How could you be just towards me?' – that is how you must speak – 'I choose your injustice as my portion.'

They throw injustice and dirt at the solitary: but, my brother, if you want to be a star, you must shine none the less brightly for them on that account!

And be on your guard against the good and just! They would like to crucify those who devise their own virtue – they hate the solitary.

Be on your guard, too, against holy simplicity! Everything which is not simple is unholy to it: and it, too, likes to play with fire – in this case, the fire of the stake.

And be on your guard, too, against the assaults your love makes upon you! The solitary extends his hand too quickly to anyone he meets.

To many men, you ought not to give your hand, but only your paw[12]: and I should like it if your paw had claws, too.

But you yourself will always be the worst enemy you can encounter; you yourself lie in wait for yourself in caves and forests.

Solitary man, you are going the way to yourself! And your way leads past yourself and your seven devils!

You will be a heretic to yourself and a witch and a prophet and an evil-doer and a villain.

You must be ready to burn yourself in your own flame: how could you become new, if you had not first become ashes?

Solitary man, you are going the way of the creator: you want to create yourself a god from your seven devils!

Solitary man, you are going the way of the lover: you love yourself and for that reason you despise yourself as only lovers can despise.

The lover wants to create, because he despises! What does he know of love who has not had to despise precisely what he loved?

Go apart and be alone with your love and your creating, my brother; and justice will be slow to limp after you.

Go apart and be alone with my tears, my brother. I love

him who wants to create beyond himself, and thus perishes.

Thus spoke Zarathustra.

Of Old and Young Women

'WHY do you slink so shyly through the twilight, Zarathustra? And what are you hiding so carefully under your cloak?

'Is it a treasure someone has given you? Or a child that has been born to you? Or are you now taking the way of thieves yourself, friend of the wicked?'

Truly, my brother! (said Zarathustra) it is a treasure that has been given me: it is a little truth that I carry.

But it is as unruly as a little child, and if I do not stop its mouth it will cry too loudly.

Today as I was going my way alone, at the hour when the sun sets, a little old woman encountered me and spoke thus to my soul:

'Zarathustra has spoken much to us women, too, but he has never spoken to us about woman.'

And I answered her: 'One should speak about women only to men.'

'Speak to me too of woman,' she said; 'I am old enough soon to forget it.'

And I obliged the little old woman and spoke to her thus:

Everything about woman is a riddle, and everything about woman has one solution: it is called pregnancy.

For the woman, the man is a means: the end is always the child. But what is the woman for the man?

The true man wants two things: danger and play. For that reason he wants woman, as the most dangerous plaything.

Man should be trained for war and woman for the recreation of the warrior: all else is folly.

The warrior does not like fruit that is too sweet. Therefore he likes woman; even the sweetest woman is still bitter.

Woman understands children better than a man, but man is more childlike than woman.

A child is concealed in the true man: it wants to play. Come, women, discover the child in man!

Let woman be a plaything, pure and fine like a precious stone illumined by the virtues of a world that does not yet exist.

Let the flash of a star glitter in your love! Let your hope be: 'May I bear the Superman!'

Let there be bravery in your love! With your love you should attack him who inspires you with fear.

Let your honour be in your love! Woman has understood little otherwise about honour. But let this be your honour: always to love more than you are loved and never to be second in this.

Let man fear woman when she loves. Then she bears every sacrifice and every other thing she accounts valueless.

Let man fear woman when she hates: for man is at the bottom of his soul only wicked, but woman is base.

Whom does woman hate most? – Thus spoke the iron to the magnet: 'I hate you most, because you attract me, but are not strong enough to draw me towards you.'

The man's happiness is: I will. The woman's happiness is: He will.

'Behold, now the world has become perfect!' – thus thinks every woman when she obeys with all her love.

And woman has to obey and find a depth for her surface. Woman's nature is surface, a changeable, stormy film upon shallow waters.

But a man's nature is deep, its torrent roars in subterranean caves: woman senses its power but does not comprehend it.

Then the little old woman answered me: 'Zarathustra has said many nice things, especially for those who are young enough for them.

'It is strange, Zarathustra knows little of women and yet he is right about them! Is this because with women nothing is impossible?

'And now accept as thanks a little truth! I am certainly old enough for it!

'Wrap it up and stop its mouth: otherwise it will cry too loudly, this little truth!'

'Give me your little truth, woman!' I said. And thus spoke the little old woman:

'Are you visiting women? Do not forget your whip!'

Thus spoke Zarathustra.

Of the Adder's Bite

ONE day Zarathustra had fallen asleep under a fig tree because of the heat, and had laid his arms over his face. An adder came along and bit him in the neck, so that Zarathustra cried out with pain. When he had taken his arm from his face he regarded the snake: it recognized Zarathustra's eyes, turned away awkwardly and was about to go. 'No, don't go,' said Zarathustra; 'you have not yet received my thanks! You have awakened me at the right time, I still have a long way to go.' 'You have only a short way to go,' said the adder sadly, 'my poison is deadly.' Zarathustra smiled. 'When did a dragon ever die from the poison of a snake?' he said. 'But take your poison back! You are not rich enough to give it me!' Then the adder fell upon his neck again and licked his wound.

When Zarathustra once told this to his disciples, they asked: 'And what, O Zarathustra, is the moral of your story?' Zarathustra answered the question thus:

The good and just call me the destroyer of morals: my story is immoral.

When, however, you have an enemy, do not requite him good for evil: for that would make him ashamed. But prove that he has done something good to you.

Better to be angry than make ashamed! And when you are cursed, I do not like it that you then want to bless. Rather curse back a little!

And should a great injustice be done you, then quickly do five little injustices besides. He who bears injustice alone is terrible to behold.

Did you know this already? Shared injustice is half justice. And he who can bear it should take the injustice upon himself.

A little revenge is more human than no revenge at all. And if the punishment be not also a right and an honour for the transgressor, then I do not like your punishment.

It is more noble to declare yourself wrong than to maintain you are right, especially when you *are* right. Only you must be rich enough for it.

I do not like your cold justice; and from the eye of your judges there always gazes only the executioner and his cold steel.

Tell me, where is the justice which is love with seeing eyes to be found?

Then devise the love that bears not only all punishment but also all guilt!

Then devise the justice that acquits everyone except the judges!

Will you learn this, too? To him who wants to be just from the very heart even a lie becomes philanthropy.

But how could I be just from the very heart? How can I give everyone what is his? Let this suffice me: I give everyone what is mine.

Finally, my brothers, guard yourselves against doing wrong to any hermit! How could a hermit forget? How could he requite?

A hermit is like a deep well. It is easy to throw a stone into it; but if it sink to the bottom, tell me, who shall fetch it out again?

Guard yourselves against offending the hermit! But if you have done so, well then, kill him as well!

Thus spoke Zarathustra.

Of Marriage and Children

I HAVE a question for you alone, my brother: I throw this question like a plummet into your soul, to discover how deep it is.

You are young and desire marriage and children. But I ask you: are you a man who *ought* to desire a child?

Are you the victor, the self-conqueror, the ruler of your senses, the lord of your virtues? Thus I ask you.

Or do the animal and necessity speak from your desire? Or isolation? Or disharmony with yourself?

I would have your victory and your freedom long for a child. You should build living memorials to your victory and your liberation.

You should build beyond yourself. But first you must be built yourself, square-built in body and soul.

You should propagate yourself not only forward, but upward![13] May the garden of marriage help you to do it!

You should create a higher body, a first motion, a self-propelling wheel – you should create a creator.

Marriage: that I call the will of two to create the one who is more than those who created it. Reverence before one another, as before the willers of such a will – that I call marriage.

Let this be the meaning and the truth of your marriage. But that which the many-too-many, the superfluous, call marriage – ah, what shall I call it?

Ah, this poverty of soul in partnership! Ah, this filth of soul in partnership! Ah, this miserable ease in partnership!

All this they call marriage; and they say their marriages are made in Heaven.

Well, I do not like it, this Heaven of the superfluous! No, I do not like them, these animals caught in the heavenly net!

And let the God who limps hither to bless what he has not joined stay far from me!

Do not laugh at such marriages! What child has not had reason to weep over its parents?

This man seemed to me worthy and ripe for the meaning of the earth: but when I saw his wife the earth seemed to me a house for the nonsensical.

Yes, I wish that the earth shook with convulsions when a saint and a goose mate together.

This man set forth like a hero in quest of truth and at last he captured a little dressed-up lie. He calls it his marriage.

That man used to be reserved in his dealings and fastidious in his choice. But all at once he spoilt his company once and for all: he calls it his marriage.

That man sought a handmaiden with the virtues of an angel. But all at once he became the handmaiden of a woman, and now he needs to become an angel too.

I have found all buyers cautious, and all of them have astute eyes. But even the most astute man buys his wife while she is still wrapped.

Many brief follies – that is called love with you. And your marriage makes an end of many brief follies with one long stupidity.

Your love for woman and woman's love for man: ah, if only it were pity for suffering and veiled gods! But generally two animals sense one another.

But even your best love too is only a passionate impersonation and a painful ardour. It is a torch which should light your way to higher paths.

One day you shall love beyond yourselves! So first *learn* to love! For that you have had to drink the bitter cup of your love.

There is bitterness in the cup of even the best love: thus it arouses longing for the Superman, thus it arouses thirst in you, the creator!

A creator's thirst, arrow, and longing for the Superman: speak, my brother, is this your will to marriage?

I call holy such a will and such a marriage.

Thus spoke Zarathustra.

Of Voluntary Death

MANY die too late and some die too early. Still the doctrine sounds strange: 'Die at the right time.'

Die at the right time: thus Zarathustra teaches.

To be sure, he who never lived at the right time could hardly die at the right time! Better if he were never to be born! – Thus I advise the superfluous.

But even the superfluous make a great thing of their dying; yes, even the hollowest nut wants to be cracked.

Everyone treats death as an important matter: but as yet death is not a festival. As yet, men have not learned to consecrate the fairest festivals.

I shall show you the consummating death, which shall be a spur and a promise to the living.

The man consummating his life dies his death triumphantly, surrounded by men filled with hope and making solemn vows.

Thus one should learn to die; and there should be no festivals at which such a dying man does not consecrate the oaths of the living!

To die thus is the best death; but the second best is: to die in battle and to squander a great soul.

But equally hateful to the fighter as to the victor is your grinning death, which comes creeping up like a thief – and yet comes as master.

I commend to you my sort of death, voluntary death that comes to me because *I* wish it.

And when shall I wish it? – He who has a goal and an heir wants death at the time most favourable to his goal and his heir.

And out of reverence for his goal and his heir he will hang up no more withered wreaths in the sanctuary of life.

Truly, I do not want to be like the rope-makers: they spin out their yarn and as a result continually go backwards themselves.

Many a one grows too old even for his truths and victories;

a toothless mouth has no longer the right to every truth.

And everyone who wants glory must take leave of honour in good time and practise the difficult art of – going at the right time.

One must stop permitting oneself to be eaten when one tastes best: this is understood by those who want to be loved long.

To be sure, there are sour apples whose fate is to wait until the last day of autumn: and they become at the same time ripe, yellow, and shrivelled.

In some the heart ages first and in others the spirit. And some are old in their youth: but those who are young late stay young long.

For many a man, life is a failure: a poison-worm eats at his heart. So let him see to it that his death is all the more a success.

Many a man never becomes sweet, he rots even in the summer. It is cowardice that keeps him fastened to his branch.

Many too many live and they hang on their branches much too long. I wish a storm would come and shake all this rottenness and worm-eatenness from the tree!

I wish preachers of *speedy* death would come! They would be the fitting storm and shakers of the trees of life! But I hear preached only slow death and patience with all 'earthly things'.

Ah, do you preach patience with earthly things? It is these earthly things that have too much patience with you, you blasphemers!

Truly, too early died that Hebrew whom the preachers of slow death honour: and that he died too early has since been a fatality for many.

As yet he knew only tears and the melancholy of the Hebrews, together with the hatred of the good and just – the Hebrew Jesus: then he was seized by the longing for death.

Had he only remained in the desert and far from the good and just! Perhaps he would have learned to live and learned to love the earth – and laughter as well!

Believe it, my brothers! He died too early; he himself

would have recanted his teaching had he lived to my age! He was noble enough to recant!

But he was still immature. The youth loves immaturely and immaturely too he hates man and the earth. His heart and the wings of his spirit are still bound and heavy.

But there is more child in the man than in the youth, and less melancholy: he has a better understanding of life and death.

Free for death and free in death, one who solemnly says No when there is no longer time for Yes: thus he understands life and death.

That your death may not be a blasphemy against man and the earth, my friends: that is what I beg from the honey of your soul.

In your death, your spirit and your virtue should still glow like a sunset glow around the earth: otherwise yours is a bad death.

Thus I want to die myself, that you friends may love the earth more for my sake; and I want to become earth again, that I may have peace in her who bore me.

Truly, Zarathustra had a goal, he threw his ball: now may you friends be the heirs of my goal, I throw the golden ball to you.

But best of all I like to see you, too, throwing on the golden ball, my friends! So I shall stay on earth a little longer: forgive me for it!

Thus spoke Zarathustra.

Of the Bestowing Virtue

I

WHEN Zarathustra had taken leave of the town to which his heart was attached and which was called 'The Pied Cow' there followed him many who called themselves his disciples and escorted him. Thus they came to a cross-road: there Zarathustra told them that from then on he wanted to go alone: for he was a friend of going-alone. But his disciples handed him in farewell a staff, upon the golden haft of which a serpent was coiled about a sun. Zarathustra was delighted with the staff and leaned upon it; then he spoke thus to his disciples:

Tell me: how did gold come to have the highest value? Because it is uncommon and useless and shining and mellow in lustre; it always bestows itself.

Only as an image of the highest virtue did gold come to have the highest value. Gold-like gleams the glance of the giver. Gold-lustre makes peace between moon and sun.

The highest virtue is uncommon and useless, it is shining and mellow in lustre: the highest virtue is a bestowing virtue.

Truly, I divine you well, my disciples, you aspire to the bestowing virtue, as I do. What could you have in common with cats and wolves?

You thirst to become sacrifices and gifts yourselves; and that is why you thirst to heap up all riches in your soul.

Your soul aspires insatiably after treasures and jewels, because your virtue is insatiable in wanting to give.

You compel all things to come to you and into you, that they may flow back from your fountain as gifts of your love.

Truly, such a bestowing love must become a thief of all values; but I call this selfishness healthy and holy.

There is another selfishness, an all-too-poor, a hungry selfishness that always wants to steal, that selfishness of the sick, the sick selfishness.

It looks with the eye of a thief upon all lustrous things; with the greed of hunger it measures him who has plenty to eat; and it is always skulking about the table of the givers.

Sickness speaks from such craving, and hidden degeneration; the thieving greed of this longing speaks of a sick body.

Tell me, my brothers: what do we account bad and the worst of all? Is it not *degeneration*? – And we always suspect degeneration where the bestowing soul is lacking.

Our way is upward, from the species across to the super-species. But the degenerate mind which says 'All for me' is a horror to us.

Our mind flies upward: thus it is an image of our bodies, an image of an advance and elevation.

The names of the virtues are such images of advances and elevations.

Thus the body goes through history, evolving and battling. And the spirit – what is it to the body? The herald, companion, and echo of its battles and victories.

All names of good and evil are images: they do not speak out, they only hint. He is a fool who seeks knowledge from them.

Whenever your spirit wants to speak in images, pay heed; for that is when your virtue has its origin and beginning.

Then your body is elevated and risen up; it enraptures the spirit with its joy, that it may become creator and evaluator and lover and benefactor of all things.

When your heart surges broad and full like a river, a blessing and a danger to those who live nearby: that is when your virtue has its origin and beginning.

When you are exalted above praise and blame, and your will wants to command all things as the will of a lover: that is when your virtue has its origin and beginning.

When you despise the soft bed and what is pleasant and cannot make your bed too far away from the soft-hearted: that is when your virtue has its origin and beginning.

When you are the willers of a single will, and you call this dispeller of need your essential and necessity: that is when your virtue has its origin and beginning.

Truly, it is a new good and evil! Truly, a new roaring in the depths and the voice of a new fountain!

It is power, this new virtue; it is a ruling idea, and around it a subtle soul: a golden sun, and around it the serpent of knowledge.

2

Here Zarathustra fell silent a while and regarded his disciples lovingly. Then he went on speaking thus, and his voice was different:

Stay loyal to the earth, my brothers, with the power of your virtue! May your bestowing love and your knowledge serve towards the meaning of the earth! Thus I beg and entreat you.

Do not let it fly away from the things of earth and beat with its wings against the eternal walls! Alas, there has always been much virtue that has flown away!

Lead, as I do, the flown-away virtue back to earth – yes, back to body and life: that it may give the earth its meaning, a human meaning!

A hundred times hitherto has spirit as well as virtue flown away and blundered. Alas, all this illusion and blundering still dwells in our bodies: it has there become body and will.

A hundred times has spirit as well as virtue experimented and gone astray. Yes, man was an experiment. Alas, much ignorance and error has become body in us!

Not only the reason of millennia – the madness of millennia too breaks out in us. It is dangerous to be an heir.

We are still fighting step by step with the giant Chance, and hitherto the senseless, the meaningless, has still ruled over mankind.

May your spirit and your virtue serve the meaning of the earth, my brothers: and may the value of all things be fixed anew by you. To that end you should be fighters! To that end you should be creators!

The body purifies itself through knowledge; experimenting with knowledge it elevates itself; to the discerning man all instincts are holy; the soul of the elevated man grows joyful.

Physician, heal yourself: thus you will heal your patient too. Let his best healing-aid be to see with his own eyes him who makes himself well.

There are a thousand paths that have never yet been trodden, a thousand forms of health and hidden islands of life. Man and man's earth are still unexhausted and undiscovered.

Watch and listen, you solitaries! From the future come winds with a stealthy flapping of wings; and good tidings go out to delicate ears.

You solitaries of today, you who have seceded from society, you shall one day be a people: from you, who have chosen out yourselves, shall a chosen people spring – and from this chosen people, the Superman.

Truly, the earth shall yet become a house of healing! And already a new odour floats about it, an odour that brings health – and a new hope!

3

When Zarathustra had said these words he paused like one who has not said his last word; long he balanced the staff doubtfully in his hand. At last he spoke thus, and his voice was different:

I now go away alone, my disciples! You too now go away and be alone! So I will have it.

Truly, I advise you: go away from me and guard yourselves against Zarathustra! And better still: be ashamed of him! Perhaps he has deceived you.

The man of knowledge must be able not only to love his enemies but also to hate his friends.

One repays a teacher badly if one remains only a pupil. And why, then, should you not pluck at my laurels?

You respect me; but how if one day your respect should tumble? Take care that a falling statue does not strike you dead!

You say you believe in Zarathustra? But of what importance is Zarathustra? You are my believers: but of what importance are all believers?

You had not yet sought yourselves when you found me. Thus do all believers; therefore all belief is of so little account.

Now I bid you lose me and find yourselves; and only when you have all denied me will I return to you.

Truly, with other eyes, my brothers, I shall then seek my lost ones; with another love I shall then love you.

And once more you shall have become my friends and children of one hope: and then I will be with you a third time, that I may celebrate the great noontide with you.

And this is the great noontide: it is when man stands at the middle of his course between animal and Superman and celebrates his journey to the evening as his highest hope: for it is the journey to a new morning.

Then man, going under, will bless himself; for he will be going over to Superman; and the sun of his knowledge will stand at noontide.

'*All gods are dead: now we want the Superman to live*' – let this be our last will one day at the great noontide!

Thus spoke Zarathustra.

PART TWO

※

'—and only when you have all denied me
will I return to you.

'Truly, with other eyes, my brothers, I
shall then seek my lost ones; with another
love I shall then love you.'

ZARATHUSTRA:
'Of the Bestowing Virtue'

The Child with the Mirror

THEN Zarathustra went back into the mountains and into the solitude of his cave and withdrew from mankind: waiting like a sower who has scattered his seed. His soul, however, became full of impatience and longing for those whom he loved: for he still had much to give them. This, indeed, is the most difficult thing: to close the open hand out of love and to preserve one's modesty as a giver.

Thus months and years passed over the solitary; but his wisdom increased and caused him pain by its abundance.

One morning, however, he awoke before dawn, deliberated long upon his bed, and at length spoke to his heart:

Why was I so frightened in my dream that I awoke? Did not a child carrying a mirror come to me?

'O Zarathustra,' the child said to me, 'look at yourself in the mirror!'

But when I looked into the mirror I cried out and my heart was shaken: for I did not see myself, I saw the sneer and grimace of a devil.

Truly, I understand the dream's omen and warning all too well: my *doctrine* is in danger, weeds want to be called wheat!

My enemies have grown powerful and have distorted the meaning of my doctrine, so that my dearest ones are ashamed of the gifts I gave them.

My friends are lost to me; the hour has come to seek my lost ones!

With these words Zarathustra sprang up – not, however, as if gasping for air, but rather like a seer and a singer whom the spirit has moved. His eagle and his serpent regarded him with amazement: for a dawning happiness lit up his face like the dawn.

What has happened to me, my animals? (said Zarathustra).

Have I not changed? Has bliss not come to me like a storm-wind?

My happiness is foolish and it will speak foolish things: it is still too young – so be patient with it!

My happiness has wounded me: all sufferers shall be physicians to me!

I can go down to my friends again and to my enemies too! Zarathustra can speak and give again, and again show love to those he loves.

My impatient love overflows in torrents down towards morning and evening. My soul streams into the valleys out of silent mountains and storms of grief.

I have desired and gazed into the distance too long. I have belonged to solitude too long: thus I have forgotten how to be silent.

I have become nothing but speech and the tumbling of a brook from high rocks: I want to hurl my words down into the valleys.

And let my stream of love plunge into impassable and pathless places! How should a stream not find its way to the sea at last!

There is surely a lake in me, a secluded, self-sufficing lake; but my stream of love draws it down with it – to the sea!

I go new ways, a new speech has come to me; like all creators, I have grown weary of the old tongues. My spirit no longer wants to walk on worn-out soles.

All speech runs too slowly for me – I leap into your chariot, storm! And even you I will whip on with my venom!

I want to sail across broad seas like a cry and a shout of joy, until I find the Blissful Islands where my friends are waiting –

And my enemies with them! How I now love anyone to whom I can simply speak! My enemies too are part of my happiness.

And when I want to mount my wildest horse, it is my spear that best helps me on to it; it is an ever-ready servant to my foot –

The spear which I throw at my enemies! How I thank my enemies that at last I can throw it!

The tension of my cloud has been too great: between laughter-peals of lightning I want to cast hail showers into the depths.

Mightily then my breast will heave, mightily it will blow its storm away over the mountains: and so it will win relief.

Truly, my happiness and my freedom come like a storm! But my enemies shall think the *Evil One* is raging over their heads.

Yes, you too, my friends, will be terrified by my wild wisdom; and perhaps you will flee from it together with my enemies.

Ah, if only I knew how to lure you back with shepherds' flutes! Ah, if only my lioness Wisdom had learned to roar fondly! And we have already learned so much with one another!

My wild Wisdom became pregnant upon lonely mountains; upon rough rocks she bore her young, her youngest.

Now she runs madly through the cruel desert and seeks and seeks for the soft grassland – my old, wild Wisdom!

Upon the soft grassland of your hearts, my friends! – upon your love she would like to bed her dearest one!

Thus spoke Zarathustra.

On the Blissful Islands

THE figs are falling from the trees, they are fine and sweet; and as they fall their red skins split. I am a north wind to ripe figs.

Thus, like figs, do these teachings fall to you, my friends: now drink their juice and eat their sweet flesh! It is autumn all around and clear sky and afternoon.

Behold, what abundance is around us! And it is fine to gaze out upon distant seas from the midst of superfluity.

Once you said 'God' when you gazed upon distant seas; but now I have taught you to say 'Superman'.

God is a supposition; but I want your supposing to reach no further than your creating will.

Could you *create* a god? – So be silent about all gods! But you could surely create the Superman.

Perhaps not you yourselves, my brothers! But you could transform yourselves into forefathers and ancestors of the Superman: and let this be your finest creating!

God is a supposition: but I want your supposing to be bounded by conceivability.

Could you *conceive* a god? – But may the will to truth mean this to you: that everything shall be transformed into the humanly-conceivable, the humanly-evident, the humanly-palpable! You should follow your own senses to the end!

And you yourselves should create what you have hitherto called the World: the World should be formed in your image by your reason, your will, and your love! And truly, it will be to your happiness, you enlightened men!

And how should you endure life without this hope, you enlightened men? Neither in the incomprehensible nor in the irrational can you be at home.

But to reveal my heart entirely to you, friends: *if* there were gods, how could I endure not to be a god! *Therefore* there are no gods.

I, indeed, drew that conclusion; but now it draws me.

God is a supposition: but who could imbibe all the anguish of this supposition without dying? Shall the creator be robbed of his faith and the eagle of his soaring into the heights?

God is a thought that makes all that is straight crooked and all that stands giddy. What? Would time be gone and all that is transitory only a lie?

To think this is giddiness and vertigo to the human frame, and vomiting to the stomach: truly, I call it the giddy sickness to suppose such a thing.

I call it evil and misanthropic, all this teaching about the one and the perfect and the unmoved and the sufficient and the intransitory.

All that is intransitory – that is but an image![14] And the poets lie too much.

But the best images and parables should speak of time and becoming: they should be a eulogy and a justification of all transitoriness.

Creation – that is the great redemption from suffering, and life's easement. But that the creator may exist, that itself requires suffering and much transformation.

Yes, there must be much bitter dying in your life, you creators! Thus you are advocates and justifiers of all transitoriness.

For the creator himself to be the child new-born he must also be willing to be the mother and endure the mother's pain.

Truly, I have gone my way through a hundred souls and through a hundred cradles and birth-pangs. I have taken many departures, I know the heart-breaking last hours.

But my creative will, my destiny, wants it so. Or, to speak more honestly: my will wants precisely such a destiny.

All *feeling* suffers in me and is in prison: but my *willing* always comes to me as my liberator and bringer of joy.

Willing liberates: that is the true doctrine of will and freedom – thus Zarathustra teaches you.

No more to will and no more to evaluate and no more to create! ah, that this great lassitude may ever stay far from me!

In knowing and understanding, too, I feel only my will's delight in begetting and becoming; and if there be innocence in my knowledge it is because will to begetting is in it.

This will lured me away from God and gods; for what would there be to create if gods – existed!

But again and again it drives me to mankind, my ardent, creative will; thus it drives the hammer to the stone.

Ah, you men, I see an image sleeping in the stone, the image of my visions! Ah, that it must sleep in the hardest, ugliest stone!

Now my hammer rages fiercely against its prison. Fragments fly from the stone: what is that to me?

I will complete it: for a shadow came to me – the most silent, the lightest of all things once came to me!

The beauty of the Superman came to me as a shadow. Ah, my brothers! What are the gods to me now!

Thus spoke Zarathustra.

Of the Compassionate

MY friends, your friend has heard a satirical saying: 'Just look at Zarathustra! Does he not go among us as if among animals?'

But it is better said like this: 'The enlightened man goes among men *as* among animals.'

The enlightened man calls man himself: the animal with red cheeks.

How did this happen to man? Is it not because he has had to be ashamed too often?

Oh my friends! Thus speaks the enlightened man: 'Shame, shame, shame – that is the history of man!'

And for that reason the noble man resolves not to make others ashamed: he resolves to feel shame before all sufferers.

Truly, I do not like them, the compassionate who are happy in their compassion: they are too lacking in shame.

If I must be compassionate I still do not want to be called compassionate; and if I am compassionate then it is preferably from a distance.

And I should also prefer to cover my head and flee away before I am recognized: and thus I bid you do, my friends!

May my destiny ever lead across my path only those who, like you, do not sorrow or suffer, and those with whom I can have hope and repast and honey in common!

Truly, I did this and that for the afflicted; but it always seemed to me I did better things when I learned to enjoy myself better.

As long as men have existed, man has enjoyed himself too little: that alone, my brothers, is our original sin!

And if we learn better to enjoy ourselves, we best unlearn how to do harm to others and to contrive harm.

Therefore I wash my hand when it has helped a sufferer, therefore I wipe my soul clean as well.

For I saw the sufferer suffer, and because I saw it I was ashamed on account of his shame; and when I helped him, then I sorely injured his pride.

Great obligations do not make a man grateful, they make him resentful; and if a small kindness is not forgotten it becomes a gnawing worm.

'Be reserved in accepting! Honour a man by accepting from him!' – thus I advise those who have nothing to give.

I, however, am a giver: I give gladly as a friend to friends. But strangers and the poor may pluck the fruit from my tree for themselves: it causes less shame that way.

Beggars, however, should be entirely abolished! Truly, it is annoying to give to them and annoying not to give to them.

And likewise sinners and bad consciences! Believe me, my friends: stings of conscience teach one to sting.

But worst of all are petty thoughts. Truly, better even to have done wickedly than to have thought pettily!

To be sure, you will say: 'Delight in petty wickedness spares us many a great evil deed.' But here one should not wish to be spared.

The evil deed is like a boil: it itches and irritates and breaks forth – it speaks honourably.

'Behold, I am disease' – thus speaks the evil deed; that is its honesty.

But the petty thought is like a canker: it creeps and hides and wants to appear nowhere – until the whole body is rotten and withered by little cankers.

But I whisper this advice in the ear of him possessed of a devil: 'Better for you to rear your devil! There is a way to greatness even for you!'

Ah, my brothers! One knows a little too much about everybody! And many a one who has become transparent to us is still for a long time invulnerable.

It is hard to live with men, because keeping silent is so hard.

And we are the most unfair, not towards him whom we do not like, but towards him for whom we feel nothing at all.

But if you have a suffering friend, be a resting-place for his suffering, but a resting-place like a hard bed, a camp-bed: thus you will serve him best.

And should your friend do you a wrong, then say: 'I forgive you what you did to me; but that you did it to *yourself* – how could I forgive that?'

Thus speaks all great love: it overcomes even forgiveness and pity.

One should hold fast to one's heart; for if one lets it go, how soon one loses one's head, too!

Alas, where in the world have there been greater follies than with the compassionate? And what in the world has caused more suffering than the follies of the compassionate?

Woe to all lovers who cannot surmount pity!

Thus spoke the Devil to me once: 'Even God has his Hell: it is his love for man.'

And I lately heard him say these words: 'God is dead; God has died of his pity for man.'

So be warned against pity: *thence* shall yet come a heavy cloud for man! Truly, I understand weather-signs!

But mark, too, this saying: All great love is above pity: for it wants – to create what is loved!

'I offer myself to my love, *and my neighbour as myself*' – that is the language of all creators.

All creators, however, are hard.

Thus spoke Zarathustra.

Of the Priests

AND one day Zarathustra made a sign to his disciples and spoke these words to them:

Here are priests: and although they are my enemies, pass them by quietly and with sleeping swords!

There are heroes even among them; many of them have suffered too much: so they want to make others suffer.

They are bad enemies: nothing is more revengeful than their humility. And he who touches them is easily defiled.

But my blood is related to theirs; and I want to know my blood honoured even in theirs.

And when they had passed by, Zarathustra was assailed by a pain; and he had not struggled long with his pain when he began to speak thus:

I pity these priests. They go against my taste, too; but that means little to me since I am among men.

But I suffer and have suffered with them: they seem to me prisoners and marked men. He whom they call Redeemer has cast them into bondage –

Into the bondage of false values and false scriptures! Ah, that someone would redeem them from their Redeemer!

Once, as the sea tossed them about, they thought they had landed upon an island; but behold, it was a sleeping monster!

False values and false scriptures: they are the worst monsters for mortal men – fate sleeps and waits long within them.

But at last it comes and awakes and eats and devours all that have built their huts upon it.

Oh, just look at these huts that these priests have built themselves. Churches they call their sweet-smelling caves!

Oh this counterfeit light! oh this musty air! here, where the soul may not fly up to its height!

On the contrary, their faith commands: 'Up the steps on your knees, you sinners!'

Truly, I would rather see men still shameless than with the distorted eyes of their shame and devotion!

Who created such caves and penitential steps? Was it not those who wanted to hide themselves and were ashamed before the clear sky?

And only when the clear sky again looks through broken roofs and down upon grass and red poppies on broken walls – only then will I turn my heart again towards the places of this God.

They called God that which contradicted and harmed them: and truly, there was much that was heroic in their worship!

And they knew no other way of loving their God than by nailing men to the Cross!

They thought to live as corpses, they dressed their corpses in black; even in their speech I still smell the evil aroma of burial vaults.

And he who lives in their neighbourhood lives in the neighbourhood of black pools, from out of which the toad, that prophet of evil, sings its song with sweet melancholy.

They would have to sing better songs to make me believe in their Redeemer: his disciples would have to look more redeemed!

I should like to see them naked: for beauty alone should preach penitence. But whom could this disguised affliction persuade!

Truly, their Redeemers themselves did not come from freedom and the seventh heaven of freedom! Truly, they themselves never trod upon the carpets of knowledge!

The spirit of their Redeemers consisted of holes; but into every hole they had put their illusion, their stop-gap, which they called God.

Their spirit was drowned in their pity, and when they swelled and overswelled with pity a great folly always swam to the top.

Zealously and with clamour they drove their herds over their bridge: as if there were only one bridge to the future! Truly, these shepherds, too, still belonged among the sheep!

These shepherds had small intellects and spacious souls: but, my brothers, what small countries have even the most spacious souls been, up to now!

They wrote letters of blood on the path they followed, and their folly taught that truth is proved by blood.

But blood is the worst witness of truth; blood poisons and transforms the purest teaching to delusion and hatred of the heart.

And if someone goes through fire for his teaching – what does that prove? Truly, it is more when one's own teaching comes out of one's own burning!

Sultry heart and cold head: where these meet there arises the blusterer, the 'Redeemer'.

Truly, there have been greater men and higher-born ones

than those whom the people call Redeemer, those ravishing and overpowering blustering winds!

And you, my brothers, must be redeemed by greater men than any Redeemer has been, if you would find the way to freedom!

There has never yet been a Superman. I have seen them both naked, the greatest and the smallest man.

They are still all-too-similar to one another. Truly, I found even the greatest man – all-too-human!

Thus spoke Zarathustra.

Of the Virtuous

ONE has to speak with thunder and heavenly fireworks to feeble and dormant senses.

But the voice of beauty speaks softly: it steals into only the most awakened souls.

Gently my mirror trembled and laughed to me today; it was beauty's holy laughter and trembling.

My beauty laughed at you, you virtuous, today. And thus came its voice to me: 'They want to be – paid as well!'

You want to be paid as well, you virtuous! Do you want reward for virtue and heaven for earth and eternity for your today?

And are you now angry with me because I teach that there is no reward-giver nor paymaster? And truly, I do not even teach that virtue is its own reward.

Alas, this is my sorrow: reward and punishment have been lyingly introduced into the foundation of things – and now even into the foundation of your souls, you virtuous!

But my words, like the snout of the boar, shall tear up the foundations of your souls; you shall call me a plough-share.

All the secrets of your heart shall be brought to light; and when you lie, grubbed up and broken, in the sunlight, then your falsehood will be separated from your truth.

For this is your truth: You are too *pure* for the dirt of the words: revenge, punishment, reward, retribution.

You love your virtue as the mother her child; but when was it heard of a mother wanting to be paid for her love?

Your virtue is your dearest self. The ring's desire is in you: to attain itself again – every ring struggles and turns itself to that end.

And every work of your virtue is like a star extinguished: its light is for ever travelling – and when will it cease from travelling?

Thus the light of your virtue is still travelling even when its task is done. Though it be forgotten and dead, its beam of light still lives and travels.

That your virtue is your Self and not something alien, a skin, a covering: that is the truth from the bottom of your souls, you virtuous!

But there are indeed those to whom virtue is a writhing under the whip: and you have listened too much to their cries!

And with others, their vices grow lazy and they call that virtue; and once their hatred and jealousy stretch themselves to rest, their 'justice' becomes lively and rubs its sleepy eyes.

And there are others who are drawn downward: their devils draw them. But the more they sink, the more brightly shines their eye and the longing for their God.

Alas, their cry, too, has come to your ears, you virtuous: 'What I am *not*, that, that to me is God and virtue!'

And there are others who go along, heavy and creaking, like carts carrying stones downhill: they speak much of dignity and virtue – their brake they call virtue!

And there are others who are like household clocks wound up; they repeat their tick-tock and want people to call tick-tock – virtue.

Truly, I have fun with these: wherever I find such clocks I shall wind them up with my mockery; let them chime as well as tick!

And others are proud of their handful of righteousness and

for its sake commit wanton outrage upon all things: so that the world is drowned in their unrighteousness.

Alas, how ill the word 'virtue' sounds in their mouths! And when they say: 'I am just,' it always sounds like: 'I am revenged!'[15]

They want to scratch out the eyes of their enemies with their virtue; and they raise themselves only in order to lower others.

And again, there are those who sit in their swamp and speak thus from the rushes: 'Virtue – that means to sit quietly in the swamp.

'We bite nobody and avoid him who wants to bite: and in everything we hold the opinion that is given us.'

And again, there are those who like posing and think: Virtue is a sort of pose.

Their knees are always worshipping and their hands are glorifications of virtue, but their heart knows nothing of it.

And again, there are those who hold it a virtue to say: 'Virtue is necessary'; but fundamentally they believe only that the police are necessary.

And many a one who cannot see the sublime in man calls it virtue that he can see his baseness all-too-closely: thus he calls his evil eye virtue.

And some want to be edified and raised up and call it virtue; and others want to be thrown down – and call it virtue too.

And in that way almost everyone firmly believes he is participating in virtue; and at least asserts he is an expert on 'good' and 'evil'.

But Zarathustra has not come to say to all these liars and fools: 'What do *you* know of virtue? What *could* you know of virtue?'

No, he has come that you, my friends, might grow weary of the old words you have learned from the fools and liars.

That you might grow weary of the words 'reward', 'retribution', 'punishment', 'righteous revenge'.

That you might grow weary of saying: 'An action is good when it is unselfish.'

Ah, my friends! That *your* Self be in the action, as the mother is in the child: let that be *your* maxim of virtue!

Truly, I have taken a hundred maxims and your virtues' dearest playthings away from you; and you scold me now, as children scold.

They were playing on the sea-shore – then came a wave and swept their playthings into the deep: now they cry.

But the same wave shall bring them new playthings and pour out new coloured sea-shells before them!

Thus they will be consoled; and you too, my friends, shall, like them, have your consolations – and new coloured sea-shells!

Thus spoke Zarathustra.

Of the Rabble

LIFE is a fountain of delight; but where the rabble also drinks all wells are poisoned.

I love all that is clean; but I do not like to see the grinning mouths and the thirst of the unclean.

They cast their eyes down into the well: now their repulsive smile glitters up to me out of the well.

They have poisoned the holy water with their lasciviousness; and when they called their dirty dreams 'delight' they poisoned even the words, too.

The flame is unwilling to burn when they put their damp hearts to the fire; the spirit itself bubbles and smokes when the rabble approaches the fire.

The fruit grows mawkish and over-ripe in their hands: the fruit tree becomes unstable and withered at the top under their glance.

And many a one who turned away from life, turned away only from the rabble: he did not wish to share the well and the flame and the fruit with the rabble.

And many a one who went into the desert and suffered

thirst with beasts of prey merely did not wish to sit around the cistern with dirty camel-drivers.

And many a one who came along like a destroyer and a shower of hail to all orchards wanted merely to put his foot into the jaws of the rabble and so stop its throat.

And to know that life itself has need of enmity and dying and martyrdoms, that was not the mouthful that choked me most.

But I once asked, and my question almost stifled me: What, does life have *need* of the rabble, too?

Are poisoned wells necessary, and stinking fires and dirty dreams and maggots in the bread of life?

Not my hate but my disgust hungrily devoured my life! Alas, I often grew weary of the spirit when I found the rabble, too, had been gifted with spirit!

And I turned my back upon the rulers when I saw what they now call ruling: bartering and haggling for power – with the rabble!

I dwelt with stopped ears among peoples with a strange language: that the language of their bartering and their haggling for power might remain strange to me.

And I went ill-humouredly through all yesterdays and todays holding my nose: truly, all yesterdays and todays smell badly of the scribbling rabble!

Like a cripple who has gone blind, deaf, and dumb: thus have I lived for a long time, that I might not live with the power-rabble, the scribbling-rabble, and the pleasure-rabble.

My spirit mounted steps wearily and warily; alms of delight were its refreshment; the blind man's life crept along on a staff.

Yet what happened to me? How did I free myself from disgust? Who rejuvenated my eyes? How did I fly to the height where the rabble no longer sit at the well?

Did my disgust itself create wings and water-divining powers for me? Truly, I had to fly to the extremest height to find again the fountain of delight!

Oh, I have found it, my brothers! Here, in the extremest

height, the fountain of delight gushes up for me! And here there is a life at which no rabble drinks with me!

You gush up almost too impetuously, fountain of delight! And in wanting to fill the cup, you often empty it again!

And I still have to learn to approach you more discreetly: my heart still flows towards you all-too-impetuously.

My heart, upon which my summer burns, a short, hot, melancholy, over-joyful summer: how my summer-heart longs for your coolness!

Gone is the lingering affliction of my spring! Gone the malice of my snowflakes in June! Summer have I become entirely, and summer-noonday!

A summer at the extremest height with cold fountains and blissful stillness: oh come, my friends, that the stillness may become more blissful yet!

For this is *our* height and our home: we live too nobly and boldly[16] here for all unclean men and their thirsts.

Only cast your pure eyes into the well of my delight, friends! You will not dim its sparkle! It shall laugh back at you with *its* purity.

We build our nest in the tree Future; eagles shall bring food to us solitaries in their beaks!

Truly, food in which no unclean men could join us! They would think they were eating fire and burn their mouths!

Truly, we do not prepare a home here for unclean men! Their bodies and their spirits would call our happiness a cave of ice!

So let us live above them like strong winds, neighbours of the eagles, neighbours of the snow, neighbours of the sun: that is how strong winds live.

And like a wind will I one day blow among them and with my spirit take away the breath from their spirit: thus my future will have it.

Truly, Zarathustra is a strong wind to all flatlands; and he offers this advice to his enemies and to all that spews and spits: 'Take care not to spit *against* the wind!'

Thus spoke Zarathustra.

Of the Tarantulas

SEE, this is the tarantula's cave! Do you want to see the tarantula itself? Here hangs its web: touch it and make it tremble.

Here it comes docilely: Welcome, tarantula! Your triangle and symbol sit black upon your back; and I know too what sits within your soul.

Revenge sits within your soul: a black scab grows wherever you bite; with revenge your poison makes the soul giddy!

Thus do I speak to you in parables, you who make the soul giddy, you preachers of *equality*! You are tarantulas and dealers in hidden revengefulness!

But I will soon bring your hiding places to light: therefore I laugh my laughter of the heights in your faces.

I pull at your web that your rage may lure you from your cave of lies and your revenge may bound forward from behind your word 'justice'.

For *that man may be freed from the bonds of revenge:* that is the bridge to my highest hope and a rainbow after protracted storms.

But, naturally, the tarantulas would have it differently. 'That the world may become full of the storms of our revenge, let precisely that be called justice by us' – thus they talk together.

'We shall practise revenge and outrage against all who are not as we are' – thus the tarantula-hearts promise themselves.

'And "will to equality" – that itself shall henceforth be the name of virtue; and we shall raise outcry against everything that has power!'

You preachers of equality, thus from you the tyrant-madness of impotence cries for 'equality': thus your most secret tyrant-appetite disguises itself in words of virtue.

Soured self-conceit, repressed envy, perhaps your fathers' self-conceit and envy: they burst from you as a flame and madness of revenge.

What the father kept silent the son speaks out; and I often found the son the father's revealed secret.

They resemble inspired men: but it is not the heart that inspires them – it is revenge. And when they become refined and cold, it is not their mind, it is their envy that makes them refined and cold.

Their jealousy leads them upon thinkers' paths too; and this is the mark of their jealousy – they always go too far: so that their weariness has at last to lie down and sleep even on the snow.

Revenge rings in all their complaints, a malevolence is in all their praise; and to be judge seems bliss to them.

Thus, however, I advise you, my friends: Mistrust all in whom the urge to punish is strong!

They are people of a bad breed and a bad descent; the executioner and the bloodhound peer from out their faces.

Mistrust all those who talk much about their justice! Truly, it is not only honey that their souls lack.

And when they call themselves 'the good and just', do not forget that nothing is lacking to make them into Pharisees except – power!

My friends, I do not want to be confused with others or taken for what I am not.

There are those who preach my doctrine of life: yet are at the same time preachers of equality, and tarantulas.

That they speak well of life, these poison spiders, although they sit in their caves and with their backs turned on life, is because they want to do harm by speaking well of life.

They want to do harm to those who now possess power: for with those the preaching of death is still most at home.

If it were otherwise, the tarantulas would teach otherwise: and it is precisely they who were formerly the best world-slanderers and heretic-burners.

I do not want to be confused with these preachers of equality, nor taken for one of them. For justice speaks thus *to me*: 'Men are not equal.'

And they should not become so, either! For what were my love of the Superman if I spoke otherwise?

They should press on to the future across a thousand bridges and gangways, and there should be more and more war and inequality among them: thus my great love makes me speak!

They should become devisers of emblems and phantoms in their enmity, and with their emblems and phantoms they should fight together the supreme fight!

Good and evil, and rich and poor, and noble and mean, and all the names of the virtues: they should be weapons and ringing symbols that life must overcome itself again and again!

Life wants to raise itself on high with pillars and steps; it wants to gaze into the far distance and out upon joyful splendour – *that* is why it needs height!

And because it needs height, it needs steps and conflict between steps and those who climb them! Life wants to climb and in climbing overcome itself.

And just look, my friends! Here, where the tarantula's cave is, there rises up the ruins of an old temple – just look at it with enlightened eyes!

Truly, he who once towered up his thoughts in stone here knew as well as the wisest about the secret of all life!

That there is battle and inequality and war for power and predominance even in beauty: he teaches us that here in the clearest parable.

How divinely vault and arch here oppose one another in the struggle: how they strive against one another with light and shadow, these divinely-striving things.

Beautiful and assured as these, let us also be enemies, my friends! Let us divinely strive *against* one another!

Ha! Now the tarantula, my old enemy, has bitten me! Divinely beautiful and assured, it bit me in the finger!

'There must be punishment and justice' – thus it thinks: 'here he shall not sing in vain songs in honour of enmity!'

Yes, the tarantula has revenged itself! And alas, now it will make my soul, too, giddy with revenge!

But so that I may *not* veer round, tie me tight to this pillar, my friends! I would rather be even a pillar-saint than a whirlpool of revengefulness!

Truly, Zarathustra is no veering wind nor whirlwind; and although he is a dancer, he is by no means a tarantella dancer!

Thus spoke Zarathustra.

Of the Famous Philosophers

You have served the people and the people's superstitions, all you famous philosophers! – you have *not* served truth! And it is precisely for that reason that they paid you reverence.

And for that reason too they endured your disbelief, because it was a joke and a bypath for the people. Thus the lord indulges his slaves and even enjoys their insolence.

But he who is hated by the people as a wolf is by the dogs: he is the free spirit, the enemy of fetters, the non-worshipper, the dweller in forests.

To hunt him from his hiding-place – the people always called that 'having a sense of right': they have always set their sharpest-toothed dogs upon him.

'For where the people are, truth is! Woe to him who seeks!' That is how it has been from the beginning.

You sought to make the people justified in their reverence: that you called 'will to truth', you famous philosophers!

And your heart always said to itself: 'I came from the people: God's voice, too, came to me from them.'

You have always been obstinate and cunning, like the ass, as the people's advocate.

And many a man of power who wanted to fare well with the people harnessed in front of his horses – a little ass, a famous philosopher.

And now I should like you to throw the lion-skin right off yourselves, you famous philosophers!

The spotted skin of the beast of prey and the matted hair of the inquirer, the seeker, the overcomer!

Ah, for me to learn to believe in your 'genuineness' you would first have to break your will to venerate.

Genuine – that is what I call him who goes into god-forsaken deserts and has broken his venerating heart.

In the yellow sand and burned by the sun, perhaps he blinks thirstily at the islands filled with springs where living creatures rest beneath shady trees.

But his thirst does not persuade him to become like these comfortable creatures: for where there are oases there are also idols.

Hungered, violent, solitary, godless: that is how the lion-will wants to be.

Free from the happiness of serfs, redeemed from gods and worship, fearless and fearful, great and solitary: that is how the will of the genuine man is.

The genuine men, the free spirits, have always dwelt in the desert, as the lords of the desert; but in the towns dwell the well-fed famous philosophers – the draught animals.

For they always, as asses, pull – the *people's* cart!

Not that I am wroth with them for that: however, they are still servants and beasts in harness, even when they glitter with golden gear.

And they have often been good and praiseworthy servants. For thus speaks virtue: 'If you must be a servant, then seek him whom you can serve best!

'The spirit and the virtue of your lord should thrive because you are his servant: thus you yourself will thrive with your lord's spirit and virtue!'

And in truth, you famous philosophers, you servants of the people, you yourselves have thrived with the spirit and virtue of the people – and the people have thrived through you! It is to your honour I say this!

But you are still of the people even in your virtue, of the people with their purblind eyes – of the people who do not know what *spirit* is!

Spirit is the life that itself strikes into life: through its own torment it increases its own knowledge – did you know that before?

And this is the spirit's happiness: to be anointed and by

tears consecrated as a sacrificial beast – did you know that before?

And the blindness of the blind man and his seeking and groping shall yet bear witness to the power of the sun into which he gazed – did you know that before?

And the enlightened man shall learn to *build* with mountains! It is a small thing for the spirit to move mountains – did you know that before?

You know only the sparks of the spirit: but you do not see the anvil which the spirit is, nor the ferocity of its hammer!

In truth, you do not know the spirit's pride! But even less could you endure the spirit's modesty, if it should ever deign to speak!

And you have never yet dared to cast your spirit into a pit of snow: you are not hot enough for that! Thus you do not know the rapture of its coldness, either.

But you behave in all things in too familiar a way with the spirit; and you have often made of wisdom a poorhouse and hospital for bad poets.

You are no eagles: so neither do you know the spirit's joy in terror. And he who is not a bird shall not make his home above abysses.

You are tepid: but all deep knowledge flows cold. The innermost wells of the spirit are ice-cold: a refreshment to hot hands and handlers.

You stand there respectable and stiff and with a straight back, you famous philosophers! – no strong wind or will propels you.

Have you never seen a sail faring over the sea, rounded and swelling and shuddering before the impetuosity of the wind?

Like a sail, shuddering before the impetuosity of the spirit, my wisdom fares over the sea – my untamed wisdom!

But you servants of the people, you famous philosophers – how *could* you fare with me?

Thus spoke Zarathustra.

The Night Song

IT is night: now do all leaping fountains speak louder. And my soul too is a leaping fountain.

It is night: only now do all songs of lovers awaken. And my soul too is the song of a lover.

Something unquenched, unquenchable, is in me, that wants to speak out. A craving for love is in me, that itself speaks the language of love.

Light am I: ah, that I were night! But this is my solitude, that I am girded round with light.

Ah, that I were dark and obscure! How I would suck at the breasts of light!

And I should bless you, little sparkling stars and glow-worms above! – and be happy in your gifts of light.

But I live in my own light, I drink back into myself the flames that break from me.

I do not know the joy of the receiver; and I have often dreamed that stealing must be more blessed than receiving.

It is my poverty that my hand never rests from giving; it is my envy that I see expectant eyes and illumined nights of desire.

Oh wretchedness of all givers! Oh eclipse of my sun! Oh craving for desire! Oh ravenous hunger in satiety!

They take from me: but do I yet touch their souls? A gulf stands between giving and receiving; and the smallest gulf must be bridged at last.

A hunger grows from out of my beauty: I should like to rob those to whom I give – thus do I hunger after wickedness.

Withdrawing my hand when another hand already reaches out to it; hesitating, like the waterfall that hesitates even in its plunge – thus do I hunger after wickedness.

Such vengeance does my abundance concoct: such spite wells from my solitude.

My joy in giving died in giving, my virtue grew weary of itself through its abundance!

The danger for him who always gives, is that he may lose his shame; the hand and heart of him who distributes grow callous through sheer distributing.

My eye no longer overflows with the shame of suppliants; my hand has become too hard for the trembling of hands that have been filled.

Where have the tears of my eye and the bloom of my heart gone? Oh solitude of all givers! Oh silence of all light-givers!

Many suns circle in empty space: to all that is dark they speak with their light – to me they are silent.

Oh, this is the enmity of light towards what gives light: unpitying it travels its way.

Unjust towards the light-giver in its inmost heart, cold towards suns – thus travels every sun.

Like a storm the suns fly along their courses; that is their travelling. They follow their inexorable will; that is their coldness.

Oh, it is only you, obscure, dark ones, who extract warmth from light-givers! Oh, only you drink milk and comfort from the udders of light!

Ah, ice is around me, my hand is burned with ice! Ah, thirst is in me, which yearns after your thirst!

It is night: ah, that I must be light! And thirst for the things of night! And solitude!

It is night: now my longing breaks from me like a well-spring – I long for speech.

It is night: now do all leaping fountains speak louder. And my soul too is a leaping fountain.

It is night: only now do all songs of lovers awaken. And my soul too is the song of a lover.

Thus sang Zarathustra.

The Dance Song

ONE evening Zarathustra was walking through the forest with his disciples; and as he was looking for a well, behold, he came upon a green meadow quietly surrounded by trees and bushes: and in the meadow girls were dancing together. As soon as the girls recognized Zarathustra they ceased their dance; Zarathustra, however, approached them with a friendly air and spoke these words:

Do not cease your dance, sweet girls! No spoil-sport has come to you with an evil eye, no enemy of girls.

I am God's advocate with the Devil; he, however, is the Spirit of Gravity. How could I be enemy to divine dancing, you nimble creatures? or to girls' feet with fair ankles?

To be sure, I am a forest and a night of dark trees: but he who is not afraid of my darkness will find rosebowers too under my cypresses.

And he will surely find too the little god whom girls love best: he lies beside the fountain, still, with his eyes closed.

Truly, he has fallen asleep in broad daylight, the idler! Has he been chasing butterflies too much?

Do not be angry with me, fair dancers, if I chastise the little god a little! Perhaps he will cry out and weep, but he is laughable even in weeping!

And with tears in his eyes, he shall ask you for a dance; and I myself will sing a song for his dance.

A dance-song and a mocking-song on the Spirit of Gravity, my supreme, most powerful devil, who they say is 'the lord of the earth'.

And this is the song Zarathustra sang as cupid and the girls danced together:

Lately I looked into your eye, O Life! And I seemed to sink into the unfathomable.

But you pulled me out with a golden rod; you laughed mockingly when I called you unfathomable.

'All fish talk like that,' you said; 'what *they* cannot fathom is unfathomable.

'But I am merely changeable and untamed and in everything a woman, and no virtuous one.

'Although you men call me "profound" or "faithful",
"eternal", "mysterious".

'But you men always endow us with your own virtues – ah,
you virtuous men!'

Thus she laughed, the incredible woman; but I never
believe her and her laughter when she speaks evil of herself.

And when I spoke secretly with my wild Wisdom, she said
to me angrily: 'You will, you desire, you love, that is the only
reason you *praise* Life!'

Then I almost answered crossly and told the truth to my
angry Wisdom; and one cannot answer more crossly than
when one 'tells the truth' to one's Wisdom.

This then is the state of affairs between us three. From the
heart of me I love only Life – and in truth, I love her most of
all when I hate her!

But that I am fond of Wisdom, and often too fond, is
because she very much reminds me of Life!

She has her eyes, her laughter, and even her little golden
fishing-rod: how can I help it that they both look so alike?

And when Life once asked me: 'Who is she then, this
Wisdom?' – then I said eagerly: 'Ah yes! Wisdom!

'One thirsts for her and is not satisfied, one looks at her
through veils, one snatches at her through nets.

'Is she fair? I know not! But the cleverest old fish are still
lured by her.

'She is changeable and defiant; I have often seen her bite
her lip and comb her hair against the grain.

'Perhaps she is wicked and false, and in everything a wench;
but when she speaks ill of herself, then precisely is she most
seductive.'

When I said this to Life, she laughed maliciously and closed
her eyes. 'But whom are you speaking of?' she asked, 'of me,
surely?

'And if you are right – should you tell me *that* to my face?
But now speak of your Wisdom, too!'

Ah, and then you opened your eyes again, O beloved Life!
And again I seemed to sink into the unfathomable.

Thus sang Zarathustra. But when the dance had ended and the girls had gone away, he grew sad.

The sun has long since set (he said at last); the meadow is damp, coolness is coming from the forests.

Something strange and unknown is about me, looking thoughtfully at me. What! are you still living, Zarathustra?

Why? Wherefore? Whereby? Whither? Where? How? Is it not folly to go on living?

Ah, my friends, it is the evening that questions thus within me. Forgive me my sadness!

Evening has come: forgive me that it has become evening!

Thus spoke Zarathustra.

The Funeral Song

'YONDER is the grave-island, the silent island; yonder too are the graves of my youth. I will bear thither an evergreen wreath of life.'

Resolving thus in my heart I fared over the sea.

O, you sights and visions of my youth! O, all you glances of love, you divine momentary glances![17] How soon you perished! Today I think of you as my dead ones.

A sweet odour comes to me from you, my dearest dead ones, a heart-easing odour that banishes tears. Truly, it moves and eases the solitary seafarer's heart.

Still am I the richest and most-to-be-envied man – I, the most solitary! For I *had* you and you have me still: tell me, to whom have such rosy apples fallen from the tree as have fallen to me?

Still am I heir and heritage of your love, blooming to your memory with many-coloured wild-growing virtues, O my most beloved ones!

Ah, we were made for one another, you gentle, strange marvels; and you came to me and my longing not as timid birds – no, you came trusting to me, who also trusted.

Yes, made for faithfulness, like me, and for tender eternities:

must I now name you by your unfaithfulness, you divine glances and moments: I have as yet learned no other name.

Truly, you perished too soon, you fugitives. Yet you did not fly from me, nor did I fly from you: we are innocent towards one another in our unfaithfulness.

They put you to death, you song-birds of my hopes, in order to kill *me*! Yes, the arrows of malice were always directed at you, my beloved ones – in order to strike at my heart!

And they struck! You were always my heart's dearest, my possession and my being-possessed: *therefore* you had to die young and all-too-early!

They shot the arrow at the most vulnerable thing I possessed: and that was you, whose skin is like down and even more like the smile that dies at a glance!

But I will say this to my enemies: What is any manslaughter compared with what you did to me!

You did a worse thing to me than any manslaughter; you took from me the irretrievable – thus I speak to you, my enemies!

You murdered my youth's visions and dearest marvels! You took from me my playfellows, those blessed spirits! To their memory do I lay this wreath and this curse.

This curse upon you, my enemies! You have cut short my eternity, as a note is cut short in the cold night! It came to me hardly as the twinkling of divine eyes – as a moment!

Thus in a happy hour my purity once spoke: 'All creatures shall be divine to me.'

Then you surprised me with foul phantoms; alas, whither has that happy hour fled now?

'All days shall be holy to me' – thus the wisdom of my youth once spoke: truly, the speech of a joyful wisdom!

But then you, my enemies, stole my nights from me and sold them to sleepless torment: alas, whither has that joyful wisdom fled now?

Once I longed for happy bird-auspices: then you led an owl-monster across my path, an adverse sign. Alas, whither did my tender longings flee then?

I once vowed to renounce all disgust; then you transformed my kindred and neighbours into abscesses. Alas, whither did my noblest vow flee then?

Once, as a blind man, I walked on happy paths; then you threw filth in the blind man's path: and now the old footpath disgusts him.

And when I achieved my most difficult task and celebrated the victory of my overcomings: then you made those whom I loved cry out that I hurt them most.

Truly, all that was your doing: you embittered my finest honey and the industry of my finest bees.

You have always sent the most insolent beggars to my liberality; you have always crowded the incurably shameless around my pity. Thus you have wounded my virtues' faith.

And when I brought my holiest thing as a sacrifice, straightway your 'piety' placed its fatter gifts beside it: so that my holiest thing choked in the smoke of your fat.

And once I wanted to dance as I had never yet danced: I wanted to dance beyond all heavens. Then you lured away my favourite singer.

And then he struck up a gruesome, gloomy melody: alas, he trumpeted into my ears like a mournful horn!

Murderous singer, instrument of malice, most innocent man! I stood prepared for the finest dance: then you murdered my ecstasy with your tones!

I know how to speak the parable of the highest things only in the dance – and now my greatest parable has remained in my limbs unspoken!

My highest hope has remained unspoken and unachieved! And all the visions and consolations of my youth are dead!

How did I endure it? How did I recover from such wounds, how did I overcome them? How did my soul arise again from these graves?

Yes, something invulnerable, unburiable is within me, something that rends rocks: it is called *my Will*. Silently it steps and unchanging through the years.

It shall go its course upon my feet, my old Will; hard of heart and invulnerable is its temper.

I am invulnerable only in my heels. You live there and are always the same, most patient one! You will always break out of all graves!

In you too still live on all the unachieved things of my youth; and you sit as life and youth, hopefully, here upon yellow grave-ruins.

Yes, you are still my destroyer of all graves: Hail, my Will! And only where there are graves are there resurrections.

Thus sang Zarathustra.

Of Self-Overcoming

WHAT urges you on and arouses your ardour, you wisest of men, do you call it 'will to truth'?

Will to the conceivability of all being: that is what *I* call your will!

You first want to *make* all being conceivable: for, with a healthy mistrust, you doubt whether it is in fact conceivable.

But it must bend and accommodate itself to you! Thus will your will have it. It must become smooth and subject to the mind as the mind's mirror and reflection.

That is your entire will, you wisest men; it is a will to power; and that is so even when you talk of good and evil and of the assessment of values.

You want to create the world before which you can kneel: this is your ultimate hope and intoxication.

The ignorant, to be sure, the people – they are like a river down which a boat swims: and in the boat, solemn and disguised, sit the assessments of value.

You put your will and your values upon the river of becoming; what the people believe to be good and evil betrays to me an ancient will to power.

It was you, wisest men, who put such passengers in this boat and gave them splendour and proud names – you and your ruling will!

Now the river bears your boat along: it has to bear it. It is of small account if the breaking wave foams and angrily opposes its keel!

It is not the river that is your danger and the end of your good and evil, you wisest men, it is that will itself, the will to power, the unexhausted, procreating life-will.

But that you may understand my teaching about good and evil, I shall relate to you my teaching about life and about the nature of all living creatures.

I have followed the living creature, I have followed the greatest and the smallest paths, that I might understand its nature.

I caught its glance in a hundredfold mirror when its mouth was closed, that its eye might speak to me. And its eye did speak to me.

But wherever I found living creatures, there too I heard the language of obedience. All living creatures are obeying creatures.

And this is the second thing: he who cannot obey himself will be commanded. That is the nature of living creatures.

But this is the third thing I heard: that commanding is more difficult than obeying. And not only because the commander bears the burden of all who obey, and that this burden can easily crush him.

In all commanding there appeared to me to be an experiment and a risk: and the living creature always risks himself when he commands.

Yes, even when he commands himself: then also must he make amends for his commanding. He must become judge and avenger and victim of his own law.

How has this come about? thus I asked myself. What persuades the living creature to obey and to command and to practise obedience even in commanding?

Listen now to my teaching, you wisest men! Test in earnest whether I have crept into the heart of life itself and down to the roots of its heart!

Where I found a living creature, there I found will to power; and even in the will of the servant I found the will to be master.

The will of the weaker persuades it to serve the stronger; its will wants to be master over those weaker still: this delight alone it is unwilling to forgo.

And as the lesser surrenders to the greater, that it may have delight and power over the least of all, so the greatest, too, surrenders and for the sake of power stakes – life.

The devotion of the greatest is to encounter risk and danger and play dice for death.

And where sacrifice and service and loving glances are, there too is will to be master. There the weaker steals by secret paths into the castle and even into the heart of the more powerful – and steals the power.

And life itself told me this secret: 'Behold,' it said, 'I am that *which must overcome itself again and again*.

'To be sure, you call it will to procreate or impulse towards a goal, towards the higher, more distant, more manifold: but all this is one and one secret.

'I would rather perish than renounce this one thing; and truly, where there is perishing and the falling of leaves, behold, there life sacrifices itself – for the sake of power!

'That I have to be struggle and becoming and goal and conflict of goals: ah, he who divines my will surely divines, too, along what *crooked* paths it has to go!

'Whatever I create and however much I love it – soon I have to oppose it and my love: thus will my will have it.

'And you too, enlightened man, are only a path and footstep of my will: truly, my will to power walks with the feet of your will to truth!

'He who shot the doctrine of "will to existence" at truth certainly did not hit the truth: this will – does not exist!

'For what does not exist cannot will; but that which is in existence, how could it still want to come into existence?

'Only where life is, there is also will: not will to life, but – so I teach you – will to power!

'The living creature values many things higher than life itself; yet out of this evaluation itself speaks – the will to power!'

Thus life once taught me: and with this teaching do I solve the riddle of your hearts, you wisest men.

Truly, I say to you: Unchanging good and evil does not exist! From out of themselves they must overcome themselves again and again.

You exert power with your values and doctrines of good and evil, you assessors of values; and this is your hidden love and the glittering, trembling, and overflowing of your souls.

But a mightier power and a new overcoming grow from out your values: egg and egg-shell break against them.

And he who has to be a creator in good and evil, truly, has first to be a destroyer and break values.

Thus the greatest evil belongs with the greatest good: this, however, is the creative good.

Let us *speak* of this, you wisest men, even if it is a bad thing. To be silent is worse; all suppressed truths become poisonous.

And let everything that can break upon our truths – break! There is many a house still to build!

Thus spoke Zarathustra.

Of the Sublime Men

STILL is the bottom of my sea: who could guess that it hides sportive monsters!

Imperturbable is my depth: but it glitters with swimming riddles and laughter.

Today I saw a sublime man, a solemn man, a penitent of the spirit: oh, how my soul laughed at his ugliness!

With upraised breast and in the attitude of a man drawing in breath: thus he stood there, the sublime man, and silent.

Hung with ugly truths, the booty of his hunt, and rich in torn clothes; many thorns, too, hung on him – but I saw no rose.

As yet he has not learned of laughter and beauty. This huntsman returned gloomily from the forest of knowledge.

He returned home from the fight with wild beasts: but a

wild beast still gazes out of his seriousness – a beast that has not been overcome!

He stands there like a tiger about to spring; but I do not like these tense souls, my taste is hostile towards all these withdrawn men.

And do you tell me, friends, that there is no dispute over taste and tasting? But all life is dispute over taste and tasting!

Taste: that is at the same time weight and scales and weigher; and woe to all living creatures that want to live without dispute over weight and scales and weigher!

If he grew weary of his sublimity, this sublime man, only then would his beauty rise up – and only then will I taste him and find him tasty.

And only if he turns away from himself will he jump over his own shadow – and jump, in truth, into *his own* sunlight.

He has sat all too long in the shadows, the cheeks of the penitent of the spirit have grown pale; he has almost starved on his expectations.

There is still contempt in his eye, and disgust lurks around his mouth. He rests now, to be sure, but he has never yet lain down in the sunlight.

He should behave like the ox; and his happiness should smell of the earth and not of contempt for the earth.

I should like to see him as a white ox, snorting and bellowing as he goes before the plough: and his bellowing, too, should laud all earthly things!

His countenance is still dark; his hand's shadow plays upon it. The sense of his eyes, too, is overshadowed.

His deed itself is still the shadow upon him: the hand darkens the doer.[18] He has still not overcome his deed.

To be sure, I love in him the neck of the ox: but now I want to see the eye of the angel, too.

He must unlearn his heroic will, too: he should be an exalted man and not only a sublime one – the ether itself should raise him up, the will-less one!

He has tamed monsters, he has solved riddles: but he should also redeem his monsters and riddles, he should transform them into heavenly children.

His knowledge has not yet learned to smile and to be without jealousy; his gushing passion has not yet grown calm in beauty.

Truly, his longing should be silenced and immersed not in satiety but in beauty! The generosity of the magnanimous man should include gracefulness.

With his arm laid across his head: that is how the hero should rest, that is also how he should overcome his rest.

But it is precisely to the hero that *beauty* is the most difficult of all things. Beauty is unattainable to all violent wills.

A little more, a little less: precisely that is much here, here that is the most of all.

To stand with relaxed muscles and unharnessed wills: that is the most difficult thing for all of you, you sublime men!

When power grows gracious and descends into the visible: I call such descending beauty.

And I desire beauty from no one as much as I desire it from you, you man of power: may your goodness be your ultimate self-overpowering.

I believe you capable of any evil: therefore I desire of you the good.

In truth, I have often laughed at the weaklings who think themselves good because their claws are blunt!

You should aspire to the virtue of the pillar: the higher it rises, the fairer and more graceful it grows, but inwardly harder and able to bear more weight.

Yes, you sublime man, you too shall one day be fair and hold the mirror before your own beauty.

Then your soul will shudder with divine desires; and there will be worship even in your vanity!

This indeed is the secret of the soul: only when the hero has deserted the soul does there approach it in dreams – the superhero.

Thus spoke Zarathustra.

Of the Land of Culture

I FLEW too far into the future: a horror assailed me.

And when I looked around, behold! time was my only contemporary.

Then I flew back, homeward – and faster and faster I flew: and so I came to you, you men of the present, and to the land of culture.

The first time I brought with me an eye to see you and healthy desires: truly, I came to you with longing in my heart.

But how did I fare? Although I was so afraid – I had to laugh! My eye had never seen anything so motley-spotted!

I laughed and laughed, while my foot still trembled and my heart as well: 'Here must be the home of all the paint-pots!' I said.

Painted with fifty blotches on face and limbs: thus you sat there to my astonishment, you men of the present!

And with fifty mirrors around you, flattering and repeating your opalescence!

Truly, you could wear no better masks than your own faces, you men of the present! Who could – *recognize* you!

Written over with the signs of the past and these signs over-daubed with new signs: thus you have hidden yourselves well from all interpreters of signs!

And if one tests your virility, one finds only sterility! You seem to be baked from colours and scraps of paper glued together.

All ages and all peoples gaze motley out of your veils; all customs and all beliefs speak motley out of your gestures.

He who tore away from you your veils and wraps and paint and gestures would have just enough left over to frighten the birds.

Truly, I myself am the frightened bird who once saw you naked and without paint; and I flew away when the skeleton made advances to me.

I would rather be a day-labourer in the underworld and

among the shades of the bygone! – Even the inhabitants of the underworld are fatter and fuller than you!

This, yes this is bitterness to my stomach, that I can endure you neither naked nor clothed, you men of the present!

And the unfamiliar things of the future, and whatever frightened stray birds, are truly more familiar and more genial than your 'reality'.

For thus you speak: 'We are complete realists, and without belief or superstition': thus you thump your chests – alas, even without having chests!

But how should you be *able* to believe, you motley-spotted men! – you who are paintings of all that has ever been believed!

You are walking refutations of belief itself and the fracture of all thought. *Unworthy of belief*: that is what *I* call you, you realists!

All ages babble in confusion in your spirits; and the dreaming and babbling of all ages was more real than is your waking!

You are unfruitful: *therefore* you lack belief. But he who had to create always had his prophetic dreams and star-auguries – and he believed in belief!

You are half-open doors at which grave-diggers wait. And this is *your* reality: 'Everything is worthy of perishing.'

Ah, how you stand there, you unfruitful men, how lean-ribbed! And, indeed, many of you have noticed that.

And they have said: 'Perhaps a god has secretly taken something from me there as I slept? Truly, sufficient to form a little woman for himself!

'Amazing is the poverty of my ribs!' That is how many a present-day man has spoken.

Yes, you are laughable to me, you men of the present! And especially when you are amazed at yourselves!

And woe to me if I could not laugh at your amazement and had to drink down all that is repulsive in your bowels.

However, I will make light of you, since I have *heavy things* to carry; and what do I care if beetles and dragonflies sit themselves on my bundle!

Truly, it shall not become heavier on that account! And the

great weariness shall not come to me from you, you men of the present.

Alas, whither shall I climb now with my longing? I look out from every mountain for fatherlands and motherlands.

But nowhere have I found a home; I am unsettled in every city and I depart from every gate.

The men of the present, to whom my heart once drove me, are strange to me and a mockery; and I have been driven from fatherlands and motherlands.

So now I love only my *children's land*, the undiscovered land in the furthest sea: I bid my sails seek it and seek it.

I will make amends to my children for being the child of my fathers: and to all the future – for *this* present!

Thus spoke Zarathustra.

Of Immaculate Perception

WHEN the moon rose yesterday I thought it was about to give birth to a sun, it lay on the horizon so broad and pregnant.

But it was a liar with its pregnancy; and I will sooner believe in the man in the moon than in the woman.

To be sure, he is not much of a man, either, this timid night-reveller. Truly, he travels over the roofs with a bad conscience.

For he is lustful and jealous, the monk in the moon, lustful for the earth and for all the joys of lovers.

No, I do not like him, this tomcat on the roofs! All who slink around half-closed windows are repugnant to me!

Piously and silently he walks along on star-carpets: but I do not like soft-stepping feet on which not even a spur jingles.

Every honest man's step speaks out: but the cat steals along over the ground. Behold, the moon comes along catlike and without honesty.

This parable I speak to you sentimental hypocrites, to you of 'pure knowledge'! *I* call you – lustful!

You too love the earth and the earthly: I have divined you

well! – but shame and bad conscience is in your love – you are like the moon!

Your spirit has been persuaded to contempt of the earthly, but your entrails have not: these, however, are the strongest part of you!

And now your spirit is ashamed that it must do the will of your entrails and follows by-ways and lying-ways to avoid its own shame.

'For me, the highest thing would be to gaze at life without desire and not, as a dog does, with tongue hanging out' – thus speaks your mendacious spirit to itself:

'To be happy in gazing, with benumbed will, without the grasping and greed of egotism – cold and ashen in body but with intoxicated moon-eyes!

'For me, the dearest thing would be to love the earth as the moon loves it, and to touch its beauty with the eyes alone' – thus the seduced one seduces himself.

'And let this be called by me *immaculate* perception of all things: that I desire nothing of things, except that I may lie down before them like a mirror with a hundred eyes.'

Oh, you sentimental hypocrites, you lustful men! You lack innocence in desire: and therefore you now slander desiring!

Truly, you do not love the earth as creators, begetters, men joyful at entering upon a new existence!

Where is innocence? Where there is will to begetting. And for me, he who wants to create beyond himself has the purest will.

Where is beauty? Where I *have to will* with all my will; where I want to love and perish, that an image may not remain merely an image.

Loving and perishing: these have gone together from eternity. Will to love: that means to be willing to die, too. Thus I speak to you cowards!

But now your emasculated leering wants to be called 'contemplation'! And that which lets cowardly eyes touch it shall be christened 'beautiful'! Oh, you befoulers of noble names!

But it shall be your curse, you immaculate men, you of pure

knowledge, that you will never bring forth, even if you lie broad and pregnant on the horizon!

Truly, you fill your mouths with noble words: and are we supposed to believe that your hearts are overflowing, you habitual liars?

But *my* words are poor, despised, halting words: I am glad to take what falls from the table at your feast.

Yet with them I can still – tell the truth to hypocrites! Yes, my fish-bones, shells, and prickly leaves shall – tickle hypocrites' noses!

There is always bad air around you and around your feasts: for your lustful thoughts, your lies and secrets are in the air!

Only dare to believe in yourselves – in yourselves and in your entrails! He who does not believe in himself always lies.

You have put on the mask of a god, you 'pure': your dreadful coiling snake has crawled into the mask of a god.

Truly, you are deceivers, you 'contemplative'! Even Zarathustra was once the fool of your divine veneer; he did not guess at the serpent-coil with which it was filled.

Once I thought I saw a god's soul at play in your play, you of pure knowledge! Once I thought there was no better art than your arts!

Distance concealed from me the serpent-filth, and the evil odour, and that a lizard's cunning was prowling lustfully around.

But I *approached* you: then day dawned for me – and now it dawns for you – the moon's love affair had come to an end!

Just look! There it stands, pale and detected – before the dawn!

For already it is coming, the glowing sun – *its* love of the earth is coming! All sun-love is innocence and creative desire!

Just look how it comes impatiently over the sea! Do you not feel the thirst and the hot breath of its love?

It wants to suck at the sea and drink the sea's depths up to its height: now the sea's desire rises with a thousand breasts.

It *wants* to be kissed and sucked by the sun's thirst; it *wants* to become air and height and light's footpath and light itself!

Truly, like the sun do I love life and all deep seas.

And this *I* call knowledge: all that is deep shall rise up – to my height!

Thus spoke Zarathustra.

Of Scholars

As I lay asleep, a sheep ate at the ivy-wreath upon my head – ate and said: 'Zarathustra is no longer a scholar.'

It spoke and went away stiffly and proud. A child told me of it.

I like to lie here where children play, beside the broken wall, among thistles and red poppies.

To children I am still a scholar, and to thistles and red poppies, too. They are innocent, even in their wickedness.

But to the sheep I am no longer a scholar: thus my fate will have it – blessed be my fate!

For this is the truth: I have left the house of scholars and slammed the door behind me.

Too long did my soul sit hungry at their table; I have not been schooled, as they have, to crack knowledge as one cracks nuts.

I love freedom and the air over fresh soil; I would sleep on ox-skins rather than on their dignities and respectabilities.

I am too hot and scorched by my own thought: it is often about to take my breath away. Then I have to get into the open air and away from all dusty rooms.

But they sit cool in the cool shade: they want to be mere spectators in everything and they take care not to sit where the sun burns upon the steps.

Like those who stand in the street and stare at the people passing by, so they too wait and stare at thoughts that others have thought.

If one takes hold of them, they involuntarily raise a dust like sacks of flour; but who could guess that their dust derived from corn and from the golden joy of summer fields?

When they give themselves out as wise, their little sayings and truths make me shiver: their wisdom often smells as if it came from the swamp: and indeed, I have heard the frog croak in it!

They are clever, they have cunning fingers: what is *my* simplicity compared with their diversity? Their fingers understand all threading and knitting and weaving: thus they weave the stockings of the spirit!

They are excellent clocks: only be careful to wind them up properly! Then they tell the hour without error and make a modest noise in doing so.

They work like mills and rammers: just throw seed-corn into them! – they know how to grind corn small and make white dust of it.

They keep a sharp eye upon one another and do not trust one another as well as they might. Inventive in small slynesses, they lie in wait for those whose wills go upon lame feet – they lie in wait like spiders.

I have seen how carefully they prepare their poisons; they always put on protective gloves.

They also know how to play with loaded dice; and I found them playing so zealously that they were sweating.

We are strangers to one another, and their virtues are even more opposed to my taste than are their falsehoods and loaded dice.

And when I lived among them I lived above them. They grew angry with me for that.

They did not want to know that someone was walking over their heads; and so they put wood and dirt and rubbish between their heads and me.

Thus they muffled the sound of my steps: and from then on the most scholarly heard me the worst.

They put all the faults and weaknesses of mankind between themselves and me – they call this a 'false flooring' in their houses.

But I walk *above* their heads with my thoughts in spite of that; and even if I should walk upon my own faults, I should still be above them and their heads.

For men are *not* equal: thus speaks justice. And what I desire *they* may not desire!

Thus spoke Zarathustra.

Of Poets

'SINCE I have known the body better,' said Zarathustra to one of his disciples, 'the spirit has been only figuratively spirit to me; and all that is "intransitory" – that too has been only an "image"'.[19]

'I heard you say that once before,' answered the disciple; 'and then you added: "But the poets lie too much." Why did you say that the poets lie too much?'

'Why?' said Zarathustra. 'You ask why? I am not one of those who may be questioned about their Why.

'Do my experiences date from yesterday? It is a long time since I experienced the reasons for my opinions.

'Should I not have to be a barrel of memory, if I wanted to carry my reasons, too, about with me?

'It is already too much for me to retain even my opinions; and many a bird has flown away.

'And now and then I find in my dove-cote an immigrant creature which is strange to me and which trembles when I lay my hand upon it.

'Yet what did Zarathustra once say to you? That the poets lie too much? – But Zarathustra too is a poet.

'Do you now believe that he spoke the truth? Why do you believe it?'

The disciple answered: 'I believe in Zarathustra.' But Zarathustra shook his head and smiled.

Belief does not make me blessed (he said), least of all belief in myself.

But granted that someone has said in all seriousness that the poets lie too much: he is right – *we* do lie too much.

We know too little and are bad learners: so we have to lie.

And which of us poets has not adulterated his wine? Many a poisonous hotch-potch has been produced in our cellars, many an indescribable thing has been done there.

And because we know little, the poor in spirit delight our hearts, especially when they are young women.

And we desire even those things the old women tell one another in the evening. We call that the eternal-womanly in us.

And we believe in the people and its 'wisdom' as if there were a special secret entrance to knowledge which is *blocked* to him who has learned anything.

But all poets believe this: that he who, lying in the grass or in lonely bowers, pricks up his ears, catches a little of the things that are between heaven and earth.

And if they experience tender emotions, the poets always think that nature herself is in love with them:

And that she creeps up to their ears, to speak secrets and amorous flattering words into them: of this they boast and pride themselves before all mortals!

Alas, there are so many things between heaven and earth of which only the poets have let themselves dream!

And especially *above* heaven: for all gods are poets' images, poets' surreptitiousness!

Truly, it draws us ever upward – that is, to cloudland: we set our motley puppets on the clouds and then call them gods and supermen.

And are they not light enough for these insubstantial seats? – all these gods and supermen.

Alas, how weary I am of all the unattainable that is supposed to be reality. Alas, how weary I am of the poets!

When Zarathustra had spoken thus, his disciple was angry with him, but kept silent. And Zarathustra, too, kept silent; and his eye had turned within him as if it were gazing into the far distance. At length he sighed and drew a breath.

I am of today and of the has-been (he said then); but there is something in me that is of tomorrow and of the day-after-tomorrow and of the shall-be.

I have grown weary of the poets, the old and the new: they all seem to me superficial and shallow seas.

They have not thought deeply enough: therefore their feeling – has not plumbed the depths.

A little voluptuousness and a little tedium: that is all their best ideas have ever amounted to.

All their harp-jangling is to me so much coughing and puffing of phantoms; what have they ever known of the ardour of tones!

They are not clean enough for me, either: they all disturb their waters so that they may seem deep.

And in that way they would like to show themselves reconcilers: but to me they remain mediators and meddlers, and mediocre and unclean men!

Ah, indeed I cast my net into their sea and hoped to catch fine fish; but I always drew out an old god's head.

Thus the sea gave a stone to the hungry man. And they themselves may well originate from the sea.

To be sure, one finds pearls in them: then they themselves are all the more like hard shell-fish. And instead of the soul I often found in them salty slime.

They learned vanity, too, from the sea: is the sea not the peacock of peacocks?

It unfurls its tail even before the ugliest of buffaloes, it never wearies of its lace-fan of silver and satin.

The buffalo looks on insolently, his soul like the sand, yet more like the thicket, but most like the swamp.

What are beauty and sea and peacock-ornaments to him? I speak this parable to the poets.

Truly, their spirit itself is the peacock of peacocks and a sea of vanity!

The poet's spirit wants spectators, even if they are only buffaloes!

But I have grown weary of this spirit: and I see the day coming when it will grow weary of itself.

Already I have seen the poets transformed; I have seen them direct their glance upon themselves.

I have seen penitents of the spirit appearing: they grew out of the poets.

Thus spoke Zarathustra.

Of Great Events

THERE is an island in the sea – not far from the Blissful Islands of Zarathustra – upon which a volcano continually smokes; the people, and especially the old women among the people, say that it is placed like a block of stone before the gate of the underworld, but that the narrow downward path which leads to this gate of the underworld passes through the volcano itself.

Now at the time Zarathustra was living on the Blissful Islands it happened that a ship dropped anchor at the island upon which the smoking mountain stood; and its crew landed in order to shoot rabbits. Towards the hour of noon, however, when the captain and his men were reassembled, they suddenly saw a man coming towards them through the air, and a voice said clearly: 'It is time! It is high time!' But as the figure was closest to them – it flew quickly past, however, like a shadow, in the direction of the volcano – they recognized, with the greatest consternation, that it was Zarathustra; for all of them had seen him before, except the captain himself, and they loved him as the people love: that is, with love and awe in equal parts.

'Just look!' said the old steersman, 'there is Zarathustra going to Hell!'

At the same time as these sailors landed on the volcano island, the rumour went around that Zarathustra had disappeared; and when his friends were questioned, they said that he had gone aboard a ship by night without saying where he intended to sail.

Thus there arose a disquiet; after three days, however, there was added to this disquiet the story of the sailors – and then all the people said that the Devil had carried Zarathustra off. Of course, his disciples laughed at this talk; and one of them even said: 'I would rather believe that Zarathustra had carried off the Devil.' But at the bottom of their souls they were all full of apprehension and longing: so great was their joy when, on the fifth day, Zarathustra appeared among them.

And this is the tale of Zarathustra's conversation with the fire-dog:

The earth (he said) has a skin; and this skin has diseases. One of these diseases, for example, is called 'Man'.

And another of these diseases is called 'the fire-dog': men have told many lies and been told many lies about *him*.

To fathom this secret I fared across the sea: and I have seen truth naked, truly! barefoot to the neck.

Now I know all about the fire-dog; and also about all the revolutionary and subversive devils which not only old women fear.

'Up with you, fire-dog, up from your depth!' I cried, 'and confess how deep that depth is! Where does it come from, that which you snort up?

'You drink deeply from the sea: your bitter eloquence betrays that! Truly, for a dog of the depths you take your food too much from the surface!

'At the best, I hold you to be the earth's ventriloquist: and when I have heard subversive and revolutionary devils speak, I have always found them like you: bitter, lying, and superficial.

'You understand how to bellow and how to darken the air with ashes! You are the greatest braggart and have sufficiently learned the art of making mud boil.

'Where you are there must always be mud around and much that is spongy, hollow, and compressed: it wants to be freed.

'"Freedom", you all most like to bellow: but I have unlearned belief in "great events" whenever there is much bellowing and smoke about them.

'And believe me, friend Infernal-racket! The greatest events – they are not our noisiest but our stillest hours.

'The world revolves, not around the inventors of new

noises, but around the inventors of new values; it revolves *inaudibly*.

'And just confess! Little was ever found to have happened when your noise and smoke dispersed. What did it matter that a town had been mummified and a statue lay in the mud!

'And I say this to the overthrowers of statues: To throw salt into the sea and statues into the mud are perhaps the greatest of follies.

'The statue lay in the mud of your contempt: but this precisely is its law, that its life and living beauty grow again out of contempt!

'And now it arises again, with diviner features and sorrow-fully-seductive; and in truth! it will even thank you for over-throwing it, you overthrowers!

'I tender, however, this advice to kings and churches and to all that is weak with age and virtue – only let yourselves be overthrown! That you may return to life, and that virtue – may return to you!'

Thus I spoke before the fire-dog: then he interrupted me sullenly and asked: 'The church? What is that then?'

'The church?' I answered. 'The church is kind of state, and indeed the most mendacious kind. But keep quiet, you hypocrite dog! You surely know your own kind best!

'Like you, the state is a hypocrite dog; like you, it likes to speak with smoke and bellowing – to make believe, like you, that it speaks out of the belly of things.

'For the state wants to be absolutely the most important beast on earth; and it is believed to be so, too!'

When I said that, the fire-dog acted as if he were mad with envy. 'What?' he cried, 'the most important beast on earth? And it is believed to be so, too?' And so much steam and hideous shrieking came from his throat I thought he would choke with vexation and envy.

At length he grew quieter and his panting ceased; as soon as he was quiet, however, I said laughing;

'You are vexed, fire-dog: therefore I am right about you!

'And that I may press my point, let me speak of another fire-dog, which really speaks from the heart of the earth.

'His breath exhales gold and golden rain: so his heart will have it. What are ashes and smoke and hot mud to him now!

'Laughter flutters from him like a motley cloud; he is ill-disposed towards your gurgling and spitting and griping of the bowels!

'Gold and laughter, however, he takes from the heart of the earth: for, that you may know it – *the heart of the earth is of gold.*'

When the fire-dog heard this he could no longer bear to listen to me. Abashed, he drew in his tail, said 'Bow-wow' in a small voice and crawled down into his cave.

Thus narrated Zarathustra. But his disciples hardly listened to him, so great was their desire to tell him about the sailors, the rabbits, and the flying man.

'What am I to think of it?' said Zarathustra. 'Am I then a ghost?

'But it will have been my shadow. Surely you have heard something of the Wanderer and his Shadow?[20]

'This, however, is certain: I must keep it under stricter control – otherwise it will ruin my reputation.'

And once again Zarathustra shook his head and wondered. 'What am I to think of it?' he said again.

'Why, then, did the phantom cry: "It is time! It is high time!"?

'*For what,* then, is it – high time?'

Thus spoke Zarathustra.

The Prophet

–AND I saw a great sadness come over mankind. The best grew weary of their works.

A teaching went forth, a belief ran beside it: Everything is empty, everything is one, everything is past!

And from every hill it resounded: Everything is empty, everything is one, everything is past!

We have harvested, it is true: but why did all our fruits turn rotten and brown? What fell from the wicked moon last night?

All our work has been in vain, our wine has become poison, an evil eye has scorched our fields and our hearts.

We have all become dry; and if fire fell upon us we should scatter like ashes – yes, we have made weary fire itself.

All our wells have dried up, even the sea has receded. The earth wants to break open, but the depths will not devour us!

Alas, where is there still a sea in which one could drown: thus our lament resounds – across shallow swamps.

Truly, we have grown too weary even to die; now we are still awake and we live on – in sepulchres!'

Thus did Zarathustra hear a prophet speak;[21] and his prophecy went to Zarathustra's heart and transformed him. He went about sad and weary; and he became like those of whom the prophet had spoken.

'Truly,' he said to his disciples, 'this long twilight is very nearly upon us. Alas, how shall I preserve my light through it?

'May it not be smothered in this sadness! It is meant to be a light to more distant worlds and to the most distant nights!'

Zarathustra went about grieving thus in his heart; and for three days he took no food or drink, had no rest and forgot speech. At length it happened that he fell into a deep sleep. And his disciples sat around him in the long watches of the night and waited anxiously to see if he would awaken and speak again and be cured of his affliction.

And this is the discourse that Zarathustra spoke when he awoke; his voice, however, came to his disciples as if from a great distance:

Listen to the dream which I dreamed, friends, and help me to read its meaning!

It is still a riddle to me, this dream; its meaning is hidden within it and imprisoned and does not yet fly above it with unconfined wings.

I dreamed I had renounced all life. I had become a night-watchman and grave-watchman yonder upon the lonely hill-fortress of death.

Up there I guarded death's coffins: the musty vaults stood

full of these symbols of death's victory. Life overcome regarded me from glass coffins.

I breathed the odour of dust-covered eternities: my soul lay sultry and dust-covered. And who could have ventilated his soul there?

Brightness of midnight was all around me, solitude crouched beside it; and, as a third, the rasping silence of death, the worst of my companions.

I carried keys, the rustiest of all keys; and I could open with them the most creaking of all doors.

When the wings of this door were opened, the sound ran through the long corridors like an evil croaking; this bird cried out ill-temperedly, it did not want to be awakened.

But it was even more fearful and heart-tightening when it again became silent and still all around and I sat alone in that malignant silence.

So did time pass with me and creep past, if time still existed: what did I know of it! But at last occurred that which awakened me.

Three blows were struck on the door like thunderbolts, the vault resounded and roared three times again: then I went to the door.

Alpa! I cried, who is bearing his ashes to the mountain? Alpa! Alpa! Who is bearing his ashes to the mountain?

And I turned the key and tugged at the door and exerted myself. But it did not open by so much as a finger's breadth:

Then a raging wind tore the door asunder: whistling, shrilling and piercing it threw to me a black coffin:

And in the roaring and whistling and shrilling, the coffin burst asunder and vomited forth a thousand peals of laughter.

And from a thousand masks of children, angels, owls, fools, and child-sized butterflies it laughed and mocked and roared at me.

This terrified me dreadfully: it prostrated me. And I shrieked with horror as I had never shrieked before.

But my own shrieking awoke me – and I came to myself.

Thus Zarathustra narrated his dream and then fell silent:

for he did not yet know the interpretation of his dream. But the disciple whom he loved most arose quickly, grasped Zarathustra's hand, and said:

Your life itself interprets to us this dream, O Zarathustra!

Are you yourself not the wind with a shrill whistling that tears open the doors of the fortress of death?

Are you yourself not the coffin full of motley wickednesses and angel-masks of life?

Truly, Zarathustra comes into all sepulchres like a thousand peals of children's laughter, laughing at these night-watchmen and grave-watchmen, and whoever else rattles gloomy keys.

You will terrify and overthrow them with your laughter; fainting and reawakening will demonstrate your power over them.

And even when the long twilight and the weariness unto death appears, you will not set in our heaven, you advocate of life!

You have shown us new stars and new glories of the night; truly, you have spread out laughter itself above us like a motley canopy.

Henceforth laughter of children will always issue from coffins; henceforth a strong wind will always come, victorious, to all weariness unto death: of that you yourself are our guarantee and prophet!

Truly, you have dreamed *your enemies themselves*: that was your most oppressive dream!

But as you awoke from them and came to yourself, so shall they awake from themselves – and come to you!

Thus spoke the disciple; and all the others then pressed around Zarathustra and grasped his hands and sought to persuade him to leave his bed and his sadness and return to them. But Zarathustra sat upon his bed erect and with an absent expression. Like one who has returned home after being long in a strange land did he look upon his disciples and examine their faces; and as yet he did not recognize them. But when they raised him and set him upon his feet, behold, his eye was suddenly transformed; he understood everything that had happened, stroked his beard, and said in a firm voice:

Well now! This has had its time; but see to it, my disciples, that we have a good meal, and quickly! Thus I mean to do penance for bad dreams!

The prophet, however, shall eat and drink beside me: and truly, I will yet show him a sea in which he can drown!

Thus spoke Zarathustra. Then, however, he gazed long into the face of the disciple who had interpreted the dream, and shook his head.

Of Redemption

As Zarathustra was going across the great bridge one day, the cripples and beggars surrounded him and a hunchback spoke to him thus:

Behold, Zarathustra! The people, too, learn from you and acquire belief in your teaching: but for the people to believe you completely, one thing is still needed – you must first convince even us cripples! Here now you have a fine selection and truly, an opportunity with more than one forelock! You can cure the blind and make the lame walk; and from him who has too much behind him you could well take a little away, too – that, I think, would be the right way to make the cripples believe in Zarathustra!

But Zarathustra replied thus to him who had spoken:

If one takes the hump away from the hunchback, one takes away his spirit – that is what the people teach. And if one gives eyes to the blind man, he sees too many bad things on earth: so that he curses him who cured him. But he who makes the lame man walk does him the greatest harm: for no sooner can he walk than his vices run away with him – that is what the people teach about cripples. And why should Zarathustra not learn from the people, if the people learn from Zarathustra?

But it is the least serious thing to me, since I have been among men, to see that this one lacks an eye and that one an ear and a third lacks a leg, and there are others who have lost their tongue or their nose or their head.

I see and have seen worse things and many of them so monstrous that I should not wish to speak of all of them; but of some of them I should not wish to be silent: and they are, men who lack everything except one thing, of which they have too much – men who are no more than a great eye or a great mouth or a great belly or something else great – I call such men inverse cripples.

And when I emerged from my solitude and crossed over this bridge for the first time, I did not believe my eyes and looked and looked again and said at last: 'That is an ear! An ear as big as a man!' I looked yet more closely: and in fact under the ear there moved something that was pitifully small and meagre and slender. And in truth, the monstrous ear sat upon a little, thin stalk – the stalk, however, was a man! By the use of a magnifying glass one could even discern a little, envious face as well; and one could discern, too, that a turgid little soul was dangling from the stalk. The people told me, however, that the great ear was not merely a man, but a great man, a genius. But I have never believed the people when they talked about great men – and I held to my belief that it was an inverse cripple, who had too little of everything and too much of one thing.

When Zarathustra had spoken thus to the hunchback and to those whose mouthpiece and advocate he was, he turned to his disciples with profound ill-humour and said:

Truly, my friends, I walk among men as among the fragments and limbs of men!

The terrible thing to my eye is to find men shattered in pieces and scattered as if over a battle-field of slaughter.

And when my eye flees from the present to the past, it always discovers the same thing: fragments and limbs and dreadful chances – but no men!

The present and the past upon the earth – alas! my friends – that is *my* most intolerable burden; and I should not know how to live, if I were not a seer of that which must come.

A seer, a willer, a creator, a future itself and a bridge to the future – and alas, also like a cripple upon this bridge: Zarathustra is all this.

And even you have often asked yourselves: Who is Zarathustra to us? What shall we call him? and, like me, you answer your own questions with questions.

Is he a promiser? Or a fulfiller? A conqueror? Or an inheritor? A harvest? Or a ploughshare? A physician? Or a convalescent?

Is he a poet? Or a genuine man? A liberator? Or a subduer? A good man? Or an evil man?

I walk among men as among fragments of the future: of that future which I scan.

And it is all my art and aim, to compose into one and bring together what is fragment and riddle and dreadful chance.

And how could I endure to be a man, if man were not also poet and reader of riddles and the redeemer of chance!

To redeem the past and to transform every 'It was' into an 'I wanted it thus!' – that alone do I call redemption!

Will – that is what the liberator and bringer of joy is called: thus I have taught you, my friends! But now learn this as well: The will itself is still a prisoner.

Willing liberates: but what is it that fastens in fetters even the liberator?

'It was': that is what the will's teeth-gnashing and most lonely affliction is called. Powerless against that which has been done, the will is an angry spectator of all things past.

The will cannot will backwards; that it cannot break time and time's desire – that is the will's most lonely affliction.

Willing liberates: what does willing itself devise to free itself from its affliction and to mock at its dungeon?

Alas, every prisoner becomes a fool! The imprisoned will, too, releases itself in a foolish way.

It is sullenly wrathful that time does not run back; 'That which was' – that is what the stone which it cannot roll away is called.

And so, out of wrath and ill-temper, the will rolls stones

about and takes revenge upon him who does not, like it, feel wrath and ill-temper.

Thus the will, the liberator, becomes a malefactor: and upon all that can suffer it takes revenge for its inability to go backwards.

This, yes, this alone is *revenge* itself: the will's antipathy towards time and time's 'It was'.

Truly, a great foolishness dwells in our will; and that this foolishness acquired spirit has become a curse to all human kind.

The spirit of revenge: my friends, that, up to now, has been mankind's chief concern; and where there was suffering, there was always supposed to be punishment.

'Punishment' is what revenge calls itself: it feigns a good conscience for itself with a lie.

And because there is suffering in the willer himself, since he cannot will backwards – therefore willing itself and all life was supposed to be – punishment!

And then cloud upon cloud rolled over the spirit: until at last madness preached: 'Everything passes away, therefore everything deserves to pass away!

'And that law of time, that time must devour her children, is justice itself': thus madness preached.

'Things are ordered morally according to justice and punishment. Oh, where is redemption from the stream of things and from the punishment "existence"?' Thus madness preached.

'Can there be redemption when there is eternal justice? Alas, the stone "It was" cannot be rolled away: all punishments, too, must be eternal!' Thus madness preached.

'No deed can be annihilated: how could a deed be undone through punishment? That existence too must be an eternally-recurring deed and guilt, this, this is what is eternal in the punishment "existence"!

'Except the will at last redeem itself and willing become not-willing – ': but you, my brothers, know this fable-song of madness!

I led you away from these fable-songs when I taught you: 'The will is a creator.'

All 'It was' is a fragment, a riddle, a dreadful chance – until the creative will says to it: 'But I willed it thus!'

Until the creative will says to it: 'But I will it thus! Thus shall I will it!'

But has it ever spoken thus? And when will this take place? Has the will yet been unharnessed from its own folly?

Has the will become its own redeemer and bringer of joy? Has it unlearned the spirit of revenge and all teeth-gnashing?

And who has taught it to be reconciled with time, and higher things than reconciliation?

The will that is the will to power must will something higher than any reconciliation – but how shall that happen? Who has taught it to will backwards, too?

But at this point of his discourse, Zarathustra suddenly broke off and looked exactly like a man seized by extremest terror. With terrified eyes he gazed upon his disciples; his eyes transpierced their thoughts and their reservations[22] as if with arrows. But after a short time he laughed again and said in a soothed voice:

'It is difficult to live among men because keeping silent is so difficult. Especially for a babbler.'

Thus spoke Zarathustra. The hunchback, however, had listened to the conversation and had covered his face the while; but when he heard Zarathustra laugh, he looked up in curiosity, and said slowly:

'But why does Zarathustra speak to us differently than to his disciples?'

Zarathustra answered: 'What is surprising in that? One may well speak in a hunchbacked manner to a hunchback!'[23]

'Very good,' said the hunchback; 'and with pupils one may well tell tales out of school.

'But why does Zarathustra speak to his pupils differently – than to himself?'

Of Manly Prudence

It is not the height, it is the abyss that is terrible!

The abyss where the glance plunges *downward* and the hand grasps *upward*. There the heart grows giddy through its twofold will.

Ah, friends, have you, too, divined my heart's twofold will?

That my glance plunges into the heights and that my hand wants to hold on to the depths and lean there – that, that is *my* abyss and my danger.

My will clings to mankind, I bind myself to mankind with fetters, because I am drawn up to the Superman: for my other will wants to draw me up to the Superman.

That my hand may not quite lose its belief in firmness: *that is why* I live blindly among men, as if I did not recognize them.

I do not recognize you men: this darkness and consolation has often spread around me.

I sit at the gateway and wait for every rogue and ask: Who wants to deceive me?

This is my first manly prudence: I let myself be deceived so as not to be on guard against deceivers.

Ah, if I were on guard against men, how could men be an anchor for my ball? It would be torn upward and away too easily!

This providence lies over my fate: I have to be without foresight.

And he who does not want to die of thirst among men must learn to drink out of all glasses; and he who wants to stay clean among men must know how to wash himself even with dirty water.

And to console myself I often spoke thus: 'Well then! Come on, old heart! A misfortune failed to harm you: enjoy that as your – good fortune!'

This, however, is my second manly prudence: I am more considerate to the *vain* than to the proud.

Is wounded vanity not the mother of all tragedies? But where pride is wounded there surely grows up something better than pride.

If life is to be pleasant to watch, its play must be well acted: for that, however, good actors are needed.

I found all vain people to be good actors: they act and desire that others shall want to watch them – all their spirit is in this desire.

They act themselves, they invent themselves; I like to watch life in their vicinity – it cures melancholy.

I am considerate to the vain because they are physicians to my melancholy and hold me fast to mankind as to a play.

And further: who can estimate the full depth of the vain man's modesty! I love and pity him on account of his modesty.

He wants to learn belief in himself from you; he feeds upon your glances, he eats praise out of your hands.

He believes even your lies when you lie favourably to him: for his heart sighs in its depths: 'What am *I*?'

And if the virtue that is unconscious of itself be the true virtue: well, the vain man is unconscious of his modesty!

This, however, is my third manly prudence: I do not let your timorousness spoil my pleasure at the sight of the *wicked*.

I am happy to see the marvels the hot sun hatches: tigers and palm trees and rattle-snakes.

Among men, too, there is a fine brood of the hot sun and much that is marvellous in the wicked.

Indeed, as your wisest man did not seem so very wise to me, so I found that human wickedness, too, did not live up to its reputation.

And I often shook my head and asked: Why go on rattling, you rattle-snakes?

Truly, there is still a future, even for evil! And the hottest South has not yet been discovered for mankind.

How many a thing is now called grossest wickedness which is only twelve feet broad and three months long! One day, however, greater dragons will come into the world.

For, that the Superman may not lack his dragon, the super-dragon worthy of him, much hot sunshine must yet burn upon damp primeval forests!

Your wild cats must have become tigers and your poison-toads crocodiles: for the good huntsman shall have a good hunt!

And truly, you good and just! There is much in you that is laughable and especially your fear of him who was formerly called the 'Devil'!

Your souls are so unfamiliar with what is great that the Superman would be *fearful* to you in his goodness!

And you wise and enlightened men, you would flee from the burning sun of wisdom in which the Superman joyfully bathes his nakedness!

You highest men my eyes have encountered! This is my doubt of you and my secret laughter: I think you would call my Superman – a devil!

Alas, I grew weary of these highest and best men: from their 'heights' I longed to go up, out, away to the Superman!

A horror overcame me when I saw these best men naked: then there grew for me the wings to soar away into distant futures.

Into most distant futures, into more southerly Souths than artist ever dreamed of: thither where gods are ashamed of all clothes!

But I want to see *you* disguised, you neighbours and fellow-men, and well-dressed and vain and worthy as 'the good and just'.

And I myself will sit among you disguised, so that I may *misunderstand* you and myself: that, in fact, is my last manly prudence.

Thus spoke Zarathustra.

The Stillest Hour

WHAT has happened to me, my friends? You behold me troubled, driven forth, unwillingly obedient, ready to go – alas, to go away from *you*!

Yes, Zarathustra must go into his solitude once again: but this time the bear goes unhappily back into his cave!

What has happened to me? Who has ordered this? – alas, my mistress will have it so, so she told me; have I ever told you her name?

Yesterday towards evening *my stillest hour* spoke to me: that is the name of my terrible mistress.

And thus it happened, for I must tell you everything, that your hearts may not harden against me for departing so suddenly!

Do you know the terror which assails him who is falling asleep?

He is terrified down to his toes, because the ground seems to give way, and the dream begins.

I tell you this in a parable. Yesterday, at the stillest hour, the ground seemed to give way: my dream began.

The hand moved, the clock of my life held its breath – I had never heard such stillness about me: so that my heart was terrified.

Then, voicelessly, something said to me: '*You know, Zarathustra?*'

And I cried out for terror at this whisper, and the blood drained from my face: but I kept silent.

Then again, something said to me voicelessly: 'You know, Zarathustra, but you do not speak!'

And I answered at last defiantly: 'Yes, I know, but I will not speak!'

Then again something said to me voicelessly: 'You *will* not, Zarathustra? Is this true? Do not hide yourself in your defiance!'

And I wept and trembled like a child and said: 'Alas, I want to, but how can I? Release me from this alone! It is beyond my strength!'

Then again something said to me voicelessly: 'Of what consequence are you, Zarathustra? Speak your teaching and break!'

And I answered: 'Ah, is it *my* teaching? Who am *I*? I await one who is more worthy; I am not worthy even to break by it.'

Then again something said to me voicelessly: 'Of what consequence are you? You are not yet humble enough. Humility has the toughest hide.'

And I answered: 'What has the hide of my humility not already endured? I live at the foot of my heights: how high are my peaks? No one has yet told me. But I know my valleys well.'

Then again something said to me voicelessly: 'O Zarathustra, he who has to move mountains moves valleys and lowlands too.'

And I answered: 'My words have as yet moved no mountains and what I have spoken has not reached men. Indeed, I went to men, but I have not yet attained them.'

Then again something said to me voicelessly: 'How do you know *that*? The dew falls upon the grass when the night is at its most silent.'

And I answered: 'They mocked me when I found and walked my own way; and in truth my feet trembled then.

'And they spoke thus to me: You have forgotten the way, now you will also forget how to walk!'

Then again something said to me voicelessly: 'Of what consequence is their mockery? You are one who has unlearned how to obey: now you shall command!

'Do you know what it is all men most need? Him who commands great things.

'To perform great things is difficult: but more difficult is to command great things.

'This is the most unpardonable thing about you: You have the power and you will not rule.'

And I answered: 'I lack the lion's voice for command.'

Then again something said to me as in a whisper: 'It is the stillest words which bring the storm. Thoughts that come on doves' feet guide the world.

'O Zarathustra, you shall go as a shadow of that which must come: thus you will command and commanding lead the way.'

And I answered: 'I am ashamed.'

Then again something said to me voicelessly: 'You must yet become a child and without shame.

'The pride of youth is still in you, you have become young late: but he who wants to become a child must overcome even his youth.'

And I considered long and trembled. At last, however, I said what I had said at first: 'I will not.'

Then a laughing broke out around me. Alas, how this laughing tore my body and ripped open my heart!

And for the last time something said to me: 'O Zarathustra, your fruits are ripe but you are not ripe for your fruits!

'So you must go back into solitude: for you shall yet grow mellow.'

And again something laughed, and fled: then it grew still round me as if with a twofold stillness. I, however, lay on the ground and the sweat poured from my limbs.

Now you have heard everything, and why I must return to my solitude. I have kept nothing back from you, my friends.

And you have heard, too, *who* is the most silent of men – and intends to remain so!

Ah, my friends! I should have something more to tell you, I should have something more to give you! Why do I not give it? Am I then mean?

When Zarathustra had said these words, however, the violence of his grief and the nearness of his departure from his friends overwhelmed him, so that he wept aloud; and no one knew how to comfort him. But that night he went away alone and forsook his friends.

PART THREE

'You look up when you desire to be exalted. And I look down, because I am exalted.

'Who among you can at the same time laugh and be exalted?

'He who climbs upon the highest mountains laughs at all tragedies, real or imaginary.'

ZARATHUSTRA:
'*Of Reading and Writing*'

The Wanderer

IT was midnight when Zarathustra made his way over the ridge of the island, so that he might arrive at the other shore with the early dawn: for there he meant to board ship. For there was a good harbour at which foreign ships, too, liked to drop anchor: they took on board many who wanted to leave the Blissful Islands and cross the sea. Now, as Zarathustra was climbing the mountain he recalled as he went the many lonely wanderings he had made from the time of his youth, and how many mountains and ridges and summits he had already climbed.

I am a wanderer and a mountain-climber (he said to his heart), I do not like the plains and it seems I cannot sit still for long.

And whatever may yet come to me as fate and experience – a wandering and a mountain-climbing will be in it: in the final analysis one experiences only oneself.

The time has passed when accidents could befall me; and what *could* still come to me that was not already my own?

It is returning, at last it is coming home to me – my own Self and those parts of it that have long been abroad and scattered among all things and accidents.

And I know one thing more: I stand now before my last summit and before the deed that has been deferred the longest. Alas, I have to climb my most difficult path! Alas, I have started upon my loneliest wandering!

But a man of my sort does not avoid such an hour: the hour that says to him: 'Only now do you tread your path of greatness! Summit and abyss – they are now united in one!

'You are treading your path of greatness: now what was formerly your ultimate danger has become your ultimate refuge!

'You are treading your path of greatness: now it must call up all your courage that there is no longer a path behind you!

'You are treading your path of greatness: no one shall steal after you here! Your foot itself has extinguished the path behind you, and above that path stands written: Impossibility.

'And when all footholds disappear, you must know how to climb upon your own head: how could you climb upward otherwise?

'Upon your own head and beyond your own heart! Now the gentlest part of you must become the hardest.

'He who has always been very indulgent with himself sickens at last through his own indulgence. All praise to what makes hard! I do not praise the land where butter and honey – flow!

'In order to see *much* one must learn to *look away* from oneself – every mountain-climber needs this hardness. '

'But he who, seeking enlightenment, is over-eager with his eyes, how could he see more of a thing than its foreground!

'You, however, O Zarathustra, have wanted to behold the ground of things and their background:[24] so you must climb above yourself – up and beyond, until you have even your stars *under* you!'

Yes! To look down upon myself and even upon my stars: that alone would I call my *summit*, that has remained for me as my *ultimate* summit!

Thus spoke Zarathustra to himself as he climbed, consoling his heart with hard sayings: for his heart was wounded as never before. And when he arrived at the top of the mountain ridge, behold, there lay the other sea spread out before him: and he stood and was long silent. But the night at this height was cold and clear and bright with stars.

I know my fate (he said at last with sadness). Well then! I am ready. My last solitude has just begun.

Ah, this sorrowful, black sea beneath me! Ah, this brooding reluctance! Ah, destiny and sea! Now I have to *go down* to you!

I stand before my highest mountain and my longest

wandering: therefore I must first descend deeper than I have ever descended,

– deeper into pain than I have ever descended, down to its blackest stream! So my destiny will have it. Well then! I am ready.

Whence arise the highest mountains? I once asked. Then I learned that they arise from the sea.

This testimony is written into their stones and into the sides of their summits. The highest must arise to its height from the deepest.

Thus spoke Zarathustra on the mountain summit, where it was cold; when he drew near to the sea, however, and at length stood alone beneath the cliffs, he had grown weary on the way and more yearning than he was before.

Everything is still asleep (he said); even the sea is asleep. Its eye looks at me drowsily and strangely.

But it breathes warmly; I feel it. And I feel, too, that it is dreaming. Dreaming, it writhes upon a hard pillow.

Listen! Listen! How it groans with wicked memories! Or with wicked expectations?

Ah, I am sad with you, dark monster, and angry even with myself for your sake.

Alas, that my hand has insufficient strength! In truth, I should dearly like to release you from your bad dreams!

And as Zarathustra thus spoke, he laughed at himself with melancholy and bitterness. What, Zarathustra! he said, do you want to sing consolation even to the sea?

Ah, you fond fool, Zarathustra, too eager to trust! But that is what you have always been: you have always approached trustfully all that is fearful.

You have always wanted to caress every monster. A touch of warm breath, a little soft fur on its paw – and at once you have been ready to love and entice it.

Love is the danger for the most solitary man, love of any thing *if only it is alive!* Indeed, my foolishness and modesty in love is laughable!

Thus spoke Zarathustra and laughed again: but then he

thought of the friends he had left, and he was angry with himself because of his thoughts, as if he had injured his friends with them. And forthwith the laughing man wept – for anger and longing did Zarathustra weep bitterly.

Of the Vision and the Riddle

I

WHEN it became rumoured among the sailors that Zarathustra was on the ship – for a man from the Blissful Islands had gone on board at the same time as he – a great curiosity and expectancy arose. But Zarathustra was silent for two days and was cold and deaf for sorrow, so that he responded neither to looks nor to questions. But on the evening of the second day he opened his ears again, although he still remained silent: for there were many strange and dangerous things to hear on this ship, which had come from afar and had yet further to go. Zarathustra, however, was a friend to all who take long journeys and do not want to live without danger. And behold! in listening his tongue was loosened, and the ice of his heart broke: then he started to speak thus:

To you, the bold venturers and adventurers and whoever has embarked with cunning sails upon dreadful seas,

to you who are intoxicated by riddles, who take pleasure in twilight, whose soul is lured with flutes to every treacherous abyss –

for you do not desire to feel for a rope with cowardly hand; and where you can *guess* you hate to *calculate* –

to you alone do I tell this riddle that I *saw* – the vision of the most solitary man.

Lately I walked gloomily through a deathly-grey twilight, gloomily and sternly with compressed lips. Not only one sun had gone down for me.

A path that mounted defiantly through boulders and rubble, a wicked, solitary path that bush or plant no longer cheered: a mountain path crunched under my foot's defiance.

Striding mute over the mocking clatter of pebbles, trampling the stones that made it slip: thus my foot with effort forced itself upward.

Upward – despite the spirit that drew it downward, drew it towards the abyss, the Spirit of Gravity, my devil and arch-enemy.

Upward – although he sat upon me, half dwarf, half mole; crippled, crippling; pouring lead-drops into my ear, leaden thoughts into my brain.

'O Zarathustra,' he said mockingly, syllable by syllable, 'you stone of wisdom! You have thrown yourself high, but every stone that is thrown must – fall!

'O Zarathustra, you stone of wisdom, you projectile, you star-destroyer! You have thrown yourself thus high, but every stone that is thrown – must fall!

'Condemned by yourself and to your own stone-throwing: O Zarathustra, far indeed have you thrown your stone, but it will fall back upon *you*!'

Thereupon the dwarf fell silent; and he long continued so. But his silence oppressed me; and to be thus in company is truly more lonely than to be alone!

I climbed, I climbed, I dreamed, I thought, but everything oppressed me. I was like a sick man wearied by his sore torment and reawakened from sleep by a worse dream.

But there is something in me that I call courage: it has always destroyed every discouragement in me. This courage at last bade me stop and say: 'Dwarf! You! Or I!'

For courage is the best destroyer – courage that *attacks*: for in every attack there is a triumphant shout.

Man, however, is the most courageous animal: with his courage he has overcome every animal. With a triumphant shout he has even overcome every pain; human pain, however, is the deepest pain.

Courage also destroys giddiness at abysses: and where does man not stand at an abyss? Is seeing itself not – seeing abysses?

Courage is the best destroyer: courage also destroys pity. Pity, however, is the deepest abyss: as deeply as man looks into life, so deeply does he look also into suffering.

Courage, however, is the best destroyer, courage that attacks: it destroys even death, for it says: 'Was *that* life? Well then! Once more!'

But there is a great triumphant shout in such a saying. He who has ears to hear, let him hear.

2

'Stop, dwarf!' I said. 'I! Or you! But I am the stronger of us two – you do not know my abysmal thought! That thought – you could not endure!'

Then something occurred which lightened me: for the dwarf jumped from my shoulder, the inquisitive dwarf! And he squatted down upon a stone in front of me. But a gateway stood just where we had halted.

'Behold this gateway, dwarf!' I went on: 'it has two aspects. Two paths come together here: no one has ever reached their end.

'This long lane behind us: it goes on for an eternity. And that long lane ahead of us – that is another eternity.

'They are in opposition to one another, these paths; they abut on one another: and it is here at this gateway that they come together. The name of the gateway is written above it: "Moment".

'But if one were to follow them further and ever further and further: do you think, dwarf, that these paths would be in eternal opposition?'

'Everything straight lies,' murmured the dwarf disdainfully. 'All truth is crooked, time itself is a circle.'

'Spirit of Gravity!' I said angrily, 'do not treat this too lightly! Or I shall leave you squatting where you are, Lame-foot – and I have carried you *high*!

'Behold this moment!' I went on. 'From this gateway Moment a long, eternal lane runs *back*: an eternity lies behind us.

'Must not all things that *can* run have already run along this lane? Must not all things that *can* happen *have* already happened, been done, run past?

'And if all things have been here before: what do you think

of this moment, dwarf? Must not this gateway, too, have been here – before?

'And are not all things bound fast together in such a way that this moment draws after it all future things? *Therefore* – draws itself too?

'For all things that *can* run *must* also run once again forward along this long lane.

'And this slow spider that creeps along in the moonlight, and this moonlight itself, and I and you at this gateway whispering together, whispering of eternal things – must we not all have been here before?

' – and must we not return and run down that other lane out before us, down that long, terrible lane – must we not return eternally?'

Thus I spoke, and I spoke more and more softly: for I was afraid of my own thoughts and reservations. Then, suddenly, I heard a dog *howling* nearby.

Had I ever heard a dog howling in that way? My thoughts ran back. Yes! When I was a child, in my most distant childhood:

– then I heard a dog howling in that way. And I saw it, too, bristling, its head raised, trembling in the stillest midnight, when even dogs believe in ghosts:

– so that it moved me to pity. For the full moon had just gone over the house, silent as death, it had just stopped still, a round glow, still upon the flat roof as if upon a forbidden place:

that was what had terrified the dog: for dogs believe in thieves and ghosts. And when I heard such howling again, it moved me to pity again.

Where had the dwarf now gone? And the gateway? And the spider? And all the whispering? Had I been dreaming? Had I awoken? All at once I was standing between wild cliffs, alone, desolate in the most desolate moonlight.

But there a man was lying! And there! The dog, leaping, bristling, whining; then it saw me coming – then it howled again, then it *cried out* – had I ever heard a dog cry so for help?[25]

And truly, I had never seen the like of what I then saw. I

saw a young shepherd writhing, choking, convulsed, his face distorted; and a heavy, black snake was hanging out of his mouth.

Had I ever seen so much disgust and pallid horror on a face? Had he, perhaps, been asleep? Then the snake had crawled into his throat – and there it had bitten itself fast.

My hands tugged and tugged at the snake – in vain! they could not tug the snake out of the shepherd's throat. Then a voice cried from me: 'Bite! Bite!

'Its head off! Bite!' – thus a voice cried from me, my horror, my hate, my disgust, my pity, all my good and evil cried out of me with a single cry.

You bold men around me! You venturers, adventurers, and those of you who have embarked with cunning sails upon undiscovered seas! You who take pleasure in riddles!

Solve for me the riddle that I saw, interpret to me the vision of the most solitary man!

For it was a vision and a premonition: *what* did I see in allegory? And *who* is it that must come one day?

Who is the shepherd into whose mouth the snake thus crawled? *Who* is the man into whose throat all that is heaviest, blackest will thus crawl?

The shepherd, however, bit as my cry had advised him; he bit with a good bite! He spat far away the snake's head – and sprang up.

No longer a shepherd, no longer a man – a transformed being, surrounded with light, *laughing*! Never yet on earth had any man laughed as he laughed!

O my brothers, I heard a laughter that was no human laughter – and now a thirst consumes me, a longing that is never stilled.

My longing for this laughter consumes me: oh how do I endure still to live! And how could I endure to die now!

Thus spoke Zarathustra.

Of Involuntary Bliss

WITH such riddles and bitterness in his heart did Zarathustra fare across the sea. When he was four days' journey from the Blissful Islands and from his friends, however, he had overcome all his pain – triumphantly and with firm feet he again accepted his destiny.[26] And then Zarathustra spoke thus to his rejoicing conscience:

I am again alone and willingly so, alone with the pure sky and the open sea; and again it is afternoon around me.

It was afternoon when I once found my friends for the first time, it was afternoon, too, when I found them a second time – at the hour when all light grows stiller.

For whatever happiness that is still travelling between heaven and earth now seeks shelter in a luminous soul: *with happiness* all light has now grown stiller.

O afternoon of my life! Once my happiness, too, climbed down into the valley to seek a shelter: there it found these open, hospitable souls.

O afternoon of my life! What have I not given away that I might possess one thing: this living plantation of my thoughts and this dawn of my highest hope!

Once the creator sought companions and children of *his* hope: and behold, it turned out that he could not find them, except he first create them himself.

Thus I am in the midst of my work, going to my children and turning from them: for the sake of his children must Zarathustra perfect himself.

For one loves from the very heart only one's child and one's work; and where there is great love of oneself, then it is a sign of pregnancy: thus have I found.

My children are still green in their first spring, standing close together and shaken in common by the winds, the trees of my garden and my best soil.

And truly! Where such trees stand together, there blissful islands *are*!

But one day I will uproot them and set each one up by itself, that it may learn solitude and defiance and foresight.

Then it shall stand by the sea, gnarled and twisted and with supple hardiness, a living lighthouse of unconquerable life.

Yonder, where storms plunge down into the sea and the mountain's snout drinks water, there each of them shall one day keep its day and night watch, for *its* testing and recogniton.

It shall be tested and recognized, to see whether it is of my kind and my race – whether it is master of a protracted will, silent even when it speaks, and giving in such a way that in giving it *takes* –

that it may one day be my companion and a fellow-creator and fellow-rejoicer of Zarathustra – such a one as inscribes my will upon my tablets: for the greater perfection of all things.

And for its sake, and for those like it, must I perfect *myself*: therefore I now avoid my happiness and offer myself to all unhappiness – for *my* ultimate testing and recognition.

And truly, it was time I went; and the wanderer's shadow and the longest sojourn and the stillest hour – all told me: 'It is high time!'

The wind blew to me through the keyhole and said: 'Come!' The door sprang cunningly open and said: 'Go!'

But I lay fettered to love of my children: desire set this snare for me, desire for love, that I might become my children's victim and lose myself through them.

To desire – that now means to me: to have lost myself. *I possess you, my children!* In this possession all should be certainty and nothing desire.

But the sun of my love lay brooding upon me, Zarathustra stewed in his own juice – then shadows and doubts flew past me.

I hankered after frost and winter: 'Oh that frost and winter would again make me crackle and crunch!' I sighed: then icy mist arose from me.

My past broke open its graves, many a pain buried alive

awoke: they had only been sleeping, concealed in winding sheets.

Thus in symbols everything called to me: 'It is time!' But I – did not hear: until at last my abyss stirred and my thought bit me.

Alas, abysmal thought that is *my* thought! When shall I find the strength to hear you boring and no longer tremble?

My heart rises to my throat when I hear you boring! Even your silence threatens to choke me, you abysmal, silent thought!

I have never yet dared to summon you *up*: it has been enough that I – carried you with me! I have not yet been strong enough for the ultimate lion's arrogance and lion's wantonness.

Your heaviness has always been fearful enough for me: but one day I shall find the strength and the lion's voice to summon you up!

When I have overcome myself in that, I will overcome myself in that which is greater; and a *victory* shall be the seal of my perfection!

In the meantime, I travel on uncertain seas; smooth-tongued chance flatters me; I gaze forward and backward, still I see no end.

The hour of my last struggle has not yet arrived – or has it perhaps just arrived? Truly, sea and life around me gaze at me with insidious beauty!

O afternoon of my life! O happiness before evening! O harbour in mid-sea! O peace in uncertainty! How I mistrust you all!

Truly, I am mistrustful of your insidious beauty! I am like the lover who mistrusts all-too-velvety smiles.

As the jealous man thrusts his best beloved from him, tender even in his hardness – thus do I thrust this blissful hour from me.

Away with you, blissful hour! With you there came to me an involuntary bliss! I stand here ready for my deepest pain – you came out of season!

Away with you, blissful hour! Rather take shelter yonder –

with my children! Hurry, and bless them before evening with *my* happiness!

There evening already approaches: the sun is sinking. Away – my happiness!

Thus spoke Zarathustra. And he waited all night for his unhappiness: but he waited in vain. The night remained clear and still and happiness itself drew nearer and nearer to him. Towards morning, however, Zarathustra laughed to his heart and said ironically: 'Happiness runs after me. That is because I do not run after women. Happiness, however, is a woman.'

Before Sunrise

O SKY above me! O pure, deep sky! You abyss of light! Gazing into you, I tremble with divine desires.

To cast myself into your height – that is *my* depth! To hide myself in your purity – that is *my* innocence!

The god is veiled by his beauty: thus you hide your stars. You do not speak: thus you proclaim to me your wisdom.

You have risen for me today, mute over the raging sea; your love and your modesty speak a revelation to my raging soul.

That you have come to me, beautiful, veiled in your beauty; that you have spoken to me mutely, manifest in your wisdom:

Oh how should I not divine all that is modest in your soul! You came to me *before* the sun, to me the most solitary man.

We have been friends from the beginning: we have grief and terror and world in common; we have even the sun in common.

We do not speak to one another, because we know too much: we are silent together, we smile our knowledge to one another.

Are you not the light of my fire? Do you not have the sister-soul of my insight?

Together we learned everything; together we learned to mount above ourselves to ourselves and to smile uncloudedly –

to smile uncloudedly down from bright eyes and from miles away when under us compulsion and purpose and guilt stream like rain.

And when I wandered alone, *what* did my soul hunger after by night and on treacherous paths? And when I climbed mountains, *whom* did I always seek, if not you, upon mountains?

And all my wandering and mountain-climbing: it was merely a necessity and an expedient of clumsiness: my whole will desires only to *fly*, to fly into *you*!

And what have I hated more than passing clouds and all that defiles you? And I have hated even my own hatred, because it defiled you!

I dislike the passing clouds, these stealthy cats of prey: they take from you and from me what we have in common – the vast and boundless declaration of Yes and Amen.

We dislike these mediators and mixers, the passing clouds: these half-and-halfers, who have learned neither to bless nor to curse from the heart.

I would rather sit in a barrel under a closed sky, rather sit in an abyss without a sky, than see you, luminous sky, defiled by passing clouds!

And often I longed to bind them fast with jagged golden wires of lightning, so that I, like the thunder, might drum upon their hollow bellies –

an angry drummer, because they rob me of your Yes! and Amen! O sky above me, you pure sky! You luminous sky! You abyss of light! – because they rob me of *my* Yes! and Amen!

For I would rather have noise and thunder and storm-curses than this cautious, uncertain feline repose; and among men, too, I hate most all soft-walkers and half-and-halfers and uncertain, hesitating passing clouds.

And 'He who cannot bless shall *learn* to curse!' – this clear teaching fell to me from the clear sky, this star stands in my sky even on dark nights.

I, however, am one who blesses and declares Yes, if only you are around me, you pure, luminous sky! You abyss of light! – then into all abysses do I carry my consecrating declaration Yes.

I have become one who blesses and one who declares Yes: and for that I wrestled long and was a wrestler, so that I might one day have my hands free for blessing.

This, however, is my blessing: To stand over everything as its own sky, as its round roof, its azure bell and eternal certainty: and happy is he who thus blesses!

For all things are baptized at the fount of eternity and beyond good and evil; good and evil themselves, however, are only intervening shadows and damp afflictions and passing clouds.

Truly, it is a blessing and not a blasphemy when I teach: 'Above all things stands the heaven of chance, the heaven of innocence, the heaven of accident, the heaven of wantonness.'[27]

'Lord Chance'[28] – he is the world's oldest nobility, which I have given back to all things; I have released them from servitude under purpose.

I set this freedom and celestial cheerfulness over all things like an azure bell when I taught that no 'eternal will' acts over them and through them.

I set this wantonness and this foolishness in place of that will when I taught: 'With all things one thing is impossible – rationality!'

A *little* reason, to be sure, a seed of wisdom scattered from star to star – this leaven is mingled with all things: for the sake of foolishness is wisdom mingled with all things!

A little wisdom is no doubt possible; but I have found this happy certainty in all things: that they prefer – to *dance* on the feet of chance.

O sky above me, you pure, lofty sky! This is now your purity to me, that there is no eternal reason-spider and spider's web in you –

that you are to me a dance floor for divine chances, that you are to me a gods' table for divine dice and dicers!

But are you blushing? Did I say something unspeakable? Did I slander you when I meant to bless you?

Or is it the shame of our being together which makes you blush? Are you telling me to go and be silent because now – *day* is coming?

The world is deep: and deeper than day has ever comprehended. Not everything may be spoken in the presence of day. But day is coming: so let us part!

O sky above me, you modest, glowing sky! O you, my happiness before sunrise! Day is coming: so let us part!

Thus spoke Zarathustra.

Of the Virtue that Makes Small

I

WHEN Zarathustra was again on firm land he did not go off straightway to his mountains and his cave, but made many journeys and asked many questions and inquired of this and that, so that he said jokingly of himself: 'Behold a river that flows back to its source through many meanderings!' For he wanted to learn what had been happening *to men* while he had been away: whether they had become bigger or smaller. And once he saw a row of new houses, and he marvelled and said:

What do these houses mean? Truly, no great soul put them up as its image!

Did a silly child perhaps take them out of its toy-box? If only another child would put them back into its box!

And these sitting-rooms and bedrooms: are *men* able to go in and out of them? They seem to have been made for dolls; or for dainty nibblers who perhaps let others nibble with them.

And Zarathustra stopped and considered. At length he said sadly: '*Everything* has become smaller!

'Everywhere I see lower doors: anyone like *me* can still pass through them, but – he has to stoop!

'Oh when shall I return to my home, where I shall no longer have to stoop – shall no longer have to stoop *before the small men*!' And Zarathustra sighed and gazed into the distance.

The same day, however, he spoke his discourse upon the virtue that makes small.

2

I go among this people and keep my eyes open: they do not forgive me that I am not envious of their virtues.

They peck at me because I tell them: For small people small virtues are necessary – and because it is hard for me to understand that small people are *necessary*!

Here I am still like a cockerel in a strange farmyard, who is pecked at even by the hens; but I am not unfriendly to these hens on that account.

I am polite towards them, as towards every small vexation; to be prickly towards small things seems to me the wisdom of a hedgehog.

They all talk of me when they sit around the fire at evening – they talk of me, but no one thinks – of me!

This is the new silence I have learned: their noise about me spreads a cloak over my thoughts.

They bluster among themselves: 'What does this gloomy cloud want with us? Let us see that it does not bring us a pestilence!'

And recently a woman pulled back her child when it was coming towards me: 'Take the children away!' she cried; 'such eyes scorch children's souls.'

They cough when I speak: they think that coughing is an objection to strong winds – they know nothing of the raging of my happiness!

'We have no time yet for Zarathustra' – thus they object; but of what consequence is a time that 'has no time' for Zarathustra?

And should they even praise me: how could I rest on *their* praise? Their praise is a barbed girdle to me: it scratches me even when I take it off.

And I have learned this, too, among them: he who praises appears to be giving back, in truth however he wants to be given more!

Ask my foot if it likes their melodies of praise and enticement!

Truly, to such a measure and tick-tock beat it likes neither to dance nor to stand still.

They would like to lure and commend me to small virtue; they would like to persuade my foot to the tick-tock measure of a small happiness.

I go among this people and keep my eyes open: they have become *smaller* and are becoming ever smaller: *and their doctrine of happiness and virtue is the cause.*

For they are modest even in virtue – for they want ease. But only a modest virtue is compatible with ease.

To be sure, even they learn in their own way how to stride and to stride forward: that is what I call their *limping*. Therewith they become a hindrance to anyone who is in a hurry.

And some of them go forward and at the same time look backward with a stiff neck: I like to run up against them.

Foot and eye should not lie, nor give one another the lie. But there is much lying among the small people.

Some of them *will*, but most of them are only *willed*. Some of them are genuine, but most of them are bad actors.

There are unconscious actors among them and involuntary actors – the genuine are always rare, especially genuine actors.

There is little manliness here: therefore their women make themselves manly. For only he who is sufficiently a man will – *redeem the woman* in woman.

And I have found this hypocrisy the worst among them: that even those who command affect the virtues of those who obey.

'I serve, you serve, we serve' – so here even the hypocrisy of the rulers intones – and alas, if the first ruler is *only* the first servant!

Ah, my eyes' curiosity has strayed even into their hypocrisies; and I have divined well all their fly-happiness and their humming around sunny window-panes.

I see as much weakness as goodness. As much weakness as justice and pity.

They are frank, honest, and kind to one another, as grains of sand are frank, honest, and kind to grains of sand.

To embrace modestly a little happiness – that they call

'submission'! And at the same time they are looking out for a new little happiness.

Fundamentally they want one thing most of all: that nobody shall do them harm. So they steal a march on everyone and do good to everyone.

This, however, is *cowardice*: although it be called 'virtue'.

And when they speak harshly, these little people, *I* hear in it only their hoarseness – every draught, in fact, makes them hoarse.

They are clever, their virtues have clever fingers. But they lack fists, their fingers do not know how to fold into fists.

To them, virtue is what makes modest and tame: with it they make the wolf into a dog and man himself into man's best domestic animal.

'We have set our chairs down in the *middle*' – that is what their smirking tells me – 'and as far away from dying warriors as from contented swine.'

This, however, is – *mediocrity*: although it be called moderation.

3

I go among this people and let fall many a word; but they know neither how to take nor to keep.

They are surprised that I have not come to rail at their lusts and vices; and truly, I have not come to warn against pickpockets, either!

They are surprised that I am not prepared to improve and sharpen their cleverness: as if they had not already sufficient wiseacres, whose voices grate on me like slate-pencils!

And when I cry: 'Curse all the cowardly devils within you who would like to whimper and clasp their hands and worship,' then they cry: 'Zarathustra is godless.'

And this is especially the cry of their teachers of submission; but it is into precisely their ears that I love to shout: Yes! I *am* Zarathustra the Godless!

These teachers of submission! Wherever there is anything small and sick and scabby, there they crawl like lice; and only my disgust stops me from cracking them.

Well then! This is my sermon for *their* ears: I am Zarathustra the Godless, who says 'Who is more godless than I, that I may rejoice in his teaching?'

I am Zarathustra the Godless: where shall I find my equal? All those who give themselves their own will and renounce all submission, they are my equals.

I am Zarathustra the Godless: I cook every chance in *my* pot. And only when it is quite cooked do I welcome it as *my* food.

And truly, many a chance came imperiously to me: but my *will* spoke to it even more imperiously, then it went down imploringly on its knees –

imploring shelter and love with me, and urging in wheedling tones: 'Just see, O Zarathustra, how a friend comes to a friend!'

But why do I speak where no one has *my* kind of ears? And so I will shout it out to all the winds:

You will become smaller and smaller, you small people! You will crumble away, you comfortable people! You will yet perish –

through your many small virtues, through your many small omissions, through your many small submissions!

Too indulgent, too yielding: that is the state of your soil! But in order to grow *big*, a tree wants to strike hard roots into hard rocks!

Even what you omit weaves at the web of mankind's future; even your nothing is a spider's web and a spider that lives on the future's blood.

And when you take, it is like stealing, you small virtuous people; but even among rogues, *honour* says: 'One should steal only where one cannot plunder.'

'It is given' – that is also a doctrine of submission. But I tell you, you comfortable people: *it is taken*, and will be taken more and more from you![29]

Oh, that you would put from you all *half* willing, and decide upon lethargy as you do upon action!

Oh, that you understood my saying: 'Always do what you will – but first be such as *can will*!'

'Always love your neighbour as yourselves – but first be such as *love themselves* –

'such as love with a great love, such as love with a great contempt!' Thus speaks Zarathustra the Godless.

But why do I speak where no one has *my* kind of ears? Here it is yet an hour too early for me.

Among this people I am my own forerunner, my own cock-crow through dark lanes.

But *their* hour is coming! And mine too is coming! Hourly will they become smaller, poorer, more barren – poor weeds! poor soil!

And *soon* they shall stand before me like arid grass and steppe, and truly! weary of themselves – and longing for *fire* rather than for water!

O blessed hour of the lightning! O mystery before noontide! One day I shall turn them into running fire and heralds with tongues of flame –

one day they shall proclaim with tongues of flame: It is coming, it is near, *the great noontide*!

Thus spoke Zarathustra.

On the Mount of Olives

WINTER, an ill guest, sits in my house; my hands are blue from his friendly handshake.

I honour him, this ill guest, but I am glad to let him sit alone. I gladly run away from him; and if you run *well* you can escape him!

With warm feet and warm thoughts do I run yonder where the wind is still, to the sunny corner of my mount of olives.

There I laugh at my stern guest and am still fond of him, for he drives the flies away and silences many little noises for me at home.

For he will not permit even a gnat to buzz about, far less two gnats; and he makes the streets lonely, so that the moonlight is afraid there at night.

He is a hard guest, but I honour him, and do not pray to a fat-bellied fire-idol, as the weaklings do.

Rather a little chattering of teeth than idol-worship! – so my nature will have it. And I especially detest all lustful, steaming, musty fire-idols.

Whom I love I love better in winter than in summer; I now mock my enemies better and more heartily, since winter sits in my home.

Heartily, in truth, even when I *crawl* into bed – even there my hidden happiness laughs and grows wanton; even my deceptive dream laughs.

I, a – crawler? Never in my life have I crawled before the powerful; and if I ever lied, I lied from love. For that reason I am joyful even in my winter bed.

A meagre bed warms me more than an opulent one, for I am jealous of my poverty. And it is most faithful to me in the winter.

I start each day with a wickedness, I mock winter with a cold bath: my stern house-companion grumbles at that.

I also like to tickle him with a wax candle: so that he may finally let the sky emerge from an ash-grey dawn.

For I am especially wicked in the morning: at the early hour when the bucket clatters at the well and horses neigh warmly in grey streets.

Then I wait impatiently, until the luminous sky at last dawns for me, the snowy-bearded winter sky, the white-haired, ancient sky –

the silent, winter sky, that often conceals even its sun!

Did I learn long, luminous silence from it? Or did it learn it from me? Or did each of us devise it himself?

The origin of all good things is thousandfold – all good, wanton things spring for joy into existence: how should they do that – once only?

Long silence is also a good, wanton thing, and to gaze like the winter sky from a luminous, round-eyed countenance –

like it, to conceal one's sun and one's inflexible sun-will: truly, I have learned *well* this art and this winter wantonness!

It is my favourite wickedness and art, that my silence has learned not to betray itself by silence.

Rattling words and dice have I outwitted the solemn attendants: my will and purpose shall elude all the stern watchers.

So that no one might see down into my profundity and ultimate will – that is why I devised my long, luminous silence.

I have found so many shrewd men who veiled their faces and troubled their waters, so that no one might see through them and under them.

But the shrewder distrusters and nut-crackers came straight to them: straightway they fished out their best-hidden fish!

But the clear, the honest, the transparent – they seem to me the shrewdest silent men: those whose *profundity* is so deep that even the clearest water does not – betray it.

You snowy-bearded winter sky, you round-eyed, white-haired sky above me! O you heavenly image of my soul and its wantonness!

And do I not *have* to hide myself, like one who has swallowed gold, so that my soul shall not be slit open?

Do I not *have* to wear stilts, so that they may *not notice* my long legs – all these envious and injurious people around me?

These reeky, cosy, worn-out, mouldy, woebegone souls – how *could* their envy endure my happiness?

So I show them only ice and winter on my peaks – and not that my mountain also winds all the girdles of sunlight around it!

They hear only the whistling of my winter storms: and *not* that I also fare over warm seas, like passionate, heavy, hot south winds.

They even pity my accidents and chances: but *my* doctrine is: 'Let chance come to me: it is as innocent as a little child!'

How *could* they endure my happiness, if I did not put accidents and the miseries of winter and fur-hats and coverings of snow-clouds around my happiness!

– if I did not myself pity their *pity*, the pity of these envious and injurious people!

– if I myself did not sigh and let my teeth chatter in their presence, and patiently *let* myself be wrapped up in their pity!

This is the wise wantonness and benevolence of my soul: it *does not hide* its winter and frosty storms; neither does it hide its chilblains.

For one person, solitude is the escape of an invalid; for another, solitude is escape *from* the invalids.

Let them *hear* me chattering and sighing with winter cold, all these poor, squint-eyed knaves around me! With such sighing and chattering have I escaped their heated rooms.

Let them pity me and sigh with me over my chilblains: 'He will yet *freeze to death* on the ice of knowledge!' – so they wail.

In the meanwhile, I run with warm feet hither and thither upon my mount of olives: in the sunny corner of my mount of olives do I sing and mock all pity.

Thus sang Zarathustra.

Of Passing By

THUS, slowly making his way among many people and through divers towns, did Zarathustra return indirectly to his mountain and his cave. And behold, on his way he came unawares to the gate of the *great city*; here, however, a frothing fool with hands outstretched sprang at him and blocked his path. But this was the fool the people called 'Zarathustra's ape': for he had learned from him something of the composition and syntax of language and perhaps also liked to borrow from his store of wisdom. The fool, however, spoke thus to Zarathustra:

O Zarathustra, here is the great city: here you have nothing to seek and everything to lose.

Why do you want to wade through this mud? Take pity on your feet! Rather spit upon the gate and – turn back!

Here is the Hell for hermits' thoughts: here great thoughts are boiled alive and cooked small.

Here all great emotions decay: here only little, dry emotions may rattle!

Do you not smell already the slaughter-houses and cook-shops of the spirit? Does this city not reek of the fumes of slaughtered spirit?

Do you not see the souls hanging like dirty, limp rags? – And they also make newspapers from these rags!

Have you not heard how the spirit has here become a play with words? It vomits out repulsive verbal swill! – And they also make newspapers from this verbal swill.

They pursue one another and do not know where. They inflame one another, and do not know why. They rattle their tins, they jingle their gold.

They are cold and seek warmth in distilled waters; they are inflamed and seek coolness in frozen spirits; they are all ill and diseased with public opinion.

All lusts and vices are at home here; but there are virtuous people here, too, there are many adroit, useful virtues:

Many adroit virtues with scribbling fingers and behinds hardened to sitting and waiting, blessed with little chest decorations and padded, rumpless daughters.

There is also much piety here and much devout spittle-licking and fawning before the God of Hosts.

Down 'from on high' drips the star and the gracious spittle; every starless breast longs to go up 'on high'.

The moon has its court, and the court has its mooncalves: to all that comes from the court, however, do the paupers and all the adroit pauper-virtues pray.

'I serve, you serve, we serve' – thus does all adroit virtue pray to the prince: so that the merited star may at last be fastened to the narrow breast.

But the moon still revolves around all that is earthly: so the prince, too, still revolves around what is most earthly of all: that, however, is the shopkeepers' gold.

The God of Hosts is not the god of the golden ingots; the prince proposes, but the shopkeeper – disposes!

By all that is luminous and strong and good in you, O Zarathustra! spit upon this city of shopkeepers and turn back!

Here all blood flows foul and tepid and frothy through all veins: spit upon the great city that is the great rubbish pile where all the scum froths together!

Spit upon the city of flattened souls and narrow breasts, of slant eyes and sticky fingers –

upon the city of the importunate, the shameless, the ranters in writing and speech, the overheated ambitious:

where everything rotten, disreputable, lustful, gloomy, over-ripe, ulcerous, conspiratorial festers together –

spit upon the great city and turn back!

But here Zarathustra interrupted the frothing fool and stopped his mouth.

Have done! (cried Zarathustra) Your speech and your kind have long disgusted me!

Why did you live so long in the swamp that you had to become a frog and toad yourself?

Does not foul, foaming swamp-blood now flow through your own veins, so that you have learned to quack and rail like this?

Why did you not go into the forest? Or plough the earth? Is the sea not full of green islands?

I despise your contempt; and since you warned me, why did you not warn yourself?

My contempt and my bird of warning shall ascend from love alone; not from the swamp!

They call you my ape, you frothing fool: but I call you my grunting pig – by grunting you are undoing even my praise of folly.

What, then, was it that started you grunting? That nobody had *flattered* you enough: therefore you sat down beside this filth, so that you might have cause for much grunting –

so that you might have cause for much *revenge*! For all your frothing, you vain fool, is revenge; I have divined you well!

But your foolish teaching is harmful to *me*, even when you are right! And if Zarathustra's teaching *were* a hundred times justified, *you* would still – *use* my teaching falsely!

Thus spoke Zarathustra; and he looked at the great city, sighed and was long silent. At length he spoke thus:

This great city, and not only this fool, disgusts me. In both there is nothing to make better, nothing to make worse.

Woe to this great city! And I wish I could see already the pillar of fire in which it will be consumed!

For such pillars of fire must precede the great noontide. Yet this has its time and its own destiny.

But I offer you in farewell this precept, you fool: Where one can no longer love, one should – *pass by*!

Thus spoke Zarathustra and passed by the fool and the great city.

Of the Apostates

I

ALAS, everything that lately stood green and motley in this meadow already lies faded and grey! And how much honey of hope have I carried from here into my beehives!

All these young hearts have already grown old – and not even old! only weary, common, comfortable: they describe it: 'We have grown pious again.'

But lately I saw them running out in the early morning with bold feet: but the feet of their knowledge grew weary and now they slander even their morning boldness!

Truly, many of them once lifted their legs like a dancer, the laughter in my wisdom beckoned to them: then they considered. And now I have seen them bent – to creep to the Cross.

Once they fluttered around light and freedom like flies and young poets. A little older, a little colder: and already they are mystifiers and mutterers and stay-at-homes.

Did their hearts perhaps despair because solitude devoured me like a whale? Did their ears perhaps listen long and longingly *in vain* for me and for my trumpet and herald calls?

Alas! They are always few whose heart possesses a long-enduring courage and wantonness; and in such, the spirit, too, is patient. The remainder, however, are *cowardly*.

The remainder: that is always the majority, the commonplace, the superfluity, the many-too-many – all these are cowardly!

He who is of my sort will also encounter experiences of my sort, so that his first companions must be corpses and buffoons.

His second companions, however, will call themselves his *believers*: a lively flock, full of love, full of folly, full of adolescent adoration.

He among men who is of my sort should not grapple his heart to these believers; he who knows fickle-cowardly human nature should not believe in these springs and many-coloured meadows!

If they *could* do otherwise, they would *choose* otherwise. The half-and-half spoil every whole. Why complain because leaves wither?

Let them fall, let them go, O Zarathustra, and do not complain! Rather blow among them with rustling winds –

blow among these leaves, O Zarathustra: so that all that is *withered* may run from you the faster.

2

'We have grown pious again' – thus these apostates confess; and many of them are still too cowardly to confess it.

I look into their eyes, then I tell them to their face and to the blushes of their cheeks: You are those who again *pray*!

But it is a disgrace to pray! Not for everyone, but for you and me and for whoever else has his conscience in his head. For *you* it is a disgrace to pray!

You know it well: the cowardly devil in you who would like to clasp his hands and to fold his arms and to take it easier: – it was this cowardly devil who persuaded you: 'There *is* a God!'

Through that, however, have you become one of those who dread the light, whom light never lets rest; now you must stick your head deeper every day into night and fog!

And truly, you have chosen well the hour: for even now the night-birds have again flown out. The hour has arrived for all people who fear the light, the evening hour of ease when there is no – 'ease' for them.

I hear and smell it: the hour for their chase and procession has arrived; not indeed for a wild chase, but for a tame, lame, snuffling, soft-walker's and soft-prayer's chase –

for a chase after soulful hypocrites: all mousetraps of the heart have now again been set! And wherever I raise a curtain, a little night-moth comes fluttering out.

Has it perhaps been crouching there with another little night-moth? For everywhere I smell little hidden communities; and wherever there are closets, there are new devotees in them and the atmosphere of devotees.

They sit together on long evenings and say: 'Let us again become as little children and say Dear God!' – ruined in mouth and stomach by the pious confectioners.

Or they observe on long evenings a cunning, lurking Cross-spider, which preaches prudence to the spiders themselves and teaches: 'There is good spinning under Crosses!'

Or they sit all day with fishing-rods beside swamps and for that reason think themselves *deep*; but he who fishes where there are no fish I do not call even superficial!

Or they learn to play the harp in pious-joyful style with a song-poet who would like to harp his way into the hearts of young women – for he has grown weary of the old women and their praises.

Or they learn to shudder with a learned half-madman who waits in darkened rooms so that the spirits may come to him – and the spirit[30] has quite departed!

Or they listen to an old, roving, whistling tramp who has learned from the distressful winds the distress of tones; now he whistles like the wind and preaches distress in distressful tones.

And some of them have even become night-watchmen: now they know how to blow horns and to go around at night and awaken old things that have long been asleep.

I heard five sayings about old things last night beside the

garden wall: they came from such old, distressed, dried-up night-watchmen:

'For a father he does not look after his children enough: human fathers do it better!'

'He is too old! He no longer looks after his children at all' – thus the other night-watchman answered.

'*Has* he any children? No one can prove it, if he doesn't prove it himself! I have long wished he would prove it thoroughly for once.'

'Prove it? As if *he* has ever proved anything! He finds it hard to prove things; he thinks it very important that people should *believe* him.'

'Yes, yes! Belief makes him happy, belief in him. Old people are like that! So shall we be, too!'

Thus the two old night-watchmen and light-scarecrows spoke together and thereupon blew their horns distressfully: so it happened last night beside the garden wall.

My heart, however, writhed with laughter and was like to break and knew not where to go and sank into the midriff.

Truly, it will yet be the death of me, to choke with laughter when I see asses intoxicated and hear night-watchmen thus doubt God.

For has not the time for all such doubts *long* since passed? Who may still awaken such old, sleeping, light-shunning things!

With the old gods, they have long since met their end – and truly, they had a fine, merry, divine ending!

They did not 'fade away in twilight'[31] – that is a lie! On the contrary: they once – laughed themselves to death!

That happened when the most godless saying proceeded from a god himself, the saying: 'There is one God! You shall have no other gods before me!' –

an old wrath-beard of a god, a jealous god, thus forgot himself:

And all the gods laughed then and rocked in their chairs and cried: 'Is not precisely this godliness, that there are gods but no God?'

He who has ears to hear, let him hear.

Thus spoke Zarathustra in the town which he loved and which is called 'The Pied Cow'. For from here he had only two days to go before arriving again at his cave and his animals; and his soul rejoiced continually at the nearness of his home-coming.

The Home-Coming

O SOLITUDE! Solitude, my *home*! I have lived too long wildly in wild strange lands to come home to you without tears!

Now shake your finger at me as mothers do, now smile at me as mothers smile, now say merely: 'And who was it that once stormed away from me like a storm-wind? –

'who departing cried: I have sat too long with Solitude, I have unlearned how to be silent! You have surely learned *that* – now?

'O Zarathustra, I know all: and that you were *lonelier* among the crowd, you solitary, than you ever were with me!

'Loneliness is one thing, solitude another: you have learned *that* – now! And that among men you will always be wild and strange:

'wild and strange even when they love you: for above all they want to be *indulged*!

'But here you are at your own hearth and home; here you can utter everything and pour out every reason, nothing is here ashamed of hidden, hardened feelings.

'Here all things come caressingly to your discourse and flatter you: for they want to ride upon your back. Upon every image you here ride to every truth.

'Here you may speak to all things straight and true: and truly, it sounds as praise to their ears, that someone should speak with all things – honestly!

'But it is another thing to be lonely. For, do you remember, O Zarathustra? When once your bird cried above you as you stood in the forest undecided, ignorant where to go, beside a corpse.

'When you said: May my animals lead me! I found it more

dangerous among men than among animals. *That* was loneliness!

'And do you remember, O Zarathustra? When you sat upon your island, a well of wine among empty buckets, giving and distributing, bestowing and out-pouring among the thirsty:

'until at last you sat alone thirsty among the intoxicated and lamented each night: "Is it not more blessed to receive than to give? And more blessed to steal than to receive?" – *That* was loneliness!

'And do you remember, O Zarathustra? When your stillest hour came and tore you forth from yourself, when it said in an evil whisper: "Speak and break!" –

'when it made you repent of all your waiting and silence and discouraged your humble courage: *That* was loneliness!'

O Solitude! Solitude, my home! How blissfully and tenderly does your voice speak to me!

We do not question one another, we do not complain to one another, we go openly together through open doors.

For with you all is open and clear; and here even the hours run on lighter feet. For time weighs down more heavily in the dark than in the light.

Here, the words and word-chests of all existence spring open to me: all existence here wants to become words, all becoming here wants to learn speech from me.

Down there, however – all speech is in vain! There, the best wisdom is to forget and pass by: I have learned *that* – now!

He who wants to understand all things among men has to touch all things. But my hands are too clean for that.

I even dislike to breathe in their breath; alas, that I lived so long among their noise and bad breath!

O blissful stillness around me! O pure odours around me! Oh, how this stillness draws pure breath from a deep breast! Oh, how it listens, this blissful stillness!

But down there – everything speaks, everything is unheard. One may ring in one's wisdom with bells – the shopkeeper in the market-place will out-ring it with pennies!

Everything among them speaks, no one knows any longer

how to understand. Everything falls away into failure, nothing falls any longer into deep wells.

Everything among them speaks, nothing prospers and comes to an end any longer. Everything cackles, but who still wants to sit quietly upon the nest and hatch eggs?

Everything among them speaks, everything is talked down. And what yesterday was still too hard for time itself and its teeth, today hangs chewed and picked from the mouth of the men of today.

Everything among them speaks, everything is betrayed. And what was once called a secret and a secrecy of profound souls, today belongs to the street-trumpeters and other butter-flies.

O humankind, you strange thing! You noise in dark streets! Now again you lie behind me – my greatest danger lies behind me!

My greatest danger always lay in indulgence and sufferance; and all humankind wants to be indulged and suffered.

With truths held back, with foolish hand and foolish-fond heart and rich in pity's little lies – that is how I used to live among men.

I sat among them disguised, ready to misunderstand *myself* so that I might endure *them,* and glad to tell myself: 'You fool, you do not know men!'

One forgets what one has learned about men when one lives among men: there is too much foreground in all men – what can far-seeing, far-seeking eyes do *there*!

And when they misunderstood me, I, like a fool, indulged them more than I did myself: for I was accustomed to being hard with myself and often even taking revenge on myself for this indulgence.

Stung by poisonous flies and hollowed out like a stone by many drops of wickedness: that is how I sat among them and still told myself: 'Everything small is innocent of its smallness!'

Especially those who call themselves 'the good' did I dis-cover to be the most poisonous flies: they sting in all innoc-ence; how *could* they be – just towards me!

Pity teaches him to lie who lives among the good. Pity

makes the air stifling for all free souls. For the stupidity of the good is unfathomable.

To conceal myself and my riches – *that* did I learn down there: for I found everybody still poor in spirit. It was my pity's lie that I knew with everybody,

that I saw and scented in everybody what was *sufficient* spirit for him and what was *too much* spirit for him!

Their pedantic wise men: I called them wise, not pedantic – thus I learned to slur words. Their gravediggers: I called them investigators and scholars – thus I learned to confound words.

Gravediggers dig diseases for themselves. Evil vapours repose beneath old rubble. One should not stir up the bog. One should live upon mountains.

With happy nostrils I breathe again mountain-freedom! At last my nose is delivered from the odour of all humankind!

My soul, tickled by sharp breezes as with sparkling wine, *sneezes* – sneezes and cries to itself: Bless you!

Thus spoke Zarathustra.

Of the Three Evil Things

I

In a dream, in my last morning dream, I stood today upon a headland – beyond the world, I held a pair of scales and *weighed* the world.

Oh, that the dawn came to me too soon! It glowed me into wakefulness, the jealous dawn! It is always jealous of the glow of my morning dreams.

Measurable to him who has time, weighable to a good weigher, accessible to strong pinions, divinable to divine nut-crackers: thus did my dream find the world.

My dream, a bold sailor, half ship half hurricane, silent as a butterfly, impatient as a falcon: how did it have time and patience today for weighing of worlds?

Did my wisdom perhaps speak secretly to it, my laughing, wakeful day-wisdom that mocks all 'infinite worlds'? For my wisdom says: 'Where power is, there *number* becomes master: it has more power.'

How confidently did my dream gaze upon this finite world, eager neither for new things nor for old; neither in awe nor in supplication –

as if a round apple presented itself to my hand, a ripe, golden apple with a soft, cool, velvety skin – thus the world presented itself to me –

as if a tree nodded to me, a wide-branching, strong-willed tree, bent for reclining and as a footstool for the way-weary: thus the world stood upon my headland –

as if tender hands brought me a casket – a casket open for the delight of modest, adoring eyes: thus the world presented himself before me today –

not so enigmatic as to frighten away human love, not so explicit as to put to sleep human wisdom – a good, human thing was the world to me today, this world of which so many evil things are said!

How grateful I am to my morning dream, that today in the early morning I thus weighed the world! It came to me as a good, human thing, this dream and comforter of the heart!

And that I may do the same as it by day and learn and imitate its best aspects, I will now place the three most evil things upon the scales and weigh them well and humanly.

He who taught how to bless also taught how to curse: which are the three most-cursed things in the world? I will place these upon the scales.

Sensual pleasure, lust for power, selfishness: these three have hitherto been cursed the most and held in the worst and most unjust repute – these three will I weigh well and humanly.

Well then! Here is my headland and there is the sea: *it* rolls towards me, shaggy, fawning, the faithful old hundred-headed canine monster that I love.

Well then! Here I will hold the scales over the rolling sea: and I choose a witness, too, to look on – you, hermit tree, you heavy-odoured, broad-arched tree that I love!

Upon what bridge does the present go over to the hereafter? What compulsion compels the high to bend to the low? And what bids even the highest – to grow higher still?

Now the scales stand level and still: I have thrown in three weighty questions, the other scale bears three weighty answers.

2

Sensual pleasure: goad and stake to all hair-shirted despisers of the body and anathematized as 'the world' by all after-worldsmen: for it mocks and makes fools of all teachers of confusion and error.

Sensual pleasure: to the rabble the slow fire over which they are roasted; to all worm-eaten wood, to all stinking tatters, the ever-ready stewing-oven of lust.

Sensual pleasure: innocent and free to free hearts, the earth's garden-joy, an overflowing of thanks to the present from all the future.

Sensual pleasure: a sweet poison only to the withered, but to the lion-willed the great restorative and reverently-preserved wine of wines.

Sensual pleasure: the great symbolic happiness of a higher happiness and highest hope. For marriage is promised to many, and more than marriage –

to many that are stranger to one another than man and woman: and who has fully conceived *how strange* man and woman are to one another!

Sensual pleasure – but I will fence my thoughts round, and my words too: so that swine and hot fanatics shall not break into my garden!

Lust for power: the scourge of fire of the hardest-hearted; the cruel torment reserved by the cruellest for himself; the dark flame of living bonfires.

Lust for power: the wicked fly seated upon the vainest peoples; the mocker of all uncertain virtue; which rides upon every horse and every pride.

Lust for power: the earthquake that breaks and bursts open all that is decayed and hollow; the rolling, growling, punitive destroyer of whitewashed sepulches; the flashing question-mark beside premature answers.

Lust for power: before its glance man crawls and bends and toils and becomes lower than the swine or the snake – until at last the cry of the great contempt bursts from him –

Lust for power: the fearsome teacher of the great contempt, who preaches in the face of cities and empires 'Away with you!' – until at last they themselves cry out 'Away with *me*!'

Lust for power: which, however, rises enticingly even to the pure and the solitary and up to self-sufficient heights, glowing like a love that paints purple delights enticingly on earthly heavens.

Lust for power: but who shall call it *lust,* when the height longs to stoop down after power! Truly, there is no sickness and lust in such a longing and descent!

That the lonely height may not always be solitary and sufficient to itself; that the mountain may descend to the valley and the wind of the heights to the lowlands –

Oh who shall find the rightful baptismal and virtuous name for such a longing! 'Bestowing virtue' – that is the name Zarathustra once gave the unnameable.

And then it also happened – and truly, it happened for the first time! – that his teaching glorified *selfishness,* the sound, healthy selfishness that issues from a mighty soul –

from a mighty soul, to which pertains the exalted body, the beautiful, victorious, refreshing body, around which everything becomes a mirror;

the supple, persuasive body, the dancer whose image and epitome is the self-rejoicing soul. The self-rejoicing of such bodies and souls calls itself: 'Virtue'.

Such self-rejoicing protects itself with its doctrines of good and bad as with sacred groves; with the names it gives its happiness it banishes from itself all that is contemptible.

It banishes from itself all that is cowardly; it says: Bad – that is to say, cowardly! He who is always worrying, sighing, complaining, and who gleans even the smallest advantage, seems contemptible to it.

It also despises all woeful wisdom: for truly, there is also a wisdom that blossoms in darkness, a night-shade wisdom, which is always sighing: 'All is vain!'

Timid mistrustfulness seems base to it, as do all who desire oaths instead of looks and hands; and all-too-mistrustful wisdom, for such is the nature of cowardly souls.

It regards as baser yet him who is quick to please, who, dog-like, lies upon his back, the humble man; and there is also a wisdom that is humble and dog-like and pious and quick to please.

Entirely hateful and loathsome to it is he who will never defend himself, who swallows down poisonous spittle and evil looks, the too-patient man who puts up with everything, is content with everything: for that is the nature of slaves.

Whether one be servile before gods and divine kicks, or before men and the silly opinions of men: it spits at slaves of *all* kinds, this glorious selfishness!

Bad: that is what it calls all that is broken-down and niggardly-servile, unclear, blinking eyes, oppressed hearts, and that false, yielding type of man who kisses with broad, cowardly lips.

And sham-wisdom: that is what it calls all wit that slaves and old men and weary men affect; and especially the whole bad, raving, over-clever priest-foolishness!

And to ill-use selfishness – precisely *that* has been virtue and called virtue. And 'selfless' – that is what, with good reason, all these world-weary cowards and Cross-spiders wished to be!

But now the day, the transformation, the sword of judgement, *the great noontide* comes to them all: then many things shall be revealed!

And he who declares the Ego healthy and holy and selfishness glorious – truly, he, a prophet, declares too what he knows: '*Behold, it comes, it is near, the great noontide!*'

Thus spoke Zarathustra.

Of the Spirit of Gravity

1

My glib tongue – is of the people; I speak too coarsely and warmly for silky rabbits. And my words sound even stranger to all inky fish and scribbling foxes.

My hand – is a fool's hand: woe to all tables and walls and whatever has room left for fool's scribbling, fool's doodling!

My foot – is a horse's foot: with it I trot and trample up hill, down dale, hither and thither over the fields, and am the Devil's own for joy when I am out at a gallop.

My stomach – is it perhaps an eagle's stomach? For it likes lamb's flesh best of all. But it is certainly a bird's stomach.

Nourished with innocent and few things, ready and impatient to fly, to fly away – that is my nature now: how should there not be something of the bird's nature in it!

And especially bird-like is that I am enemy to the Spirit of Gravity: and truly, mortal enemy, arch-enemy, born enemy! Oh where has my enmity not flown and strayed already!

I could sing a song about that – and I *will* sing one, although I am alone in an empty house and have to sing it to my own ears.

There are other singers, to be sure, whose voices are softened, whose hands are eloquent, whose eyes are expressive, whose hearts are awakened, only when the house is full: I am not one of them.

2

He who will one day teach men to fly will have moved all boundary-stones; all boundary-stones will themselves fly into the air to him, he will baptize the earth anew – as 'the weightless'.

The ostrich runs faster than any horse, but even he sticks his head heavily into heavy earth: that is what the man who cannot yet fly is like.

He calls earth and life heavy: and so *will* the Spirit of Gravity have it! But he who wants to become light and a bird must love himself – thus do *I* teach.

Not with the love of the sick and diseased, to be sure: for with them even self-love stinks!

One must learn to love oneself with a sound and healthy love, so that one may endure it with oneself and not go roaming about – thus do I teach.

Such roaming about calls itself 'love of one's neighbour': these words have been up to now the best for lying and dissembling, and especially for those who were oppressive to everybody.

And truly, to *learn* to love oneself is no commandment for today or for tomorrow. Rather is this art the finest, subtlest, ultimate, and most patient of all.

For all his possessions are well concealed from the possessor; and of all treasure pits, one's own is the last to be digged – the Spirit of Gravity is the cause of that.

Almost in the cradle are we presented with heavy words and values: this dowry calls itself 'Good' and 'Evil'. For its sake we are forgiven for being alive.

And we suffer little children to come to us, to prevent them in good time from loving themselves: the Spirit of Gravity is the cause of that.

And we – we bear loyally what we have been given upon hard shoulders over rugged mountains! And when we sweat we are told: 'Yes, life is hard to bear!'

But only man is hard to bear! That is because he bears too many foreign things upon his shoulders. Like the camel, he kneels down and lets himself be well laden.

Especially the strong, weight-bearing man in whom dwell respect and awe: he has laden too many *foreign* heavy words and values upon himself – now life seems to him a desert!

And truly! Many things that are *one's own* are hard to bear, too! And much that is intrinsic in man is like the oyster, that is loathsome and slippery and hard to grasp –

so that a noble shell with noble embellishments must

intercede for it. But one has to learn this art as well: to *have* a shell and a fair appearance and a prudent blindness!

Again, it is deceptive about many things in man that many a shell is inferior and wretched and too much of a shell. Much hidden goodness and power is never guessed at; the most exquisite dainties find no tasters!

Women, or the most exquisite of them, know this: a little fatter, a little thinner – oh, how much fate lies in so little!

Man is difficult to discover, most of all to himself; the spirit often tells lies about the soul. The Spirit of Gravity is the cause of that.

But he has discovered himself who says: This is *my* good and evil: he has silenced thereby the mole and dwarf who says: 'Good for all, evil for all.'

Truly, I dislike also those who call everything good and this world the best of all. I call such people the all-contented.

All-contentedness that knows how to taste everything: that is not the best taste! I honour the obstinate, fastidious tongues and stomachs that have learned to say 'I' and 'Yes' and 'No'.

But to chew and digest everything – that is to have a really swinish nature! Always to say Ye-a[32] – only the ass and those like him have learned that.

Deep yellow and burning red: that is to *my* taste – it mixes blood with all colours. But he who whitewashes his house betrays to me a whitewashed soul.

One loves mummies, the other phantoms; and both alike enemy to all flesh and blood – oh, how both offend my taste! For I love blood.

And I do not want to stay and dwell where everyone spews and spits: that is now *my* taste – I would rather live among thieves and perjurers. No one bears gold in his mouth.

More offensive to me, however, are all lickspittles; and the most offensive beast of a man I ever found I baptized Parasite: it would not love, yet wanted to live by love.

I call wretched all who have only one choice: to become an evil beast or an evil tamer of beasts: I would build no tabernacles among these men.

I also call wretched those who always have to *wait* – they offend my taste: all tax-collectors and shopkeepers and kings and other keepers of lands and shops.

Truly, I too have learned to wait, I have learned it from the very heart, but only to wait for *myself*. And above all I have learned to stand and to walk and to run and to jump and to climb and to dance.

This, however, is my teaching: He who wants to learn to fly one day must first learn to stand and to walk and to run and to climb and to dance – you cannot learn to fly by flying!

With rope-ladders I learned to climb to many a window, with agile legs I climbed up high masts: to sit upon high masts of knowledge seemed to me no small happiness –

to flicker like little flames upon high masts: a little light, to be sure, but yet a great comfort to castaway sailors and the shipwrecked!

I came to my truth by diverse paths and in diverse ways: it was not upon a single ladder that I climbed to the height where my eyes survey my distances.

And I have asked the way only unwillingly – that has always offended my taste! I have rather questioned and attempted the ways themselves.

All my progress has been an attempting and a questioning – and truly, one has to *learn* how to answer such questioning! That however – is to my taste:

not good taste, not bad taste, but *my* taste, which I no longer conceal and of which I am no longer ashamed.

'This – is now *my* way: where is yours?' Thus I answered those who asked me 'the way'. For *the* way – does not exist!

Thus spoke Zarathustra.

Of Old and New Law-Tables

I

HERE I sit and wait, old shattered law-tables around me and also new, half-written law-tables. When will my hour come?

– the hour of my down-going, my descent: for I want to go to men once more.

For that I now wait: for first the sign that it is *my* hour must come to me – namely, the laughing lion with the flock of doves.

Meanwhile I talk to myself, as one who has plenty of time. No one tells me anything new; so I tell myself to myself.

2

When I visited men, I found them sitting upon an old self-conceit. Each one thought he had long since known what was good and evil for man.

All talk of virtue seemed to them an ancient wearied affair; and he who wished to sleep well spoke of 'good' and 'evil' before retiring.

I disturbed this somnolence when I taught that *nobody yet knows* what is good and evil – unless it be the creator!

But he it is who creates a goal for mankind and gives the earth its meaning and its future: he it is who *creates* the quality of good and evil in things.

And I bade them overturn their old professorial chairs, and wherever that old self-conceit had sat. I bade them laugh at their great masters of virtue and saints and poets and world-redeemers.

I bade them laugh at their gloomy sages, and whoever had sat as a black scarecrow, cautioning, on the tree of life.

I sat myself on their great grave-street, and even beside carrion and vultures – and I laughed over all their 'past' and its decayed expiring glory.

Truly, like Lenten preachers and fools did I cry anger and

shame over all their great and small things – their best is so very small! Their worst is so very small! – thus I laughed.

Thus from out of me cried and laughed my wise desire, which was born on the mountains, a wild wisdom, in truth! – my great desire with rushing wings.

And often it tore me forth and up and away and in the midst of laughter: and then indeed I flew, an arrow, quivering with sun-intoxicated rapture:

out into the distant future, which no dream has yet seen, into warmer Souths than artists have ever dreamed of, there where gods, dancing, are ashamed of all clothes –

so that I might speak in parables, and hobble and stutter like poets: and truly, I am ashamed that I still have to be a poet!

Where all becoming seemed to me the dancing of gods and the wantonness of gods, and the world unrestrained and abandoned and fleeing back to itself –

as many gods eternally fleeing and re-seeking one another, as many gods blissfully self-contradicting, communing again and belonging again to one another –

Where all time seemed to me a blissful mockery of moments, where necessity was freedom itself, which blissfully played with the goad of freedom –

Where I found again my old devil and arch-enemy, the Spirit of Gravity, and all that he created: compulsion, dogma, need and consequence and purpose and will and good and evil:

For must there not exist that which is danced *upon*, danced across? Must there not be moles and heavy dwarfs – for the sake of the nimble, the nimblest?

3

There it was too that I picked up the word 'Superman' and that man is something that must be overcome,

that man is a bridge and not a goal; counting himself happy for his noontides and evenings, as a way to new dawns:

Zarathustra's saying of the great noontide, and whatever

else I have hung up over men, like a purple evening afterglow.

Truly, I showed them new stars, together with new nights – and over cloud and day and night I spread out laughter like a coloured canopy.

I taught them all *my* art and aims: to compose into one and bring together what is fragment and riddle and dreadful chance in man –

as poet, reader of riddles, and redeemer of chance, I taught them to create the future, and to redeem by creating – all that *was past*.

To redeem that past of mankind and to transform every 'It was', until the will says: 'But I willed it thus! So shall I will it –'

this did I call redemption, this alone did I teach them to call redemption.

Now I await *my* redemption – that I may go to them for the last time.

For I want to go to man once more: I want to go under *among* them, I want to give them, dying, my richest gift!

From the sun when it goes down, that superabundant star, I learned this: then, from inexhaustible riches it pours out gold into the sea –

so that the poorest fisherman rows with *golden* oars! For once I saw this, and did not tire of weeping to see it.

Like the sun, Zarathustra also wants to go down: now he sits here and waits, old shattered law-tables around him and also new law-tables – half-written.

4

Behold, here is a new law-table: but where are my brothers, to bear it with me to the valley and to fleshly hearts?

Thus commands my great love for the most distant men: *Do not spare your neighbour!* Man is something that must be overcome.

There are diverse paths and ways to overcoming: just look to it! But only a buffoon thinks: 'Man can also be *jumped over*.'

Overcome yourself even in your neighbour: and a right that you can seize for yourself you should not accept as a gift!

What you do, no one can do to you. Behold, there is no requital.

He who cannot command himself should obey. And many a one *can* command himself but be very remiss in obeying what he commands!

5

This is the will of those of noble soul: they desire nothing *gratis,* least of all life.

He who is of the mob wants to live gratis; we others, however, to whom life has given itself – we are always considering what we can best give *in return*!

And truly, it is a noble speech that says: 'What life has promised *us, we* shall keep that promise – to life!'

One should not wish to enjoy where one has not given enjoyment. And – one should not *wish* to enjoy!

For enjoyment and innocence are the most modest things: neither want to be looked for. One should *have* them – but one should *look* rather for guilt and pain!

6

O my brothers, he who is a first-born is always sacrificed. Now we are first-born.

We all bleed at secret sacrificial tables, we all burn and roast to the honour of ancient idols.

Our best is still young: this excites old palates. Our flesh is tender, our skin is only a lamb-skin: – how should we not excite old idol-priests!

He still lives on *in us ourselves*, the old idol-priest, who roasts our best for his feast. Alas, my brothers, how should the first-born not be sacrifices!

But our kind will have it thus; and I love those who do not wish to preserve themselves. I love with my whole love those who go down and perish: for they are going beyond.

7

To be truthful – few *can* do it! And those who can, will not! Least of all, however, can the good be truthful.

Oh these good men! *Good men never tell the truth;* to be good in that way is a sickness of the spirit.

They yield, these good men, they acquiesce, their hearts imitate, they obey from the heart: but he who obeys *does not listen to himself!*

All that the good call evil must come together that one truth may be born: O my brothers, are you, too, evil enough for *this* truth?

The bold attempt, prolonged mistrust, the cruel No, satiety, the cutting into the living – how seldom do *these* come together! But from such seed is – truth raised.

Hitherto all *knowledge* has grown up *beside* the bad conscience! Shatter, you enlightened men, shatter the old law-tables!

8

When water is planked over so that it can be walked upon, when gangway and railings span the stream: truly, he is not believed who says: 'Everything is in flux.'[33]

On the contrary, even simpletons contradict him. 'What?' say the simpletons, 'everything in flux? But there are planks and railings *over* the stream!

'*Over* the stream everything is firmly fixed, all the values of things, the bridges, concepts, all "Good" and "Evil": all are *firmly fixed!*'

But when hard winter comes, the animal-tamer of streams, then even the cleverest learn mistrust; and truly, not only the simpletons say then: 'Is not everything meant to – stand still?'

'Fundamentally, everything stands still' – that is a proper winter doctrine, a fine thing for unfruitful seasons, a fine consolation for hibernators and stay at-homes.

'Fundamentally, everything stands still' – the thawing wind, however, preaches to the *contrary!*

The thawing wind, an ox that is no ploughing ox – a raging ox, a destroyer that breaks ice with its angry horns! Ice, however – *breaks gangways*!

O my brothers, is everything not *now in flux*? Have not all railings and gangways fallen into the water and come to nothing? Who can still *cling to* 'good' and 'evil'?

'Woe to us! Hail to us! The thawing wind is blowing!' – Preach thus, O my brothers, through every street!

9

There is an old delusion that is called good and evil. Up to now, this delusion has orbited about prophets and astrologers.

Once people *believed* in prophets and astrologers: and *therefore* people believed: 'Everything is fate: you shall, for you must!'

Then again people mistrusted all prophets and astrologers: and *therefore* people believed: 'Everything is freedom: you can, for you will!'

O my brothers, up to now there has been only supposition, not knowledge, concerning the stars and the future: and *therefore* there has hitherto been only supposition, not knowledge, concerning good and evil!

10

'You shall not steal! You shall not kill!' – such words were once called holy; in their presence people bowed their knees and their heads and removed their shoes.

But I ask you: Where have there ever been better thieves and killers in the world than such holy words have been?

Is there not in all life itself – stealing and killing? And when such words were called holy was not *truth* itself – killed?

Or was it a sermon of death that called holy that which contradicted and opposed all life? – O my brothers, shatter, shatter the old law-tables!

11

My pity for all that is past is that I see: It has been handed over –

handed over to the favour, the spirit, the madness of every generation that comes and transforms everything that has been into its own bridge!

A great despot could come, a shrewd devil, who with his favour and disfavour could compel and constrain all that is past, until it became his bridge and prognostic and herald and cock-crow.

This, however, is the other danger and my other pity: he who is of the mob remembers back to his grandfather – with his grandfather, however, time stops.

Thus all that is past is handed over: for the mob could one day become master, and all time be drowned in shallow waters.

Therefore, O my brothers, is a *new nobility* needed: to oppose all mob-rule and all despotism and to write anew upon new law-tables the word: 'Noble'.

For many noblemen are needed, and noblemen of many kinds, *for nobility to exist*! Or, as I once said in a parable: 'Precisely this is godliness, that there are gods but no God!'

12

O my brothers, I direct and consecrate you to a new nobility: you shall become begetters and cultivators and sowers of the future –

truly, not to a nobility that you could buy like shopkeepers with shopkeepers' gold: for all that has a price is of little value.

Let where you are going, not where you come from, henceforth be your honour! Your will and your foot that desires to step out beyond you – let them be your new honour!

Truly, not that you have served a prince – of what account are princes now! – or have become a bulwark to that which stands, that it may stand more firmly!

Not that your family have grown courtly at courts and you

have learned to stand for long hours in shallow pools, motley-coloured like a flamingo:

for *being able* to stand is a merit with courtiers; and all courtiers believe that part of the bliss after death is – *being allowed* to sit!

And not that a ghost, called holy, led your ancestors into promised lands that *I* do not praise: for in the land where the worst of all trees, the Cross, grew – there is nothing to praise! –

and truly, wherever this 'Holy Ghost' led its knights, goats and geese and Cross-eyed and wrong-headed fellows always – ran *at the head* of the procession!

O my brothers, your nobility shall not gaze backward, but *outward*! You shall be fugitives from all fatherlands and fore-fatherlands!

You shall love your *children's land*: let this love be your new nobility – the undiscovered land in the furthest sea! I bid your sails seek it and seek it!

You shall *make amends* to your children for being the children of your fathers: *thus* you shall redeem all that is past! This new law-table do I put over you!

13

'Wherefore live? All is vanity! To live – that means to thrash straw; to live – that means to burn oneself and yet not become warm.'

Ancient rigmarole like this still counts as 'wisdom'; and it is the more honoured *because* it is old and smells damp. Even mould ennobles.

Children might speak in this way: they *shrink* from the fire because it has burned them! There is much childishness in the old books of wisdom.

And how should he who is always 'thrashing straw' be allowed to slander thrashing! Such a fool would have to have his mouth stopped!

Such people sit down to dinner and bring nothing with them, not even a good appetite – and now they say slander-ously: 'All is vanity!'

But to eat and drink well, O my brothers, is truly no vain art! Shatter, shatter the law-tables of the never-joyful!

14

'To the pure all things are pure' – thus speaks the people. But I say to you: To the swine all things become swinish!

That is why the fanatics and hypocrites with bowed heads whose hearts too are bowed down preach: 'The world itself is a filthy monster.'

For they all have an unclean spirit; but especially those who have no peace or rest except they see the world *from behind* – these afterworldsmen!

I tell *these* to their faces, although it does not sound pleasant: The world resembles man in that it has a behind – *so much* is true!

There is much filth in the world: *so much* is true! But the world itself is not yet a filthy monster on that account!

There is wisdom in the fact that much in the world smells ill: disgust itself creates wings and water-divining powers!

Even in the best there is something to excite disgust; and even the best is something that must be overcome!

O my brothers, there is much wisdom in the fact that there is much filth in the world!

15

These sayings I heard pious afterworldsmen say to their consciences, and truly without deceit or falsehood, although there is nothing more false or deceitful in the world.

'Let the world be! Do not raise even a finger against it!'

'Let him who wants to slaughter and kill and harass and swindle the people: do not raise even a finger against it! Thus they will yet learn to renounce the world.'

'And your own reason – you shall yourself choke and throttle; for it is a reason of this world – thus you shall yourself learn to renounce the world.'

Shatter, O my brothers, shatter these ancient law-tables of

the pious! Shatter by your teachings the sayings of the world-calumniators!

16

'He who learns much, unlearns all violent desiring' – people whisper that to one another today in all dark streets.

'Wisdom makes weary, nothing is worth while; you shall not desire!' – I found this new law-table hanging even in public market-places.

Shatter, O my brothers, shatter this new law-table too! The world-weary and the preachers of death hung it up, and so did the jailers: for behold, it is also a sermon urging slavery:

They have learned badly and the best things not at all, they have learned everything too early and too fast: they have *eaten* badly – that is how they got that stomach-ache –

for their spirit is stomach-ache: *it* counsels death! For truly, my brothers, the spirit *is* a stomach!

Life is a fountain of delight: but all wells are poisoned for him from whom an aching stomach, the father of affliction, speaks.

To know: that is *delight* to the lion-willed! But he who has grown weary is only 'willed', he is the sport of every wave.

And that is always the nature of weak men: they lose themselves on their way. And at last their weariness asks: 'Why have we ever taken any way? It is a matter of indifference!'

It sounds pleasant to *their* ears when it is preached: 'Nothing is worth while! You shall not will!' This, however, is a sermon urging slavery.

O my brothers, Zarathustra comes as a fresh, blustering wind to all the way-weary; he will yet make many noses sneeze!

My liberal breath blows even through walls and into prisons and imprisoned spirits!

Willing liberates: for willing is creating: thus I teach. And you should learn *only* for creating!

And you should first *learn* from me even how to learn, how to learn well! – He who has ears to hear, let him hear!

17

There stands the boat – over there is perhaps the way to the great Nothingness. But who wants to step into this 'perhaps'?

None of you wants to step into the death-boat! How then could you be *world-weary*?

World-weary! And you have not yet even parted from the earth! I have always found you still greedy for the earth, still in love with your own weariness of the earth!

Your lip does not hang down in vain – a little earthly wish still sits upon it! And in your eye – does not a little cloud of unforgotten earthly joy swim there?

There are many excellent inventions on earth, some useful, some pleasant: the earth is to be loved for their sake.

And there are many things so well devised that they are like women's breasts: at the same time useful and pleasant.

But you world-weary people! You should be given a stroke of the cane! Your legs should be made sprightly again with cane-strokes!

For: if you are not invalids and worn-out wretches of whom the earth is weary, you are sly sluggards or dainty, sneaking lust-cats. And if you will not again *run about* merrily, you shall – pass away!

One should not want to be physician to the incurable: thus Zarathustra teaches: so you shall pass away!

But to make an end requires more *courage* than to make a new verse: all physicians and poets know that.

18

O my brothers, there are law-tables framed by weariness and law-tables framed by laziness, indolent laziness: although they speak similarly they want to be heard differently.

Look here at this languishing man! He is only an inch from his goal, but from weariness he has laid himself defiantly here in the dust: this valiant man!

He yawns from weariness at the path and the earth and the

goal and at himself: he refuses to take another step – this valiant man!

Now the sun burns down upon him and the dogs lick his sweat: but he lies there in his defiance and prefers to languish –

to languish an inch from his goal! Truly, he will have to be pulled into his heaven by the hair – this hero!

Better to leave him lying where he has laid himself, so that sleep, the comforter, may come to him with cooling, murmuring rain:

Let him lie until he awakes of his own accord, until of his own accord he disavows all weariness and what weariness has taught through him!

Only, my brothers, scare away the dogs from him, the indolent skulkers, and all the swarming vermin –

all the swarming 'cultured' vermin who feast upon the sweat of every hero!

19

I form circles and holy boundaries around myself; fewer and fewer climb with me upon higher and higher mountains: I build a mountain-range out of holier and holier mountains.

But wherever you would climb with me, O my brothers, see to it that no *parasite* climbs with you!

Parasite: that is a worm, a creeping, supple worm, that wants to grow fat on your sick, sore places.

And it is its art to divine the weary spots in climbing souls: it builds its loathsome nest in your grief and dejection, in your tender modesty.

Where the strong man is weak, where the noble man is too gentle, there it builds its loathsome nest: the parasite dwells where the great man possesses little sore places.

Which is the highest type of being and which the lowest? The parasite is the lowest type; but he who is of the highest type nourishes the most parasites.

For the soul which possesses the longest ladder and can descend the deepest: how should the most parasites not sit upon it?

the most spacious soul, which can run and stray and roam

the farthest into itself; the most necessary soul, which out of joy hurls itself into chance –

the existing soul which plunges into becoming; the possessing soul which *wants* to partake in desire and longing –

the soul fleeing from itself which retrieves itself in the widest sphere; the wisest soul, to which foolishness speaks sweetest –

the soul that loves itself the most, in which all things have their current and counter-current and ebb and flow: – oh how should *the highest soul* not possess the worst parasites?

20

O my brothers, am I then cruel? But I say: That which is falling should also be pushed!

Everything of today – it is falling, it is decaying: who would support it? But I – want to push it too!

Do you know the delight that rolls stones into precipitous depths? – These men of today: just see how they roll into my depths!

I am a prologue to better players, O my brothers! An example![34] Follow my example!

And him you do not teach to fly, teach – *to fall faster*!

21

I love the brave: but it is not enough to be a swordsman, one must also know *against* whom to be a swordsman!

And there is often more bravery in containing oneself and passing by: *in order* to spare oneself for a worthier enemy!

You should have enemies whom you hate but not enemies whom you despise: you must be proud of your enemy: thus I taught once before.

You should spare yourselves, O my friends, for a worthier enemy: therefore you must pass many things by,

especially must you pass by many of the rabble who din in your ears about people and peoples.

Keep your eye clear of their For and Against! There is much right, much wrong in it: whoever looks on grows angry.

To look in, to weigh in – that comes to the same thing in this case: therefore go off into the forests and lay your sword to sleep!

Go *your* ways! And let people and peoples go theirs! – dark ways, to be sure, on which not one hope lightens any longer!

Let the shopkeeper rule where everything that still glisters is – shopkeeper's gold! The age of kings is past: what today calls itself the people deserves no king.

Just see how these people themselves now behave like shopkeepers: they glean the smallest advantage from sweepings of every kind.

They lie in wait for one another, they wheedle things out of one another – they call that 'good neighbourliness'. Oh blessed, distant time when a people said to itself: 'I want to be – *master* over peoples!'

For, my brothers: the best shall rule, the best *wants* to rule! And where it is taught differently, there – the best is *lacking*.

22

If *they* – had bread for nothing, alas! – what would *they* cry for! Their maintenance – that is their proper entertainment;[35] and life shall be hard for them!

They are beasts of prey: even in their 'working' – there is robbery, even in their 'earning' – there is fraud! Therefore life shall be hard for them!

Thus they shall become finer beasts of prey, subtler, cleverer, *more man-like* beasts of prey: for man is the finest beast of prey.

Man has already robbed all beasts of their virtues: that is why, of all beasts, life is the hardest for man.

Only the birds are still beyond him. And if man should learn to fly, alas! *to what height* – would his rapaciousness fly!

23

This is how I would have man and woman: the one fit for war, the other fit for bearing children, but both fit for dancing with head and heels.

And let that day be lost to us on which we did not dance once! And let that wisdom be false to us that brought no laughter with it!

24

Your marriage-contracting: see it is not a bad *contracting*! You have decided too quickly: from that *follows* – break up of marriage.[36]

And yet rather break up of marriage than bending of marriage, lying in marriage! – A woman said to me: 'True, I broke up my marriage, but first my marriage – broke me up!'

I have always found the badly-paired to be the most revengeful: they make everybody suffer for the fact that they are no longer single.

For that reason I want honest people to say to one another: 'We love each other: let us *see to it* that we stay in love! Or shall our promise be a mistake?'[37]

'Allow us a term and a little marriage, to see if we are fit for the great marriage! It is a big thing always to be with another!'

Thus I counsel all honest people; and what would be my love for the Superman and for everything to come if I should counsel and speak otherwise!

To propagate yourselves not only forward but *upward* – may the garden of marriage assist you, O my brothers!

25

He who has grown wise concerning old origins, behold, he will at last seek new springs of the future and new origins.

O my brothers, it will not be long before *new peoples* shall arise and new springs rush down into new depths.

For the earthquake – that blocks many wells and causes much thirst – also brings to light inner powers and secret things.

The earthquake reveals new springs. In the earthquake of ancient peoples new springs break forth.

And around him who cries: 'Behold here a well for many who are thirsty, one heart for many who long, one will for many instruments' – around him assembles a *people*, that is to say: many experimenters.

Who can command, who can obey – *that is experimented here*! Alas, with what protracted searching and succeeding, and failing and learning and experimenting anew!

Human society: that is an experiment, so I teach – a long search:[38] it seeks, however, the commander! –

an experiment, O my brothers! And *not* a 'contract'! Shatter, shatter that expression of the soft-hearted and half-and-half!

26

O my brothers! With whom does the greatest danger for the whole human future lie? Is it not with the good and just? –

with those who say and feel in their hearts: 'We already know what is good and just, we possess it too; woe to those who are still searching for it!'

And whatever harm the wicked may do, the harm the good do is the most harmful harm!

And whatever harm the world-calumniators may do, the harm the good do is the most harmful harm.

O my brothers, someone who once looked into the heart of the good and just said: 'They are the Pharisees.' But he was not understood.

The good and just themselves could not understand him: their spirit is imprisoned in their good conscience. The stupidity of the good is unfathomably clever.

But it is the truth: the good *have* to be Pharisees – they have no choice!

The good *have* to crucify him who devises his own virtue! That *is* the truth!

But the second man to discover their country, the country, heart, and soil of the good and just, was he who asked: 'Whom do they hate the most?'

They hate the *creator* most: him who breaks the law-tables and the old values, the breaker – they call him the law-breaker.

For the good – *cannot* create: they are always the beginning of the end: –

they crucify him who writes new values on new law-tables, they sacrifice the future *to themselves* – they crucify the whole human future!

The good – have always been the beginning of the end.

27

O my brothers, have you understood this saying, too? And what I once said about the 'Ultimate Man'?

With whom does the greatest danger to the whole human future lie? Is it not with the good and just?

Shatter, shatter the good and just! – O my brothers, have you understood this saying, too?

28

Do you flee from me? Are you frightened? Do you tremble at this saying?

O my brothers, when I bade you shatter the good and the law-tables of the good, only then did I embark mankind upon its high seas.

And only now does the great terror, the great prospect, the great sickness, the great disgust, the great sea-sickness come to it.

The good taught you false shores and false securities; you were born and kept in the lies of the good. Everything has been distorted and twisted down to its very bottom through the good.

But he who discovered the country of 'Man', also discovered the country of 'Human Future'. Now you shall be seafarers, brave, patient seafarers!

Stand up straight in good time, O my brothers, learn to stand up straight! The sea is stormy: many want to straighten themselves again by your aid.

The sea is stormy: everything is at sea. Well then! Come on, you old seaman-hearts!

What of fatherland! Our helm wants to fare *away*, out to

where our *children's land* is! Out, away, more stormy than the sea, storms our great longing!

29

'Why so hard?' the charcoal once said to the diamond; 'for are we not close relations?'

Why so soft? O my brothers, thus *I* ask you: for are you not – my brothers?

Why so soft, so unresisting and yielding? Why is there so much denial and abnegation in your hearts? So little fate in your glances?

And if you will not be fates, if you will not be inexorable: how can you – conquer with me?

And if your hardness will not flash and cut and cut to pieces: how can you one day – create with me?

For creators are hard. And it must seem bliss to you to press your hand upon millennia as upon wax,

bliss to write upon the will of millennia as upon metal – harder than metal, nobler than metal. Only the noblest is perfectly hard.

This new law-table do I put over you, O my brothers: *Become hard!*

30

O my Will! My essential, *my* necessity, dispeller of need! Preserve me from all petty victories!

O my soul's predestination, which I call destiny! In-me! Over-me! Preserve and spare me for a great destiny!

And your last greatness, my Will, save for your last – that you may be inexorable *in* your victory! Ah, who has not succumbed to his own victory!

Ah, whose eye has not dimmed in this intoxicated twilight! Ah, whose foot has not stumbled and in victory forgotten – how to stand!

That I may one day be ready and ripe in the great noontide: ready and ripe like glowing ore, like cloud heavy with lightning and like swelling milk-udder –

ready for myself and my most secret Will: a bow eager for its arrow, an arrow eager for its star –

a star, ready and ripe in its noontide, glowing, transpierced, blissful through annihilating sun-arrows –

a sun itself and an inexorable sun-will, ready for annihilation in victory!

O Will, my essential, *my* necessity, dispeller of need! Spare me for one great victory!

Thus spoke Zarathustra.

The Convalescent

I

ONE morning, not long after his return to the cave, Zarathustra sprang up from his bed like a madman, cried with a terrible voice, and behaved as if someone else were lying on the bed and would not rise from it; and Zarathustra's voice rang out in such a way that his animals came to him in terror and from all the caves and hiding-places in the neighbourhood of Zarathustra's cave all the creatures slipped away, flying, fluttering, creeping, jumping, according to the kind of foot or wing each had been given. Zarathustra, however, spoke these words:

Up, abysmal thought, up from my depths! I am your cockerel and dawn, sleepy worm: up! up! My voice shall soon crow you awake!

Loosen the fetters of your ears: listen! For I want to hear you! Up! Up! Here is thunder enough to make even the graves listen!

And wipe the sleep and all the dimness and blindness from your eyes! Hear me with your eyes, too: my voice is a medicine even for those born blind.

And once you are awake you shall stay awake for ever. It is not *my* way to awaken great-grandmothers from sleep in order to bid them – go back to sleep![39]

Are you moving, stretching, rattling? Up! Up! You shall

not rattle, you shall – speak to me! Zarathustra the Godless calls you!

I, Zarathustra, the advocate of life, the advocate of suffering, the advocate of the circle – I call you, my most abysmal thought!

Ah! you are coming – I hear you! My abyss *speaks*, I have turned my ultimate depth into the light!

Ah! Come here! Give me your hand – ha! don't! Ha, ha! – Disgust, disgust, disgust – woe is me!

2

Hardly had Zarathustra spoken these words, however, when he fell down like a dead man and remained like a dead man for a long time. But when he again came to himself, he was pale and trembling and remained lying down and for a long time would neither eat nor drink. This condition lasted seven days; his animals, however, did not leave him by day or night, except that the eagle flew off to fetch food. And whatever he had collected and fetched he laid upon Zarathustra's bed: so that at last Zarathustra lay among yellow and red berries, grapes, rosy apples, sweet-smelling herbs and pinecones. At his feet, however, two lambs were spread, which the eagle had, with difficulty, carried off from their shepherd.

At last, after seven days, Zarathustra raised himself in his bed, took a rosy apple in his hand, smelt it, and found its odour pleasant. Then his animals thought the time had come to speak with him.

'O Zarathustra,' they said, 'now you have lain like that seven days, with heavy eyes: will you not now get to your feet again?

'Step out of your cave: the world awaits you like a garden. The wind is laden with heavy fragrance that longs for you; and all the brooks would like to run after you.

'All things long for you, since you have been alone seven days – step out of your cave! All things want to be your physicians!

'Has perhaps a new knowledge come to you, a bitter, oppressive knowledge? You have lain like leavened dough, your soul has risen and overflowed its brim.'

'O my animals,' answered Zarathustra, 'go on talking and let me listen! Your talking is such refreshment: where there is talking, the world is like a garden to me. How sweet it is, that words and sounds of music exist: are words and music not rainbows and seeming bridges between things eternally separated?

'Every soul is a world of its own; for every soul every other soul is an afterworld.

'Appearance lies most beautifully among the most alike; for the smallest gap is the most difficult to bridge.

'For me – how could there be an outside-of-me? There is no outside! But we forget that, when we hear music; how sweet it is, that we forget!

'Are things not given names and musical sounds, so that man may refresh himself with things? Speech is a beautiful foolery: with it man dances over all things.

'How sweet is all speech and all the falsehoods of music! With music does our love dance upon many-coloured rainbows.'

'O Zarathustra,' said the animals then, 'all things themselves dance for such as think as we: they come and offer their hand and laugh and flee – and return.

'Everything goes, everything returns; the wheel of existence rolls for ever. Everything dies, everything blossoms anew; the year of existence runs on for ever.

'Everything breaks, everything is joined anew; the same house of existence builds itself for ever. Everything departs, everything meets again; the ring of existence is true to itself for ever.

'Existence begins in every instant; the ball There rolls around every Here. The middle is everywhere. The path of eternity is crooked.'

'O you buffoons and barrel-organs!' answered Zarathustra and smiled again; 'how well you know what had to be fulfilled in seven days:

'and how that monster crept into my throat and choked me! But I bit its head off and spat it away.

'And you – have already made a hurdy-gurdy song of it? I, however, lie here now, still weary from this biting and spitting away, still sick with my own redemption.

'*And you looked on at it all?* O my animals, are you, too, cruel? Did you desire to be spectators of my great pain, as men do? For man is the cruellest animal.

'More than anything on earth he enjoys tragedies, bull-fights, and crucifixions; and when he invented Hell for himself, behold, it was his heaven on earth.

'When the great man cries out, straightway the little man comes running; his tongue is hanging from his mouth with lasciviousness. He, however, calls it his "pity".

'The little man, especially the poet – how zealously he accuses life in words! Listen to it, but do not overlook the delight that is in all accusation!

'Such accusers of life: life overcomes them with a glance of its eye. "Do you love me?" it says impudently; "just wait a little, I have no time for you yet."

'Man is the cruellest animal towards himself; and with all who call themselves "sinners" and "bearers of the Cross" and "penitents" do not overlook the sensual pleasure that is in this complaint and accusation!

'And I myself – do I want to be the accuser of man? Ah, my animals, this alone have I learned, that the wickedest in man is necessary for the best in him,

'that all that is most wicked in him is his best *strength* and the hardest stone for the highest creator; and that man must grow better *and* wickeder:

'To know: Man is wicked; *that* was to be tied to no torture-stake – but I cried as no one had cried before:

'"Alas, that his wickedest is so very small! Alas, that his best is so very small!"

'The great disgust at man – *it* choked me and had crept into my throat: and what the prophet prophesied: "It is all one, nothing is worth while, knowledge chokes."

'A long twilight limps in front of me, a mortally-weary, death-intoxicated sadness which speaks with a yawn.

'"The man of whom you are weary, the little man, recurs eternally" – thus my sadness yawned and dragged its feet and could not fall asleep.

'The human earth became to me a cave, its chest caved in, everything living became to me human decay and bones and mouldering past.

'My sighs sat upon all the graves of man and could no longer rise; my sighs and questions croaked and choked and gnawed and wailed by day and night:

'"Alas, man recurs eternally! The little man recurs eternally!"

'I had seen them both naked, the greatest man and the smallest man: all too similar to one another, even the greatest all too human!

'The greatest all too small! – that was my disgust at man! And eternal recurrence even for the smallest! that was my disgust at all existence!

'Ah, disgust! Disgust! Disgust!' Thus spoke Zarathustra and sighed and shuddered; for he remembered his sickness. But his animals would not let him speak further.

'Speak no further, convalescent!' – thus his animals answered him, 'but go out to where the world awaits you like a garden.

'Go out to the roses and bees and flocks of doves! But go out especially to the song-birds, so that you may learn *singing* from them!

'For convalescents should sing; let the healthy talk. And when the healthy man, too, desires song, he desires other songs than the convalescent.'

'O you buffoons and barrel-organs, do be quiet!' answered Zarathustra and smiled at his animals. 'How well you know what comfort I devised for myself in seven days!

'That I have to sing again – *that* comfort and *this* convalescence did I devise for myself: do you want to make another hurdy-gurdy song out of that, too?'

'Speak no further,' his animals answered once more; 'rather first prepare yourself a lyre, convalescent, a new lyre!

'For behold, O Zarathustra! New lyres are needed for your new songs.

'Sing and bubble over, O Zarathustra, heal your soul with new songs, so that you may bear your great destiny, that was never yet the destiny of any man!

'For your animals well know, O Zarathustra, who you are and must become: behold, *you are the teacher of the eternal recurrence*, that is now *your* destiny!

'That you have to be the first to teach this doctrine – how should this great destiny not also be your greatest danger and sickness!

'Behold, we know what you teach: that all things recur eternally and we ourselves with them, and that we have already existed an infinite number of times before and all things with us.

'You teach that there is a great year of becoming, a colossus of a year: this year must, like an hour-glass, turn itself over again and again, so that it may run down and run out anew:

'so that all these years resemble one another, in the greatest things and in the smallest, so that we ourselves resemble ourselves in each great year, in the greatest things and in the smallest.

'And if you should die now, O Zarathustra: behold, we know too what you would then say to yourself – but your animals ask you not to die yet!

'You would say – and without trembling, but rather gasping for happiness: for a great weight and oppression would have been lifted from you, most patient of men!

'"Now I die and decay," you would say, "and in an instant I shall be nothingness. Souls are as mortal as bodies.

'"But the complex of causes in which I am entangled will recur – it will create me again! I myself am part of these causes of the eternal recurrence.

'"I shall return, with this sun, with this earth, with this eagle, with this serpent – *not* to a new life or a better life or a similar life:

'"I shall return eternally to this identical and self-same life, in the greatest things and in the smallest, to teach once more the eternal recurrence of all things,

'"to speak once more the teaching of the great noontide of earth and man, to tell man of the Superman once more.

'"I spoke my teaching, I broke upon my teaching: thus my eternal fate will have it – as prophet do I perish!

'"Now the hour has come when he who is going down shall bless himself. Thus – *ends* Zarathustra's down-going."'

When the animals had spoken these words they fell silent and expected that Zarathustra would say something to them: but Zarathustra did not hear that they were silent. On the contrary, he lay still with closed eyes like a sleeper, although he was not asleep: for he was conversing with his soul. The serpent and the eagle, however, when they found him thus silent, respected the great stillness around him and discreetly withdrew.

Of the Great Longing

O MY soul, I taught you to say 'today' as well as 'once' and 'formerly' and to dance your dance over every Here and There and Over-there.

O my soul, I rescued you from all corners, I brushed dust, spiders, and twilight away from you.

O my soul, I washed the petty shame and corner-virtue away from you and persuaded you to stand naked before the eyes of the sun.

With the storm which is called 'spirit' I blew across your surging sea; I blew all clouds away, I killed even that killer-bird[40] called 'sin'.

O my soul, I gave you the right to say No like the storm and to say Yes as the open sky says Yes: now, silent as light you stand, and you pass through denying storms.

O my soul, I gave you back freedom over created and un-created things: and who knows as you know the delight of things to come?

O my soul, I taught you contempt that comes not as the

gnawing of a worm, the great, the loving contempt which loves most where it despises most.

O my soul, I taught you so to persuade that you persuade the elements themselves to come to you: like the sun that persuades the sea to rise even to its height.

O my soul, I took from you all obeying, knee-bending, and obsequiousness; I myself gave you the names 'Dispeller of Care' and 'Destiny'.

O my soul, I gave you new names and many-coloured toys, I called you 'destiny' and 'encompassment of encompassments' and 'time's umbilical cord' and 'azure bell'.

O my soul, I gave your soil all wisdom to drink, all new wines and also all immemorially ancient strong wines of wisdom.

O my soul, I poured every sun and every night and every silence and every longing upon you: – then you grew up for me like a vine.

O my soul, now you stand superabundant and heavy, a vine with swelling udders and close-crowded golden-brown wine-grapes:

oppressed and weighed down by your happiness, expectant from abundance and yet bashful because of your expectancy.

O my soul, now there is nowhere a soul more loving and encompassing and spacious! Where could future and past be closer together than with you?

O my soul, I have given you everything and my hands have become empty through you: and now! now you ask me smiling and full of melancholy: 'Which of us owes thanks?

'does the giver not owe thanks to the receiver for receiving? Is giving not a necessity? Is taking not – compassion?'

O my soul, I understand the smile of your melancholy: your superabundance itself now stretches out longing hands!

Your fullness looks out over raging seas and searches and waits; the longing of over-fullness gazes out of the smiling heaven of your eyes!

And truly, O my soul! Who could behold your smile and not dissolve into tears? The angels themselves dissolve into tears through the over-kindness of your smile.

It is your kindness and over-kindness that wishes not to complain and weep: and yet your smile longs for tears, O my soul, and your trembling mouth for sobs.

'Is all weeping not a complaining? And all complaining not an accusing?' Thus you speak to yourself, and because of that, O my soul, you will rather smile than pour forth your sorrow,

pour forth in gushing tears all your sorrow at your fullness and at all the desire of the vine for the vintager and the vine-knife!

But if you will not weep nor alleviate in weeping your purple melancholy, you will have to *sing*, O my soul! Behold, I smile myself, who foretold you this:

to sing with an impetuous song, until all seas grow still to listen to your longing,

until, over still, longing seas, the boat glides, the golden marvel around whose gold all good, bad, marvellous things leap:

and many great and small beasts also, and everything that has light, marvellous feet that can run upon violet paths,

towards the golden marvel, the boat of free will, and to its master: he, however, is the vintager who waits with diamond-studded vine-knife,

your great redeemer, O my soul, the nameless one for whom only future songs will find a name! And truly, your breath is already fragrant with future songs,

already you glow and dream, already you drink thirstily from all deep, resounding wells of comfort, already your melancholy reposes in the bliss of future songs!

O my soul, now I have given you everything and even the last thing I had to give, and my hands have become empty through you: – *that I bade you sing,* behold, that was the last thing I had to give!

That I bade you sing, now say, say: *Which* of us now – owes thanks? But better still: sing for me, sing, O my soul! And let me pay thanks!

Thus spoke Zarathustra.

The Second Dance Song

I

LATELY I gazed into your eyes, O Life: I saw gold glittering in your eyes of night – my heart stood still with delight:

I saw a golden bark glittering upon dark waters, a submerging, surging, re-emerging golden tossing bark!

At my feet, my dancing-mad feet, you threw a glance, a laughing, questioning, melting tossing glance:

Twice only did you raise your castanets in your little hands – then my feet were already tossing in a mad dance.

My heels raised themselves, my toes listened for what you should propose: for the dancer wears his ears – in his toes!

I sprang to your side: then you fled back from my spring; towards me the tongues of your fleeing, flying hair came hissing!

Away from you and from your serpents did I retire: then at once you stood, half turned, your eyes full of desire.

With your crooked smile – you teach me crooked ways, upon crooked ways my feet learn – guile!

I fear you when you are near, I love you when you are far; your fleeing allures me, your seeking secures me: I suffer, but for you what would I not gladly endure!

For you whose coldness inflames, whose hatred seduces, whose flight constrains, whose mockery – induces:

who would not hate you, great woman who binds us, enwinds us, seduces us, seeks us, finds us! Who would not love you, you innocent, impatient, wind-swift, child-eyed sinner!

Where now do you take me, you unruly paragon? And again you forsake me, you sweet, ungrateful tomboy!

I dance after you, I follow you even when only the slightest traces of you linger. Where are you? Give me your hand! Or just a finger!

Here are caves and thickets: we shall go astray! Stop! Stand still! Do you not see owls and bats flitting away?

Would you befool me? You bat! You owl! Where are we? Did you learn from the dogs thus to bark and howl?

Your little white teeth you sweetly bare at me, from under your curly little mane your wicked eyes stare at me!

This is a dance over dale and hill: I am the hunter – will you be my hound or will you be my kill?

Now beside me! And quickly, you wicked rover! Now spring up! And across! – Help! In springing I myself have gone over!

Oh see me lying, you wanton companion, and begging for grace! I long to follow you in – a sweeter chase! –

love's chase through flowery bushes, still and dim! Or there beside the lake, where goldfishes dance and swim!

Are you now weary? There yonder are sheep and evening: let us end our pursuit: is it not sweet to sleep when the shepherd plays his flute?

Are you so very weary? I will carry you there, just let your arms sink! And if you are thirsty – I should have something, but you would not like it to drink! –

Oh this accursed, nimble, supple snake and slippery witch! Where have you gone? But on my face I feel from your hand two spots and blotches itch!

I am truly weary of being your shepherd, always sheepish and meek! You witch, if I have hitherto sung for you, now for me *you* shall – shriek!

To the rhythm of my whip you shall shriek and trot! Did I forget my whip? – I did not!

2

Then Life answered me thus, keeping her gentle ears closed:

'O Zarathustra! Do not crack your whip so terribly! You surely know: noise kills thought – and now such tender thoughts are coming to me.

'We are both proper ne'er-do-wells and ne'er-do-ills. Beyond good and evil did we discover our island and our green meadow – we two alone! Therefore we must love one another!

'And even if we do not love one another from the very

heart, do people have to dislike one another if they do not love one another from the very heart?

'And that I love you and often love you too well, that I know: and the reason is that I am jealous of your Wisdom. Ah, this crazy old fool, Wisdom!

'If your Wisdom should one day desert you, alas! then my love would quickly desert you too.'

Thereupon, Life gazed thoughtfully behind her and around her and said gently: 'O Zarathustra, you are not faithful enough to me!

'You do not love me nearly as much as you say; I know you are thinking of leaving me soon.

'There is an old, heavy, heavy booming bell: it booms out at night up to your cave:

'when you hear this bell beat the hour at midnight, then you think between one and twelve –

'you think, O Zarathustra, I know it, you think of leaving me soon!'

'Yes,' I answered hesitatingly, 'but you also know....' And I said something into her ear, in the midst of her tangled, yellow, foolish locks.

'You *know* that, O Zarathustra? No one knows that.'

And we gazed at one another and looked out at the green meadow, over which the cool evening was spreading, and wept together. But then Life was dearer to me than all my Wisdom had ever been.

Thus spoke Zarathustra.

3

One!
O Man! Attend!
Two!
What does deep midnight's voice contend?
Three!
'I slept my sleep,
Four!
'And now awake at dreaming's end:

243

Five!

'The world is deep,

Six!

'Deeper than day can comprehend.

Seven!

'Deep is its woe,

Eight!

' Joy – deeper than heart's agony:

Nine!

'Woe says: Fade! Go!

Ten!

'But all joy wants eternity,

Eleven!

' – wants deep, deep, deep eternity!'

Twelve!

The Seven Seals

(or: The Song of Yes and Amen)

I

IF I be a prophet and full of that prophetic spirit that wanders on high ridges between two seas,

wanders between past and future like a heavy cloud, enemy to sultry lowlands and to all that is weary and can neither die nor live:

ready for lightning in its dark bosom and for redeeming beams of light, pregnant with lightnings which affirm Yes! laugh Yes! ready for prophetic lightning-flashes:

but blessed is he who is thus pregnant! And, in truth, he who wants to kindle the light of the future must hang long over the mountains like a heavy storm!

Oh how should I not lust for eternity and for the wedding ring of rings – the Ring of Recurrence!

Never yet did I find the woman by whom I wanted children,

unless it be this woman, whom I love: for I love you, O Eternity!

For I love you, O Eternity!

2

If ever my anger broke graves open, moved boundary-stones, and rolled old shattered law-tables into deep chasms:

if ever my mockery blew away mouldered words, and if I came like a broom to the Cross-spiders and as a scouring wind to old sepulchres:

if ever I sat rejoicing where old gods lay buried, world-blessing, world-loving, beside the monuments of old world-slanderers:

for I love even churches and the graves of gods, if only heaven is looking, pure-eyed, through their shattered roofs; I like to sit like grass and red poppies on shattered churches:

Oh how should I not lust for eternity and for the wedding ring of rings – the Ring of Recurrence!

Never yet did I find the woman by whom I wanted children, unless it be this woman, whom I love: for I love you, O Eternity!

For I love you, O Eternity!

3

If ever a breath of the creative breath has come to me, and a breath of that heavenly necessity that compels even chance to dance in star-rounds:

if ever I have laughed with the laugh of the creative lightning, which the thunder of the deed, grumbling but obedient, follows:

if ever I have played dice with the gods at their table, the earth, so that the earth trembled and broke open and streams of fire snorted forth:

for the earth is a table of the gods, and trembling with creative new words and the dice throws of the gods:

Oh how should I not lust for eternity and for the wedding ring of rings – the Ring of Recurrence!

Never yet did I find the woman by whom I wanted children, unless it be this woman, whom I love: for I love you, O Eternity!

For I love you, O Eternity!

4

If ever I have drunk a full draught from that foaming mixing-bowl of spice, in which all things are well compounded:

if ever my hand has welded the furthest to the nearest, and fire to spirit and joy to sorrow and the wickedest to the kindest:

if I myself am a grain of that redeeming salt that makes everything mix well together in the bowl:

for there is a salt that unites good with evil; and even the most evil is worthy to be a spice and a last over-foaming:

Oh how should I not lust for eternity and for the wedding ring of rings – the Ring of Recurrence!

Never yet did I find the woman by whom I wanted children, unless it be this woman, whom I love: for I love you, O Eternity!

For I love you, O Eternity!

5

If I love the sea and all that is sealike, and love it most when it angrily contradicts me:

if that delight in seeking that drives sails towards the undiscovered is in me, if a seafarer's delight is in my delight:

if ever my rejoicing has cried: 'The shore has disappeared – now the last fetter falls from me,

'the boundless roars around me, far out glitter space and time, well then, come on! old heart!'

Oh how should I not lust for eternity and for the wedding ring of rings – the Ring of Recurrence!

Never yet did I find the woman by whom I wanted children, unless it be this woman, whom I love: for I love you, O Eternity!

For I love you, O Eternity!

6

If my virtue is a dancer's virtue, and if I often leap with both feet in golden-emerald rapture:

if my wickedness is a laughing wickedness, at home among rose bowers and hedges of lilies:

for in laughter all evil is present, but sanctified and absolved through its own happiness:

and if it be my Alpha and Omega that everything heavy shall become light, every body a dancer, all spirit a bird: and, truly, that is my Alpha and Omega!

Oh how should I not lust for eternity and for the wedding ring of rings – the Ring of Recurrence!

Never yet did I find the woman by whom I wanted children, unless it be this woman, whom I love: for I love you, O Eternity!

For I love you, O Eternity!

7

If ever I spread out a still sky above myself and flew with my own wings into my own sky:

if, playing, I have swum into deep light-distances and bird-wisdom came to my freedom:

but thus speaks bird-wisdom: 'Behold, there is no above, no below! Fling yourself about, out, back, weightless bird! Sing! speak no more!

'are not all words made for the heavy? Do not all words lie to the light? Sing! speak no more!'

Oh how should I not lust for eternity and for the wedding ring of rings – the Ring of Recurrence!

Never yet did I find the woman by whom I wanted children, unless it be this woman, whom I love: for I love you, O Eternity!

For I love you, O Eternity!

PART FOUR

❋

Alas, where in the world have there been greater follies than with the compassionate? And what in the world has caused more suffering than the follies of the compassionate?

Woe to all lovers who cannot surmount pity!

Thus spoke the Devil to me once: Even God has his Hell: it is his love for man.

And I lately heard him say these words: God is dead; God has died of his pity for man.

ZARATHUSTRA:
'*Of the Compassionate*'

The Honey Offering

AND again months and years passed over Zarathustra's soul, and he did not heed it; his hair, however, grew white. One day, as he was sitting upon a stone before his cave and gazing silently out – but the outlook there is of the sea and tortuous abysses – his animals went thoughtfully around him and at last placed themselves in front of him.

'O Zarathustra,' they said, 'are you perhaps looking out for your happiness?' – 'Of what account is happiness?' he answered. 'For long I have not aspired after happiness, I aspire after my work.' 'O Zarathustra,' said the animals then, 'you say that as one who has too many good things. Do you not lie in a sky-blue lake of happiness?' 'You buffoons,' answered Zarathustra and smiled, 'how well you chose that image! But you know too that my happiness is heavy and not like a liquid wave: it oppresses me and will not leave me, and behaves like molten pitch.'

Then his animals again went thoughtfully around him and placed themselves once more in front of him. 'O Zarathustra,' they said, 'is *that* why you yourself are growing ever darker and more sallow, although your hair looks white and flaxen? Behold, you are sitting in your pitch!' 'What are you saying, my animals?' said Zarathustra laughing. 'Truly, I spoke slander when I spoke of pitch. What is happening to me happens to all fruits that grow ripe. It is the *honey* in my veins that makes my blood thicker, and my soul quieter.' 'It will be so, O Zarathustra,' answered the animals and pressed towards him; 'but would you not like to climb a high mountain today? The air is clear, and today one can see more of the world than ever.' 'Yes, my animals,' he answered, 'your advice is admirable and after my own inclination: today I will climb a high mountain! But take care that I have honey ready to hand there, yellow, white, fine, ice-cool golden honey in the comb. For I intend to offer the honey offering.'

But when Zarathustra had reached the summit he sent home the animals which had accompanied him, and found that he was now alone: then he laughed with his whole heart, looked around him and spoke thus:

That I spoke of offerings and honey offerings was merely a ruse and, truly, a useful piece of folly! Up here I can speak more freely than before hermits' caves and hermits' pets.

Offer – what? I squander what is given me, I, a squanderer with a thousand hands: how could I call that – an offering!

And when I desired honey, I desired only bait and sweet syrup and gum, which even grumbling bears and strange, sullen, wicked birds are greedy for:

the finest bait, such as huntsmen and fishermen need. For although the world is like a dark animal-jungle and a pleasure-ground for all wild huntsmen, it seems to me to be rather and preferably an unfathomable, rich sea,

a sea full of many-coloured fishes and crabs for which even the gods might long and become fishers and casters of nets: so rich is the world in strange things, great and small!

Especially the human world, the human sea: now I cast my golden fishing-rod into *it* and say: Open up, human abyss!

Open up and throw me your fishes and glistening crabs! With my finest bait shall I bait today the strangest human fish!

My happiness itself shall I cast far and wide, between sunrise, noontide, and sunset, to see if many human fishes will not learn to kick and tug at my happiness,

until they, biting on my sharp, hidden hooks, have to come up to *my* height, the most multicoloured groundlings of the abyss to the most wicked of all fishers of men.

For I am *he*, from the heart and from the beginning, drawing, drawing towards me, drawing up to me, raising up, a drawer, trainer, and taskmaker who once bade himself, and not in vain: 'Become what you are!'

Thus men may now come *up* to me: for I am still waiting for the signs that it is time for my descent; as yet I do not myself go down, as I must, among men.

Therefore I wait here, cunning and scornful upon high mountains, not impatient, not patient, on the contrary one who has unlearned even patience, because he no longer 'suffers in patience'.[41]

For my destiny is allowing me time: has it forgotten me? Or is it sitting in the shadows behind a great stone catching flies?

And truly, I am grateful to my eternal destiny for not hunting and harrying me and for allowing me time for buffooneries and mischief: so that today I have climbed this high mountain to catch fish.

Has a man ever caught fish on a high mountain? And if what I want and do up here is a stupidity, better to do it than to become solemn and green and sallow by waiting down there,

to become by waiting a pompous snorter of wrath, a holy howling storm from the mountains, an impatient man crying down into the valleys: 'Listen, or I shall lash you with the scourge of God!'

Not that I should be angry with such wrathful men on that account! They are good enough for a laugh! How impatient they must be, these great alarm-drums that must find a voice today or never!

But I and my destiny – we do not speak to Today, neither do we speak to the Never: we have patience and time and more than time. For it must come one day and may not pass by.

What must come one day and may not pass by? Our great Hazar, our great, far-off empire of man, the thousand-year empire of Zarathustra.

How far off may that 'far off' be? What do I care! But I am not less certain of it on that account – I stand securely with both feet upon this foundation,

upon this eternal foundation, upon hard, primordial rock, upon this highest, hardest primordial hill to which all the winds come as to the dividing-place of storms, asking Where? and Whence? and Whither?

Here laugh, laugh my bright and wholesome wickedness! Down from high mountains cast your glistening, mocking laughter. With your glistening bait for me the fairest human fish!

And what belongs to *me* in all seas, my in-and-for-me in all things – fish *it* out for me, bring *it* here to me: I wait for it, I the wickedest of all fishermen.

Away, away my hook! In, down, bait for my happiness! Drop down your sweetest dew, honey of my heart! Bite, my hook, into the belly of all black affliction!

Gaze out, gaze out, my eye! Oh how many seas round about me, what dawning human futures! And above me – what rosy stillness! What cloudless silence!

The Cry of Distress

THE following day Zarathustra was again sitting upon the stone before his cave while the animals were roving about in the world outside fetching fresh food – and fresh honey, too: for Zarathustra had consumed and squandered the old honey to the last drop. But as he was sitting there with a stick in his hand, tracing the shadow of his figure in the ground, thinking (and truly!) not about himself and his shadow – all at once he started back in alarm: for he saw another shadow beside his own. And as he quickly rose and looked around, behold, there stood beside him the prophet, the same that had once eaten and drunk at his table, the prophet of the great weariness who taught: 'It is all one, nothing is worth while, the world is without meaning, knowledge chokes.' But his face had changed in the interim; and when Zarathustra looked into the prophet's eyes, his heart was again startled: so many evil prophecies and ashen lightning-flashes passed across this face!

The prophet, who had perceived what was going on in Zarathustra's soul, wiped his hand over his face, as if he wanted to wipe it away; Zarathustra did the same. And when each had silently composed and reassured himself, they shook hands as a sign that they wanted to recognize one another.

'Welcome to you,' said Zarathustra, 'you prophet of the great weariness; not in vain shall you once have been guest at my table. Eat and drink with me today also, and forgive a cheerful old man for sitting down at table with you!' 'A cheerful old man?' answered the prophet, shaking his head. 'But whoever you are or want to be, O Zarathustra, you have little time left up here to be it – in a little time your boat shall no longer sit in the dry!' 'Am I then sitting in the dry?' asked Zarathustra, laughing. 'The waves around your mountain rise and rise,' answered the prophet, 'waves of great distress and affliction: soon they will lift your boat too, and carry you away.' Thereupon Zarathustra was silent and wondered. 'Do you still hear nothing?' the prophet went on. 'Does not the sound of rushing and roaring arise from the depths?' Zarathustra was again silent and listened: then he heard a long, protracted cry, which the abysses threw from one to another, for none of them wanted to retain it, so evil did it sound.

'You preacher of evil,' said Zarathustra at last, 'that is a cry of distress and a human cry, perhaps it comes from out a black sea. But what is human distress to me! The ultimate sin that is reserved for me – perhaps you know what it is called?'

'*Pity!*' answered the prophet from an overflowing heart, and raised both hands aloft – 'O Zarathustra, I come to seduce you to your ultimate sin!' –

And hardly were these words spoken than the cry rang out again, and more protracted and more distressful than before, and much nearer. 'Do you hear? Do you hear, O Zarathustra?' cried the prophet. 'The cry is meant for you, it calls to you: Come, come, come, it is time, it is high time!'

Hereupon Zarathustra was silent, confused, and deeply shaken; at last he asked like one undecided: 'And who is it that calls me?'

'But you know who it is,' answered the prophet vehemently, 'why do you hide yourself? It is the *Higher Man* that cries for you!'

'The Higher Man?' cried Zarathustra, horror-struck. 'What does *he* want? What does *he* want? The Higher Man! What does he want here?' – and his skin was covered with sweat.

The prophet, however, did not respond to Zarathustra's anguish, but listened intently towards the depths. But when it had remained quiet there for a long time, he turned his gaze back and saw Zarathustra standing and trembling.

'O Zarathustra,' he began in a scornful voice, 'you do not stand there like one made giddy by happiness: you will have to dance if you are not to fall over!

'But even if you were to dance before me and indulge in all your tricks, no one could say: "Behold, here dances the last happy man!"

'Anyone who sought *him* here would visit these heights in vain: he would find caves, certainly, and backwood-caves, hiding-places for the hidden, but not mines of happiness and treasure-houses and new gold-veins of happiness.

'Happiness – how could man find happiness with such buried men and hermits! Must I yet seek ultimate happiness upon blissful islands and far away among forgotten seas?

'But it is all one, nothing is worth while, seeking is useless, and there are no blissful islands any more!'

Thus sighed the prophet; with his last sigh, however, Zarathustra again became cheerful and assured, like one emerging from a deep chasm into the light. 'No! No! Thrice No!' he cried vigorously, and stroked his beard. 'I know better! There still are blissful islands! Do not talk about such things, you sighing sack-cloth!

'Cease to splash about such things, you morning rain-cloud! Do I not stand here already wet with your affliction and drenched as a dog?

'Now I shall shake myself and run away from you, so that I may become dry again: you must not be surprised at that! Do you think me discourteous? But this is *my* court.

'But concerning your Higher Man: very well! I shall seek him at once in those forests: his cry came from *there*. Perhaps he is being attacked by an evil beast.

'He is in *my* domain: here he shall not come to harm! And truly, there are many evil beasts about me.'

With these words Zarathustra turned to go. Then the prophet said: 'O Zarathustra, you are a rogue!

'I know it: you want to be rid of me! You would rather run into the forests and waylay evil beasts!

'But what good will it do you? In the evening you will have me back; I shall sit in your own cave, patient and heavy as a log – and wait for you!'

'So be it!' Zarathustra shouted behind him as he departed: 'and whatever in my cave belongs to me also belongs to you, my guest!

'But should you discover honey in there, very well! just lick it up, you growling bear, and sweeten your soul! For in the evening we must both be in good spirits,

'in good spirits and glad that this day has ended! And you yourself shall dance to my songs as my dancing bear.

'You do not believe it? You are shaking your head? Very well! Go on, old bear! But I too – am a prophet!'

Thus spoke Zarathustra.

Conversation with the Kings

I

ZARATHUSTRA had not been going an hour through his mountains and forests when all at once he saw a strange procession. Along just that path that he was going down came two kings, adorned with crowns and purple sashes and bright as flamingos: they drove before them a laden ass. 'What do these kings want in my kingdom?' said Zarathustra in astonishment to his heart, and quickly concealed himself behind a bush. But as the kings drew abreast of him, he said, half aloud like someone talking to himself: 'Strange! Strange! I cannot make this out! I see two kings – and only one ass!'

Then the two kings halted, smiled, gazed at the place from which the voice had come, and then looked one another in the face. 'No doubt people think such things as that at home, too,' said the king on the right, 'but they do not utter them.'

The king on the left shrugged his shoulders and answered: 'It is probably a goat-herd. Or a hermit who has lived too long among trees and rocks. For no company at all also corrupts good manners.'

'Good manners?' replied the other king indignantly and bitterly. 'What is it we are avoiding, then? Is it not "good manners"? Our "good company"?

'Truly, better to live among hermits and goat-herds than with our gilded, false, painted rabble – although it calls itself "good company",

'although it calls itself "nobility". But there everything is false and rotten, most of all the blood, thanks to old, evil diseases and worse quacks.

'I think the finest and dearest man today is a healthy peasant, uncouth, cunning, obstinate, enduring: that is the noblest type today.

'The peasant is the finest man today; and the peasantry should be master! But ours is the kingdom of the rabble – I no longer let myself be taken in. Rabble, however, means: hotchpotch.

'Rabble-hotchpotch: in that everything is mixed up with everything else, saint and scoundrel and gentleman and Jew and every beast out of Noah's Ark.

'Good manners! Everything is false and rotten with us. Nobody knows how to be respectful any more: it is from precisely *this* that we are running away. They are honey-mouthed, importunate dogs, they gild palm-leaves.

'It is this disgust that chokes me, that we kings ourselves have become false, arrayed and disguised in the old, yellowed pomp of our grandfathers, show-pieces for the stupidest and the craftiest and whoever today traffics with power!

'We *are not* the first of them – yet we have to *pretend* to be: we have at last become tired and disgusted with this deception.

'Now we are avoiding the mob, all these ranters and scribbling-bluebottles, the stench of shopkeepers, the struggles of ambition, the foul breath: faugh, to live among the mob,

'faugh, to pretend to be the first among the mob! Ah, disgust! disgust! disgust! What do we kings matter any more!'

'Your old illness is assailing you,' the king on the left said at this point, 'disgust is assailing you, my poor brother. But you know that someone can overhear us.'

Hereupon Zarathustra, who had kept his ears and eyes open to these speeches, rose from his hiding-place, stepped towards the kings and began:

'He who has overheard you, he who likes to overhear you, O kings, is called Zarathustra.

'I am Zarathustra, who once said: "What do kings matter any longer!" Forgive me, but I was glad when you said to one another: "What do we kings matter!"

'This, however, is *my* kingdom and dominion: what might you be seeking in my kingdom? But perhaps on your way you have *found* what I am *seeking*: that is, the Higher Man.'

When the kings heard this they beat their breasts and said in a single voice: 'We have been recognized!

'With the sword of these words you have cut through the thickest darkness of our hearts. You have discovered our distress, for behold! we are on our way to find the Higher Man –

'the man who is higher than we: although we are kings. We are leading this ass to him. For the Highest Man shall also be the highest lord on earth.

'There is no harder misfortune in all human destiny than when the powerful of the earth are not also the first men. Then everything becomes false and awry and monstrous.

'And when they are even the last men and more beast than man, then the value of the rabble rises higher and higher and at last the rabble-virtue says: Behold, I alone am virtue!'

'What do I hear?' answered Zarathustra; 'what wisdom from kings! I am enchanted, and truly, I already feel the urge to compose a verse about it:

'even if it should be a verse not suited to everyone's ears. I long ago unlearned consideration for long ears. Very well! Come on!

(But here it happened that the ass, too, found speech: it said clearly and maliciously 'Ye-a'.)

> 'Once on a time – 'twas A.D. One, I think –
> Thus spoke the Sybil, drunken without drink:
> "How bad things go!
> Decay! Decay! Ne'er sank the world so low!
> Rome is now a harlot and a brothel too,
> Rome's Caesar's a beast, and God himself – a Jew!"'

2

The kings were delighted with these lines of Zarathustra's; and the king on the right said: 'O Zarathustra, how well we did to come out and see you!

'For your enemies have shown us your image in their mirror, from which you gazed with the grimace of a devil and with mocking laughter, so that we were afraid of you.

'But what good was it! Again and again you stung our ears and hearts with your sayings. Then at last we said: What does it matter how he looks!

'We must *hear* him, him who teaches: You should love peace as a means to new wars and a short peace more than a long!

'No one ever spoke such warlike words: What is good? To be brave is good. It is the good war that hallows every cause.

'O Zarathustra, at such words the blood of our fathers stirred in our bodies: it was like spring speaking to old wine-casks.

'Our fathers loved life when swords were crossed like red-flecked serpents; they thought all suns of peace faint and feeble, but the long peace made them ashamed.

'How they sighed, our fathers, when they saw resplendent, parched swords upon the wall! Like them, they thirsted for war. For a sword wants to drink blood and sparkles with its desire.'

As the kings thus eagerly talked and babbled of the happiness of their fathers, Zarathustra was overcome by no small desire to mock their eagerness: for they were apparently very peaceable kings that he saw before him, with aged, refined faces. But he controlled himself. 'Very well!' he said, 'yonder leads the way to Zarathustra's cave; and this day shall have a long evening! But now a cry of distress calls me hurriedly away from you.

'My cave will be honoured if kings would sit and wait in it: but, to be sure, you will have to wait a long time!

'But really! What does it matter! Where today does one learn to wait better than in courts? And the whole virtue still remaining to kings – is it not today called: *being able* to wait!'

Thus spoke Zarathustra.

The Leech

AND Zarathustra walked thoughtfully farther and deeper through forests and past swampy places; but, as happens with those who think on difficult things, on his way he unintentionally trod on a man. And behold, all at once a cry of pain and two curses and twenty little invectives spurted up into his face: so that in his fright he raised his stick and brought it down on the man he had trodden on. But he immediately came to his senses; and his heart laughed at the folly he had just committed.

'Forgive me,' he said to the man he had trodden on, who had angrily risen and sat down again, 'forgive me and first of all accept a parable.

'How a wanderer dreaming of distant things unintentionally stumbles over a dog on a lonely road, a dog lying in the sun:

'how they both start up and let fly at one another like mortal enemies, these two, frightened to death: thus it happened with us.

'And yet! And yet – how little was lacking for them to caress one another, this dog and this solitary! For they are both – solitaries!'

'Whoever you may be,' said the trodden-on man, still angry, 'you have come too near me with your parable and not only with your foot!

'For look, am I a dog?' – and thereupon the sitting man arose and drew his naked arm from the swamp. For previously he had lain stretched out on the ground, concealed and unrecognizable, like someone lying in wait for swamp game.

'But what are you doing!' cried Zarathustra in alarm, for he saw that a great deal of blood was running down the naked arm, 'what has happened to you? Has an evil beast bitten you, unhappy man?'

The bleeding man laughed, still irritated. 'What is it to do with you!' he said, and made to go off. 'Here I am at home and in my domain. Whoever wants to question me, let him: but I shall hardly reply to a blockhead!'

'You are wrong,' said Zarathustra compassionately, and held him fast, 'you are wrong: here you are not in your own home but in my kingdom, and I will have no one come to harm here.

'But none the less, call me what you like – I am what I must be. I call myself Zarathustra.

'Very well! Up yonder leads the way to Zarathustra's cave: it is not far – will you not tend your wounds in my home?

'Things have gone ill with you in this life, you unhappy man: first a beast bit you, and then – a man trod on you!'

But when the trodden-on man heard the name of Zarathustra, he changed. 'What has happened to me!' he cried; '*who* concerns me in this life except this one man, Zarathustra, and that one beast that lives on blood, the leech?

'For the sake of the leech I have lain here beside this swamp like a fisherman, and already my outstretched arm has been bitten ten times; now a fairer leech bites for my blood, Zarathustra himself!

'Oh happiness! Oh wonder! Praised be this day, that lured me to this swamp! Praised be the best, liveliest cupping-glass alive today, praised be the great leech of conscience, Zarathustra!'

Thus spoke the man who had been trodden on; and Zarathustra rejoiced at his words and their fine, respectful manner. 'Who are you?' he asked, and offered him his hand, 'between us there is still much to elucidate and clear up: but already, it seems to me, it is bright, broad daylight.'

'I am the *conscientious man of the spirit*,' answered the other, 'and scarcely anyone is sterner, stricter, and more severe in things of the spirit than I, apart from him from whom I learned, Zarathustra himself.

'Better to know nothing than half-know many things! Better to be a fool on one's own account than a wise man at the approval of others! I – go to the root of things:

'what matter if it be great or small? If it be swamp or sky? A hand's breadth of ground is enough for me: if only it be thoroughly firm ground!

'a hand's breadth of ground: one can stand upon that. In truly conscientious knowledge there is nothing great and nothing small.'

'So perhaps you are an expert on the leech?' asked Zarathustra. 'And do you probe the leech down to its ultimate roots, conscientious man?'

'O Zarathustra,' answered the man who was trodden on, 'that would be a colossal task, how could I undertake it!

'But what I am master of and expert on is the leech's *brain* – that is *my* world!

'And that too is a world! But forgive me that my pride here speaks out, for here I have not my equal. That is why I said "Here I am at home".

'How long have I probed this one thing, the brain of the leech, so that slippery truth should here no longer slip away from me! Here is *my* kingdom!

'For its sake I have cast away all others, for its sake I have grown indifferent to all others; and close beside my knowledge couches my black ignorance.

'The conscience of my spirit demands of me that I know one thing and apart from that know nothing: I am disgusted by all the semi-intellectual, all the vaporous, hovering, visionary.

'Where my honesty ceases I am blind and want to be blind. But where I want to know I also want to be honest, that is, severe, stern, strict, cruel, inexorable.

'Because *you*, O Zarathustra, once said: "Spirit is the life that itself cuts into life", that led and seduced me to your teaching. And truly, with my own blood have I increased my own knowledge!'

'As the evidence indicates,' Zarathustra interposed; for blood continued to run down the naked arm of the man of conscience. For ten leeches had bitten into it.

'Oh you strange fellow, how much this evidence tells me, for it tells me about yourself! And perhaps I could not pour all of it into your stern ears!

'Very well! Let us part here! But I should like to meet you again. Up yonder leads the way to my cave: tonight you shall there be my welcome guest!

'And I should also like to make amends to your body for treading upon you: I shall think about that. But now a cry of distress calls me hurriedly away from you.'

Thus spoke Zarathustra.

The Sorcerer

I

WHEN Zarathustra had turned the corner around a rock, however, he saw not far below him on the same pathway a man who was throwing his arms about as if in a frenzy and who finally hurled himself to earth flat on his belly. 'Stop!' said Zarathustra then to his heart, 'he yonder must surely be the Higher Man, that evil cry of distress came from him – I will see if he can be helped.' But when he ran to the spot where the man lay on the ground, he found a trembling old man with staring eyes; and however much Zarathustra tried to raise him and set him upon his legs, it was in vain. Neither did the unfortunate man seem to notice that there was anyone with him; on the contrary, he continually looked around him with pathetic gestures, like one forsaken by and isolated from all the world. Eventually, however, after much trembling, quivering, and self-contortion, he began to wail thus:

> Who still warms me, who still loves me?
> Offer me hot hands!
> Offer me coal-warmers for the heart!
> Spread-eagled, shuddering,
> Like a half-dead man whose feet are warmed –
> Shaken, alas! by unknown fevers,
> Trembling with sharp icy frost-arrows,
> Pursued by you, my thought!
> Unutterable, veiled, terrible one!
> Huntsman behind the clouds!
> Struck down by your lightning-bolt,
> You mocking eye that stares at me from the darkness –
>   thus I lie,
> Bend myself, twist myself, tortured
> By every eternal torment,
> Smitten
> By you, cruel huntsman,
> You unknown – God!

> Strike deeper!
> Strike once again!
> Sting and sting, shatter this heart!
> What means this torment
> With blunt arrows?
> Why do you look down,
> Unwearied of human pain,
> With malicious divine flashing eyes?
> Will you not kill,
> Only torment, torment?
> Why – torment *me*,
> You malicious, unknown God?

> Ha ha! Are you stealing near?
> At such a midnight hour
> What do you want? Speak!
> You oppress me, press me –

Ha! far too closely!
Away! Away!
You hear me breathing,
You overhear my heart,
You jealous God –
Yet, jealous of what?
Away! Away! Why the ladder?
Would you climb
Into my heart,
Climb into my most secret
Thoughts?
Shameless, unknown – thief!
What would you get by stealing?
What would you get by listening?
What would you get by torturing,
You torturer?
You – Hangman-god!
Or shall I, like a dog,
Roll before you?
Surrendering, raving with rapture,
Wag – love to you?

In vain! Strike again,
Cruellest knife! No,
Not dog – I am only your game,
Cruellest huntsman!
Your proudest prisoner,
You robber behind the clouds!
For the last time, speak!
What do you want, waylayer, from me?
You God veiled in lightning! Unknown One! Speak,
What do you want, unknown – God?

What? Ransom?
How much ransom?
Demand much – thus speaks my pride!
And be brief – thus speaks my other pride!

Ha ha!

Me – you want me?
Me – all of me? ...

Ha ha!
And you torment me, fool that you are,
You rack my pride?
Offer me love – who still warms me?
Who still loves me? – offer me hot hands!
Offer me coal-warmers for the heart,
Offer me, the most solitary,
Whom ice, alas! sevenfold ice
Has taught to long for enemies,
For enemies themselves,
Offer, yes yield to me,
Cruellest enemy –
Yourself!

He is gone!
He himself has fled,
My last, sole companion,
My great enemy,
My unknown,
My Hangman-god!

No! Come back,
With all your torments!
Oh come back
To the last of all solitaries!
All the streams of my tears
Run their course to you!
And the last flame of my heart –
It burns up to *you*!
Oh come back,
My unknown God! My pain! My last – happiness!

2

At this point, however, Zarathustra could restrain himself no longer; he took his stick and struck the wailing man with all his force. 'Stop!' he shouted at him with furious laughter, 'stop, you actor! You fabricator! You liar from the heart! I know you well!

'I will warm your legs for you, you evil sorcerer, I well know how to make things warm for such as you!'

'Leave off,' said the old man and jumped up from the ground, 'beat me no more, O Zarathustra! I was doing it only in fun!

'Such things are part of my art; I wanted to put you yourself to the proof when I gave you this exhibition![42] And truly, you have seen well through me!

'But you, too, have given me no small proof of yourself: you are *hard*, you wise Zarathustra! You strike hard with your "truths", your cudgel forced from me – *this* truth!'

'Do not flatter,' answered Zarathustra, still excited and frowning, 'you actor from the heart! You are false: why speak – of truth!

'You peacock of peacocks, you ocean of vanity, *what* did you play before me, you evil sorcerer, in *whom* was I supposed to believe when you wailed in such a fashion?'

'*The penitent of the spirit*,' said the old man, 'it was *he* I played: you yourself once invented this expression – the poet and sorcerer who at last turns his spirit against himself, the transformed man who freezes through his bad knowledge and bad conscience.

'And just confess it: it took a long time, O Zarathustra, for you to see through my trick and lie! You *believed* in my distress when you took my head in your hands,

'I heard you wail: "He has been too little loved, too little loved!" My wickedness rejoiced within me that I had deceived you so far.'

'You may have deceived subtler men than me,' said Zarathustra severely. 'I am not on my guard against deceivers, I *must* be without caution: so my fate will have it.

'You, however, *must* deceive: I know you so far. You must always be ambiguous, with two, three, four, five meanings! And what you just confessed was not nearly true enough and not nearly false enough for me!

'You evil fabricator, how could you do otherwise! You would even deck your disease if you showed yourself naked to your physician.

'Thus you decked your lie before me when you said "I was doing it *only* in fun!" There was also *earnestness* in it, you *are* something of a penitent of the spirit!

'I have divined you well: you have become the enchanter of everyone, but against yourself you have no lie and no cunning left – you are disenchanted with yourself!

'You have reaped disgust as your single truth. With you, no word is genuine any more, but your mouth is genuine: that is, the disgust that clings to your mouth.'

'But who are you!' the old sorcerer cried at this point in a defiant voice, 'who dares to speak like this to *me*, the greatest man living today?' – and a green lightning-flash shot from his eye at Zarathustra. But immediately he changed and said sadly:

'O Zarathustra, I am tired of it, my arts disgust me, I am not *great*, why do I pretend! But, you know it well – I sought greatness!

'I wanted to appear a great man and I convinced many: but this lie has been beyond my strength. I am collapsing under it.

'O Zarathustra, everything about me is a lie; but that I am collapsing – this is *genuine*!'

'It honours you,' said Zarathustra gloomily, casting down his eyes, 'it honours you that you sought greatness, but it also betrays you. You are not great.

'You evil old sorcerer, *this* is the best and most honest thing that I honour in you, that you have grown weary of yourself and have declared "I am not great".

'In *that* do I honour you as a penitent of the spirit: and, if only for a passing breath, in this one moment you were – genuine.

'But say, what do you seek here among *my* forests and cliffs? And when you laid yourself in *my* path, what proof did you want of me?

'What did you test *me* in?'

Thus spoke Zarathustra and his eyes sparkled. The old

sorcerer was silent for a time, then he said: 'Did I test you? I
– only seek.

'O Zarathustra, I seek a genuine man, a proper, simple man,
a man of one meaning and of all honesty, a repository of wisdom, a saint of knowledge, a great man!

'For do you not know, O Zarathustra? *I seek Zarathustra.*'

And at this point a long silence arose between the two; Zarathustra, however, became deeply absorbed, so that he closed
his eyes. Then, however, returning to his companion, he
grasped the sorcerer's hand and said, with much politeness
and guile:

'Very well! Up yonder leads the way to where Zarathustra's
cave lies. You may seek there him you wish to find.

'And ask advice of my animals, my eagle and my serpent:
they shall help you seek. But my cave is big.

'I myself, to be sure – I have never yet seen a great man.
The eye of the subtlest is crude today for what is great. It is
the kingdom of the mob.

'I have found so many who stretched and inflated themselves, and the people cried: "Behold a great man!" But what
good are all bellows! The wind escapes from them at last.

'A frog that has blown itself out too long explodes at last:
then the wind escapes. To prick the belly of a puffed-up wind-
bag I call a fine sport. Hear that, lads!

'Today belongs to the mob: who still *knows* what is great,
what small! Who could successfully seek greatness there!
Only a fool: a fool would succeed.

'Do you seek great men, you strange fool? Who *taught* you
to? Is today the time for it? Oh, you evil seeker, why – do
you tempt[43] me?'

Thus spoke Zarathustra, comforted at heart, and continued,
laughing, on his way.

Retired from Service

NOT long after Zarathustra had freed himself from the sorcerer, however, he again saw someone sitting beside the path he was going: a tall, dark man with a pale, haggard face; *this* man greatly vexed him. 'Alas,' he said to his heart, 'there sits disguised affliction, he seems to be of the priestly sort: what do *they* want in my kingdom?

'What! I have hardly escaped from that sorcerer: must another magician cross my path,

'some wizard who operates by laying on hands, some gloomy miracle-worker by the grace of God, some anointed world-slanderer: may the Devil take him!

'But the Devil is never in his proper place: he always comes too late, that confounded dwarf and club-foot!'

Thus cursed Zarathustra impatiently in his heart and considered how, with averted gaze, he might slip past the dark man: but behold, it turned out differently. For at the same moment the sitting man had already seen him; and not unlike someone whom an unexpected happiness has befallen, he jumped up and went towards Zarathustra.

'Whoever you may be, traveller,' he said, 'help one who has gone astray, a seeker, an old man who may easily come to harm here!

'The world here is strange and remote to me, and I hear the howling of wild animals; and he who could have afforded me protection is himself no more.

'I was seeking the last pious man, a saint and hermit who, alone in his forest, had as yet heard nothing of what all the world knows today.'

'*What* does all the world know today?' asked Zarathustra. 'This, perhaps: that the old God in whom all the world once believed no longer lives?'

'That is so,' answered the old man sadly. 'And I served that old God until his last hour.

'Now, however, I am retired from service, without master,

and yet I am not free, neither am I merry even for an hour, except in memories.

'That is why I climbed into these mountains, that I might at last celebrate a festival once more, as becomes an old pope and church-father: for know, I am the last pope! – a festival of pious memories and divine services.

'But now he himself is dead, the most pious of men, that saint in the forest who used continually to praise his God with singing and muttering.

'When I found his hut I no longer found him himself, but I did find two wolves in it, howling over his death – for all animals loved him. Then I hurried away.

'Had I come into these forests and mountains in vain? Then my heart decided to seek another, the most pious of all those who do not believe in God – to seek Zarathustra!'

Thus spoke the old man and gazed with penetrating eyes at him who stood before him; Zarathustra, however, took the old pope's hand and for a long time regarded it admiringly.

'Behold, venerable man,' he said then, 'what a long and beautiful hand! It is the hand of one who has always distributed blessings. But now it holds fast him you seek, me, Zarathustra.

'It is I, the godless Zarathustra, the same who says: Who is more godless than I, that I may rejoice in his teaching?'

Thus spoke Zarathustra and pierced with his glance the thoughts and reservations of the old pope. At last the latter began:

'He who loved and possessed him most, he has now lost him the most also:

'behold, am I myself not the more godless of us two now? But who could rejoice in that!'

'You served him to the last,' asked Zarathustra thoughtfully, after a profound silence, 'do you know *how* he died? Is it true what they say, that pity choked him,

'that he saw how *man* hung on the Cross and could not endure it, that love for man became his Hell and at last his death?'

The old pope, however, did not answer, but looked away shyly and with a pained and gloomy expression.

'Let him go,' said Zarathustra after prolonged reflection, during which he continued to gaze straight in the old man's eye.

'Let him go, he is finished. And although it honours you that you speak only good of this dead god, yet you know as well as I *who* he was; and that he followed strange paths.'

'Between ourselves,' said the old pope, becoming cheerful, 'or, as I may say, spoken beneath three eyes'[44] (for he was blind in one eye) 'in divine matters I am more enlightened than Zarathustra himself – and may well be so.

'My love served him long years, my will obeyed all his will. A good servant, however, knows everything, and many things, too, that his master hides from himself.

'He was a hidden god, full of secrecy. Truly, he even came by a son through no other than secret and indirect means. At the door of faith in him stands adultery.

'Whoever honours him as a god of love does not think highly enough of love itself. Did this god not also want to be judge? But the lover loves beyond reward and punishment.

'When he was young, this god from the orient, he was hard and revengeful and built himself a Hell for the delight of his favourites.

'But at length he grew old and soft and mellow and compassionate, more like a grandfather than a father, most like a tottery old grandmother.

'Then he sat, shrivelled, in his chimney corner, fretting over his weak legs, world-weary, weary of willing, and one day suffocated through his excessive pity.'

'Old pope,' Zarathustra interposed at this point, 'did you see *that* with your own eyes? It certainly could have happened like that: like that, *and* also otherwise. When gods die, they always die many kinds of death.

'But very well! One way or the other, one way and the other – he is gone! He offended the taste of my ears and eyes, I will say no worse of him.

'I love everything that is clear-eyed and honest of speech.

But he – you must know it, old priest, there was something of your nature about him, something of the priestly nature – he was ambiguous.

'He was also indistinct. How angry he was with us, this snorter of wrath, because we mistook his meaning! But why did he not speak more clearly?

'And if our ears were to blame, why did he give us ears that were unable to hear him properly? If there was dirt in our ears, very well! who put it there?

'He had too many failures, this potter who had not learned his craft! But that he took vengeance on his pots and creations because they had turned out badly – that was a sin against *good taste*.

'There is also good taste in piety: *that* said at last: Away with *such* a god! Better no god, better to produce destiny on one's own account, better to be a fool, better to be God oneself!'

'What do I hear!' the old pope said at this point, pricking up his ears; 'O Zarathustra, you are more pious than you believe, with such an unbelief! Some god in you has converted you to your godlessness.

'Is it not your piety itself that no longer allows you to believe in a god? And your exceeding honesty will yet carry you off beyond good and evil, too!

'For behold, what has been reserved for you? You have eyes and hand and mouth destined for blessing from eternity. One does not bless with the hand alone.

'In your neighbourhood, although you would be the most godless, I scent a stealthy odour of holiness and well-being that comes from long benedictions: it fills me with joy and sorrow.

'Let me be your guest, O Zarathustra, for a single night! Nowhere on earth shall I be happier now than with you!'

'Amen! So shall it be!' said Zarathustra in great astonishment, 'up yonder leads the way, there lies Zarathustra's cave.

'Indeed, I would gladly lead you there myself, venerable man, for I love all pious men. But now a cry of distress calls me hurriedly away from you.

'I will have no one come to harm in my domain; my cave is an excellent refuge. And most of all I should like to set every sad and sorrowful person again on firm land and firm legs.

'Who, however, could lift *your* melancholy from your shoulders? I am too weak for that. Truly, we should have to wait a long time before someone reawakened your god for you.

'For this old god no longer lives: he is quite dead.'

Thus spoke Zarathustra.

The Ugliest Man

AND again Zarathustra's feet ran through forests and mountains, and his eyes sought and sought, but him they desired to see, the great sufferer and crier of distress, was nowhere to be seen. All the time he was on his way, however, he rejoiced in his heart and was thankful. 'What good things this day has given me,' he said, 'as recompense for having begun so badly! What strange discoursers I have found!

'Now I will long chew their words as if they were fine corn; my teeth shall grind and crunch them small, until they flow into my soul like milk!'

But when the path again rounded a rock, all at once the scenery changed, and Zarathustra stepped into a kingdom of death. Here black and red cliffs projected up: no grass, no tree, no cry of birds. For it was a valley which all beasts avoided, even the beasts of prey; except that a kind of ugly, thick, green serpent, when it grew old, came here to die. Therefore the shepherds called this valley 'Serpent's Death'.

Zarathustra, however, was plunged into dark recollections, for it seemed to him as if he had stood in this valley once before. And many heavy things settled upon his mind: so that he went slowly and ever slower and at last stopped. Then, however, as he opened his eyes, he saw something sitting on the pathway, shaped like a man and yet hardly like a man, something unutterable. And all at once Zarathustra was overcome by the great shame of having beheld such a thing: blushing to his white hair, he turned his glance away and lifted his foot to leave this evil spot. But then the dead wilderness resounded: for from the ground issued a gurgling, rasping sound such as water makes in stopped-up water-pipes at night; and at last a human voice and human speech emerged from it: it sounded thus:

'Zarathustra! Zarathustra! Read my riddle! Speak, speak! What is the *revenge on the witness*?

'I entice you back, here is slippery ice! Take care, take care that your pride does not here break its legs!

'You think yourself wise, proud Zarathustra! So read the riddle, you hard nut-cracker – the riddle that I am! So speak: who am I?'

But when Zarathustra had heard these words, what do you think then happened to his soul? *Pity overcame him*; and all at once he sank down, like an oak tree that has long withstood many woodchoppers, heavily, suddenly, to the terror even of those who wanted to fell it. But at once he arose from the ground and his countenance grew stern.

'I know you well,' he said in a brazen voice: '*you are the murderer of God!* Let me go.

'You could not *endure* him who saw *you* – who saw you unblinking and through and through, you ugliest man! You took revenge upon this witness!'

Thus spoke Zarathustra and made to depart; but the unutterable creature grasped for a corner of his garment and began again to gurgle and grope for speech. 'Stay!' he said at last,

'stay! Do not go by! I have divined what axe it was that struck you to earth: Hail to you, O Zarathustra, that you are standing again!

'You have divined, I know it well, how he feels who killed God – how the murderer of God feels. Stay! Sit beside me; it is not to no purpose.

'To whom did I intend to go if not to you? Stay, sit down! But do not look at me! Honour thus – my ugliness!

'They persecute me: now *you* are my last refuge. *Not* with their hatred, *not* with their henchmen – oh, I would mock such persecution, I would be proud and glad of it!

'Has not all success hitherto been with the well-persecuted? And he who persecutes well easily learns to *follow*[45] – for he is already – at the heels of others. But it is their *pity*,

'it is their pity from which I flee and flee to you. O Zarathustra, my last refuge, protect me; you, the only one who can divine me:

'you have divined how he feels who has killed *him*. Stay! And if you will go, impatient man, do not go the way I came. *That* way is bad.

'Are you angry with me because I have mangled language too long? Because I have advised you? But know: it is I, the ugliest man,

'who also have the biggest, heaviest feet. Where I have gone, the way is bad. I tread all roads to death and to destruction.

'But that you went past me, silent; that you blushed, I saw it well: by that I knew you for Zarathustra.

'Anyone else would have thrown me his alms, his pity, in glance and speech. But for that – I am not enough of a beggar, you have divined that –

'for that I am too *rich*, rich in big things, in fearsome things, in the ugliest things, in the most unutterable things! Your shame, O Zarathustra, *honoured* me!

'I escaped with difficulty from the importunate crowd of those who pity, that I might find the only one who today teaches "Pity is importunate" – you, O Zarathustra!

' – be it the pity of a god, be it human pity: pity is contrary to modesty. And unwillingness to help may be nobler than that virtue which comes running with help.

'*That* however, pity, is called virtue itself with all little people – they lack reverence for great misfortune, great ugliness, great failure.

'I look beyond all these, as a dog looks over the backs of swarming flocks of sheep. They are little, well-meaning, well-woolled, colourless people.

'As a heron looks contemptuously over shallow ponds, with

head thrown back: so do I look over the swarm of colourless little waves and wills and souls.

'Too long have they been allowed right, these little people: *thus* at last they have been allowed power, too – now they teach: "Only that is good which little people call good."

'And "truth" today is what the preacher said who himself sprang from them, that strange saint and advocate of the little people who testified of himself "I – am the truth".

'This immodest man has long made the cock's comb of the little people rise up in pride – he who taught no small error when he taught "I – am the truth".

'Was an immodest man ever answered more politely? But you, O Zarathustra, passed him by and said: "No! No! Thrice No!"

'You warned against his error, as the first to do so, you warned against pity – no one else, only you and those of your kind.

'You are ashamed of the shame of the great sufferer; and truly, when you say "A great cloud emerges from pity, take care mankind!"

'When you teach "All creators are hard, all great love is beyond pity": O Zarathustra, how well-read in weather-omens you seem to me!

'You yourself, however – warn yourself too against *your* pity! For many are on their way to you, many suffering, doubting, despairing, drowning, freezing people –

'I warn you too against myself. You have read my best, my worst riddle, me myself, and what I have done. I know the axe that fells you.

'But he – *had* to die: he looked with eyes that saw *everything* – he saw the depths and abysses of man, all man's hidden disgrace and ugliness.

'His pity knew no shame: he crept into my dirtiest corners. This most curious, most over-importunate, over-compassionate god had to die.

'He always saw *me*: I desired to take revenge on such a witness – or cease to live myself.

'The god who saw everything, *even man*: this god had to die! Man could not *endure* that such a witness should live.'

Thus spoke the ugliest man. Zarathustra, however, rose and prepared to go: for he was chilled to his very marrow.

'You unutterable creature,' he said, 'you warned me against your road. As thanks for that, I recommend you mine. Behold, up yonder lies Zarathustra's cave.

'My cave is big and deep and possesses many corners; there the best hidden man can find his hiding place. And close by it are a hundred secret and slippery ways for creeping, fluttering, and jumping beasts.

'You outcast who cast yourself out, do you not wish to live among men and the pity of men? Very well, do as I do. Thus you will also learn from me; only the doer learns.

'And first of all and above all speak with my animals! The proudest animal and the wisest animal – they may well be the proper counsellors for both of us!'

Thus spoke Zarathustra and went his way, even more thoughtfully and slowly than before: for he asked himself many things and did not easily know what to answer.

How poor is man! (he thought in his heart) how ugly, how croaking, how full of secret shame!

They tell me that man loves himself: ah, how great must this self-love be! How much contempt is opposed to it!

Even this man has loved himself as he has despised himself – he seems to me a great lover and a great despiser.

I have yet found no one who has despised himself more deeply: even *that* is height. Alas, was *he* perhaps the Higher Man whose cry I heard?

I love the great despisers. Man, however, is something that must be overcome.

The Voluntary Beggar

WHEN Zarathustra had left the ugliest man he felt chilled and alone: for he had absorbed much coldness and loneliness, to such an extent that even his limbs had grown colder. But he climbed on, up hill, down dale, past green pastures but also over wild, stony courses where no doubt an impatient brook had formerly made its bed: then all at once he grew warmer and more cheerful.

'What has happened to me?' he asked himself. 'Something warm and living refreshes me, it must be nearby.

'Already I am less alone; unknown companions and brothers circle about me, their warm breath touches my soul.'

But when he peered about him and sought the comforters of his loneliness, behold, they were cows standing together on a hillock; it was their nearness and odour that had warmed his heart.

These cows, however, seemed to be listening eagerly to a speaker, and paid no heed to him who approached. And when Zarathustra was quite near them he clearly heard a human voice speaking from out the midst of the cows; and apparently they had all turned their heads towards the speaker.

Then Zarathustra eagerly sprang up the hillock and pulled the animals away, for he feared that here someone had had an accident, which the sympathy of cows could hardly remedy. But in this he was deceived; for behold, there on the ground sat a man who appeared to be persuading the animals to have no fear of him, a peaceable man and mountain sermonizer out of whose eyes goodness itself preached. 'What do you seek here?' cried Zarathustra in surprise.

'What do I seek here?' he answered: 'the same as you seek, you peace-breaker! That is, happiness on earth.

'To that end, however, I may learn from these cows. For, let me tell you, I have already been talking to them half a morning and they were just about to reply to me. Why do you disturb them?

'If we do not alter and become as cows, we shall not enter into the kingdom of heaven. For there is one thing we should learn from them: rumination.

'And truly, if a man should gain the whole world and not learn this one thing, rumination: what would it profit him! He would not be free from his affliction,

'his great affliction: that, however, is today called *disgust*.

Who today has not his heart, mouth, and eyes filled with disgust? You too! You too! But regard these cows!'

Thus spoke the mountain sermonizer and then turned his glance upon Zarathustra, for up to then it had rested lovingly upon the cows: at that, however, he changed. 'Who is that I am speaking with?' he cried, startled, and jumped up from the ground.

'This is the man without disgust, this is Zarathustra himself, the overcomer of the great disgust, this is the eye, this is the mouth, this is the heart of Zarathustra himself.'

And as he spoke thus he kissed the hands of him to whom he spoke with overflowing eyes, and behaved like someone to whom a valuable gift and jewel has unexpectedly fallen from heaven. The cows, however, looked on and were amazed.

'Do not speak of me, you strange, friendly man!' said Zarathustra, restraining his affection, 'first speak to me of yourself! Are you not the voluntary beggar who once threw away great riches,

' – who was ashamed of his riches and of the rich, and fled to the poor that he might give them his abundance and his heart? But they received him not.'

'But they received me not,' said the voluntary beggar, 'you know that. So at last I went to the animals and to these cows.'

'Then you learned', Zarathustra interrupted the speaker, 'how it is harder to give well than to take well, and that to give well is an *art* and the ultimate, subtlest master-art of kindness.'

'These days especially,' answered the voluntary beggar: 'for today everything base has become rebellious and reserved and in its own way haughty: that is, in the mob's way.

'For the hour has come, you know it, for the great, evil, protracted, slow rebellion of the mob and the slaves: it grows and grows!

'Now all benevolence and petty giving provokes the base; and let the over-rich be on their guard!

'Whoever today lets drops fall like a big-bellied bottle out of a too-narrow neck – people like to break the necks of such bottles today.

'Lustful greed, bitter envy, sour vindictiveness, mob pride:

all this threw itself in my face. It is no longer true that the poor are blessed. The kingdom of heaven, however, is with the cows.'

'And why is it not with the rich?' asked Zarathustra, tempting him, as he restrained the cows which were sniffing familiarly at the man of peace.

'Why do you tempt me?' answered the latter. 'You yourself know better even than I. For what drove me to the poorest, O Zarathustra? Was it not disgust with our richest?

' – disgust with those punished by riches, who glean advantage from all kinds of sweepings, with cold eyes, rank thoughts, disgust with this rabble that stinks to heaven,

'disgust with this gilded, debased mob whose fathers were pick-pockets or carrion-birds or ragmen with compliant, lustful, forgetful wives – for they are all of them not far from whores –

'mob above, mob below! What are "poor" and "rich" today! I unlearned this distinction – then I fled away, far away and ever farther, until I came to these cows.'

Thus spoke the man of peace and himself snorted and perspired as he spoke: so that the cows were again amazed. Zarathustra, however, looked him in the face with a smile all the while he was speaking so sternly, and then silently shook his head.

'You do violence to yourself, mountain sermonizer, when you use such stern words. Neither your mouth nor your eyes were made for such sternness.

'Nor your stomach either, as I think: *that* opposes all such raging and hating and over-frothing. Your stomach wants gentler things: you are no butcher.

'On the contrary, you seem to me a man of plants and roots. Perhaps you grind corn. But you are certainly disinclined to fleshy pleasures and love honey.'

'You have divined me well,' answered the voluntary beggar with lightened heart. 'I love honey, I also grind corn, for I have sought what tastes well and produces sweet breath:

'also what takes a long time, a day's work and a day's chewing for gentle idlers and sluggards.

'To be sure, these cows have attained the greatest proficiency in it: they have devised rumination and lying in the sun. And they abstain from all heavy thoughts that inflate the heart.'

'Very well!' said Zarathustra: 'you shall see *my* animals, too, my eagle and my serpent – there is not their like on earth today.

'Behold, yonder leads the way to my cave: be its guest tonight. And speak with my animals of the happiness of animals,

'until I return home myself. For now a cry of distress calls me hurriedly away from you. You will find new honey, too, at my cave, golden honey in the comb, cold as ice: eat it!

'But now straightway take leave of your cows, you strange, friendly man! although it may be hard for you. For they are your warmest friends and teachers!'

'Except one, whom I love more,' answered the voluntary beggar. 'You yourself are good, and even better than a cow, O Zarathustra!'

'Away, away with you! you arrant flatterer!' cried Zarathustra mischievously, 'why do you spoil me with such praise and honey of flattery?'

'Away, away from me!' he cried again and swung his stick at the affectionate beggar; he, however, ran nimbly away.

The Shadow

BUT hardly had the voluntary beggar run off and was Zarathustra alone again than he heard a new voice behind him calling: 'Stop! Zarathustra! Wait! It is I, O Zarathustra, I, your shadow!' But Zarathustra did not wait, for a sudden ill-humour overcame him on account of all the crowding and thronging on his mountains. 'Where has my solitude fled?' he said.

'Truly, it is becoming too much for me; these mountains are swarming, my kingdom is no longer of *this* world, I need new mountains.

'Does my shadow call me? Of what account is my shadow! Let it run after me! I – shall run away from it.'

Thus spoke Zarathustra to his heart and ran off. But he who was behind him followed after: so that forthwith there were three runners one behind the other, that is, foremost the voluntary beggar, then Zarathustra, and thirdly and hindmost his shadow. They had not been running thus for long when Zarathustra became conscious of his folly and at once shook off his ill-humour and disgust.

'What!' he said, 'have not the most laughable things always happened with us old hermits and saints?

'Truly, my folly has grown high in the mountains! Now I hear six foolish old legs clattering one behind the other!

'But can Zarathustra really be afraid of a shadow? And anyway, I think it has longer legs than I.'

Thus spoke Zarathustra, laughing with his eyes and his entrails, then stopped and turned quickly around – and behold, in doing so he almost threw his follower and shadow to the ground, the latter followed so closely upon his heels and was so weak. For when Zarathustra inspected him with his eyes, he was as terrified as if he had suddenly seen a ghost, so slight, dark, hollow, and spent did this follower appear.

'Who are you?' Zarathustra asked furiously, 'what are you doing here? And why do you call yourself my shadow? I do not like you.'

'Forgive me,' answered the shadow, 'that it is I; and if you do not like me, very good, O Zarathustra! I praise you and your good taste in that.

'I am a wanderer, who has already walked far at your heels: always going but without a goal and without a home: so that, truly, I am almost the eternal Wandering Jew, except that I am neither eternal nor a Jew.

'What? Must I always be going? Whirled by every wind, restless, driven onward? O Earth, you have grown too round for me!

'I have sat on every surface, like weary dust I have fallen asleep upon mirrors and window-panes: everything takes from me, nothing gives, I have become thin – I am almost like a shadow.

'But I have fled to you and followed you longest, O Zarathustra, and although I have hidden myself from you, yet I was your best shadow: where you have sat there I sat too.

'I have travelled with you in the remotest, coldest worlds, like a ghost that voluntarily walks over snow and winter roofs.

'I have striven with you into all that was forbidden, worst, most remote: and if anything in me be a virtue, it is that I have feared no prohibition.

'I have broken up with you whatever my heart revered. I have overthrown boundary stones and statues, I have pursued the most dangerous desires – truly, I once went beyond every crime.

'I have unlearned with you belief in words and values and great names. When the Devil casts his skin does his name not also fall away? For that too is a skin. The Devil himself is perhaps – a skin.

'"Nothing is true, everything is permitted": thus I told myself. I plunged into the coldest water, with head and heart. Alas, how often I stood naked, like a red crab, on that account!

'Alas, where have all my goodness and shame and belief in the good fled! Alas, where is that mendacious innocence that I once possessed, the innocence of the good and their noble lies!

'Truly, too often did I follow close by the feet of truth: then it kicked me in the face. Sometimes I intended to lie, and behold! only then did I hit – the truth.

'Too much has become clear to me: now I am no longer concerned with it. No longer is there anything living that I love – how should I still love myself?

'"To live as I desire to live or not to live at all": that is what I want, that is what the most saintly man wants. But alas! how can I still have – a desire?

'Have I – still a goal? A haven to which my sail races?

'A good wind? Alas, only he who knows where he is going knows which wind is a good and fair wind for him.

'What is left to me? A heart weary and insolent; a restless will; infirm wings; a broken backbone.

'This seeking for *my* home: O Zarathustra, do you know this seeking was *my* affliction,[46] it is consuming me.

'Where is – *my* home? I ask and seek and have sought for it, I have not found it. Oh eternal Everywhere, oh eternal Nowhere, oh eternal – Vanity!'

Thus spoke the shadow, and Zarathustra's face lengthened at his words. 'You are my shadow!' he said at length, sorrowfully.

'Your danger is no small one, you free spirit and wanderer! You have had a bad day: see you do not have a worse evening!

'Even a prison at last seems bliss to such restless people as you. Have you ever seen how captured criminals sleep? They sleep peacefully, they enjoy their new security.

'Take care that you are not at last captured by a narrow belief, a hard, stern illusion! For henceforth everything that is narrow and firm will entice and tempt you.

'You have lost your goal: alas, how will you get over and laugh away that loss? By losing your goal – you have lost your way, too!

'You poor traveller, wanderer, you weary butterfly! Would you this evening have a resting place and homestead? So go up to my cave!

'Yonder leads the way to my cave. And now I will run quickly away from you again. Already it is as if a shadow were lying upon me.

'I will run alone, so that it may again grow bright around me. For that I still have to be a long time merrily on my legs. In the evening, however, we shall – dance!'

Thus spoke Zarathustra.

At Noontide

AND Zarathustra ran and ran and found no one else and was alone and found himself again and again and enjoyed and relished his solitude and thought of good things, for hours on end. About the hour of noon, however, when the sun stood exactly over Zarathustra's head, he passed by an old gnarled and crooked tree which was embraced around by the abundant love of a vine and hidden from itself: from the vine an abundance of yellow grapes hung down to the wanderer. Then he felt a desire to relieve a little thirst and to pluck himself a grape; but when he had already extended his arm to do so, he felt an even greater desire to do something else: that is, to lie down beside the tree at the hour of perfect noon and sleep.

This Zarathustra did; and no sooner had he lain down upon the ground, in the stillness and secrecy of the multicoloured grass, than he forgot his little thirst and fell asleep. For, as Zarathustra's saying has it: One thing is more necessary than another. Only his eyes remained open – for they were not wearied of seeing and admiring the tree and the love of the vine. In falling asleep, however, Zarathustra spoke thus to his heart:

Soft! Soft! Has the world not just become perfect? What has happened to me?

As a delicate breeze, unseen, dances upon the smooth sea, light, light as a feather: thus – does sleep dance upon me.

My eyes it does not close, my soul it leaves awake. It is light, truly! light as a feather.

It persuades me, I know not how; it inwardly touches me with a caressing hand, it compels me. Yes, it compels me, so that my soul stretches itself out:

how lengthy and weary my soul has grown, my strange soul! Has a seventh day's evening come to it just at noontide? Has it wandered too long, blissfully, among good and ripe things?

It stretches itself out, long, long – longer! it lies still, my strange soul. It has tasted too many good things, this golden sadness oppresses it, it makes a wry mouth.

Like a ship that has entered its stillest bay – now it leans against the earth, weary of long voyages and uncertain seas. Is the earth not more faithful?

As such a ship lies against the shore, nestles against the

shore – there it suffices for a spider to spin its thread out to it from the land. No stronger ropes are needed.

As such a weary ship rests in the stillest bay: thus do I now rest close to the earth, faithful, trusting, waiting, fastened to it by the finest threads.

Oh happiness! Oh happiness! Would you sing, O my soul? You lie in the grass. But this is the secret, solemn hour when no shepherd plays his flute.

Take care! Hot noontide sleeps upon the fields. Do not sing! Soft! The world is perfect.

Do not sing, you grass bird, O my soul! Do not even whisper! Just see – soft! old noontide sleeps, it moves its mouth: has it not just drunk a drop of happiness

– an ancient brown drop of golden happiness, of golden wine? Something glides across it, its happiness laughs. Thus – does a god laugh. Soft!

'Happiness; how little attains happiness!' Thus I spoke once and thought myself wise. But it was a blasphemy: I have learned *that* now. Wise fools speak better.

Precisely the least thing, the gentlest, lightest, the rustling of a lizard, a breath, a moment, a twinkling of the eye – *little* makes up the quality of the *best* happiness. Soft!

What has happened to me? Listen! Has time flown away? Do I not fall? Have I not fallen – listen! into the well of eternity?

What is happening to me? Still! Is it stinging me – alas – in the heart? In the heart! oh break, break, heart, after such happiness, after such stinging!

What? Has the world not just become perfect? Round and ripe? Oh, golden round ring[47] – whither does it fly? Away, after it! Away!

Soft – (and at this point Zarathustra stretched himself and felt that he was asleep).

Up! (he said to himself) up, sleeper! You noontide sleeper! Very well, come on, old legs! It is time and past time, you have still a good way to go.

You have slept your fill, how long? Half an eternity! Very well, come on, my old heart! For how long after such a sleep may you – wake your fill?

(But then he fell asleep again, and his soul contradicted him and resisted and again lay down.) 'Let me alone! Soft! Has the world not just become perfect? Oh perfect as a round golden ball!'

Get up (said Zarathustra), you little thief, you lazybones![48] What! Still stretching, yawning, sighing, falling into deep wells?

But who are you then, O my soul? (And at this point he started, for a ray of sunlight had glanced down from the sky on to his face.)

O sky above me (he said, sighing, and sat upright), are you watching me? Are you listening to my strange soul?

When will you drink this drop of dew that has fallen upon all earthly things – when will you drink this strange soul

– when, well of eternity! serene and terrible noontide abyss! when will you drink my soul back into yourself?

Thus spoke Zarathustra and raised himself from his bed beside the tree as from a strange intoxication: and behold, the sun was still standing straight above his head. One might rightly gather from that, however, that Zarathustra had not been sleeping for long.

The Greeting

IT was only in the late afternoon that Zarathustra, after long, vain searching and roaming about, returned home to his cave. But when he was opposite it, not twenty paces away, then occurred that which he now least expected: he heard again the great *cry of distress*. And astonishing thing! this time it came from his own cave. It was a protracted, manifold, strange cry, however, and Zarathustra clearly distinguished that it was composed of many voices: although, heard from a distance, it might sound like a cry from a single throat.

Thereupon, Zarathustra sprang towards his cave, and behold! what a spectacle awaited him after that concert! For all those whom he had passed by that day were seated together: the king on the right and the king on the left, the old sorcerer, the pope, the voluntary beggar, the shadow, the conscientious man of the spirit, the sorrowful prophet, and the ass; the ugliest man, however, had placed a crown upon his head and slung two purple sashes around him, for, like all the ugly, he loved to disguise and embellish himself. But in the midst of this melancholy company stood Zarathustra's eagle, agitated and with feathers ruffled, for he had been expected to answer too much for which his pride had no answer; the wise serpent, however, hung about its neck.

Zarathustra beheld all this with great amazement; then, however, he examined each of his guests with gentle curiosity, read what was in their souls, and was amazed anew. In the meantime the assembled guests had risen from their seats and were respectfully waiting for Zarathustra to speak. Zarathustra, however, spoke thus:

You despairing men! You strange men! So was it *your* cry of distress I heard? And now I know, too, where to seek him whom I sought today in vain: *the Higher Man*

– he sits in my own cave, the Higher Man! But why am I surprised! Have I myself not enticed him to me with honey offerings and cunning bird-calls of my happiness?

But it seems to me you are ill adapted for company, you disturb one another's hearts, you criers of distress, when you sit here together? First of all someone else must come,

someone to make you laugh again, a good, cheerful Jack Pudding, a dancer and breeze and madcap, some old fool or other: – what do you think?

But forgive me, you despairing men, that I speak before you such petty words, truly unworthy of such guests! But you do not guess *what* makes my heart wanton:

you yourselves do it, and the sight of you, forgive me for it! For anyone beholding a man in despair grows brave. To encourage a despairing man – anyone thinks himself strong enough for that.

To me have you given this strength – a goodly guest-gift, my exalted guests! Very well, do not be angry with me if I offer you something of mine.

This is my kingdom and my domain: but what is mine shall be yours for this evening and this night. My animals shall serve you: let my cave be your resting place!

No one shall despair at my hearth and home, I protect everyone from his wild animals in my preserve. And that is the first thing I offer you: security!

The second, however, is: my little finger. And when you have that, take the whole hand, very well! and the heart in addition! Welcome to this place, welcome, my guests!

Thus spoke Zarathustra and laughed with love and mischievousness. After this greeting, his guests bowed themselves again and held a respectful silence; the king on the right, however, replied to him in their name.

By the manner in which you have offered us hand and greeting, O Zarathustra, do we recognize you as Zarathustra. You have humbled yourself before us; you have almost injured our respect:

but who could have humbled himself with such pride as you? *That* uplifts us ourselves, it is a refreshment to our eyes and hearts.

Just to see this would we climb higher mountains than this mountain. For we have come as sightseers, we wanted to see what makes sad eyes bright.

And behold, already all our distressful crying is over. Already our hearts and minds are opened and delighted. Little is needed for our hearts to grow wanton.

Nothing more gladdening grows on earth, O Zarathustra, than an exalted, robust will: it is the earth's fairest growth. A whole landscape is refreshed by one such tree.

To the pine-tree, O Zarathustra, do I compare him who grows up like you: tall, silent, hard, alone, of the finest, supplest wood, magnificent

– at last, however, reaching out with strong, green branches for *its* domain, asking bold questions of the winds and storms and whatever is at home in the heights,

replying more boldly, a commander, a victor: oh who would not climb high mountains to behold such trees?

The gloomy man, too, and the ill-constituted, refresh themselves at your tree, O Zarathustra; at your glance even the restless man grows secure and heals his heart.

And truly, many eyes today are raised to your mountain and your tree; a great longing has arisen, and many have learned to ask: Who is Zarathustra?

And he into whose ear you have ever poured your song and your honey: all the hidden men, the hermits and hermit-couples, say all at once to their hearts:

'Does Zarathustra still live? There is no longer any point in living, it is all one, everything is in vain: except we live with Zarathustra!'

'Why does he not come, he who has proclaimed himself so long?' thus many ask. 'Has solitude devoured him? Or should we perhaps go to him?'

Now solitude itself yields and breaks apart and can no longer contain its dead. The resurrected are to be seen everywhere.

Now the waves rise and rise around your mountain, O Zarathustra. And however high your height may be, many must reach up to you: your boat shall not sit in the dry for much longer.

And that we despairing men have now come into your cave and are already no longer despairing: that is only a sign and omen that better men are on their way to you;

for this itself is on its way to you, the last remnant of God among men, that is: all men possessed by great longing, great disgust, great satiety,

all who do not want to live except they learn to *hope* again – except they learn from you, O Zarathustra, the *great* hope!

Thus spoke the king on the right and grasped Zarathustra's hand to kiss it; but Zarathustra resisted his adoration and stepped back startled, silently and abruptly, as if escaping into the far distance. But after a short while he was again with his guests, regarded them with clear, questioning eyes, and said:

My guests, you Higher Men, I will speak clearly and in

plain German to you.[49] It is not for *you* that I have been wait-ing in these mountains.

('Clearly and in plain German? God help us!' said the king on the left to himself at this point; 'it is clear he does not know the good Germans, this wise man from the East!

'But he means "uncouthly and in German" – very well! Nowadays that is not in quite the worst taste!')

Truly, you may all be Higher Men (Zarathustra went on): but for me – you are not high and strong enough.

For me, that is to say: for the inexorable that is silent within me but will not always be silent. And if you belong to me, it is not as my right arm.

For he who himself stands on sick and tender legs, as you do, wants above all, whether he knows it or conceals it from himself: to be *spared*.

My arms and my legs, however, I do not spare, I do not spare *my warriors*: how, then, could you be fit for *my* warfare?

With you I should still spoil every victory. And some of you would give in simply on hearing the loud beating of my drums.

Neither are you handsome enough nor sufficiently well-born for me. I need pure, smooth mirrors for my teaching; upon your surface even my own reflection is distorted.

Many a burden, many a memory weighs down your shoul-ders; many an evil dwarf crouches in your corners. And there is hidden mob in you, too.

And although you are high and of a higher type, much in you is crooked and malformed. There is no smith in the world who could hammer you straight and into shape for me.

You are only bridges: may higher men than you step across upon you! You are steps: so do not be angry with him who climbs over you into *his* height!

From your seed there may one day grow for me a genuine son and perfect heir: but that is far ahead. You yourselves are not those to whom my heritage and name belong.

It is not for you that I wait here in these mountains, it is not with you that I may go down for the last time. You have come to me only as omens that higher men are already on their way to me,

not men possessed of great longing, great disgust, great satiety, and that which you called the remnant of God,

No! No! Thrice No! It is for *others* that I wait here in these mountains and I will not lift my foot from here without them,

for higher, stronger, more victorious, more joyful men, such as are square-built in body and soul: *laughing lions* must come!

O my guests, you strange men, have you yet heard nothing of my children? And that they are on their way to me?

Speak to me of my gardens, of my Blissful Islands, of my beautiful new race, why do you not speak of them?

This guest-gift do I beg of your love, that you speak to me of my children. In them I am rich, for them I became poor: what have I not given,

what would I not give, to possess one thing: *these* children, *this* living garden, *these* trees of life of my will and of my highest hope!

Thus spoke Zarathustra and suddenly halted in his discourse: for his longing overcame him and he closed his eyes and mouth because his heart was so moved. And all his guests, too, remained silent and stood still and dismayed: except that the old prophet started to make signs with his hands and his features.

The Last Supper

FOR at this point the prophet interrupted the greeting of Zarathustra and his guests: he thrust himself forward like one with no time to lose, grasped Zarathustra's hand and cried: 'But Zarathustra!

'One thing is more necessary than another, so you say yourself: very well, one thing is now more necessary to *me* than all others.

'A word in season: did you not invite me to a *meal*? And

here are many who have travelled far. You don't intend to fob us off with speeches, do you?

'Besides, you have all been thinking too much about freezing, drowning, choking, and other physical dangers: no one, however, has thought about *my* danger, that is, starving – '

(Thus spoke the prophet; but when Zarathustra's animals heard his words they ran off in terror. For they saw that all they had brought home during the day would not suffice to cram this one philosopher.)

'And dying of thirst,' the prophet went on. 'And although I have heard water splashing here like speeches of wisdom, plenteous and unceasing: I – want *wine*!

'Not everyone is a born water-drinker, like Zarathustra. Neither is water of any use to weary and drooping men: *we* ought to have wine – *that* alone brings sudden recovery and unpremeditated health!'

On this occasion, when the prophet desired wine, it happened that the king on the left, the silent one, also found speech for once. 'We have provided for wine,' he said, 'I and my brother, the king on the right: we have wine enough – a whole ass's load of it. So nothing is lacking but bread.'

'Bread?' replied Zarathustra laughing. 'It is precisely bread that hermits do not have. But man does not live by bread alone, but also by the flesh of good lambs, of which I have two.

'Let us quickly slaughter *these* and prepare them spicily with sage: that is how I like it. And neither is there any lack of roots and fruits, fine enough even for gourmets and epicures; nor of nuts and other riddles that need cracking.

'Thus we shall very shortly partake of an excellent meal. But whoever wants to eat with us must also lend a hand, even the kings. For with Zarathustra even a king may be a cook.'

Everyone heartily agreed with this suggestion: except that the voluntary beggar exclaimed against flesh and wine and spices.

'Just listen to this glutton Zarathustra!' he said jokingly: 'does one take to caves and high mountains in order to partake of such meals?

'To be sure, I now understand what he once taught us:

295

"Praised be a moderate poverty!" and why he wants to abolish beggars.'

'Be of good cheer,' Zarathustra replied to him, 'as I am. Stick to your usual custom, admirable man: grind your corn, drink your water, praise your own cooking: if only it makes you happy!

'I am a law only for my own, I am not a law for all. But he who belongs to me must be strong-limbed and nimble-footed,

'merry in war and feasting, no mournful man, no dreamy fellow, ready for what is hardest as for a feast, healthy and whole.

'The best belongs to me and mine; and if we are not given it, we take it: the best food, the purest sky, the most robust thoughts, the fairest women!'

Thus spoke Zarathustra; the king on the right, however, replied: 'Strange! Did one ever hear such clever things from the mouth of a philosopher?

'And truly, it is the rarest thing to find a philosopher clever as well as wise, and not an ass.'

Thus spoke the king on the right and wondered; the ass, however, maliciously replied to his speech with 'Ye-a.' This, however, was the beginning of that long meal which is called 'The Last Supper'[50] in the history books. And during that meal nothing was spoken of but the *Higher Man*.

Of the Higher Man

I

WHEN I went to men for the first time, I committed the folly of hermits, the great folly: I set myself in the market-place.

And when I spoke to everyone, I spoke to no one. In the evening, however, tight-rope walkers and corpses were my companions; and I myself was almost a corpse.

With the new morning, however, came to me a new truth: then I learned to say: 'What are the market-place and the mob and the mob's confusion and the mob's long ears to me!'

You Higher Men, learn this from me: In the market-place no one believes in Higher Men. And if you want to speak there, very well, do so! But the mob blink and say: 'We are all equal.'

'You Higher Men' – thus the mob blink – 'there are no Higher Men, we are all equal, man is but man, before God – we are all equal!'

Before God! But now this God has died. And let us not be equal before the mob. You Higher Men, depart from the market-place!

2

Before God! But now this God has died! You Higher Men, this God was your greatest danger.

Only since he has lain in the grave have you again been resurrected. Only now does the great noontide come, only now does the Higher Man become – lord and master!

Have you understood this saying, O my brothers? Are you terrified: do your hearts fail? Does the abyss here yawn for you? Does the hound of Hell here yelp at you?

Very well! Come on, you Higher Men! Only now does the mountain of mankind's future labour. God has died: now *we* desire – that the Superman shall live.

3

The most cautious people ask today: 'How may man still be preserved?' Zarathustra, however, asks as the sole and first one to do so: 'How shall man be *overcome*?'

The Superman lies close to my heart, *he* is my paramount and sole concern – and *not* man: not the nearest, not the poorest, not the most suffering, not the best.

O my brothers, what I can love in man is that he is a going-across and a going-down. And in you, too, there is much that makes me love and hope.

That you have despised, you Higher Men, that makes me hope. For the great despisers are the great reverers.

That you have despaired, there is much to honour in that.

For you have not learned how to submit, you have not learned petty prudence.

For today the petty people have become lord and master: they all preach submission and acquiescence and prudence and diligence and consideration and the long *et cetera* of petty virtues.

What is womanish, what stems from slavishness and especially from the mob hotchpotch: *that* now wants to become master of mankind's entire destiny – oh disgust! disgust! disgust!

That questions and questions and never tires: 'How may man preserve himself best, longest, most agreeably?' With that – they are the masters of the present.

Overcome for me these masters of the present, O my brothers – these petty people: *they* are the Superman's greatest danger!

Overcome, you Higher Men, the petty virtues, the petty prudences, the sand-grain discretion, the ant-swarm inanity, miserable ease, the 'happiness of the greatest number'!

And rather despair than submit. And truly, I love you because you do not know how to live today, you Higher Men! For thus do *you* – live best!

4

Do you possess courage, O my brothers? Are you stout-hearted? *Not* courage in the presence of witnesses, but hermits' and eagles' courage, which not even a god observes any more?

I do not call cold-spirited, mulish, blind, or intoxicated men stout-hearted. He possesses heart who knows fear but *masters* fear; who sees the abyss, but sees it with *pride*.

He who sees the abyss, but with an eagle's eyes – he who *grasps* the abyss with an eagle's claws: *he* possesses courage.

5

'Man is evil' – all the wisest men have told me that to comfort me. Ah, if only it be true today! For evil is man's best strength.

'Man must grow better and more evil' – thus do *I* teach. The most evil is necessary for the Superman's best.

It may have been good for that preacher of the petty people to bear and suffer the sin of man. I, however, rejoice in great sin as my great *consolation*.

But these things are not said for long ears. Neither does every word belong in every mouth. They are subtle, remote things: sheep's hooves ought not to grasp for them!

6

You Higher Men, do you think I am here to put right what you have done badly?

Or that I mean henceforth to make more comfortable beds for you sufferers? Or show you restless, erring, straying men new, easier footpaths?

No! No! Thrice No! More and more, better and better men of your kind must perish – for life must be harder and harder for you. Only thus,

only thus does man grow to the height where the lightning can strike and shatter him: high enough for the lightning!

My mind and longing go out to the few, the protracted, the remote things: what are your many, little, brief miseries to me!

You have not yet suffered enough! For you suffer from yourselves, you have not yet suffered *from man*. You would lie if you said otherwise! None of you suffer from what *I* have suffered.

7

It does not suffice me that the lightning no longer does harm. I do not want to conduct it away: it shall learn – to work for *me*.

My wisdom has long collected itself like a cloud, it is growing stiller and darker. Thus does every wisdom that shall one day give birth to lightnings.

I do not want to be *light* for these men of the present, or be called light by them. *These men* – I want to blind: lightning of my wisdom! put out their eyes!

8

Do not will beyond your powers: there is an evil falsity about those who will beyond their powers.

Especially when they will great things! For they awaken mistrust of great things, these subtle fabricators and actors:

until at last they are false to themselves, squint-eyed, whitewashed rottenness, cloaked with clever words, with pretended virtues, with glittering, false deeds.

Guard yourselves well against that, you Higher Men! For I count nothing more valuable and rare today than honesty.

Does this present not belong to the mob? The mob, however, does not know what is great or small, what is straight and honest: it is innocently crooked, it always lies.

9

Have a healthy mistrust today, you Higher Men, you stout-hearted, open-hearted men! And keep your reasons secret! For this present belongs to the mob.

Who could overturn with reasons what the mob has once learned to believe without reasons?

And in the market-place one convinces with gestures. But reasons make the mob mistrustful.

And when truth has triumphed for once, then you have asked with healthy mistrust: 'What mighty error has fought for it?'

Be on your guard, too, against the learned! They hate you: for they are unfruitful! They have cold, dried-up eyes, before which all birds lie stripped of their feathers.

They boast that they do not tell lies: but inability to lie is far from being love of truth. Be on your guard!

Freedom from fever is far from being knowledge! I do not believe frozen spirits. He who cannot lie does not know what truth is.

10

If you want to rise high, use your own legs! Do not let yourselves be carried up, do not sit on the backs and heads of strangers!

But did you mount horse? Do you now ride pell-mell up to your goal? Very well, my friend! But your lame foot also sits with you on your horse!

When you reach your goal, when you jump from your horse: precisely upon your *height*, you Higher Man, will you stumble!

11

You creators, you Higher Men! One is pregnant only with one's own child.

Let nothing impose upon you, nothing persuade you! For who is *your* neighbour? And if you do things 'for your neighbour', still you do not create for him!

Unlearn this 'for', you creators: your very virtue wants you to have nothing to do with 'for' and 'for the sake of' and 'because'. You should stop your ears to these false little words.

This 'for one's neighbour' is the virtue only of petty people: there they say 'birds of a feather' and 'one good turn deserves another' – they have neither right to nor strength for *your* selfishness!

The prudence and providence of pregnancy is in your selfishness! What no one has yet seen, the fruit: that is protected and indulged and nourished by your whole love.

Where your whole love is, with your child, there too is your whole virtue! Your work, your will is *your* 'neighbour': let no false values persuade you otherwise!

12

You creators, you Higher Men! Whoever has to give birth is sick; but whoever has given birth is unclean.

Ask the women: one does not give birth for pleasure. The pain makes hens and poets cackle.

You creators, there is much in you that is unclean. That is because you have to be mothers.

A new child: oh how much new filth has also entered the world! Go aside! And whoever has given birth should wash his soul clean!

13

Do not be virtuous beyond your powers! And do not ask anything improbable of yourselves!

Follow in the footsteps of your fathers' virtue! How would you climb high if the will of your fathers did not climb with you?

But he who wants to be a first-born should see that he does not also become a last-born! And you should not pretend to be saints in those matters in which your fathers were vicious!

He whose fathers passed their time with women, strong wine, and roast pork, what would it be if he demanded chastity of himself?

It would be a piece of folly! Truly, I think it would be much for such a one to be the husband of one or two or three women.

And if he founded monasteries and wrote above the doors: 'The way to holiness', I should still say: What of it! it is another piece of folly!

He has founded for himself a house of refuge and correction: much good may it do him! But I have no faith in it.

It is what one takes into solitude that grows there, the beast within included. And so, many should be dissuaded from solitude.

Has there ever been anything filthier on earth than the saints of the desert? Not only the devil was loose around *them* – but the swine, too.

14

Timid, ashamed, awkward, like a tiger whose leap has failed: this is how I have often seen you slink aside, you Higher Men. A *throw* you made had failed.

But what of that, you dice-throwers! You have not learned to play and mock as a man ought to play and mock! Are we not always seated at a great table for play and mockery?

And if great things you attempted have turned out failures, does that mean you yourselves are – failures? And if you yourselves have turned out failures, does that mean – man is a failure? If man has turned out a failure, however: very well! come on!

15

The higher its type, the less often does a thing succeed. You Higher Men here, are you not all – failures?

Be of good courage, what does it matter! How much is still possible! Learn to laugh at yourselves as a man ought to laugh!

And no wonder you have failed and half succeeded, you half-broken men! Does there not strive and struggle in you – mankind's *future*?

Mankind's most distant, most profound questions, his reaching to the furthest stars, his prodigious power: does all that not foam together in your pot?

No wonder many a pot is shattered! Learn to laugh at yourselves, as a man ought to laugh. You Higher Men, oh how much is still possible!

And truly, how much has already succeeded! How rich this earth is in good little perfect things, in well-constituted things!

Set good little perfect things around you, you Higher Men! Things whose golden ripeness heals the heart. Perfect things teach hope.

16

What has been the greatest sin here on earth? Was it not the saying of him who said: 'Woe to those who laugh!'

Did he himself find on earth no reason for laughter? If so, he sought badly. Even a child could find reasons.

He – did not love sufficiently: otherwise he would also have loved us, the laughers! But he hated and jeered at us, he promised us wailing and gnashing of teeth.

Does one then straightway have to curse where one does not love? That – seems to me bad taste. But that is what he did, this uncompromising man. He sprang from the mob.

And he himself did not love sufficiently: otherwise he would not have been so angry that he was not loved. Great love does not *desire* love – it desires more.

Avoid all such uncompromising men! They are a poor, sick type, a mob type: they look upon this life with an ill will, they have an evil eye for this earth.

Avoid all such uncompromising men! They have heavy feet and sultry hearts – they do not know how to dance. How could the earth be light to such men!

17

All good things approach their goal crookedly. Like cats they arch their backs, they purr inwardly at their approaching happiness – all good things laugh.

His step betrays whether a man is stepping along *his own* path: so watch me walk! But he who approaches his goal, dances.

And truly, I have not become a statue, I do not stand here stiff, stumpy, stony, a pillar; I love to run fast.

And although there are swamps and thick afflictions on earth, he who has light feet runs even across mud and dances as upon swept ice.

Lift up your hearts, my brothers, high, higher! And do not

forget your legs! Lift up your legs, too, you fine dancers:
and better still, stand on your heads!

18

This laugher's crown, this rose-wreath crown: I myself have
set this crown on my head, I myself have canonized my
laughter. I have found no other strong enough for it
today.

Zarathustra the dancer, Zarathustra the light, who beckons
with his wings, ready for flight, beckoning to all birds, prepared and ready, blissfully light-hearted:

Zarathustra the prophet, Zarathustra the laughing prophet,
no impatient nor uncompromising man, one who loves
jumping and escapades;[51] I myself have set this crown on my
head!

19

Lift up your hearts, my brothers, high! higher! And do not
forget your legs! Lift up your legs, too, you fine dancers: and
better still, stand on your heads!

There are beasts who are heavy-footed even in happiness,
there are those who are clumsy-footed from birth. They exert
themselves strangely, like an elephant trying to stand on its
head.

But better to be foolish with happiness than foolish with
misfortune, better to dance clumsily than to walk lamely. So
learn from me my wisdom: even the worst thing has two good
sides,

even the worst thing has good dancing legs: so learn, you
Higher Men, how to stand on your own proper legs!

So unlearn trumpeting of affliction and all mob-sorrow-
fulness! Oh how sad the Jack Puddings of the mob seem
to me at present! This present, however, belongs to the
mob.

20

Be like the wind when it rushes forth from its mountain caves: it will dance to its own pipe, the seas tremble and leap under its footsteps.

That which gives wings to asses and milks lionesses, all praise to that unruly spirit that comes to all the present and all the mob like a storm-wind,

– that is enemy to all thistle-heads and prying noses and to all withered leaves and weeds: all praise to that wild, good, free storm-spirit that dances upon swamps and afflictions as upon meadows!

That hates the wasted dogs of the mob and all the ill-constituted brood of gloom: all praise to this spirit of all free spirits, the laughing storm that blows dust in the eyes of all the dim-sighted and ulcerated.

You Higher Men, the worst about you is: none of you has learned to dance as a man ought to dance – to dance beyond yourselves! What does it matter that you are failures!

How much is still possible! So *learn* to laugh beyond yourselves! Lift up your hearts, you fine dancers, high! higher! and do not forget to laugh well!

This laugher's crown, this rose-wreath crown: to you, my brothers, do I throw this crown! I have canonized laughter; you Higher Men, *learn* – to laugh!

The Song of Melancholy

I

ZARATHUSTRA was standing near the door of his cave as he spoke this discourse; with the final words, however, he escaped from his guests and fled for a short while into the open air.

'Oh pure odours around me,' he exclaimed, 'oh blissful stillness around me! But where are my animals? Come here, come here, my eagle and my serpent!

'Tell me, my animals: all these Higher Men – do they perhaps not *smell* well? Oh pure odours around me! Only now do I know and feel how I love you, my animals.'

And Zarathustra said again: 'I love you, my animals!' But the eagle and the serpent pressed around him when he said these words, and looked up at him. All three stood silently together in this attitude, and sniffed and breathed in the good air together. For the air here outside was better than with the Higher Men.

2

Hardly had Zarathustra left his cave, however, when the old sorcerer got up, looked cunningly around, and said: He has gone out!

And already, you Higher Men – if I may tickle you with this name of praise and flattery, as he does – already my evil spirit of deceit and sorcery attacks me, my melancholy devil,

who is an adversary of this Zarathustra from the very heart: forgive him for it! Now he *insists* on working charms before you, now he has *his* hour; I wrestle in vain with this evil spirit.

To all of you, whatever honours you may bestow upon yourselves with words, whether you call yourselves 'the free spirits' or 'the truthful' or 'the penitents of the spirit' or 'the unfettered' or 'the great desirers',

to all of you, like me, suffer *from the great disgust*, for whom the old God has died and as yet no new God lies in cradles and swaddling clothes – to all of you is my evil spirit and sorcery-devil well-disposed.

I know you, Higher Men, I know him – I also know this demon whom I love despite myself, this Zarathustra: he himself often seems to me like the beautiful mask of a saint,

like a strange, new masquerade in which my evil spirit, the melancholy devil, takes pleasure – I love Zarathustra, so I often think, for the sake of my evil spirit.

But already *he* is attacking me and compelling me, this spirit of melancholy, this evening-twilight devil: and truly, you Higher Men, he has a desire

– just open your eyes! – he has a desire to come *naked,*
whether as man or woman I do not yet know: but he is coming, he is compelling me, alas! Open your senses!

Day is fading away, now evening is coming to all things,
even to the best things; listen now, and see, you Higher Men,
what devil, whether man or woman, this spirit of evening
melancholy is!

Thus spoke the old sorcerer, looked cunningly around and
then seized his harp.

3

When the air grows clear,
When the dew's comfort
Rains down upon the earth,
Invisible and unheard –
For dew the comforter
Wears tender shoes like all that gently comforts:
Do you then remember, do you, hot heart,
How once you thirsted
For heavenly tears and dew showers,
Thirsted, scorched and weary,
While on yellow grassy paths
Wicked evening sunlight-glances
Ran about you through dark trees,
Blinding, glowing sunlight-glances, malicious?

'The wooer of *truth*? You?' – so they jeered –
'No! Only a poet!
An animal, cunning, preying, creeping,
That has to lie,
That knowingly, wilfully has to lie:
Lusting for prey,
Motley-masked,
A mask to itself,
A prey to itself –
That – the wooer of truth?
No! Only a fool! Only a poet!
Only speaking motley,

Crying out of fools-masks,
Stalking around on deceitful word-bridges,
On motley rainbows,
Between a false heaven
And a false earth,
Soaring, hovering about –
Only a fool! *Only* a poet!

That – the wooer of truth?
Not still, stiff, smooth, cold,
Become an image,
Become a god's statue,
Not set up before temples,
A god's watchman:
No! enemy to such statues of truth,
More at home in any wilderness than before temples,
Full of cat's wantonness,
Leaping through every window,
Swiftly! into every chance,
Sniffing out every jungle,
Sniffing with greedy longing,
That you may run,
Sinfully-healthy and motley and fair,
In jungles among motley-speckled beasts of prey,
Run with lustful lips,
Happily jeering, happily hellish, happily blood-thirsty,
Preying, creeping, lying:

Or like the eagle staring
Long, long into abysses,
Into *its* abysses:
Oh how they circle down,
Under and in,
Into ever deeper depths!
Then,
Suddenly, with straight aim,
Quivering flight,
They pounce on *lambs*,
Headlong down, ravenous,

Lusting for lambs,
Angry at all lamb-souls,
Fiercely angry at all that look
Sheepish, lamb-eyed, curly-woolled,
Grey with lamb-sheep kindliness!

Thus,
Eaglelike, pantherlike,
Are the poet's desires,
Are *your* desires under a thousand masks,
You fool! You poet!

You saw man
As God and sheep:
To rend the God in man
As the sheep in man,
And in rending *to laugh* –

That, that is your blessedness!
A panther's and eagle's blessedness!
A poet's and fool's blessedness!'

When the air grows clear,
When the moon's sickle
Creeps along, green,
Envious, in the purple twilight:
Enemy to day,
With every step secretly
Sickling down
The hanging rose-gardens,
Until they sink,
Sink down, pale, down to night:

So sank I once
From my delusion of truth,
From my daytime longings,
Weary of day, sick with light,
Sank downwards, down to evening, down to shadows:
Scorched and thirsty
With one truth:

Do you remember, do you, hot heart,
How you thirsted then?
That I am banished
From all truth,
Only a fool!
Only a poet!

Of Science

THUS sang the sorcerer; and all who were present went like birds unawares into the net of his cunning and melancholy voluptuousness. Only the conscientious man of the spirit was not captured: he quickly snatched the harp away from the sorcerer and cried: 'Air! Let in good air! Let Zarathustra in! You are making this cave sultry and poisonous, you evil old sorcerer!

'You seduce to unknown desires and wildernesses, you false, subtle man. And alas, when such as you chatter and make ado about *truth*!

'Woe to all free spirits who are not on their guard against *such* sorcerers! Their freedom is done with: you teach and lure back into prisons,

'you old melancholy devil, a luring bird-call sounds from your lamenting, you are like those who with their praise of chastity secretly invite to voluptuousness!'

Thus spoke the conscientious man of the spirit; the old sorcerer, however, looked around him, enjoyed his victory, and on that account swallowed the displeasure the conscientious man had caused him. 'Be quiet!' he said in a modest voice, 'good songs want to echo well; one should be long silent after good songs.

'That is what all of them are doing, these Higher Men. But you, perhaps, have understood little of my song? There is little of the spirit of sorcery in you.'

'You praise me', replied the conscientious man, 'when you separate me from yourself. Very well! But you others, what do I see? You are all sitting there with lustful eyes:

'You free souls, where has your freedom fled! You almost

seem like men who have been gazing long at wicked girls dancing naked: your very souls are dancing!

'There must be more of that which the sorcerer called his evil spirit of sorcery and deceit in you, you Higher Men – we must surely be different.

'And truly, we talked and thought together enough, before Zarathustra came home to his cave, for me to know: we *are* different.

'We *seek* different things – even up here, you and I. For I seek more *security*, that is why I came to Zarathustra. For he is still the surest tower and will

' – today, when everything is tottering, when all the earth quakes. But you, when I see what eyes you make, almost seem to me to be seeking *more insecurity*,

'more horror, more danger, more earthquaking. You have a desire, I almost think, forgive me my presumption, you Higher Men,

'you have a desire for the worst, most dangerous kind of life that terrifies me the most, for the life of wild animals, for the forests, caves, steep mountains, and labyrinths.

'And it is not those who lead *out* of danger that please you best, but those who lead you astray from all paths, the misleaders. But if you *actually* harbour such desires, they seem to me, nevertheless, to be *impossible*.

'For fear – that is man's original and fundamental sensation; everything is explained by fear, original sin and original virtue. From fear grew also *my* virtue, which is called: science.

'For fear of wild animals – that has been fostered in man the longest, including the animal he hides and fears within himself – Zarathustra calls it "the beast within".

'This protracted, ancient fear at length grown subtle, spiritual, intellectual – today, it seems to me, it is called: *science.*'

Thus spoke the conscientious man; but Zarathustra, who had just come back to his cave and had heard and understood the last discourse, threw the conscientious man a handful of roses and laughed at his 'truths'. 'What,' he cried, 'what did I just hear? Truly, I think you are a fool, or I myself am one: and I shall straightway stand your "truth" on its head.

'For *fear* – is the exception with us. Courage, however, and adventure and joy in the unknown, the unattempted – *courage* seems to me the whole pre-history of man.

'He has envied the wildest, most courageous animals all their virtues and robbed them of them: only thus did he become – man.

'*This* courage, at length grown subtle, spiritual, intellectual, this human courage with eagle's wings and serpent's wisdom: *this*, it seems to me, is today called – '

'*Zarathustra!*' all those sitting together cried as if from a single mouth and burst into a great peal of laughter; and it was as if a heavy cloud had risen from off them. Even the sorcerer laughed and said prudently: 'Well! My evil spirit has departed!

'And did I myself not warn you against him, when I said he was a deceiver, a spirit of deceit and lies?

'And especially when he shows himself naked. But how can *I* prevent his pranks! Did *I* create him and the world?

'Very well! Let us be good again and of good cheer! And although Zarathustra looks ill-temperedly – just see him! he is angry with me:

'before night comes he will again learn to love and praise me, he cannot live long without committing such follies.

'*He* – loves his enemies: he understands this art better than anyone I have seen. But he takes revenge for that – on his friends!'

Thus spoke the old sorcerer, and the Higher Men applauded him: so that Zarathustra went round and mischievously and lovingly shook hands with his friends, like one who has to make amends and apologize to everyone for something. As he came to the door of his cave, however, he already felt again a desire for the good air outside and for his animals, and he was about to slip out.

Among the Daughters of the Desert

I

Do not go! (said then the wanderer who called himself Zarathustra's shadow) stay with us, otherwise the old, dull affliction may again assail us.

That old sorcerer has already done his worst for our benefit, and just look, the good, pious pope there has tears in his eyes and has again embarked on the sea of melancholy.

These kings there may still put on a brave face before us: for *they* have learned that better than any of us today! But had they no witnesses, I wager that with them, too, the bitter business would begin again – the bitter business of drifting clouds, of damp melancholy, of veiled skies, of stolen suns, of howling autumn winds,

the bitter business of our howling and cries of distress: stay with us, O Zarathustra! Here there is much hidden misery that wants to speak out, much evening, much cloud, much damp air!

You have fed us with strong man's fare and nourishing sayings: do not let us, for dessert, be assailed again by delicate, effeminate spirits!

You alone make the air around you robust and clear! Have I ever found on earth such good air as with you in your cave?

I have seen many lands, my nose has learned to test and appraise many kinds of air: but with you my nostrils taste their greatest delight!

Except, except – oh forgive an old memory! Forgive me an old after-dinner song that I once composed among the daughters of the desert –

for with them there was the same good, clear, oriental air; there I was farthest away from cloudy, damp, melancholy Old Europe!

In those days I loved such oriental girls and other blue

314

kingdoms of heaven, over which no clouds and no thoughts hung.

You would not believe how prettily they sat there when they were not dancing, deep but without thoughts, like little secrets, like ribboned riddles, like after-dinner nuts –

motley and strange indeed! but without clouds: riddles that one can read: to please such girls I then devised an after-dinner psalm.

Thus spoke the wanderer and shadow; and before anyone could answer him he had seized the old sorcerer's harp, crossed his legs, and looked calmly and sagely about him – with his nostrils, however, he drew in the air slowly and inquiringly, like someone tasting strange air in strange lands. Thereupon he began to sing with a kind of roaring.

2

Deserts grow: woe to him who harbours deserts!

> Ha! Solemnly!
> Solemnly indeed!
> A worthy beginning!
> Solemnly in an African way!
> Worthy of a lion
> Or of a moral screech-ape
> – but it is nothing for you,
> You desert maidens,
> At whose feet I,
> For the first time,
> A European under palm-trees,
> Am permitted to sit. Selah.
>
> Wonderful, truly!
> Here I now sit,
> Beside the desert, and
> Yet so far from the desert,
> And in no way devastated:
> For I am swallowed down

By this smallest oasis:
- it simply opened, yawning,
Its sweetest mouth,
The sweetest-smelling of all little mouths:
Then I fell in,
Down, straight through – among you,
You dearest maidens! Selah.

All hail to that whale
If it made things so pleasant
For its guests! – you understand
My learned allusion?
All hail to his belly
If it was
As sweet an oasis-belly
As this is: which, however, I call in question,
– since I come from Europe,
Which is more sceptical than
Any little old wife.
May God improve it!
Amen!

Here I now sit
In this smallest oasis
Like a date,
Brown, sweet, oozing golden,
Longing for a girl's rounded mouth,
But longing more for girlish,
Ice-cold, snow-white, cutting
Teeth: for these do
The hearts of all hot dates lust. Selah.

Like, all too like
That aforesaid southern fruit
Do I lie here, by little
Flying insects
Sniffed and played around,
And by even smaller,
More foolish and more sinful

Wishes and notions,
Besieged by you,
You silent girl-kittens
Full of misgivings,
Dudu and Suleika,
Sphinxed round, that I may cram
Much feeling into two words:
(May God forgive me
This sin of speech!)
I sit here sniffing the finest air,
Air of Paradise, truly,
Bright, buoyant air, gold-streaked,
As good air as ever
Fell from the moon –
Came it by chance,
Or did it happen by wantonness,
As the old poets tell?
I, doubter, however, call it
In question; since I come
From Europe,
Which is more sceptical than any
Little old wife.
May God improve it!
Amen.

Drinking in the fairest air,
With nostrils swollen like goblets,
Without future, without memories,
Thus do I sit here, you
Dearest maidens,
And regard the palm-tree,
And watch how, like a dancer,
It bends and bows and sways at the hips,
– if one watches long one follows suit!
Like a dancer who, it would seem,
Has stood long, dangerously long,
Always on one little leg?
– so that she has forgotten, it would seem,

Her other leg?
At least, in vain
I sought the missing
Twin-jewel
– that is, the other leg –
In the sacred vicinity
Of her dearest, daintiest
Little fluttering, flickering, fan-swirling skirt.
Yes, if you would quite believe me,
You sweet maidens:
She has lost it!
It has gone!
Gone for ever!
That other leg!
Oh, what a shame about that other dear leg!
Where can it now be, sorrowing forsaken?
That lonely leg?
Perhaps in fear before an
Angry, blonde-maned
Lion-monster? Or perhaps even
Gnawed off, broken in pieces –
Pitiable, alas! alas! broken in pieces! Selah.

Oh do not weep,
Gentle hearts!
Do not weep, you
Date-hearts! Milk-bosoms!
You heart-caskets
Of sweetwood!
Do not weep,
Pale Dudu!
Be a man, Suleika! Courage! Courage!
– Or would perhaps
Something bracing, heart-bracing,
Be in place here?
An anointed proverb?
A solemn exhortation?

Ha! Up, dignity!
Virtuous dignity! European dignity!
Blow, blow again,
Bellows of virtue!
Ha!
Roar once again,
Roar morally!
Roar like a moral lion
Before the daughters of the desert!
For virtuous howling,
You dearest maidens,
Is loved best of all by
European ardour, European appetite!
And here I stand now,
As European,
I cannot do otherwise, so help me God![52]
Amen!

Deserts grow: woe to him who harbours deserts!

The Awakening

I

AFTER the song of the wanderer and shadow, the cave suddenly became full of noise and laughter: and as the assembled guests were all speaking together and even the ass no longer remained silent in the face of such encouragement, Zarathustra was overcome by a little repugnance and scorn towards his visitors: although, at the same time, he rejoiced at their gaiety. For it seemed to him to be a sign of recovery. So he stole out into the open air and spoke with his animals.

'Where is their distress now?' he said, and already he was breathing again after his little disgust, 'it seems that in my home they have unlearned distressful crying!

'although, unhappily, not yet crying itself.' And Zarathustra stopped his ears, for just then the 'Ye-a' of the ass mingled strangely with the loud rejoicing of these Higher Men.

'They are merry,' he began again, 'and, who knows, perhaps at the expense of their host. And if they have learned laughing from me, still it is not *my* laughter they have learned.

'But what of it! They are old men: they recover in their own way, they laugh in their own way; my ears have suffered worse things and not been annoyed.

'This day is a victory: it wavers already, it flees, *the Spirit of Gravity,* my old arch-enemy! How well this day is ending, that began so ill and so gravely!

'And it *is* ending. Evening has already come: it is riding over the sea to us; that excellent horseman! How it sways, joyfully returning, in its purple saddle!

'The sky gazes, clear, upon it, the world lies deep: O all you strange men who have come to me, it is already worth while to live with me!'

Thus spoke Zarathustra. And then the shouting and laughter of the Higher Men again came from the cave: it had started again.

'They are biting, my bait is effective, before them too their enemy, the Spirit of Gravity, is wavering. Already they are learning to laugh at themselves: do I hear aright?

'My man's fare, my succulent and strengthening discourse, is effective: and truly, I did not feed them with distending vegetables! But with warriors' food, with conquerors' food: I awakened new desires.

'There are new hopes in their arms and legs, their hearts are stretching themselves. They are discovering new words, soon their spirits will breathe wantonness.

'To be sure, such food may not be for children, or for fond little women, old or young. Their stomachs are persuaded otherwise; I am not their teacher and physician.

'These Higher Men's disgust is wavering: very well! that is my victory. They are growing assured in my kingdom, all stupid shame is leaving them, they are unburdening themselves.

'They are unburdening their hearts, good hours are coming

back to them, they take their ease and ruminate – they grow *thankful*.

'This I take for the best sign: they grow thankful. Before long they will be devising festivals and erecting memorials to their old joys.

'They are *convalescents*!' Thus spoke Zarathustra gaily to his heart and gazed out; his animals, however, pressed around him and respected his happiness and his silence.

2

But suddenly Zarathustra's ear was startled: for the cave, which had been full of noise and laughter, all at once became deathly still; his nose, however, smelt a sweet-smelling vapour and incense, as if of burning pine-cones.

'What is happening? What are they doing?' he asked himself, and stole to the entrance, so that he might behold his guests unobserved. But, wonder upon wonders! what did he then see with his own eyes!

'They have all become *pious* again, they are *praying*, they are mad!' he said, and was astounded beyond measure. And indeed, all these Higher Men, the two kings, the retired pope, the evil sorcerer, the voluntary beggar, the wanderer and shadow, the old prophet, the conscientious man of the spirit, and the ugliest man: they were all kneeling like children and credulous old women, and worshipping the ass. And at that very moment the ugliest man began to gurgle and snort, as if something unutterable was trying to get out of him; but when he actually reached the point of speech, behold, it was a strange, pious litany in praise of the worshipped and perfumed ass. The litany went thus:

Amen! And praise and honour and wisdom and thanks and glory and strength be to our God for ever and ever!
The ass, however, brayed 'Ye-a'.
He bears our burden, he has taken upon himself the likeness of a slave, he is patient from the heart and he never says Nay; and he who loves his God, chastises him.

The ass, however, brayed 'Ye-a'.

He does not speak, except always to say Yea to the world he created: thus he praises his world. It is his subtlety that does not speak: thus he is seldom thought wrong.

The ass, however, brayed 'Ye-a'.

He goes through the world unpretentiously. Grey is the favourite colour[53] in which he wraps his virtue. If he has spirit, he conceals it; but everyone believes in his long ears.

The ass, however, brayed 'Ye-a'.

What hidden wisdom it is, that he wears long ears and says only Yea and never Nay! Has he not created the world after his own image, that is, as stupid as possible?

The ass, however, brayed 'Ye-a'.

You go straight and crooked ways; you care little what we men think straight or crooked. Your kingdom is beyond good and evil. It is your innocence not to know what innocence is.

The ass, however, brayed 'Ye-a'.

For behold, how you spurn no one, not beggars nor kings. You suffer little children to come to you, and when bad boys bait you, you simply say Yea.

The ass, however, brayed 'Ye-a'.

You love she-asses and fresh figs, you eat anything. A thistle titillates your heart, if you happen to be hungry. The wisdom of a god is in that.

The ass, however, brayed 'Ye-a'.

The Ass Festival

I

AT this point in the litany, however, Zarathustra could no longer master himself; he cried out 'Ye-a' louder even than the ass, and sprang into the midst of his guests gone mad. 'But what are you doing, my friends?' he cried, pulling the worshippers up from the ground. 'Woe to you if anyone else but Zarathustra had seen you.

'Everyone would adjudge you, with your new faith, to be the worst blasphemers or the most foolish of old women!

'And you, old pope, how can you reconcile yourself to worshipping an ass as God in this way?'

'O Zarathustra,' answered the pope, 'forgive me, but in divine matters I am even more enlightened than you. That stands to reason.

'Better to worship God in this shape than in no shape at all! Consider this saying, my exalted friend: you will quickly see that there is wisdom in such a saying.

'He who said "God is a spirit" took the biggest step and leap towards unbelief yet taken on earth: such a saying is not easily corrected!

'My old heart leaps and bounds to know that there is something left on earth to worship. Forgive a pious old pope's heart that, O Zarathustra!'

'And you,' said Zarathustra to the wanderer and shadow, 'you call and think yourself a free spirit? And do you carry on here such priestly idolatries?

'Truly, you behave here even worse than you did with your wicken brown maidens, you evil new believer!'

'It is bad enough,' answered the wanderer and shadow, 'you are right: but what can I do! The old God lives again, O Zarathustra, you may say what you will.

'It is all the fault of the ugliest man: he has awakened him again. And if he says that he once killed him: with gods, *death* is always only a prejudice.'

'And you,' said Zarathustra, 'you evil old sorcerer, what were you doing? Who in this free age shall believe in you henceforth, if *you* believe in such godly asininities?

'What you did was a stupidity; how could you, prudent man, do anything so stupid!'

'O Zarathustra,' answered the prudent sorcerer, 'you are right, it was a stupidity, and it was hard enough to do it.'

'And even you,' said Zarathustra to the conscientious man of the spirit, 'just consider, and lay your finger on your nose! For is there nothing here against your conscience? Is your spirit not too pure for this praying and the exhalations of these devotees?'

'There is something in it,' answered the conscientious man

and laid his finger on his nose, 'there is something in this spectacle which even does my conscience good.

'I may not believe in God, perhaps: but it is certain that God seems to me most worthy belief in this form.

'God is supposed to be eternal according to the testimony of the most pious: he who has so much time takes his time. As slow and as stupid as possible: but such a one can in that way go very far, none the less.

'And he who has too much spirit might well become infatuated with stupidity and folly. Consider yourself, O Zarathustra!

'You yourself – truly! even you could become an ass through abundance and wisdom.

'Does a consummate philosopher not like to walk on the most crooked paths? Appearance teaches it, O Zarathustra – *your* appearance!'

'And you yourself, finally,' said Zarathustra and turned towards the ugliest man, who was still lying on the ground raising his arm up to the ass (for he was giving it wine to drink). 'Speak, you unutterable creature, what have you been doing?

'You seem changed, your eyes are glowing, the mantle of the sublime covers your ugliness: *what* did you do?

'Is it true what they say, that you have awakened him again? And why? Was he not with reason killed and done away with?

'You yourself seem awakened: what did you do? Why did *you* reform? Why were *you* converted? Speak, you unutterable creature!'

'O Zarathustra,' answered the ugliest man, 'you are a rogue.

'Whether *he* still lives or lives again or is truly dead, which of us two knows that best? I ask you.

'But one thing I know – I once learned it from you yourself, O Zarathustra: He who wants to kill most thoroughly – *laughs*.

'"One kills, not by anger but by laughter" – that is what you once said. O Zarathustra, you obscure man, you destroyer without anger, you dangerous saint, you are a rogue!'

2

Then, however, Zarathustra, amazed at such purely roguish answers, leaped back to the door of his cave and, turning towards all his guests, cried in a loud voice:

'O all you clowns, you buffoons! Why do you pretend and dissemble before me!

'How the heart of each of you writhed with joy and mischievousness, because you had at last again become as little children, that is, pious,

'because you at last again behaved as children do, that is, prayed, clasped your hands and said "Dear God"!

'But now leave *this* nursery, my own cave, where today every kind of childishness is at home. Come out here and cool your hot childish wantonness and the clamour of your hearts!

'To be sure: except you become as little children you shall not enter into *this* kingdom of heaven.' (And Zarathustra pointed upwards with his hands.)

'But we certainly do not want to enter into the kingdom of heaven: we have become men, *so we want the kingdom of earth.*'

3

And Zarathustra began to speak once more. 'O my new friends,' he said, 'you strange men, you Higher Men, how well you please me now,

'since you have become joyful again! Truly, you have all blossomed forth: for such flowers as you, I think, *new festivals* are needed.

'a little brave nonsense, some divine service and ass festival, some joyful old Zarathustra-fool, a blustering wind to blow your souls bright.

'Do not forget this night and this ass festival, you Higher Men! You devised *that* at my home, I take that as a good omen – only convalescents devise such things!

'And if you celebrate it again, this ass festival, do it for

love of yourselves, do it also for love of me! And in re
membrance of *me*!'

Thus spoke Zarathustra.

The Intoxicated Song

I

MEANWHILE, however, one after another had gone out
into the open air and the cool, thoughtful night; but Zarathustra himself led the ugliest man by the hand, to show him
his nocturnal world and the big, round moon and the silver
waterfalls beside his cave. There at last they stood silently
together, just a group of old folk, but with comforted, brave
hearts and amazed in themselves that it was so well with
them on earth; but the mystery of the night drew nearer and
nearer their hearts. And Zarathustra thought to himself
again: 'Oh, how well they please me now, these Higher
Men!' – but he did not say it, for he respected their happiness
and their silence.

Then, however, occurred the most astonishing thing in
that long, astonishing day: the ugliest man began once more
and for the last time to gurgle and snort, and when he at
last came to the point of speech, behold, a question leaped
round and pure from his mouth, a good, deep, clear question,
which moved the hearts of all who heard it.

'My assembled friends,' said the ugliest man, 'what do you
think? For the sake of this day – *I* am content for the first
time to have lived my whole life.

'And it is not enough that I testify only this much. It is
worth while to live on earth: one day, one festival with
Zarathustra has taught me to love the earth.

'"Was *that* – life?" I will say to death. "Very well! Once
more!"

'My friends, what do you think? Will you not, like me,
say to death: "Was *that* – life? For Zarathustra's sake, very
well! Once more!"'

Thus spoke the ugliest man; and it was not long before midnight. And what would you think then took place? As soon as the Higher Men had heard his question, they were all at once conscious of their transformation and recovery, and of who had given them these things: then they leaped towards Zarathustra, thanking, adoring, caressing, kissing his hands, each after his own fashion: so that some laughed, some wept. The old prophet, however, danced with pleasure; and even if he was then full of sweet wine, as some narrators believe, he was certainly fuller still of sweet life and had renounced all weariness. There are even those who tell that the ass danced at that time: for not in vain had the ugliest man given it wine to drink. This may be the case, or it may be otherwise; and if in truth the ass did not dance that evening, greater and stranger marvels than the dancing of an ass occurred. In brief, as Zarathustra's saying has it: 'What does it matter!'

2

Zarathustra, however, when this incident with the ugliest man occurred, stood there like one intoxicated: his eyes grew dim, his tongue stammered, his feet tottered. And who could divine what thoughts then passed over Zarathustra's soul? But it seemed that his soul fell back and fled before him and was in remote distances and as if 'upon a high ridge', as it is written,

'wandering like a heavy cloud between past and future.' But gradually, while the Higher Men were holding him in their arms, he came to himself a little and his hands restrained the adoring and anxious throng; yet he did not speak. All at once, however, he swiftly turned his head, for he seemed to hear something: then he laid a finger to his lips and said: '*Come!*'

And at once it grew still and mysterious all around; from the depths, however, there slowly arose the sound of a bell. Zarathustra listened to it, as the Higher Men did; then he laid a finger to his lips a second time and said again: '*Come! Come! Midnight is coming on!*' and his voice had altered. But still he did not move from his place: then it grew yet more still and mysterious, and everything listened, even the ass and Zarathustra's animals of honour, the eagle and the serpent, likewise Zarathustra's cave and the great, cool moon and the night itself. Zarathustra, however, laid his hand to his lips for the third time and said:

Come! Come! Come! Let us walk now! The hour has come: let us walk into the night!

3

You Higher Men, midnight is coming on: so I will say something in your ears, as that old bell says it in my ear,

as secretly, as fearfully, as warmly as that midnight-bell tells it to me, which has experienced more than one man:

which has already counted your fathers' painful heartbeats – ah! ah! how it sighs! how in dreams it laughs! the ancient, deep, deep midnight!

Soft! Soft! Then many a thing can be heard which may not speak by day; but now, in the cool air, when all the clamour of your hearts, too, has grown still,

now it speaks, now it is heard, now it creeps into nocturnal, over-wakeful souls: ah! ah! how it sighs! how in dreams it laughs!

do you not hear, how secretly, fearfully, warmly it speaks to you, the ancient, deep, deep midnight?

O Man! Attend!

4

Woe is me! Where has time fled? Did I not sink into deep wells? The world is asleep –

Ah! Ah! The dog howls, the moon is shining. I will rather die, die, than tell you what my midnight-heart is now thinking.

Now I am dead. It is finished. Spider, why do you spin your web around me? Do you want blood? Ah! Ah! The dew is falling, the hour has come

– the hour which chills and freezes me, which asks and asks and asks: 'Who has heart enough for it?

' – who shall be master of the world? Who will say: Thus shall you run, you great and small streams!'

– the hour approaches: O man, you Higher Man, attend! this discourse is for delicate ears, for your ears – *what does deep midnight's voice contend?*

5

I am borne away, my soul dances. The day's task! The day's task! Who shall be master of the world?

The moon is cool, the wind falls silent. Ah! Ah! Have you flown high enough? You dance: but a leg is not a wing.

You good dancers, now all joy is over: wine has become dregs, every cup has grown brittle, the graves mutter.

You have not flown high enough: now the graves mutter: 'Redeem the dead! Why is it night so long? Does the moon not intoxicate us?'

You Higher Men, redeem the graves, awaken the corpses! Alas, why does the worm still burrow? The hour approaches, it approaches,

the bell booms, the heart still drones, the woodworm, the heart's worm, still burrows. Alas! *The world is deep!*

6

Sweet lyre! Sweet lyre! Your sound, your intoxicated, ominous sound, delights me! – from how long ago, from how far away does your sound come to me, from a far distance, from the pools of love!

You ancient bell, you sweet lyre! Every pain has torn at your heart, the pain of a father, the pain of our fathers, the pain of our forefathers; your speech has grown ripe,

ripe like golden autumn and afternoon, like my hermit's heart – now you say: The world itself has grown ripe, the grapes grow brown,

now they want to die, to die of happiness. You Higher Men, do you not smell it? An odour is secretly welling up,

a scent and odour of eternity, an odour of roseate bliss, a brown, golden wine odour of ancient happiness,

329

of intoxicated midnight's dying happiness, which sings:
The world is deep: deeper than day can comprehend!

7

Let me be! Let me be! I am too pure for you. Do not touch me! Has my world not just become perfect?

My skin is too pure for your hands. Let me be, stupid, doltish, stifling day! Is midnight not brighter?

The purest shall be master of the world; the least known, the strongest, the midnight souls, who are brighter and deeper than any day.

O day, do you grope for me? Do you feel for my happiness? Do you think me rich, solitary, a pit of treasure, a chamber of gold?

O world, do you desire me? Do you think me worldly? Do you think me spiritual? Do you think me divine? But day and world, you are too clumsy,

have cleverer hands, reach out for deeper happiness, for deeper unhappiness, reach out for some god, do not reach out for me:

my unhappiness, my happiness is deep, you strange day, but yet I am no god, no divine Hell: *deep is its woe.*

8

God's woe is deeper, you strange world! Reach out for God's woe, not for me! What am I? An intoxicated, sweet lyre

– a midnight lyre, a croaking bell which no one understands but which *has* to speak before deaf people, you Higher Men! For you do not understand me!

Gone! Gone! Oh youth! Oh noontide! Oh afternoon! Now come evening and midnight; the dog howls, the wind:

is the wind not a dog? It whines, it yelps, it howls. Ah! Ah! how it sighs! how it laughs, how it rasps and gasps, the midnight hour!

How it now speaks soberly, this intoxicated poet! perhaps

it has overdrunk its drunkenness? perhaps it has grown over-wakeful? perhaps it ruminates?

it ruminates upon its woe in dreams, the ancient, deep midnight hour, and still more upon its joy. For joy, though woe be deep: *Joy is deeper than heart's agony.*

9

You grape-vine! Why do you praise me? For I cut you! I am cruel, you bleed: what means your praise of my intoxicated cruelty?

'What has become perfect, everything ripe – wants to die!' thus you speak. Blessed, blessed be the vine-knife! But everything unripe wants to live: alas!

Woe says: 'Fade! Be gone, woe!' But everything that suffers wants to live, that it may grow ripe and merry and passionate,

passionate for remoter, higher, brighter things. 'I want heirs,' thus speaks everything that suffers, 'I want children, I do not want *myself*.'

Joy, however, does not want heirs or children, joy wants itself, wants eternity, wants recurrence, wants everything eternally the same.

Woe says: 'Break, bleed, heart! Walk, legs! Wings, fly! Upward! Upward, pain!' Very well! Come on! my old heart: *Woe says: Fade! Go!*

10

What do you think, you Higher Men? Am I a prophet? A dreamer? A drunkard? An interpreter of dreams? A midnight bell?

A drop of dew? An odour and scent of eternity? Do you not hear it? Do you not smell it? My world has just become perfect, midnight is also noonday,

pain is also joy, a curse is also a blessing, the night is also a sun – be gone, or you will learn: a wise man is also a fool.

Did you ever say Yes to one joy? O my friends, then you

said Yes to *all* woe as well. All things are chained and entwined together, all things are in love;

if ever you wanted one moment twice, if ever you said: 'You please me, happiness, instant, moment!' then you wanted *everything* to return!

you wanted everything anew, everything eternal, everything chained, entwined together, everything in love, O that is how you *loved* the world,

you everlasting men, loved it eternally and for all time: and you say even to woe: 'Go, but return!' *For all joy wants – eternity!*

II

All joy wants the eternity of all things, wants honey, wants dregs, wants intoxicated midnight, wants graves, wants the consolation of graveside tears, wants gilded sunsets,

what does joy not want! it is thirstier, warmer, hungrier, more fearful, more secret than all woe, it wants *itself*; it bites into *itself*, the will of the ring wrestles within it,

it wants love, it wants hatred, it is superabundant, it gives, throws away, begs for someone to take it, thanks him who takes, it would like to be hated;

so rich is joy that it thirsts for woe, for Hell, for hatred, for shame, for the lame, for the *world* – for it knows, oh it knows this world!

You Higher Men, joy longs for you, joy the intractable, blissful – for your woe, you ill-constituted! All eternal joy longs for the ill-constituted.

For all joy wants itself, therefore it also wants heart's agony! O happiness! O pain! Oh break, heart! You Higher Men, learn this, learn that joy wants eternity,

joy wants the eternity of all things, *wants deep, deep, deep eternity!*

12

Have you now learned my song? Have you divined what it means? Very well! Come on! You Higher Men, now sing my roundelay!

Now sing yourselves the song whose name is 'Once more', whose meaning is 'To all eternity!' – sing, you Higher Men, Zarathustra's roundelay!

> *O Man! Attend!*
> *What does deep midnight's voice contend?*
> *'I slept my sleep,*
> *'And now awake at dreaming's end:*
> *'The world is deep,*
> *'Deeper than day can comprehend.*
> *'Deep is its woe,*
> *'Joy – deeper than heart's agony:*
> *'Woe says: Fade! Go!*
> *'But all joy wants eternity,*
> *'Wants deep, deep, deep eternity!'*

The Sign

ON the morning after this night, however, Zarathustra sprang up from his bed, girded his loins, and emerged from his cave, glowing and strong, like a morning sun emerging from behind dark mountains.

'Great star,' he said, as he had said once before, 'you profound eye of happiness, what would all your happiness be if you did not have *those* for whom you shine!

'And if they remained in their rooms while you were already awake and had come, giving and distributing: how angry your proud modesty would be!

'Very well! they are still asleep, these Higher Men, while *I* am awake: *they* are not my rightful companions! It is not for them I am waiting in my mountains.

'I want to go to my work, to my day: but they do not understand what are the signs of my morning, my step – is no awakening call for them.

'They are still sleeping in my cave, their dream still drinks at my intoxicated songs. Yet the ear that listens to *me*, the *obeying* ear, is missing from them.'

Zarathustra had said this to his heart when the sun rose:

then he looked inquiringly aloft, for he heard above him the sharp cry of his eagle. 'Very well!' he cried up, 'so do I like it, so do I deserve it. My animals are awake, for I am awake.

'My eagle is awake and, like me, does honour to the sun. With eagle's claws it reaches out for the new light. You are my rightful animals: I love you.

'But I still lack my rightful men!'

Thus spoke Zarathustra; then, however, he suddenly heard that he was surrounded by countless birds, swarming and fluttering – the whirring of so many wings and the throng about his head, however, were so great that he shut his eyes. And truly, it was as if a cloud had fallen upon him, a cloud of arrows discharged over a new enemy. And behold, in this case it was a cloud of love, and over a new friend.

'What is happening to me?' thought Zarathustra, in his astonished heart, and slowly lowered himself on to the great stone that lay beside the exit of his cave. But, as he was clutching about, above and underneath himself, warding off the tender birds, behold, then something even stranger occurred: for in doing so he clutched unawares a thick, warm mane of hair; at the same time, however, a roar rang out in front of him – the gentle, protracted roar of a lion.

'*The sign has come*,' said Zarathustra, and his heart was transformed. And in truth, when it grew clear before him, there lay at his feet a sallow, powerful animal that lovingly pressed its head against his knee and would not leave him, behaving like a dog that has found his old master again. The doves, however, were no less eager than the lion with their love; and every time a dove glided across the lion's nose, the lion shook its head and wondered and laughed.

While this was happening, Zarathustra said but one thing: '*My children are near, my children*,' then he grew quite silent. His heart, however, was loosened, and tears fell from his eyes down upon his hands. And he no longer paid attention to anything, and sat there motionless and no longer warding off the animals. Then the doves flew back and forth and sat upon his shoulder and fondled his white hair and did not weary of tenderness and rejoicing. The mighty lion, however, continually licked the tears that fell down upon Zarathustra's hands, roaring and growling shyly as he did so. Thus did these animals.

All this lasted a long time, or a short time: for, properly speaking, there is *no* time on earth for such things. In the meantime, however, the Higher Men in Zarathustra's cave had awakened and arranged themselves for a procession, that they might go to Zarathustra and offer him their morning greeting: for they had discovered when they awoke that he was no longer among them. But when they reached the door of the cave, and the sound of their steps preceded them, the lion started violently, suddenly turned away from Zarathustra, and leaped up to the cave, roaring fiercely; the Higher Men, however, when they heard its roaring, all cried out as with a single throat and fled back and in an instant had vanished.

But Zarathustra himself, bewildered and spell-bound, raised himself from his seat, gazed about him, stood there amazed, questioned his heart, recollected, and saw he was alone. 'What was it I heard?' he slowly said at last, 'what has just happened to me?'

And at once his memory returned and he comprehended in a glance all that had happened between yesterday and today. 'This here is the stone,' he said and stroked his beard, 'on *this* did I sit yesterday morning; and here did the prophet come to me, and here I first heard the cry which I heard even now, the great cry of distress.

'O you Higher Men, it was of *your* distress that old prophet prophesied to me yesterday morning,

'he tried to seduce and tempt me to your distress: O Zarathustra, he said to me, I have come to seduce you to your ultimate sin.

'To my ultimate sin?' cried Zarathustra and laughed angrily at his own words. '*What* has been reserved for me as my ultimate sin?'

And once more Zarathustra became absorbed in himself

and sat himself again on the great stone and meditated. Suddenly, he leaped up –

'*Pity! Pity for the Higher Man!*' he cried out, and his countenance was transformed into brass. 'Very well! *That* – has had its time!

'My suffering and my pity – what of them! For do I aspire after *happiness*? I aspire after my *work*!

'Very well! The lion has come, my children are near, Zarathustra has become ripe, my hour has come!

'This is *my* morning, *my* day begins: *rise up now, rise up, great noontide!*'

Thus spoke Zarathustra and left his cave, glowing and strong, like a morning sun emerging from behind dark mountains.

Notes

NOTES

1. *Untergehen* has three meanings: to descend or go down; to set (as of the sun); and to be destroyed or to go under. There is much play upon this triple meaning throughout the book. The noun *Untergang* is treated in a similar way.

2. *Übergang und Untergang.* The antithesis *über* (over) and *unter* (under) is very frequently employed. It is not always possible to bring this out fully in translation.

3. *Rede* = discourse; *Vorrede* = prologue. The play on words is lost in translation.

4. *Brecher* = breaker; *Verbrecher* normally = criminal. 'Law-breaker' retains the verbal repetition.

5. *Hinterweltler* is a coinage meaning 'those who believe in an after life'. It gains force from its similarity to the word *Hinter-wäldler* = backwoodsmen.

6. The Danish writer Sören Kierkegaard (1813–55), who advocated a return to Christianity by means of a 'leap' from unbelief into belief, is perhaps being criticized here. Much in this chapter reads like a refutation of Kierkegaard.

7. The phrase derives from the expression *Mit dem Kopfe durch die Wand wollen* = to run full tilt at everything.

8. *Geist* means spirit, mind, and intellect – the human understanding. I have generally rendered it as spirit because this seems to me to include intellect and mind while intellect is too narrow in meaning and understanding too cumbrous for the contexts in which *Geist* occurs. In *Thus Spoke Zarathustra*, *Geist* never has any supernatural connotation. Where spirit in the sense of soul (*Seele*) is intended, I have used the word soul.

9. *Denken* = to think, *bedenklich* = suspicious – a neat play upon words lost in translation.

10. The people referred to are the Persians. The two following are the Jews and the Germans.

11. *Nächsten* = neighbour and nearest, and throughout this chapter *Fernsten* (= the most distant), the opposite of nearest, is also made to mean the opposite of neighbour, i.e. the people of the most distant future. Hence the continual antithesis between

339

'neighbour' and 'most distant' – an antithesis not quite so clear in translation as in the original.

12. An untranslatable pun. 'To give a person a paw' means to strike him across the hand with a cane.

13. There is a play upon words here that can hardly be transmitted in translation. '*Nicht nur fort sollst du dich pflanzen, sondern hinauf!*' '*Fortpflanzen*' means to propagate (biological) and to transplant (botanical); '*hinpflanzen*' means to plant out (in the sense of planting out cuttings from a single, original plant). The sentence means: You should not only propagate yourself, transplant yourself in the future just as you are; you should see to it that your children are something higher and less confined than you.

14. The reference is to the first line of the final verse of Goethe's *Faust* Part Two: All that is transitory is but an image. See also note 19.

15. In German *gerecht* (just) and *gerächt* (revenged) are pronounced identically.

16. *Hoch und steil leben* means literally to live in a high and steep place, figuratively to live nobly and boldly.

17. *Blicke* = glances; *Augenblicke* = moments. But by a quibble '*Augenblicke*' can be made to mean 'glances of the eyes' (*Augen* = eyes). This word-play is lost in translation.

18. 'Doer' is in German (in this case) *Handelnden* – giving a play upon the word 'hand'.

19. The final 'Mystic Chorus' of Goethe's *Faust* Part Two is burlesqued in this chapter. Verbal references to it will be clear from the following literal translation:

> All that is transitory
> Is but an image;
> The unattainable
> Here becomes reality;
> The indescribable
> Here it is done!
> The eternal-womanly
> Draws up upward!

20. *The Wanderer and his Shadow* is the title of one of Nietzsche's books (the Third Part of *Human, All Too Human*).

21. The prophet is Arthur Schopenhauer (1788–1860), who also appears in Part Four.

22. *Gedanken und Hintergedanken:* the antithesis is lost in translation.

23. *Bucklichte* = hunchback; *bucklicht reden* = to speak crossly.

24. *Grund* = ground and reason. The pun is amplified in 'foreground' (superficial reasons) and 'background' (fundamental reasons).

25. This scene is a memory from Nietzsche's childhood. Nietzsche's father died following a fall, and it seems that Nietzsche was attracted to the scene by the frightened barking of a dog: he found his father lying unconscious. It is not entirely clear why the scene should have been evoked at this point. The most likely suggestion is that Nietzsche at one time thought that events recurred within historical time, and was troubled by the idea that he might meet the same death as his father. (The idea seems to have assumed the nature of an obsession: its origin probably lay in Nietszche's fear of madness, which was strengthened by the fact that his father died insane. The insanity was caused by the fall, but Nietzsche was probably doubtful whether the fall did not merely bring to the surface an inherited weakness.) This old idea may have come into the author's mind at this point, and have been included in the text as a cryptic 'history' of the theory of the eternal recurrence. What follows is, of course, symbolic and not actual.

26. For 'accepted his destiny' the author here uses the idiom 'stood upon his destiny', giving point to the words 'with firm feet', which in translation may seem puzzling.

27. *Himmel* means both 'sky' and 'heaven'.

28. *Von Ohngefähr* means 'by chance' – but the author treats the noun as a proper name and ennobles it by adding '*von*', the ordinary designation of nobility.

29. I have left this paragraph as it stands because a properly idiomatic translation would alter the original more than is justified. *Es gibt sich*, as well as meaning 'it is given', is employed idiomatically to mean 'it will get better', or simply as the verbal equivalent of a shrug of the shoulders. *Es nimmt sich* – 'it is taken' – has no such idiomatic connotation, and is employed by the author simply as an (untranslatable) antithesis to *es gibt sich*.

30. A pun on the two meanings of *Geist* – spirit and intellect.

31. *Dämmerten* – a scornful reference to Wagner's *Götterdämmerung* (The Twilight of the Gods).

32. The bray of an ass is rendered in German *Ia* (pronounced ee-ah), which sounds and looks very much like *Ja* = yes. I have adopted Thomas Common's translation of this as 'Ye-a' (the best that can be done, I think). Thomas Common always translates *Ja* as 'yea', in accordance with the notion that *Thus Spoke Zarathustra*

is mock-Biblical throughout. The author employs this humorous device to great effect in Part Four.

33. The imagery of this section derives from the saying *Wasser hat keine Balken* = Water is not planked over, Praise the sea but keep on dry land. *Im Fluss* means 'in flux', but also 'in the river' and 'flowing'. Later in the same section, 'Have not all railings and gangways fallen into the water and come to nothing' refers to the expression *ins Wasser fallen*, which means to melt away, to come to nothing, as well as, literally, to fall into the water. This method of reducing an abstract idea to a concrete image by means of everyday idioms is of the essence of Nietzsche's art – and one reason why the vividness of his style is often dimmed in translation.

34. A play upon *Vorspiel* = prologue, and *Beispiel* = example.

35. A play upon *Unterhalt* = maintenance, and *Unterhaltung* = entertainment.

36. A play upon *Eheschliessen* = marriage contract, and *Ehebrechen* = literally marriage breaking, usually adultery. The literal meaning of *Ehebrechen* is played upon in the following paragraphs.

37. A play upon *Versprechen* = promise, and *Versehen* = mistake. The words balance one another because *sprechen* by itself means 'to speak', and *sehen* means 'to see'.

38. A play, frequent in *Thus Spoke Zarathustra*, upon *versuchen* = to experiment, to attempt, and *suchen* = to seek.

39. A malicious reference to the opening of Act Three of Wagner's *Siegfried*, in which the Wanderer (Wotan) calls up Erda, the Earth Mother, from her sleep, and after a fifteen-minute colloquy bids her return to sleep. The style of this whole passage imitates that of the Wanderer's summons.

40. *Würgerin* is the feminine form of 'strangler' or 'throttler'; but the word also means the 'shrike'. It is in the feminine form because *die Sünde* = sin, is feminine.

41. A play upon *Geduld* = patience, and *dulden* = to endure, to suffer in patience.

42. A play upon two meanings of *Probe*: 'proof or test' and 'exhibition'.

43. *Versuchen* means both 'to test' and 'to tempt'.

44. *Unter vier Augen gesprochen* = between ourselves (literally 'spoken beneath four eyes'). The last pope, however, is blind in one eye.

45. A play upon *verfolgen* = to persecute, and *folgen* = to follow.

46. A play upon *Suchung* = seeking, *Heim* = home, and *Heimsuchung* = affliction.

47. *Reif* means both 'ring' and 'ripe'.

48. *Tagedieb* (lazy bones) means literally 'thief of daytime'.

49. A play upon the similar sound of *deutsch* = German, and *deutlich* = clearly. *Deutsch reden*, used idiomatically, means 'to speak clearly' (compare 'in plain English').

50. *Abendmahl*, the word employed here and in the title of the chapter, is an old form of *Abendessen*, that is, 'supper'. But it is also the normal word for 'Holy Communion', which is of course an imitation of Christ's last meal with his followers, called in English 'The Last Supper'. The pun upon 'supper' and 'Holy Communion' is not translatable, except perhaps in the way I have attempted.

51. A play upon *Sprünge* = leaps, and *Seitensprünge* = literally 'side leaps', idiomatically 'escapades'.

52. *Ich kann nicht anders, Gott helfe mir!* – Luther's famous words before the Diet of Worms.

53. *Leib-Farbe* means literally 'body colour', but idiomatically 'favourite colour'.

THE JOYOUS SCIENCE

Friedrich Nietzsche

'God is dead; but given the ways of men, perhaps for millennia to
come there will be caves in which His shadow will be shown'

Friedrich Nietzsche described *The Joyous Science* as a book of
'exuberance, restlessness, contrariety and April showers'. A deeply
personal and affirmative work, it straddles his middle and late
periods and contains some of the most important ideas he would
ever express in his writing. Moving from a critique of conventional
morality, the arts and modernity to an exhilarating doctrine of
self-emancipation, this playful combination of aphorisms, poetry
and prose is a treasure trove of philosophical insights, brought to
new life in R. Kevin Hill's clear, graceful translation.

Translated and edited with an Introduction and Notes by
R. Kevin Hill

ISBN: 978 0 14 119 539 1

THUS SPOKE ZARATHUSTRA

Friedrich Nietzsche

'Yes! I am Zarathustra the Godless'

Nietzsche was one of the most revolutionary and subversive thinkers in Western philosophy, and *Thus Spoke Zarathustra* remains his most famous and influential work. It describes how the ancient Persian prophet Zarathustra descends from his solitude in the mountains to tell the world that God is dead and that the Superman, the human embodiment of divinity, is his successor. With blazing intensity and poetic brilliance, Nietzsche argues that the meaning of existence is not to be found in religious pieties or meek submission, but in all-powerful life force: passionate, chaotic and free.

Translated and edited with an Introduction by R. J. Hollingdale

ISBN: 978 0 14 044 118 5

CRITIQUE OF PURE REASON

Immanuel Kant

'The purpose of this critique of pure speculative reason consists
in the attempt to change the old procedure of metaphysics and to
bring about a complete revolution'

Kant's *Critique of Pure Reason* (1781) is the central text of modern
philosophy. It presents a profound and challenging investigation
into the nature of human reason, its knowledge and its illusions.
Reason, Kant argues, is the seat of certain concepts that precede
experience and make it possible, but we are not therefore entitled
to draw conclusions about the natural world from these concepts.
The *Critique* brings together two opposing schools of philosophy:
rationalism, which grounds all our knowledge in reason, and
empiricism, which traces all our knowledge to experience. Kant's
transcendental idealism indicates a third way that goes beyond
these alternatives.

Translated, edited and with an introduction by Marcus Weigelt
Based on the translation by Max Müller

ISBN: 978 0 14 044 747 7

CANDIDE, OR OPTIMISM

Voltaire

'You have been to England ... Are they as mad as in France?'

Brought up in the household of a German Baron, Candide is an open-minded young man whose tutor, Pangloss, has instilled in him the belief that 'all is for the best'. But when his love for the Baron's rosy-cheeked daughter is discovered, Candide is cast out to make his own fortune. As he and his various companions roam over the world, an outrageous series of disasters befall them – earthquakes, syphillis, a brush with the Inquisition, murder – sorely testing the young hero's optimism. In *Candide*, Voltaire threw down an audacious challenge to the philosophical views of his time, to create one of the most glorious satires of the eighteenth century.

Translated by Theo Cuffe
with an Introduction by Michael Wood

ISBN: 978 0 14 045 510 6

DEMOCRACY IN AMERICA

Alexis de Tocqueville

'A new political science is needed for a totally new world'

In 1831 Alexis de Tocqueville, a young French aristocrat and civil servant, made a nine-month journey through eastern America. The result was *Democracy in America*, a monumental study of the strengths and weaknesses of the nation's evolving politics. Tocqueville looked to the flourishing democratic system in America as a possible model for post-revolutionary France, believing its egalitarian ideals reflected the spirit of the age – even that they were the will of God. His insightful work has become one of the most influential political texts ever written on America and an indispensable authority for anyone interested in the future of democracy. This volume includes the rarely translated 'Two Weeks in the Wilderness', an evocative account of Tocqueville's travels among the Iroquois and Chippeway and 'Exclusion to Lake Oneida'.

Translated by Gerald Bevan
with an Introduction and Notes by Isaac Kram

ISBN: 978 0 14 044 760 6

THE GOLDEN BOWL

Henry James

'You think ... that I had better get married just in order to be as I
was before'

Maggie Verver, a young American heiress, and her widowed father
Adam, a billionaire collector of objets d'art, lead a life of wealth
and refinement in London. They are both getting married: Maggie
to Prince Amerigo, an impoverished Italian aristocrat, and Adam
to the beautiful but penniless Charlotte Stant, a friend of his daughter. But both father and daugther are unaware that their new
conquests share a secret – one for which all concerned must pay
the price. Henry James's late, great work is a highly charged study
of adultery, jealousy and possession that both continues and chal-
lenged his theme of confrontation between American innocence
and European experience.

'One of the greatest pieces of fiction ever written'
A. N. Wilson

ISBN: 978 0 14 1441 127 6

FEAR AND TREMBLING

Søren Kierkegaard

'He who loved himself became great in himself, and he who loved
others became great through his devotion, but he who loved God
became greater than all'

In *Fear and Trembling* Kierkegaard, writing under the pseudonym
Johannes de silentio, expounds his personal view of religion
through a discussion of the scene in Genesis in which Abraham
prepares to sacrifice his son at God's command. Believing Abraham's unreserved obedience to be the essential leap of faith needed
to make a full commitment to his religion. Kierkegaard himself
made great sacrifices in order to dedicate his life entirely to his
philosophy and to God. The conviction shown in this religious
polemic – that a man can have an exceptional mission in his life
– informed all Kierkegaard's later writings, and was also hugely
influential for both Protestant theology and the existentialist
movement.

Translated with an Introduction by Alastair Hannay

ISBN: 978 0 14 044 449 0